Praise for
Path of Fate

"What's better than a story about a stubborn, likable heroine thrust into events fraught with danger, wizards, and gods? Well, all of the above, plus a goshawk. . . . I thoroughly enjoyed *Path of Fate* by the talented Diana Pharaoh Francis and look forward to more of the adventures of Reisil and her goshawk, Saljane."

—Kristen Britain, bestselling
author of *Green Rider*

"This is an entertaining book—at times compelling—from one of fantasy's promising new voices."

—David B. Coe, award-winning
author of *Seeds of Betrayal*

"In this delightful debut, Diana Pharaoh Francis caught me with a compelling story, intrigued me with the magic of her ahalad-kaaslane, and swept me away with her masterful feel for the natural world."

—Carol Berg, critically acclaimed
author of *Restoration*

Path of Fate

Diana Pharaoh Francis

A ROC BOOK

Acknowledgments

First I want to thank my parents, Bill and Vi Pharaoh, for encouraging and funding my reading habit from the moment I learned what words were. They taught me to love language. Next I want to thank Jennifer Stevenson and the "book in a week" group that got me started on *Path of Fate* in the first place. Thanks also to Kevin Kvalvik for teaching me how to build a Web site: www.sff.net/people/di-francis.

It is said that writing is a lonely experience, and that is true, but a lot of people contributed to this book, including Sharman Horwood, Lyn McConchie, Megan Glasscock, MJean Harvey, and Elizabeth Covington, who all read *Path of Fate* in draft and offered wonderful aid. Thank you for your encouragement, advice and friendship. Thanks also to Jack Kirkley for introducing me to goshawks and answering all sorts of questions. I'd also like to thank the members of Broad Universe and the Roundtable, for humor, support, interest, and information, especially Fighter Guy.

Next I'd like to thank Lucienne Diver and Jennifer Heddle for your support, advice and hard work. This is a much better book because of you both, and Jen, thanks especially for the inspiring "prune generously" editorial advice—you have no idea what that did for my writing. Thanks also to Kristen Britain, David Coe and Carol Berg for generously reading my manuscript and offering wonderful reviews and helpful critiques.

One other person who had little to do with my book,

and yet everything to do with enabling me to write it needs to be mentioned: Dr. Gerald Dorros. You are my hero and my friend. There will never be words to thank you enough.

And last but not least, to the two loves of my life, Tony and Quentin. For believing in me, for making me laugh, for making sure my world keeps running even when I'm too mired in words to know, for all your unconditional support. This book is yours as much as mine.

As always, any mistakes are mine alone. I hope you enjoy reading this book as much as I enjoyed writing it.

Chapter 1

Reisil's spine twinged protest as she lurched into a shadowed wagon rut. Her next step caught the lip of the uneven furrow and she sprawled on the hard-baked road, scraping her chin and inhaling a mouthful of powdery dust. Coughing, she struggled to her feet. She brushed the graze on her chin with tender fingers, pleased when they came away unbloodied. An anxious glance revealed that no one had witnessed her clumsiness. She sighed, licking the dust from her lips.

Not that she wasn't willing to be the brunt of a joke, but people in Kallas still saw her as the child she had been thirteen years ago, rather than as a capable tark. Tripping over her own feet didn't do much to revise that perspective. She snorted. The fever that had swept through the town three months ago had done even less. Never mind that it was one of those illnesses that had no cure, and could be treated only with sleep, fluids and time. Never mind that only two men had died—one with a weak heart and the other with bad lungs. Many more would have died if Reisil hadn't been there.

She shook her head. All Kallas knew was that there had been a major illness three months after her arrival and she'd been helpless against it.

No, she admonished, pulling herself up short. That wasn't fair. The townspeople knew well enough that things would have been worse without her. But she had wanted to shine. She wanted them to see her as a rock in the storm, not as the little abandoned girl they'd fostered.

Reisil bent and dusted herself off, scowling at the tear in her trousers. If only the fever hadn't been so recalcitrant . . .

But she still had time, she reassured herself for the umpteenth time. She had six more months before the council voted on accepting her. They'd paid for her upbringing and her training. Surely they'd want some return on their investment? Surely they wouldn't decide they'd prefer to have no tark at all.

Strain pulled the corners of her mouth down. The fact was, the council could very well vote against throwing good money after bad in support of a less than competent tark. After all, for the seven years since her predecessor's death, Kallas had made do with wandering tarks who preferred the rambling life. Which was *not* what she wanted to do. She meant to settle down, and right here.

Humor wriggled up through the morass of her fears. Certainly tripping over her own feet would not make them reject her, she chided herself. She giggled. Any more than dribbling food on her shirt or bumping into furniture. It was her skills that counted, and she had confidence in those.

She gripped the handles of her pack firmly. Six more months. Plenty of time. She nodded sharply and strode forward, her back straight as she set her feet carefully on the uneven ground.

Alone in the predawn, Reisil approached the gate, fishing a handful of nut mix from the pouch dangling from her belt. Behind her, the empty road rolled toward the river like an elegant pearl snake in the moonlit morning. Rising from the gauzy darkness, Reisil heard rumbling voices from the river as captains rousted their crews out of bed. From the wall above came the jingle and thump of armor and booted feet as the watch changed shift.

She halted before the inset pedestrian gate beneath the portcullis and yanked firmly on the chain. Within, dull tin bells tinked and clanked. After a few moments the spyhole slid back, revealing a lantern-lit square. Reisil could see a pair of bushy salt-and-pepper eyebrows below a wrinkled brow. She stood on tiptoe to be seen better, though in truth she was not particularly short.

"Reisiltark! Is there an emergency?" The guard scratched his beard and yawned, while Reisil scrambled to recall his name.

"No emergency, Beren," she replied, triumph at the memory brightening her voice. "I'm just going to replenish supplies. Aftermath of Lady Day," she said with a little shrug and a grin. The wrinkles in Beren's brow smoothed and he chuckled understanding.

"Just a minute," he said. The spyhole snapped shut and Reisil heard the bars slide back one at a time.

He waved her inside, the metal plates on his shoulders and chest clanking together softly, the boiled leather beneath it squeaking.

"Lady Day is one of rest. But I never lived one, but that it was the day after that saw a lot more rest than not." His teeth were uneven as he smiled.

"*I* didn't rest," Reisil said with a little sigh and a roll of her eyes. Beren laughed and clapped her on the shoulder.

"Reckon not. Folks like to celebrate the Lady's day. Get a little boisterous with it, I suppose. Give themselves sour stomachs and such."

Reisil nodded. "Used up a lot of my stores."

"Where are you headed?"

"East gate and up into the hills. I could go around, but it's so much faster to cut through town."

"True enough. But you be careful. That bunch of squatters in the copse is getting bigger. Made themselves a regular village. They haven't got much and they don't mind taking what they need from a body. Nobody's complained yet, and until one of them crosses the line, there's nothing we can do to roust them out. But Kallas doesn't need its tark being the one they take after. Mark my words and be careful."

"Thanks, Beren. I hadn't realized there were so many. What brings them here?" Reisil could have bitten her tongue. As if it weren't obvious. The war had never come to Kallas. Why wouldn't refugees come here, running from the burned-out shells of their homes and the fields trampled and scorched, the wells poisoned with a stew of dead animals, salt and lye? They were looking for a new start, and the isolated town of Kallas had more to offer than most places. "I mean, now that there's a truce, I'd have thought they might have gone home to rebuild," she explained lamely.

"Some have. Patverseme soldiers didn't taint much as they could have. Didn't have the supplies and wanted to leave themselves some good lands and wells. But what they did was enough to drive folks away. Can't fight if you can't eat.

"As for our squatter folk, fact is, we feed 'em. Kallas is tender about that," he declared proudly. "We're generous to those as don't have much. They know it and so they stick around, keep coming back, 'stead of going back home and breaking their backs to build up what they lost. Wouldn't be so bad, but a lot more have come the past month or two. Nest of beggars is what they really are. But now that the *ahalad-kaaslane* are here . . ." He trailed away, shrugging eloquently.

The *ahalad-kaaslane* were the Blessed Lady's eyes and hands in Kodu Riik, dispensing justice, setting wrongs to right. No one disobeyed the *ahalad-kaaslane* without reprisal from the Blessed Lady. If even one ordered the squatters to leave, they would. Or face the Lady's wrath.

Reisil shuddered. Those poor, ravaged people had already suffered too much. She hoped they would listen and obey. The Blessed Amiya was as generous as the sun and the earth, as unforgiving as the wind and the cold. The war had already inflicted a heavy toll on them, but the Lady's retribution would be far greater if the squatters did not accept the judgment of Her *ahalad-kaaslane*.

Reisil's mind skipped to Juhrnus and she nearly groaned. Newly chosen *ahalad-kaaslane,* he had been the bane of her childhood. Time had done little to make him grow up. He was as malicious and hateful as ever, more so now with the power of being *ahalad-kaaslane*.

To have him sit in judgment of those devastated people . . . Reisil shuddered again. "They're back? When?" The four of them—two newly minted and two experienced *ahalad-kaaslane*—had departed nine weeks before, and Reisil had been grateful for the respite from Juhrnus's endless pestering.

"Last night, just as we were shutting the gates. Not that they can't come and go as they please. I expect Varitsema will talk to them first thing this morning about the squatter problem. He's been frothing at the mouth about it."

"That's good. Until then, I'll be careful," Reisil said with a ghost of a smile, uncertain that running the refugees off was the right answer, and departed with a little wave.

The streets of Kallas were mostly deserted. Lady Day ribbons and streamers still decorated doors, windows, trees and lampposts. The smell of cedar burned in the Lady's honor wafted through the still air. Here a figure skulked along, huddled in a cloak too warm for the balmy morning, hastening home before an illicit absence was noticed. There a stray dog galloped after a scent, whining eagerly.

Upstairs above a cobbler shop, a rectangular window glowed, and from it emanated the wailing cry of a baby mingled with the sobbing of a woman. Reisil hesitated on the walk below, wondering if she should offer aid. The baby shrieked and Reisil made up her mind. In all likelihood she would be summoned later, after daybreak, but they would not find her then and she was here now. The baby was Shen's and Ulla's first child, only three months old, born in the last days of the fever. The boy's unrelenting wail, despairing and frantic at once, told Reisil his colic had not not subsided in the week since her last visit.

Reisil rapped on the door, then dug in her supplies for what she might offer. She hadn't brought much, intending to fill the pack with her harvest.

The door swung open. Inside stood a young woman clutching her hastily donned wrap tightly at her throat, her wide eyes shadowed, her sleep-tousled hair framing her face in a fuzzy halo.

"Yes? Oh, bright morning, Reisiltark!" Relief washed her voice and Reisil smiled sympathy. She doubted the neighbors had had much sleep in the night, much less the servants.

"I was passing," she explained. "I have some things that might help your mistress, if you would take them to her?"

"Oh, but . . . don't you want to come up?"

Reisil shook her head. "It's not really necessary." And Ulla would not welcome being seen in such a state. She was a young wife, and Shen was his mother's favorite son. Though she desperately desired Nevaline's approval, Ulla knew Shen's mother found her wanting. And certainly as soon as news reached Nevaline about yet another wakeful night, she would bustle over to take charge, once again proving how deficient a wife Ulla was. All Reisil wanted to do was quiet the baby and let Ulla and Shen have a few hours' sleep before the invasion.

"Give these to your mistress," she said, handing the girl a jar and a pouch. "One spoonful of each into a cup of water every four hours. No more than that."

Reisil made the girl repeat back her instructions twice.

"I'll return later to see how he is," she said, then shooed the maid upstairs.

The sky had begun to lighten, though the moon still leached color from the world. Reisil hurried along the side streets like a ghost, keeping her eyes fixed on the walk in front of her. Old pain pricked as she passed a narrow brownstone with deep windows and a dark door. The home of Bassien and his wife Kivi. When had she lived there? Maybe when she was seven or eight? Reisil shook her head. She couldn't remember.

There had been so many houses, so many families. Dozens. Good families with money. No one who took Reisil in was forced to. Every three months she would move to another house—so that no one family would have to bear the burden of her keep for too long. They fed her, clothed her, kept her clean, gave her a place to sleep. As much as they'd do for any stray they took pity on. But she wasn't one of theirs. They never forgot that. Neither did Reisil.

She sighed. It hadn't been all bad. Not even mostly bad. The adults had always been kind. The worst had been the children, who had been . . . children. They had liked to tease her about having no parents: that she'd been found in a horse trough, the dustbin, a midden wagon, the gutter, a rain barrel. She made an easy target.

Reisil had also been a slight girl, all bones and angles. The children, often led by her nemesis, Juhrnus, called her a walking skeleton, and just as deaf and dumb, for her habit of restraint. Nor was it wise to invite further persecution by protesting or tattling. When they tired of name-calling, they liked to pelt her with the crab apples and juniper berries that grew abundantly in town, chanting rhymes like:

Who is Reisil's mother?
Who is Reisil's father?
Who is going to feed her?
Who is going to bother?

And,

Naughty little Reisil,
Aren't you so ashamed?
Scaring off your mommy.
You're too ugly to claim!

She could hear them even now, and remembered running away, remembered the black bruises from the hard-thrown missiles.

Kolleegtark's cottage had become Reisil's refuge. He'd always let her in without any questions, leaving his back door open when he wasn't home. He encouraged her to sit at his table as he worked, to watch as he treated his patients. It was there she'd learned to love healing. She'd coveted Kolleegtark's independence and the esteem the townspeople showed him. She envied the way everyone seemed to be his friend. She swiftly concluded that being a tark meant a person's background didn't matter. Kolleegtark's father had been a ragpicker, his mother a laundress. No one cared. Tarks were welcomed and respected everywhere.

Reisil scrubbed her hands over her face, surprised to find her cheeks wet. Idiot. That had all been long ago. It didn't matter anymore. Or it wouldn't, once she was confirmed as Kallas's tark. Most of those who had teased her so unmercifully hadn't done so out of real malice. She had just been different and an easy target. Usually Juhrnus started it and the rest just followed like sheep. Now those same children invited her into their homes, confiding their secrets, entrusting her with the care of their families.

Reisil squared her shoulders. She was no longer a child to cry over old hurts. No, her tears were in honor of Kolleegtark, who had died while she was away. He had been her first friend, kind and gentle, and he deserved the tears far more than the scrawny memory of Reisil, who now had so much.

Kallas continued to wake around her. Maidservants appeared with swinging baskets, heading to market. Fragrant scents of baking bread and roasting meats drifted tantalizingly in the air. Bells jingled, doors slammed, and birds erupted into song.

The eastern gate bustled with wagons loaded with vegetables and meat for market. Many of the farmers carried long-knives, cudgels and bows. Several of them surrounded the gate guards, voices raised in complaint about the squatters village.

Reisil edged past a sweet-smelling cargo of melons, carrots, radishes and lettuce. Good as it smelled, she couldn't help but notice the melons were tiny, the carrots thin and leathery, the lettuce stunted. The farms were too far from the river to make use of its water, and there had been little rain.

Just outside the gate, Reisil paused at the common well, saving the water in her flask for her ramble. Situated just beyond the walls, the well was a kindness to thirsty travelers. Reisil selected a chipped pottery mug from those dangling from wire hooks around the well-house roof and scooped a cup from the already full bucket.

The wind brushed dry fingers over Reisil's moist brow as she drank. She closed her eyes and lifted her face into it, drawing a deep breath, tasting dust. It was looking like a third drought year. Added to the damage caused by the Patverseme invaders, there would be precious little food for people like the squatters who already had nothing. Even Kallas was feeling the pinch, with a number of its wells running low and gritty. Several enterprising men had begun hauling water from the river in wagons and selling it in town. At least the truce meant an end to the fighting for a while. If only it would rain, there was still time to salvage crops before winter.

Reisil opened her eyes. The sky glowed sapphire, and she squinted against the sun's fiery brilliance as it crested the eastern hills. Feeling time pressing at her, she drained the water from the cup, making a face. It tasted like metal. She replaced the cup on its hook and set off over a grassy swell, avoiding the traffic and dust on the road.

By the time the sun had risen overhead and the shadows had shrunk away, Reisil's pack bulged with collected booty, as did the string sack she'd brought with her. Sweat dampened her undertunic and her stomach growled. She munched more nut mix from the pouch at her waist. Her day had been profitable. She was most excited about the seedlings she'd collected to plant in her garden. Growing the plants herself would not only save time and energy hunting for them, but it was another claim laid on her cottage and on Kallas.

She ambled down the crease of a hill, following a deer track. The sun flickered through the rustling leaves overhead, dappling her skin. Grateful for the shade, Reisil made no effort to speed her steps. Though she had worn a wide-brimmed canvas hat over her black hair, she felt prickly with the heat, and dirty. She wanted a swim in the river and some cream for her mosquito bites.

Throughout the morning, Reisil had worked her way through the hills in a long, sweeping arc, and now descended to the road east of Kallas. She waded through the hedgerow of purple vetch and betony, pausing on the dirt to adjust the straps digging into her shoulders. As she walked, puffs of dust rose about her feet and powdered her legs brown.

The road rose before her in a long, steady hill. Halfway up, Reisil stopped to unclip her flask and drink the last of the tepid water, pushing her hat back to wipe her brow with her sleeve.

The Lady Day celebration two days before had been boisterous, with games and dancing following the bonfire in the Lady's grove. Everyone in town had contributed food or drink to the feast after, and the festivities lasted well into the night. Reisil had spent the next day attending to countless little injuries and maladies stemming from the previous day's revelry. In all the excitement, she had not had a quiet moment to offer the Lady her own thanks.

"A tark is the Lady's right hand," Elutark always said. "The *ahalad-kaaslane* dispense Her justice; tarks dispense Her healing. Our gifts come direct from the Blessed Amiya Herself."

Kolleegtark had said much the same thing, and like Elutark, each night at dusk he had lit a rosemary-scented candle for the Lady, saying She cupped Her hands around Kodu Riik's fragile light and kept the land safe from darkness. Reisil had marveled at the candles. Always set in a window to guide the sick and injured, neither wind nor rain ever doused the flame. This, to Reisil, had always been the definitive sign of the Lady's endorsement of a tark. The night of her return to Kallas, Reisil had lit her own candle for the first time, setting it in the wind and watching into the early hours to see if it would blow out. She had fallen asleep, and her joy in finding her candle still burning the next morning continued to bubble in her veins even now.

The Lady Day celebration and aftermath had not

given Reisil the opportunity she wanted to properly offer her gratitude to the Lady. Reisil had therefore planned to break her noontime fast in the green silence of the festival grove, where she could also make her devotions. Thus, despite the heat and her fatigue, she continued to trudge along the dusty road, mouth dry, sweat trickling down her back and between her breasts.

She had forgotten the squatters in her fatigue and so was startled when she crested another hill and found herself suddenly in the midst of the "village," which in reality was little more than a squalid camp.

She trailed to a halt. Bits of ragged clothing hung from bushes. Reisil supposed they had been hung there to dry after a wash, but they appeared dingy with dirt. Bloat-flies rose and fell in lazy swarms, while dogs and children chased each other in the dust. Woodsmoke stung Reisil's lungs and there was a smell of burned porridge and rancid meat. The shelters were rude at best. A blanket spread over a framework of cut branches. A lean-to made by fastening green boughs to the lowhanging branches of a traveler's pine. A sagging wagon box given privacy by attaching a quiltwork skirting of dried animal skins.

The village seemed entirely populated by shrieking children and barking dogs, and Reisil supposed that many of the adults had gone to Kallas or the surrounding farms looking for work, or foraged for food in the hills. As she wandered through, the children stopped their play and clustered around, eyeing her curiously, with a hint of both hope and fear.

Before Reisil could do more than offer a smile, there came an agonized groan from within the trees along the north side of the road. It started low and rose to a howl before dying away in a wrenching wail, sending goose bumps prickling along Reisil's arms and legs.

"What's that?" she asked, pushing through the crowd of children toward the source of the sound.

A boy of perhaps twelve years stepped in front of her and put a grimy hand on her arm, his brown eyes flat and unyielding.

"This ain't your business. You best get along."

Reisil brushed his hand off as the tortured cry came again. This time he grabbed her pack and yanked, twisting her around. His lips curled like those of a cornered weirmart, his head hunching low.

"I said, you git," he growled, and his tongue was wet and pink against his dust-browned lips.

Reisil paused, taken aback by his hostility. But when the cry came again, she jerked her pack out of his hands, shoving him back with the heel of her hand.

"Get out of my way, boy," she said, already looking over her shoulder for the source of the cry. "I'm a tark, and someone here surely needs me."

His voice changed, sounding hopeful. "Yer a tark? Why dinya say so? Come on!"

She followed after him as he darted ahead into the trees. He led her to a shelter at the confluence of three close-growing spruce trees. She would have missed it if she hadn't had a guide. The sweeping branches of the trees had been propped and tied together to form the braces of a roof. On top of those had been spread more branches as thatching. A series of bushes and vines had been planted and woven together to form a latticework that would eventually grow into thick, leafy walls. From the outside, the shelter appeared to be nothing more than dense undergrowth.

But the boy offered no hesitation as he dropped to his knees and squirmed inside. Reisil followed quickly.

The only light filtered feebly through the dense foliage. In the gloom Reisil saw a woman reclining on a pallet, clutching her stomach as she curled up into herself. Her voice rose razor thin and her neck tented with strain as she wailed. Beside her another woman, equally young, clung to the stricken woman's hand, bending to murmur soothing words against her ear.

"How long has she been like this?" Reisil asked the boy as she shrugged out of her pack.

"This morning. Not this bad, though. Been getting worse all day."

"Has she got family?"

"Me. My brother."

"She's your sister?"

"Nah. Carden's wife."

Carden, Reisil supposed, was the boy's brother.

"Better go get him," she said, taking in the woman's sweating pallor, ragged breathing and unceasing writhing.

"She gonna die?" There was a matter-of-factness about his question that made Reisil's stomach curl. But there was no time for him.

"Not if I can help it. Now get going." After a tiny pause, he did as she asked. The rustle of leaves was the only indication that he'd left.

"What's your name?" Reisil asked the sick woman's attendant. She looked up, fear stretching the skin around her red-rimmed eyes.

"Ginle," she said, her voice cracking.

"And who is she?"

"Detta."

Reisil crawled over to the pallet and ran deft fingers over the squirming woman's stomach, pressing against the hard expanse. Detta moaned and flung out her hands in defense of the probing. Reisil gave a little nod to herself.

"Try not to let her twist, Ginle. I know it hurts, but she's only making it worse."

Reisil once again dug into the limited supplies of the emergency kit she kept at the bottom of her pack. Working quickly, she measured ingredients carefully into a flat-bottomed wooden bowl, mixing them together with a pestle. With her fingers, she formed two pastilles from the moist mass. The first she put between the agonized Detta's cheek and gum, straddling her chest to hold her still.

"Detta, you must not swallow this. Do you understand? Chew it, and swallow the juice, but nothing else. All right?"

Detta whimpered and nodded, the whites of her eyes like shining moons in the gloom.

"Good. Now there's another one. We have to insert it below. So I'm going to undress you. It won't hurt, but you're going to have to pull your knees up and spread them apart. Can you do that?"

Reisil completed her ministrations, then dabbed Detta's face with cool water mixed with crushed mint leaves. She didn't know if her treatment would work. It depended on what had caused Detta's innards to block up. But the pastilles contained both a very strong aperient and an antispasmodic. If they were going to have an effect, it would be very soon.

And soon it was. A half hour later, Detta sat up, wanting help outside, refusing to soil her home. A short time later, Reisil departed just as the worried Carden returned in the company of the boy.

"My wife, how is she?" Sweat runneled the dirt on his florid face, and he panted with the effort of his hurried return. His left hand was missing, as well as his left ear. Scars of the war, Reisil thought, disturbed by the brutality of the old wounds.

"She's better. Give her broth with a little bread floating in it, maybe add a bit of grain or vegetable in a day or so. She needs a lot of water. Try to keep her quiet. She should rest for a couple of days. I'll check back later."

Reisil's stomach growled and she flushed as Carden took it as a signal to begin gabbling about food and payment.

"It's not necessary," she said, her voice revealing nothing of her impatience to be on her way. If Detta had continued to need her, she'd have stayed by her side without hesitation. But now that her patient was on the mend, Reisil wanted to be about her business. She still wanted to make her devotions to the Lady.

"I have my lunch," she assured Carden, patting her pack with a tired smile. "And I am a tark. I am pleased to help anyone in need."

She departed the village at last, having accepted Carden's offer to refill her water flask. He did so clumsily. He had been lefthanded, Reisil realized, watching him hold the flask under his elbow to unstopper it before sinking it in a bucket of water, bubbles rushing out as the water ran in. What work could a one-handed man find? How would he rebuild a decimated home? Plow a field? Scythe a crop?

The afternoon sun had grown hotter, and Reisil's steps were slow on the rutted road. The heat intensified her weariness, but the relief of Detta's recovery gave her energy enough to struggle on. She thought of the pitiful village, remembering Beren's prediction—that the *ahalad-kaaslane* would drive them all away. She shook her head. The village had not been so deserted because the people were lazy beggars. Only those too young or ill had remained behind, while everyone else went in search of work and food. Even Carden with his one hand.

Reisil wiped away sudden tears with an irritated hand. Tarks who got too involved didn't survive long as tarks. Swallowing, she resolutely put the plight of the squatters from her mind. There wasn't anything she could do about it. The *ahalad-kaaslane* would make that decision.

The Lady's grove was as cool and restful as Reisil could desire. A shrine stood on the western edge of the clearing. Its simple, square lines were faced with colorfully glazed tiles with pictures of wild animals. Banding the top was a series of green tiles with red-eyed gryphons gamboling around. A crystal spring bubbled from an opening at its base. The water collected in a red-tile pool and then ran off into a rill, the same one that ran near Reisil's cottage.

The smell of charred wood clung to the clearing, and a large scorched spot opposite the shrine told why. Four times a year a fire was kindled before the shrine to celebrate the Lady's generosity, and Her victorious light holding back the Demonlord's night. The Lady Day fire always burned highest and longest. It was the longest day of the year, when the Lady's power waxed greatest.

Reisil skirted around the scorch and knelt before the shrine, pulling off her hat. So tired was she that she sat for several minutes, unable to focus on a prayer. She opened her mouth and then closed it. Finally she bowed her head and let her thoughts tumble together, swirling and rolling like a quick-running river. With them came her fears, her hopes, her pity for the squatters, her desperation to stay in Kallas. Above all else was her gratitude.

"My heart and my hands belong to you, Blessed Lady. You have given me so much. A home at last. Let it be your will that it remain so," Reisil whispered fervently. And then she dug a rosemary candle out of her pack and set it on the shrine. She lit it with a steel and flint, watching the flame lengthen and flicker.

Her stomach growled again, reminding her of just how hungry she was. Pressing a hand to her heart, Reisil bowed a deep obeisance to the shrine and then retreated to a fallen log nestled in a hollow just beyond the clearing. She smiled and sighed as she sat back against it, stretching her legs out before her. The lush grasses were matted here, the leafmeal furrowed. Someone had completed an assignation here during the Lady Day celebration. She chewed, wondering who it had been, and if they had been married, or hoped to. Her mind flew to Kaval, leagues and leagues away. She blushed in the leafy silence. If he were here now, what they would do! Her flush deepened, remembering the warm, sleek skin wrapping his ribs, the swell of his buttocks, the rough warmth of his chest.

A belligerent voice shattered her daydream and made her stomach clench. She tensed to flee, but didn't have time to escape without being seen.

"Haven't you been listening at all? The Patversemese are monsters. They didn't just invade; they *spoiled*. Look at what's happened to these squatters! Look at Mysane Kosk! How can you defend them?"

There were the sounds of scuffling boots and crackling twigs and then four figures—no, Reisil corrected herself, eight figures: four human, four animal—entered the Lady's grove. Juhrnus stalked in first, his jaw jutting like an angry bull. He carried his *ahalad-kaaslane* draped across his shoulders. The green-and-yellow-striped sisalik splayed contentedly on its pale belly, black claws clamped around Juhrnus's bicep in a gentle grip. The lizard's long, prehensile tail wrapped Juhrnus's other arm three times down to his wrist.

Juhrnus was dressed like his companions, in sturdy leathers with a sword on one hip, a long knife on the other. Everything he wore was new—a sign of his recent choosing. He was taller than Reisil by a few inches, with a wide, muscular chest, powerful legs and a square, boyish face. Thick brown hair fell in shaggy locks over his forehead and past his collar. If Reisil hadn't known him, if he hadn't spent her entire childhood tormenting her, she might have thought him attractive. She knew many girls did. But she did know him, and the very sight of him made her blood boil.

After came Felias. She was about the same height as Juhrnus, dressed nearly identically. Her round face was framed by curly brown hair. Like Upsakes, who followed, her *ahalad-kaaslane* was a weirmart. It crouched on her shoulder, hissing at Juhrnus, needle-sharp teeth clacking together as it snapped at the air. The minklike animal lashed its thin tail from side to side, the hair on its back standing on end. By the look on Felias's face, she was as angry as her *ahalad-kaaslane*.

Reisil's lips tightened in a sympathetic grimace; she had too often been on the receiving end of Juhrnus's attacks.

"I'm not defending them!" Felias retorted hotly, facing Juhrnus across the firepit, hands on her hips. "All I'm saying is that peace is better than letting the war go on."

"At any cost? Have you eyes? Look at the squatters village! Most of the men missing hands and ears and eyes. The women and girls swollen with their rapists' babies. Do you think they want the Patversemese to get away with that? And what about Mysane Kosk? What's to stop the wizards from doing that everywhere?"

Reisil blinked, startled by his genuine anger and concern. This was a side of Juhrnus she had never suspected.

"The Lady is," said Sodur mildly, wiping his brow with a ragged square of linen he pulled from his pocket. Lanky, stooped, with thinning hair, he looked older than his years. Adding to the impression were his patched boots, threadbare elbows and limp, battered hat. He had a pinched face as though perpetually hungry, his thin, crooked nose and squinting eyes adding to the effect. His *ahalad-kaaslane,* a silver lynx, lapped water from the spring before sprawling in the shade, panting.

"The wizards destroyed Mysane Kosk because it was on the border and they somehow managed to breach the Lady's protection. But their magic does not, as a rule, work inside the bounds of Kodu Riik. Only the Lady's hand is at work here. The siege of Koduteel failed largely because the wizards could only aid the attacks from ships, and the force of their magic wilted before reaching the walls. And because the Lady answered our prayers and sent aid. The rivers outside of Koduteel diverted so that there was no fresh water outside the walls. The firewood in the Patversemese camp would not burn, and the snows came early. Mud bogs appeared in the middle of camps, and moles and ground squirrels burrowed fields of holes to trap their horses' legs. Wolves and bears prowled the camps, and any game in the vicinity retreated beyond the reach of hunters. The Patversemese had no choice but to withdraw." A slight smile creased Sodur's lips with the memory.

Reisil might have smiled at Juhrnus's dumbfounded expression, if Sodur's revelation hadn't astonished her equally as much. Felias, too, gazed openmouthed at the elder *ahalad-kaaslane.* Sodur chuckled and patted her on the shoulder, flashing a quick grin at Juhrnus.

"You have heard stories all your lives of what the *ahalad-kaaslane* can do. Do not be so surprised. We are the Lady's eyes and hands and we protect Kodu Riik— all of it, human and not. We are not defenseless against the wizards. You're both *ahalad-kaaslane* now and must learn our secrets if you are to serve."

"But I don't understand. Why is it a secret?" Juhrnus blurted.

"You question the Lady?" Upsakes demanded. He had paused in the shade at the edge of the grove, listening to the other three with lowered brows, arms crossed over his broad chest. He differed from Sodur

like the sun to the moon. His clothing was clean and
soft with wear. He stood upright with a military bearing
and his gaze was sharp and darting. His weirmart
crouched on his shoulder, clutching the pad sewn there
for that purpose. At his reprimand, Juhrnus stiffened
and hung his head. Reisil startled herself with an unexpected surge of defensiveness for the bully who'd made
her childhood so miserable. The question deserved an
answer.

"No, of course not. I—But I don't understand," Juhrnus
said, uneasy fingers stroking his sisalik's gray-and-green
head. The lizard bumped his head encouragingly under
Juhrnus's hand, eyes half-closed.

"And you don't need to. The Lady would inform you
if you did," Upsakes said.

Despite her sudden and alien feeling of protectiveness
for Juhrnus against Upsakes's pomposity, seeing his expression, Reisil had to bite her lips to keep from chor-
tling. How she wished she could be the one to put that
look of consternation on his face!

Sodur frowned at Upsakes, and then turned to Felias
and Juhrnus.

"Come on, both of you. It's time we announced ourselves. We'll need a good pile of wood, and you might
have to search a ways out. Everything close by was
burned on the Lady Day fire."

Felias and Juhrnus departed in opposite directions,
Juhrnus red-necked and stiff-legged. Luckily neither approached Reisil's hollow, and she gathered herself to
sneak away as soon as chance provided. She did not
want to be discovered eavesdropping on the *ahalad-
kaaslane,* even accidentally.

"What was that about?" Sodur asked his companion
as he sat cross-legged on the ground, drawing out a small
knife and a chunk of wood.

Upsakes turned a sharp look on Sodur and then gave
a gusty sigh, lifting his weirmart down to the ground.

"Those two are enough to send the Demonlord
screaming for mercy. Must they bicker *all* the time?"

Sodur chuckled. "Apparently. But did you really mean

to hide the wizards' inability to practice magic in Kodu Riik from them?"

"No. But I don't want new *ahalad-kaaslane* to count on it either. What happened at Mysane Kosk shouldn't have been possible. And maybe if we hadn't been so busy congratulating ourselves on our invulnerability, we might have done something to prevent the massacre. All those people, women and children, the weak and the sick, all dead."

The bitterness and pain in his voice was raw and hard to witness. Reisil felt her throat tighten, knowing this was too private a moment for her to be intruding on. But neither could she escape without calling attention to herself.

Sodur's hands dropped into his lap and he gave Upsakes a steady look. "It wasn't your fault. You had no idea the wizards could attack like that when you sent those people there. None of us did. We all would have done the same thing."

Though deeply sincere, the words sounded worn and thin, as if repeated too often.

"But it was the wrong thing, and everyone in Mysane Kosk paid the price. Because I sent all those refugees there to be *safe*."

The self-recrimination in his voice struck deep in Reisil's heart and tears rose in her eyes. Pity for him, pity for those who had fled to Mysane Kosk, thinking they'd be safe. Whole families had been slaughtered there.

"There isn't anything that says the Wizard Guild couldn't do something like that again. We can't just assume the Lady is strong enough to hold against their attack. She wasn't last time. We can't have new *ahalad-kaaslane* wandering about thinking we're safe from the Patversemese wizards when it isn't true!" Upsakes strode up and down, chopping the air with his hands, while Sodur looked on from his seat on the ground. At last Upsakes paused and hunkered down on the ground facing his friend. He pulled a small bottle from the pouch at his waist and took a swallow, making a face at the taste. Sodur watched him return the bottle to its pouch and lean back against a spreading maple tree, eyes closed.

Rustling green silence drifted between them for a long minute. Bees buzzed in the clover and robins twittered overhead. Sodur bent over his wood, scraping his knife over the pale wood in his hand.

"A treaty might be what's needed," he said, not looking up. Upsakes reacted if yanked by a string attached to the top of his head.

"What?" he barked. "You're not serious!"

"I know it's not the popular solution. I know most of Kodu Riik would rather lose every one of their sons than make a deal with Patverseme. Even here in Kallas, and they suffered nothing from the war. Even those miserable squatters in that pisshole they call a village would slit their own throats before they'd sign a treaty with Patverseme. And Lady knows they've plenty of cause, but continued fighting will only make their lives worse. As it is, even with a treaty, they'd be hard-put to rebuild their lives with all they've lost.

"We're *ahalad-kaaslane*. We're not supposed to let our feelings influence our duty to protect and preserve Kodu Riik. Don't you think peace is for the best? Look at the difference just a few months of truce have made. Imagine what a permanent peace could do."

Upsakes launched to his feet and resumed his pacing, shaking his head furiously. "I'll tell you what I told Geran. Patverseme can't be trusted. This treaty is a ruse, buying time until the Wizard Guild finds a way to extend its power inside Kodu Riik."

"I don't think so. Our *magilanes* have managed to uncover a great deal of information inside Patverseme. Their intelligence shows that we've done a great deal to cripple Patverseme, even as they have us. The drought hurts them also. And it appears that the Karalis is no longer on good of terms with the Wizard Guild. In fact, there's a split of some sort within the Guild itself. No, this may be the best opportunity we have for peace. If we wait, the Guild will surely collect itself and push to undermine the Karalis, or be rid of him altogether.

Imagine the puppet they might replace him with. Or worse, one of their own."

Reisil could tell that Upsakes was unconvinced, though the last prospect worried him. But he ceased pacing and propped himself against a tree, scratching at the stubble on his cheeks.

"So how do you think the squatters are going to take our news?" he asked Sodur in a sudden change of subject.

"The river is close by for water and there is open, fertile land. It's a good place to start over, even with a drought. They will be content."

"I hope so. I dislike having to uproot them after all they've suffered. First the Patversemese soldiers and then us."

"Juhrnus, Felias and I will stay with them for a while and give what aid we can. Try to ready them for winter. I'm sure we can convince Kallas to send supplies and labor as well. If only to get rid of their unwelcome guests," he added mordantly.

"Varitsema isn't going to be too happy having a new town spring up so close," Upsakes said.

"He doesn't have a choice about it, does he? And better twelve leagues away than on his doorstep. He'll come around."

Just then the underbrush crackled as either Felias or Juhrnus returned. Reisil took advantage of the distraction to withdraw.

The sun was sinking over Kallas, turning the pink walls fiery crimson. Reisil made her way quickly through the town, stopping for a moment at the cobbler shop to check on Ulla and the baby. All was well and she continued homeward, her pack made heavier with a loaf of bread and a crock of fresh-churned butter.

Outside the walls she followed the road's zigzagging course, turning off where the path to her cottage cut away at a right angle. Despite her desire to be home, Reisil paused on the path, finding her gaze drawn farther down, to the narrow bridge over the Sadelema that joined Kodu Riik to Patverseme. There were guardhouses on both sides—matching stone buildings broken here and there by arrow loops. Behind each one stood an archer. A reminder that the truce was only a truce and not peace. She thought of what she'd overheard in the Lady's grove. Sodur thought it could be peace.

Reisil's breath caught on a sudden surge of hope.

News of the truce had come at the end of winter. A promise of hope for the new year, ushered in by the warmth of spring. Reisil remembered spinning around her garden, arms outflung, laughing aloud.

If only it *could* turn into real peace. So many lives would be saved. Not that Kallas would see much difference. Ironic that the town had never seen a battle in all the five years the war had raged. Situated as it was, right on the border, it would have seemed like a prime plum for the picking. But in truth Kallas was just too small, too far out of the way, too uninteresting. It had no strategic value whatsoever, and certainly no monetary significance, not compared to the wealthier trade cities and more populated lands to the south. Maybe that was why so many townspeople raged against the truce, against anything that smacked of giving in to Patverseme. They hadn't lost what others lost; they didn't feel the pain of the war as others did.

Reisil sighed, thinking of the angry outbursts she'd witnessed from those she would have thought eager for the war to end. Even Kaval's father, the tightfisted trader Rikutud, though peace would mean a flourishing of his stunted trade. If not for Mysane Kosk—but that had changed everything. So many lives lost there.

And it wasn't just Kallas. Even Sodur had acknowledged how against a treaty people like the squatters would be; people who'd lost hands and ears, like Carden; people who'd lost their homes and their families; people who'd been raped and maimed. They didn't want peace. They wanted justice.

Reisil glanced over her shoulder, watching the plume of smoke curling up from the Lady's grove. Not for the first time did she thank the Lady she was only a simple tark.

"Let the *ahalad-kaaslane* take care of Kodu Riik, and I'll take care of Kallas," she said aloud. And then she hurried home to set her seedlings in the ground before the light faded.

Chapter 2

Kek-kek-kek-kek!

K The shrill, strident call echoed imperatively down the river gorge. The hot midmorning sun slanted across neat garden rows. A sable shadow flicked through the branches of the fruit trees marching along the edge of the cliff, winking across Reisil's sun-browned face as she dribbled water over newly planted hempnettle seedlings.

Startled by sound and shadow, she spun around, dropping her bucket and sieve.

Kek-kek-kek-kek!

The cry scraped like a razor over Reisil's nerves.

Whistling sliced the leafy silence like the wail of a swung sickle. Wind across wings, Reisil realized as a large female goshawk alighted into the branches of a gnarled buckthorn, just beyond the reach of her fingertips. At two feet tall, the goshawk was the picture of lethal beauty. She spread her slate wings to full length, looking like some sort of avenging spirit. Her white-and-black-barred underbelly gleamed like ermine, fading streaks of brown revealing her youth.

Reisil jumped as the bird snapped her wings closed then clacked her short, wickedly hooked beak, tipping her head to the side. The amber eye beneath a flaring white brow fixed the slender healer in place, scrutinizing the spare planes of her tanned face, her serious green eyes, her wide lips bracketed by lines of humor, all framed starkly by pitch-colored hair scraped back from her face in a thick, straight plait.

Reisil endured the inspection, standing braced against the onslaught. She felt at once as if she'd been pierced through by a spear, and engulfed by the depthless waters of a volcanic lake.

And she felt fear.

It rose up in her stomach and clawed at her throat.

"No," she whispered. "No, no, no."

She heard words in her mind, steel and velvet.

~*I am Saljane,* ahalad-kaaslane. *I have found you at last!*

A welter of emotion flung itself over Reisil like a storm-driven wave—love, eagerness, friendship, exultation, hunger. Her mind merged with Saljane's like water touching water, knowing her, being known. There was no hiding, no secrets, nothing that wasn't open and exposed, raw and vulnerable. Reisil froze, paralyzed by the moment: such unrestrained welcome, such joy and adoration, completeness and repletion. Never before had Reisil experienced such feelings. She tasted them on her tongue like forbidden delicacies: sugar and lemon, blood and metal, fire and wind.

~*I am yours! You are mine! We are* ahalad-kaaslane!

The words fizzed in Reisil's blood for a heart-stealing moment, and then jagged shards of pain and fury ripped through the marrow of her bones.

Deserted by her parents before she was even one hour old, left to the mercy of Kallas, Reisil had grown up perpetually out of place, knowing she had nowhere she was supposed to be; and everywhere she went, and every moment of every day reminded her of that. She had never belonged anywhere, never felt as if she shouldn't apologize for taking up too much time or food or space. Not until she had become a tark. Not until she had earned her own cottage. A purpose and a place.

The old anger and bitterness for the nameless, faceless parents who'd left her behind flared up like a spouting flame, blistering and seething, thrusting everything out ahead of its raging heat. Reisil felt a shocked Saljane reel out of her mind. For a heartbeat she felt fleeting remorse for the bird's sudden agony. Then there was

nothing but grim triumph. The flames blew hotter and
Reisil let them incinerate the residue of the soul-fulfilling
contact with Saljane. Being a tark was fulfilling. She
didn't need or want to be *ahalad-kaaslane*.

She didn't realize she was shouting the words until she
bit her tongue. The pain brought her back to herself. As
if waking from a long fever, she blinked dazedly and
peered about her. The spilled bucket, the crushed hempnettle seedlings, plumes of white yarrow between the
flowering fruit trees, the stalwart buckthorn.

Empty now.

A white-and-black-speckled feather lay on the ground
at its foot. She looked away, scrutinizing the clearing,
seeking Saljane, hoping not to find her. Her gaze drifted
slowly as she studied her home with the greediness of
having almost lost it, for had not Saljane nearly stolen
it from her? She felt a spurt of anger at the bird, forgetting the other's shock and anguish.

Reisil's gaze returned to the buckthorn tree and the
feather in the dirt beneath it.

"No." It came out in a shaky whisper. She licked her
lips and said it again. Louder, firmer. "No. Blessed Lady,
I thank you. But no, I am not *ahalad-kaaslane*. I am
a tark."

Even as she spoke, the magnitude of her refusal struck
her. Her knees gave way and she dropped heavily to
the ground.

"What have I done?" she whispered through
trembling lips. "Blessed Lady, what have I done?"

Hearing herself, Reisil flushed red and pressed a hand
over her mouth as if to press the words back inside. The
Lady would not be sympathetic. Why should She? Reisil
couldn't bring herself to regret her choice. Feeling so,
how could she have the gall to ask the Lady's forgiveness?

The Blessed Amiya gifted but a few of Her precious
children to the people of Kodu Riik. Most hoped and
prayed fervently for a questing animal to seek them out,
but only a small portion were fortunate enough to be
chosen *ahalad-kaaslane*.

Most dreamed of bonding. Reisil shuddered. Being *ahalad-kaaslane* meant unending demands and constant travel. She did not want that, any of it, for herself.

But who was she to refuse such a gift?

Nothing but a stray, abandoned by her parents in the hour of her birth, a worthless foundling. Except for her talent to heal.

"They need me here," she argued to the still morning, willing the Lady to hear. "What do I know of being *ahalad-kaaslane*? I don't know how to shoot an arrow or use a sword, ride a horse or spy. But I am a good tark. Besides, I owe this town. Kallas raised me, paid for my schooling and apprenticeship. They didn't have to do that. They could have indentured me, or sent me to the Temple orphanage to become a scullery maid or a serving girl." Reisil shook her head and licked dry lips, her heart still racing as she tried to convince both the Lady and herself. "I know I can serve better here as a tark than wandering across Kodu Riik. I *know* it."

She stopped, staring up at the featureless azure sky as if waiting for a response. None came. She waited a few more seconds, then drew a steadying breath. She clambered to her feet, turning her mind with effort to practical matters.

"All right then. It's all over. I've made my choice. The bird is gone and won't be coming back. Time to get back to work."

Reisil took up her empty bucket and lugged it to the well.

She hadn't gone more than a dozen feet when she was halted by the sound of the city bells clanging an emergency. *Hurry, hurry,* they cried. *Trouble, trouble.*

Reisil dashed to her cottage. She snatched up her pack, already well stocked in readiness for her afternoon rounds, and then glanced at her shelves. What could have happened? Fire? An accident? What catastrophe? Something big to ring the bells. What would she need?

With knowing fingers she sorted through her carefully harvested stores, snatching up several pouches and a half dozen wax-sealed jars. She added these to the supplies in her pack before securing the flap. Then she was running back out the door, yanking her pack over her shoulders as she went.

The path from her cottage led along the river bluff and disappeared into a shady wood. Reisil raced along beneath the box elders, hawthorns and maples, the bells continuing to peal, goading her faster. Her booted feet pounded over the moist leafmeal, silencing crickets and songbirds. She leaped over the rivulet bisecting the path, missing the bank and splashing her legs. Her breath rasped between her lips as she ran. In what seemed like an hour, but was no more than a few minutes, she emerged from the wood out onto the crown of a sloping hill. Above her perched Kallas, circled by its dusky-pink stone walls.

Reisil followed the footpath around the hill and out through the exterior commons to the road. A wagon rumbled by, kicking up a plume of dust. Down by the quay Reisil could see a motley swarm of well-dressed merchants, sweat-stained stevedores and shaggy-haired river rats hurrying up the road in response to the summons of the bells.

Reisil hurried after the retreating wagon. Sweat dampened the collar of her tunic and trickled down her back. Puffs of dust rose with every step. The wind brushed her face with thirsty fingers, and on its back rode the pungent scent of white hellebore—an ominous odor. The poisonous plant flourished in the brackish flats north of Kallas on the Patverseme side, where treacherous bogs pooled with fetid water, despite the drought.

Wrinkling her nose at the cloying smell, she jogged faster. The flowers' odor seemed to hint at something dire. But just as she arrived at the gates, the sound of the bells ceased, the air still reverberating with their clarion call.

"What has happened?" she demanded of a guard whose name she did not know.

"No one's hurt, Reisiltark. There's news from Koduteel. Something about the war," he said, his face stern. "The mayor's called a meeting up at Raim's kohvhouse."

Reisil stared at the man for a moment, taken aback.

Sodur had said that a peace could be coming soon. Was this it then? Or did the ringing of the emergency bells indicate the war was beginning again?

Aware that the guard was watching her, she schooled her expression into one of cool professionalism, nodded and passed inside the gate.

Out of sight, she leaned against the corner of a brick warehouse, her legs trembling. No accident. No injury or fire. She closed her eyes, relief surging through her, followed quickly by concern. She stiffened. The war. Had Patverseme broken the truce? Was it coming to Kallas at last? Or—

Reisil's mind fled to Kaval as it did a dozen times a day since he'd left to steward his first caravan. Her mouth flattened, thinking of bandits. Every trader and tinker who came through Kallas told terrible stories of butchery and depredations—from outlaw soldiers to desperate, homeless crofters to mythic wild beasts—*nokulas*, they called them. Spirit beasts. But no, Rikutud, Kaval's father, was no fool. He didn't take chances. He would have sent his goods with ample guards. Kaval would be home soon, back in her arms, safe and sound.

Unless the war had begun again. Would he have to fight? Kaval had passed the last years of fighting watching after the business, while his father ran supply wagons for the Kodu Riikian army. Her heart stuttered. Her joy at the prospect of peace had as much to do with Kaval as anything else.

Reisil made her way through the mostly deserted streets of Kallas, forgetting all about Saljane and her refusal of the Lady's gift, absorbed by a nightmarish wash of dreadful possibilities: of Kaval surrounded by a pack of Patversemese soldiers with shining red eyes and black holes for mouths; of Kaval lying on the ground, eyes blank, his chest crushed; of Kaval fending off the blazing magic of a wizard attack, blood matting his hair and drenching his clothing crimson.

At last she came out of her dark ruminations to realize she had missed her turn and was wandering off in the wrong direction. With a muttered imprecation, she ducked

through a narrow alley between the mercantile and Taktitu's jewelry shop. She emerged onto the wide circular
avenue forming the hub from which the streets of Kallas
branched out in spokes. At the center lay a wide grass-
and-paved plaza dotted with trees. Skirting its edges
were a number of the town's more upscale businesses.
Among them was Raim's kohv-house. Raim served the
best food Reisil had ever eaten, and he always had a
ready plate for Reisil, which she took advantage of as
often as possible. It was here that she was headed,
though it appeared she was one of the last stragglers
to arrive.

Too aware that until she was confirmed as tark, her
position in Kallas was tenuous, Reisil swung into a fast
walk, trying to appear composed and serene. If they
were going to let her stay, the townspeople must believe
in her, trust her to be steady, controlled and capable in
a crisis. Such were the hallmarks of a good tark, and
this news from Koduteel—whatever it was—might be an
excellent chance to really show her abilities.

An accusing voice niggled in her mind. What would
they do if they knew that less than an hour ago she had
refused to become *ahalad-kaaslane,* the greatest honor
in the land? Her mouth went dry. If anyone in Kallas
should find out—

They'd despise her. They really would turn her out so
as not to incur the Blessed Lady's wrath.

So make sure it was worth it, she told herself firmly,
refusing to consider the possibility, refusing to let fear
and guilt undermine her decision. *Be the tark you know
you are and both the town and the Lady will forgive you.*

Sunk in the mire of her anxiety, she was caught up
short when a bony hand on her sleeve stopped her.

"Please, is there work? My children have to eat."

Reisil guessed the woman was about her own age,
though she looked a decade older. Her straw-colored
hair was unevenly cropped short, eyes beginning to look
bugged in her emaciated face. She bore a boy child on
her hip, maybe two years old. His bones protruded
sharply beneath his papery skin and his belly pouched

out, distended with hunger. Two more children clung to her ragged skirts with gaunt fingers, lips dry and cracking, flies crawling along their cheeks to the corners of their eyes.

Seeing them, Reisil felt a shudder of repulsion and a simultaneous wash of pity. They'd come a long way to get to Kallas, to get away from the war and find refuge. But the town had absorbed all the refugees it wanted. And so with superficial generosity, it fed and clothed the rest and then firmly sent them on their way, closing the gates at night and shooing loiterers away at the point of a pike, at least as far as the squatters village in the copse.

Reisil remembered the conversation she'd overheard between Sodur and Upsakes. Maybe there *was* something they could do for her. She opened her mouth to speak, but the woman forestalled her, anticipating refusal.

"Please. There must be work here. Something. Anything. You have so much. The war hasn't come here." The woman might have cried, if she had any tears left, if her body didn't need every resource just to keep her standing.

"Let me find you something to eat," Reisil said, grasping the woman's hand to steady her as she swayed.

The woman shook her head violently and yanked her hand away.

"We need work, a home. What is the other? A meal? A moment? What then? Go on to the next town? And they have less, and they struggle just to survive. The wind blows hot and dry. There will be little this year, even if the fields aren't burned or ravaged in battle. This place has plenty. Surely there must be work. I work very hard. Very hard," she begged.

In Kallas there was no work. And no real charity. If the *ahalad-kaaslane* hadn't decided to do something for these people, there would be nothing Reisil could do. But Reisil hesitated to speak of the overheard conversation. She might not have heard correctly. She might be offering false hope.

"Please, take these and eat," Reisil said, digging in her pack for the raisins and bread she carried against emergencies. "Your children are hungry." She thrust the food into the woman's reluctant hands. The woman continued to stare at Reisil and she flushed, feeling the stirrings of anger. The woman needed work, but her children needed food, and right now. They were starving for their mother's willfulness. Reisil reined in her spurting anger, the gray and faceless specter of her unknown parents rising in her mind. She thrust the image away. It wasn't a fair comparison. At least this woman was trying to take care of her children and she had enough pride to hate handouts.

Reluctantly she said, "There may be something for you. I don't know what exactly, not right now. But the *ahalad-kaaslane* may have something planned. For you, and others like you."

The woman stared at Reisil, unsure whether this was merely a way of brushing her off.

Reisil nodded. "It is true, but I will have to find out more."

The certainty and reassurance in Reisil's voice convinced the woman and she smiled, her lips trembling. Reisil fingered the silver tree-and-circle brooch on her collar. Helping people, healing, this was what she was meant to do.

"Reisiltark! Why aren't you at Raim's? Didn't you hear the bells?"

A middle-aged woman with a braided crown of graying blond hair thrust open the doors of the jewelry shop, wringing her apron in her hands. Her voice sounded high and breathy, as if she'd been running, and her face was pale beneath her freckles. Normally staid and unflappable, Meelaru trembled with emotion.

"I heard them, Meelaru. I'm going to Raim's now. Do you know what has happened?" Reisil spoke in soothing tones. When Reisil was growing up, Meelaru had been a buoy of comfort. Though she had little time to spare from her own family, she always made time for the stray girl, always had a hug and a smile, a cup of milk and a slice of sweet bread.

"It's a herald. All the way from Koduteel. He's brought awful news, just awful."

"The truce is over? Was there an attack?" Reisil's jaw

tightened and she crossed her arms over her stomach. Kaval had gone to Koduteel. The capital city was desperate for goods after the winter, and the long trek fraught with bandits was worth the return, or so Kaval's father had said as he waved his son out of the gates. Was the herald to report an attack on the caravan? Reisil kept her face expressionless as fear clutched her throat.

"I don't know." Meelaru put her fingers to her trembling lips. "Taktitu wouldn't tell me, but I've never seen my husband so upset. Everyone is."

"I'd better go then." Reisil looked at the beggar woman and her children as if she'd never seen them before. For a split second she didn't recall them at all. She turned back to Meelaru. "This woman and her children need to eat, a place to rest. Can you look after them? I'll come back for them later."

Meelaru gave them a hard look then a short nod, her round cheeks jiggling. Her expression firmed and color seeped back into her cheeks. Reisil almost smiled. Meelaru could be depended on to get things done in a crisis, and she never turned away needy children. Reisil ought to know. Meelaru motioned the woman and her children into the shop, *tsk*ing at the dirt and dust.

"Mind you come back and tell me what you hear. Taktitu's bound to forget," she said to Reisil, her voice sounding more like herself.

"Yes, mind you do, little sister!" came a taunting voice behind Reisil. She spun around, clenching her teeth. Juhrnus.

He stood opposite her, a spiteful grin stretching his lips, his legs braced wide, his head tipped in challenge.

He watched her, his lip curling as he stroked the yellow-and-green-striped head of his *ahalad-kaaslane*. He cradled the sisalik on one arm, its claws clamped around his wrist. The lizard's black, fleshy tongue whispered across the back of Juhrnus's hand affectionately. Mean-spirited and malicious as he was, she still couldn't understand why the Blessed Lady had chosen him.

Or me either.

"Poor girlie, missing your Kaval? Afraid he'll get lost

on the way home? Or maybe you're worried that he's bedded every serving wench, merchant's daughter and trull between here and Koduteel and has caught himself a pox. Got your potions all ready for that, have you? The ladies do so love our handsome Kaval, don't they?" He shook his head and *tsk*ed. "He has such a hard time keeping his . . . eyes . . . from wandering. I do hope he's got enough strength left to wave his flag for you."

Reisil kept her expression composed with some effort, though she flushed at Juhrnus's none-too-subtle crudity. She and Kaval weren't a secret. But that really wasn't the point. Juhrnus had made it his personal mission to harass and embarrass her since the first moment she'd returned from her apprenticeship. Six months and he'd dogged her heels every single day as if she hadn't been gone for thirteen years, as if she were still ten years old. She'd hoped after being chosen *ahalad-kaaslane* he might have better things to do, something more important to occupy his time, but apparently she was wrong.

Her glance flicked to Meelaru, who watched the exchange with avid curiosity. There was a frown between her eyes, as if she were waiting for Reisil to put Juhrnus in his proper place.

And just what is that? she thought wrathfully. *He's ahalad-kaaslane. Who can speak against him? Who can bring him to heel? He's the Blessed Lady's own chosen. Bad choice as that might be,* she brooded, trying to sort out some reply that wouldn't damn her in Meelaru's eyes, but might give her back a little of her own.

In the back of her mind, a malicious voice wondered what he'd say if he'd knew she'd been chosen too. She quashed the thought with a spurt of fear. She must not ever reveal that to anyone! Least of all Juhrnus!

"Come, little sister. Cat got your tongue?" Juhrnus smiled, daring her to say something. Reisil's fingers curled. He'd taken to calling her his little sister when they were very young, disguising his attacks on her under the name of familial sport, all good-natured and affectionate, just brotherly teasing. After all, she belonged to everyone's family and nobody's, moving house to house as she had. Even after years away, whenever she encountered him, she felt as if she were a child again, homeless and helpless.

"Hadn't *you* better get up to Raim's, Juhrnus? You ought to buckle down, now that you're *ahalad-kaaslane*. What would your grandmother say if she knew what a wild thing you still were, and here with all this responsibility?" Meelaru asked suddenly, and Reisil felt a rush of relief clash headlong against a staggering sense of humiliation. Meelaru was *rescuing* her.

Red seeped into Juhrnus's cheeks and his eyes narrowed. But he flashed Meelaru an impudent, bitter-edged grin. "She'd be speechless with surprise that I hadn't yet drunk myself into the river like my mother, or got myself killed in the war like my father." He sauntered forward past Reisil, then turned back and gestured for her to accompany him.

Left with little choice, Reisil fell in beside him, her jaw tight with anger. He chuckled softly.

"Little sister, what will you do when I leave Kallas?"

"It can't be soon enough for me," she gritted between her teeth.

"Ah, you don't mean that. But never fear. I plan to devote all my attention to you before I go."

"Some *ahalad-kaaslane* you are," she returned. "If you are so intent on me, how will you find time to help Kallas and Kodu Riik?"

Reisil was gratified to see him wince as her dagger hit home.

"I am not the only *ahalad-kaaslane* in Kallas. There are three others," he said stiffly, not looking at her.

Reisil snorted. "Felias is no more experienced than you. And you want to spend your time bullying me."

"Make hay while the sun shines."

"Whyever did the Blessed Lady choose you?"

Juhrnus jeered at her. "Hidden depths, little sister. My talents are valuable to the Lady, as no doubt Kaval's are to you," he added with a suggestive wag of his brows. He bent and made a kissing sound next to her ear and then brushed past, dashing up the wide flagstone steps to disappear inside the double doors of Raim's kohv-house.

Reisil stood on the bottom step for a moment, taking several calming breaths. Once again he'd gotten the better of her. When would she figure out how to handle him? Maybe she wouldn't have to. He would be leaving soon. She had only to wait him out.

Inside she could hear the clamor of shouting voices. The place must be full to the bursting. Her mouth watered as she smelled the welcoming aromas of rhubarb tarts, honey bread, mori-spice soup and rich kohv blended with thick cream and dusted on top with golden nussa, a tangy-bitter spice harvested on the upper slopes of Suur Hunnik in spring. She'd watched the sun rise as she ate her breakfast on her front porch and she hadn't eaten since. And from the sound of things, she doubted she'd be eating anytime soon.

The delectable scents contrasted incongruously against the tumult within. She eyed the polished oak doors, wishing she could return to her cottage, to the quiet tilling of her garden and the tending of her patients, and let the leaders of Kallas work this problem out on their own.

But she couldn't. Because with the mantle of tark came leadership, or at least the responsibilities of good counsel, and she must walk up those stairs and prove her abilities.

What was it Elutark used to tell her when she doubted herself? *You are what you pretend to be.* Well, then, she'd pretend to be composed, thoughtful and brave, instead of nervous of her own shadow. Reisil grinned wryly to herself as she smoothed her clothing and then marched up the steps.

On a normal day, the gaily colored ceiling, the arcaded walls open to a breezy courtyard, and the fragrant rushes strewn over the floors sent her spirits zooming. But today a wall of bodies blocked the entrance as a swarm of townspeople besieged Varitsema, the mayor of Kallas. She could see him above the crowd, standing on a bench in the center of the melee, the expression on his face a mix of anger, frustration and stubbornness.

Reisil recognized many faces: people she'd treated,

people who'd taken her in as a child. But their expressions were closed and harsh like the teeth of the mountains in winter. She shivered at the tangible rage rising from the group.

Sodur and Upsakes stood quietly with folded arms. Upsakes's chocolate-furred weirmart coiled about his neck, her long-whiskered nose twitching below his chin, sharp claws clutching into the leather pads on his shoulders. Reisil couldn't see Sodur's silver lynx, but it was certain to be close by. Their presence was comforting.

Varitsema raised his hands. A whispering hush fell, broken here and there by the sounds of coughing, shuffling feet and muttered invectives.

"You may yell all you like, but the Iisand Samir's own herald brought the proclamation and there is little to be done about it. I only repeat to you what he said.

"In fourteen days, a Patversemese envoy arrives in Kallas on his way to sign a permanent treaty in the names of their majesties Karalis Vasalis and Karaliene Pavadone. The Dure Vadonis, his family and entourage, will spend one day and night here. We are commanded to receive them with joy and courtesy and give them all the consideration of our own royal family."

An ugly eruption threatened. Varitsema lifted his hand again for silence. When the voices subsided, he said in a cajoling tone, "It means the end of the war. It means we won't have to send our sons off to die anymore. It means trade and prosperity for us all." His voice shifted and became commanding. "I know you don't like it, but hear me! If we should break the truce, fragile as it is, the Iisand has declared that all our lands and homes will be confiscated and we shall be made as homeless as those miserable squatters out there in the copse. We won't be allowed to take away any more than the clothes on our backs."

Stunned silence filled the room. Reisil's mouth fell open. She looked at Upsakes and Sodur for reassurance. Upsakes stroked his weirmart with a tense hand and Reisil noticed a feverish flush to his face. His eyes were wide and bloodshot. Sodur frowned and rubbed his chin.

Reisil began to shake her head. It was impossible. There must be a mistake.

"That's . . . that's insane! He can't do that!"

Reisil didn't see who spoke, but dozens of voices rose up in support.

"I'm afraid he can," Sodur said in a flat voice.

"You would support this? The *ahalad-kaaslane*? You're supposed to protect the people of Kodu Riik!"

"We would pray to the Blessed Amiya and follow Her guidance as we always do," Sodur said. "But you must realize that the crown is bound to the Lady as the *ahalad-kaaslane* are. I doubt Iisand Samir would promise such a possibility if he did not believe She would permit it. I would advise you to take the warning seriously, for your own sakes. Geran Samir is not known to threaten idly."

"Is that why you're here? To make sure we cooperate? So that we let the wolves into our gates?" demanded someone, Reisil could not see who.

"Peace, friend. We are here sorting out the new crop of *ahalad-kaaslane* and making arrangements for the squatters. Our presence is mere chance, but I promise you we will stay and aid in whatever manner we may," Upsakes replied in an easy voice that did much to soothe the angry tension.

But his next words, delivered like the lashes of a whip, sparked it again.

"I have no doubt that the Iisand will keep his word and you will all be turned from house and home, penniless and dishonored, should you not receive the ambassador from Patverseme with proper ceremony. With no horses or goats, cattle or sheep, what will you eat? Where will you go? How will you earn a living?"

For a single moment there was shocked, menacing stillness, like the eye of a tornado. Reisil heard her heart beat, and then a single indrawn breath as the crowd breathed together.

Shouts shattered the silence. Reisil felt herself wilt away from the fury that stormed the room. She took a step back toward the door and then caught herself, an-

noyed at her own timidity. She stiffened her back and
pushed herself forward, squirming through the mass of
rigid bodies, clenched fists and jutting elbows. At last
she arrived at the edge of the circle surrounding Varitsema, sweat dampening her ribs, her breath rasping in
her throat.

The mayor's thin face was pale but set. With every
sally from the crowd, he reiterated reassuring words of
loyalty, peace and prosperity. They had little effect. The
people behind Reisil surged forward like storm-driven
waves, their angry words tangling into nonsense as they
berated him. Sodur and Upsakes had been drawn into
little pockets of their own and each spoke fervently to
those who surrounded them.

Reisil didn't know what to do. If anything, her voice
would only add more sound to the fury. Nor could she
just stand there. She turned. She almost didn't recognize
the snarling, red faces, mouths sharp-edged and glistening like snapping wolves. For a moment Reisil wavered,
stunned by the ferocity of the townspeople. Then she
caught herself and began to scan the faces before her.
She knew these people. Some she had known her entire life.

"Paber!" she called to a florid butcher on her left. On
arriving back in Kallas, she had removed porcupine
quills from his son's leg. He started at the sound of his
name and swung his head from side to side like a bull
stung by gnats. "Paber," Reisil said more gently. "Is this
such a bad thing? To have peace at last? Think of your
sons. Soon they will be of an age to fight. Do you want
to see them march off, maybe never to come back?"

Her words struck home and he swallowed. Beside him,
Torm, a maker of glass beads, overheard and his own
lips clenched together. Reisil felt a thrill of pride and
hope as the two men looked at each other and then
away.

She turned quickly to the next man, a grandfather.
She remembered him from her childhood. He used to
run logs down the Sadelema until he'd caught his foot
in between two spinning trunks. He'd lost the leg, but

not his sense of humor. Reisil remembered sitting on his lap on the bank of the river, listening to his outrageous tales of adventure. That was years ago. Before the war.

She reached out and put a hand on his tanned forearm.

"Habelik—do you really want the war to go on? You've already lost your brother and two nephews. Do you want to lose your grandsons too?"

His head snapped around, eyes bulging.

"That's why, Reisiltark. A treaty means they've won, all those deaths for nothing. Nothing! And what about Mysane Kosk? Do we just let them get away with slaughter?"

Reisil was aware that a dozen pairs of eyes rested on her in a pocket of silence. She licked her lips. Then she gave a little shrug, spreading her hands.

"You are right, Habelik. What was done at Mysane Kosk cannot be undone and they will get away with it. They already have." She paused, letting that sink in.

"Even if we keep fighting, what happened at Mysane Kosk doesn't change. All the dead stay dead and Kodu Riik will bury many more. So I ask you again, is that what you want? Is it worth it?" She shook her head. "It's no easy decision and yet you must decide, you who lost family and friends. But I wonder, will you choose for the rest of Kodu Riik? For the towns and villages that have been burned to the ground, for the men and women and children who fight over moldy crusts like mongrel dogs? You have seen the squatters. Do you think that they would rather eat and heal than die for what cannot be changed? Does not that decision rightfully belong in the hands of Iisand Samir?"

Her voice cut with a flinty edge and she paused, her green eyes raking over the rigid faces before her. A circle of quiet rippled out from her words as if they were stones splashing into a still pool. She let her voice soften. "I do not disparage your losses. You have a right to your hurt and anger. But I marvel that you would willingly sacrifice any more."

"Well spoken," Varitsema said, resting a long-fingered

hand on her shoulder. He was a talented weaver, as
Juhrnus's mother had been, and his fingers were laced
with fine white scars and calluses. "Listen to our tark's
wisdom, my friends, even if you will not hear mine. The
Iisand Samir has entrusted us with this great task. Let
us not fail him. Let us show the Patverseme vermin that
we have prospered during this war, that we open our
gates because we are strong and unvanquished. Let us
welcome them as a Kaj of the first tier welcomes a peti-
tioner, and let them stand in awe of us!"

His voice rang with charismatic power and Reisil felt
her own heart swell in response, relishing his praise and
the way he'd said "our tark."

Just then, a flickering shadow swept like lightning beneath an arcade arch. Reisil paled as Saljane lighted on
one of the carved roof beams, her wings outstretched,
looking once again like an avenging spirit, her amber
eyes glowing like embers.

She let out one of her cries, the strident *kek-kek-kek-
kek* echoing in the sudden silence.

Again.

Kek-kek-kek-kek.

Demanding. Haughty. Proud.

Everyone gazed up at the goshawk in wonder. She
screeched again and mantled, shifting back and forth on
the beam, the wood splintering in her grip. Beneath the
white streak across her brow, amber eyes darted over
the assembly below, her beak wide in a silent scream.

"Sweet Lady! She's magnificent! And so big!"

"Blessed Amiya, have you ever seen such a thing!"

"Look at her eyes! She's got a head of steam about
something. Raim! Have you got something to feed her?"

At Varitsema's request, the tall, spiderthin proprietor
vanished into his kitchen only to reappear several minutes later with a pan of roasted meat. Behind him came
two boys dragging a cadge that they had quickly retrieved from Raim's cellar storeroom of *ahalad-kaaslane*
equipment. Every kohv-house owner and innkeeper in
Kodu Riik kept such a storeroom.

The portable perch's crossbar was as big around as

Reisil's leg, and only lightly used. She wondered a little wildly when was the last time Raim had needed it.

Hoping to avoid Saljane's notice, she tried to squirm back through the oscillating tide of bodies behind her. They hemmed her in, shoving her forward, eager for a glimpse of the goshawk. Slowly she found herself pushed nearer and nearer. Nearly crying with desperation, she turned and scrabbled at the bodies blocking her.

Too late.

Chapter 3

So close, Reisil could see every fine detail of Saljane's crisp, slate-gray wing feathers, showing here and there a trace of immature brown. Saljane gave another of her strident cries, and it seemed to Reisil to be an accusation.

The young tark held herself still, forcing herself to meet Saljane's fiery gaze, waiting for the bird to reveal her perfidy to the town. Despite Reisil's fear, she felt a certain relief and a thin sliver of regret that she experienced nothing of the unbearable intimate connection they'd shared only that morning. Just ashy gray vacancy. Yet spitted on the molten steel of those eyes, Reisil couldn't help herself. Words rose in her mind, placating and defensive.

~*Please understand. I am fated to be a tark. I cannot be* ahalad-kaaslane. *I am not for you and you are not for me.*

There was no sign that Saljane heard or understood her. The goshawk blinked slowly and then a sound caught her attention and she jerked away. Reisil felt herself go limp as relief turned her bones to water.

Raim set up the cadge and attached a feeding tray amidst the sudden joviality occasioned by Saljane. He piled the meat on the tray and tipped his dark head to the bird, sweat from the heat of the kitchen dampening his brow.

"Bright morning, Lady of the heavens. Welcome to my kohv-house. May it please you to break your fast with us." He gave a graceful little bow to the goshawk and gestured to the cadge and meat, and then stepped back, giving Saljane plenty of room to land if she so chose.

She did.

Reisil bit back a protest, her momentary relief evaporating like morning mist as Saljane lunged off the beam. The goshawk clutched the wooden crossbar, talons gouging into the oak as her tail flared for balance.

Kek-kek-kek-kek.

Saljane swiveled her head, gazing unblinkingly at the hushed crowd. Reisil held her breath, her heart stopping as those fierce eyes skimmed over the room.

Reisil almost sobbed with relief when Saljane turned to the feeding tray, snatching hungrily at the meat and bolting it down in choking gobs. A wave of muted clapping swept the room and then the murmurings of excited conversations.

"Upsakes, Sodur—can you say, has she come here for one of us?"

Sodur eyed the voracious goshawk with a crooked grin. "Undoubtedly. She's been traveling a long way and not bothering to eat. I would guess she was in a hurry, and now is not. Whoever she's looking for must be here."

Upsakes nodded agreement. "I expect her *ahalad-kaaslane* is very close by." Reisil stumbled as he thrust past her to view the feeding goshawk more closely. "It won't be long before Kallas gives Kodu Riik a new *ahalad-kaaslane*. Three in just this year. The Lady smiles on you all!"

"It is a sign," Varitsema pronounced suddenly. He stood back on a bench so all could see him. He spread his thin arms, hands lifted high, his long robes billowing. A broad smile lit his pale, hatchet face. "Can it be a coincidence? The Lady has sent this goshawk to bless this treaty between Kodu Riik and Patverseme. She wishes us to welcome the Dure Vadonis into our walls. We cannot disappoint Her, not after such a token!"

A rumbling murmur and scattered clapping met his

shouted last words. Varitsema nodded, pleased. Now, instead of feeling coerced into welcoming the Patverseme delegation, Kallas would be convinced that is was a celebration of the Lady's favor. Blessed Amiya indeed.

Reisil took advantage of the moment to escape, easing her way through the thicket of townspeople. There was nothing else for her to do here and she didn't want to give Saljane the opportunity to notice her again.

But first she had a gift for Raim—all the repayment he would take for the meals he had given her over these last months.

She stood on tiptoe, searching for the kohv-house proprietor. She caught sight of him across the room, propped against the kitchen doorway, intent upon the commotion. Reisil grimaced.

It would be easier to go out under the arches and return through the kitchen. But jealous of his domain, Raim allowed no one nonessential to its workings within the inner sanctums of his kitchen. Only Roheline, his wife, did he allow within, and then with strict dictums against touching or interfering. The potboys and scullery staff he suffered from necessity, but he prevented intrusion of the serving maids by passing prepared food through the window between the kitchen and the dining room.

Reisil edged her way around the inner wall by the enormous fireplace, empty except for an arrangement of dried flowers and brilliantly colored ribbons. Roheline's handiwork, as were the delicate paintings of flowers, fruits, grains and grasses twining up the pillars and tracing the edges of all the doors and arches. Reisil often came to the kohv-house before dawn to have breakfast and watch the rising sun touch life to the rich hues of Roheline's paintings.

Someone lurched into her and she stumbled. Ale splashed the side of her face and trickled down her neck.

Her face burned hot and her teeth clamped together, hearing Juhrnus snigger beside her.

She spun around and he held up empty hands.

"Not my doing, little sister."

Anger hardened Reisil's jaw. Maybe he hadn't done it, but his pleasure in her embarrassment was galling.

She raised her chin, green eyes hard as agates. She was not an imposing figure, but neither was she small, and she refused to feel like a mouse to his cat. She faced Juhrnus squarely, her mouth flat, her eyes narrowed.

"Is there a problem, little sister?" he asked in that sneering tone of his. Reisil gritted her teeth. She was so tired of him getting away with that "little sister" business! Words boiled up and burst on her lips, searing her tongue, but she closed her teeth on them, refusing to cause a scene by railing at an *ahalad₌kaaslane*. Even Juhrnus.

Then an idea struck her and she paused. How simple! How had she not thought of it sooner?

She smiled.

"Big brother, I must apologize. I have been remiss. I haven't yet congratulated you." She gestured at the sisalik, her smile widening at his nonplussed expression. "May the sun shine on you both all your lives." *Until you burn red and your skin peels and splits and your hair falls out and*— "I am preparing a gift for you. You will need a medicine pouch for your journeying. I have only to label things carefully so that you will not poison yourself, or give yourself the flux—accidentally."

His eyes narrowed and he crossed his arms.

"So the kitten has claws. Who'd have thought?"

"And who'd have thought I'd find you standing so far back, in the rear of trouble. But then, you're always *behind* the trouble, aren't you?"

"Careful how you go, little sister. Don't forget I'm *ahalad-kaaslane*."

"And don't *you* forget you're *ahalad-kaaslane,* big brother," Reisil retorted, her heart thundering. It wasn't much, but standing up to Juhrnus after all these years was like climbing to the top of a mountain or swimming across the ocean. Exhilarating, empowering.

"Please, don't let me keep you from your work," she said, gesturing to where Upsakes, Sodur and Felias continued to mollify the townspeople. "You've been so helpful today. Almost like you were actually here."

He flushed and opened his mouth, but she didn't wait for his response. Hugging her victory to herself, she tunneled away through the crowd.

She found Raim in his kitchen. He smiled welcome as she leaned in the serving window but did not stop kneading his dough.

"Bright day to you, Reisil. A blessed day indeed. You have seen?"

She nodded. "The Lady is generous." She changed the subject, not wanting to talk any more about Saljane, not wanting to even think about her. "I have brought you some of that perin thistle we talked about, and berigroot." She put the two pouches on the counter. She'd harvested them on a recent overnight trip up the Sadelema.

Raim dusted off his hands and took the pouches reverently in his hands. "Magnificent! You are the tark of my heart," he said, opening the perin thistle and sniffing. "Ah, like a blessing from heaven. I thank you. Will you sit and eat?"

"I'd like to, but I've more errands." She no longer felt hungry.

"Do you think anyone will mind?" He waved a flour-dusted hand at the thickening crowd. "Today is a new holiday."

"Teemart has a fever and I promised his mother I would look in," she said, trying to sound regretful.

"Nurema? I would not be late to her door for all the world. Such a tongue she has, like a whip of nails. Ah, well, such is the life of the tark. Sun shine bright on you, and thank you for these." He tapped the pouches. "I will set you a feast next time."

"Then I will make sure next time comes soon."

Reisil remembered Meelaru. "Raim, when all this settles down, could you ask Sodur to go see Meelaru? There's a woman there, another refugee—I think he can help her."

"Another one?" Raim shook his head. "My heart

weeps for them all. I heard of this plan to begin a new town. Varitsema does not like it, but it is a good thing. I shall tell Sodur. You had better go before Nurema gnaws herself into a frenzy."

Reisil waved good-bye and squeezed out through one of the arches. She turned her feet back toward the main gate, swinging into a swift walk, padding past shops built of gray flagstone, bright Lady Day banners fluttering in the wind.

As she walked, the specters of Saljane and Juhrnus rose in her mind. She felt a certain amount of elation. She had finally confronted Juhrnus. And she had twice stood her ground and rebuffed Saljane.

Rebuffed the Lady, she reminded herself and suddenly her elation drained away, her shoulders slumping. She trudged on, her stomach roiling.

The *ahalad-kaaslane* were heroes, each and every one. With the noted exception of Juhrnus, she thought dryly. Each shop in Kodu Riik kept a small area set aside for the *ahalad-kaaslane* where proprietors would offer food and drink and whatever supplies might be needed. These gifts were given without reservation or hesitation. The *ahalad-kaaslane* were bound to take no more than need required, forsaking personal gain or possessions.

So did tarks! Reisil gave all she had freely. She tended the ill—human and animal alike. She was a healer, a midwife and a counselor. She could do no more as *ahalad-kaaslane* than she could as tark. Indeed, she would do less. What did such as she know of that life? She knew nothing of battles or weapons. She'd never hunted except for plants, never stretched a bowstring, never hurt anyone. She was a tark!

She shook her head, rubbing at the ache in her forehead. She had made the right decision. The only decision.

The crowded shops with their second-story residential apartments and rooftop gardens faded into imposing houses with tall trees and wide grounds full of flowers. There were few walls inside Kallas. Its dusky-pink curtain wall built upon imposing earthworks made it a fortress, but within it was open-aired, with wide streets and courtyards.

Snow never fell on Kallas. The winters brought warm drenching rains. The runoff ran into storm sewers, which fed into a marvelous natural formation called the Sink. During the summer it was merely a rivulet running through a ravine, disappearing into an underground cavern. The water reappeared half a league away in a large pool before draining into the Sadelema. Once, in an effort to discover how long it took the water to run its course to the pool, the mayor of Kallas had ordered a crimson dye to be dropped into the Sink. Almost a full day had passed before the red-dyed water had filtered into the pool. It still remained a mystery what lengthy path the stream took in its journey. Yet no matter how much rain fell, Kallas never flooded. The Sink absorbed it all.

Reisil glanced up at the sun and realized how late it was. She hastened past the commons and the Sink and through the main gate. She smiled a distracted hello at the gatekeep and attendant guards, then trotted out along the road, following it as it curved out of sight around the shoulder of the wooded hillside, then dropped in lazy switchbacks to the river bottom. She passed the path leading to her cottage and continued down to a narrow trail through close-growing woods. The shady walk lent Reisil tranquillity. Songbirds twittered in the canopy and the sweet scent of carnillions, lupine, honey-roses, and starflowers wound together on the warm breeze. The Sadelema sparkled at her through the trees, last fall's leaves crunching beneath her feet adding a tangy fragrance to the air.

The path ended in a clearing where a small croft nestled. Tumble-stone fences hemmed in a kitchen garden and two paddocks, where grazed an assortment of chickens, goats, pigs and a milk cow. A hive of bees hummed merrily in one corner, and butterfly wings winked from wildflowers. Smoke curled from the chimney, the shutters and door closed despite the warmth of the day. Reisil knocked on the green-painted door. Moments later it swung open and she stepped inside, squinting in the gloom.

"It's about time," a wire-twist of a woman said, gray hair caught behind her head in a strict bun, black eyes snapping. Her wrinkled skin was dark, as if she was not native to Kodu Riik, but she had been a fixture of Kallas since Reisil could remember. "My son's hotter than a frying pan. That tea of yours hasn't done a lick of good. Can't hardly talk, his throat's so swollen. Suppose you've been up in Kallas dawdling about instead of tending the sick. Racket of those bells woke Teemart just when I finally got him asleep. Now he's coughing and sounding like a half-dead dog."

"My apologies, Nurema," Reisil said, setting her pack on the kitchen table, clearing her throat on the thick, dry air. "I had planned to be here sooner."

Nurema was a sharp-spoken woman, but kind and generous for all that. She had a special affection for her mild middle son, who, though now grown into a young man, had not yet married and instead took care of his widowed mother. For all her rough edges, Reisil appreciated Nurema's genuine fondness for Teemart. A mother's love. *Would that mine had shown the tiniest speck of feeling for me that Nurema has for her son!* As soon as she thought it, Reisil suppressed it. Now was not the time.

"Open these windows and the door," she ordered. "I know I said to keep him covered, but he needs fresh air. This smoke and heat don't do anything for him at all."

Reisil fit actions to words and flung open the shutters, turning to the cot in the corner where Teemart huddled beneath a thick layer of wool blankets, his breathing stertorous. She wrinkled her nose at his ripe odor, then touched her hand to his flushed forehead and cheeks. "You're right. The tea hasn't been able to do much. I brought some other things that should do the trick. Boil some water for me."

"No doubt he's being laggardly, and right now when there's so much work to be done," Nurema groused, snatching up the bucket and heading out to the well.

She sloshed water on her skirts on her hurried return. "Place is falling apart and there he is napping, lazy as a snake." Reisil wasn't deceived by the old woman's sour tirade and smiled to herself.

Nurema hovered over Reisil as she pawed through her pack, pulling out the things she needed: a vial of goris root extract, a clay jar of crushed teris and another of powdered oleaven leaves. There was a ball of red clay wrapped in damp cloth, and a bottle of fermented jess berries. Measuring carefully, Reisil prepared a brew that should break Teemart's fever. She then had Nurema hold him upright as she coaxed him to drink it.

"Easy now, Teemart. It tastes bad, I know, but it will make you feel better so that you can have a bath and stop drawing flies." A weak smile flickered across his face and he drank the foul-tasting concoction obediently. Nurema tucked the blankets in around him, stroking his hair from his forehead.

"Lazy brute," she murmured.

"He'll need another dose tonight and then in the morning," Reisil said. "I'll come around tomorrow to see how he's doing. Now to speed things up, we'll make a plaster."

She kneaded ground mustard and eucalyptus into the block of damp clay and pressed it onto the sick man's chest, laying a hot, damp cloth over it. "Don't let that dry out, or the mud will crack off. Hopefully he won't toss and turn too much. Give him some broth next time he wakes up, as much as he'll take. Float some bread in it. He needs both fluid and nourishment."

Nurema nodded, and Reisil knew the other woman would follow instructions precisely. She packed her supplies back in her pack and then arched her back, hearing it crack.

"Have a seat on the bench outside there and relax. I'll make some tea," Nurema ordered brusquely. Reisil obeyed gratefully. Her hunger had returned with a vengeance and her head pounded.

The bench had been made by Teemart for his mother and had a comfortably curved seat with a high back.

Nurema had woven rag cushions for it, and Reisil dropped down onto them with a sigh, kicking her feet out before her. The older woman soon followed, carrying a tray with two cups of tea, a plate of bread and sharp goat cheese.

"So what was this foolishness of the bells? Taktitu making a ruckus with Imeilus again?"

Reisil smiled. Meelaru's temperamental husband often went head-to-head with the tanner over an assorted variety of complaints: smell, noise, dirt, rude apprentices, wagons blocking the street and so forth. They'd a long history of bickering, and at least once a month the entire town of Kallas was drawn to one of their arguments.

"There was a herald from Koduteel. He says there's going to be peace." Reisil described the events in the kohv-house, ending with Saljane's arrival.

"The Blessed Lady is indeed generous," Nurema murmured when Reisil finished her dissertation. "Tell me again what Varitsema said about this truce and the ambassador from Patverseme."

Reisil did so in careful detail. She had been trained to pay careful attention to her constituents; their ills were often caused or made worse by events in their lives, and the tark must treat the spirit as well as the flesh. She ended with Varitsema's proclamation that the goshawk was a sign from the Blessed Lady.

"Hmph. He's a clever one, that Varitsema. Could have been a thief. Almost married him—did you know? Courted me for nigh on two years, but he was too pigheaded." She chuckled. "Pot calling the kettle black, I suppose. Least I had sense enough to know better. Varitsema and I would have been like Taktitu and Imeilus. Every morning a battle, every night a war. But trust him to take good advantage of that bird's arrival. Maybe he's right; maybe it really is a sign from Amiya. Either way, he'll stir the pot into a boil. No half measures. Got to show off for those Patversemese. Strutting like cocks in the butcher's yard. Just you wait, girl. By morning there will be all sorts of projects going on. Won't be a single soul with a moment to set and talk, but everyone will be dashing around dusting, polishing, painting, fixing, arranging, decorating—chickens with no heads. Good thing we live a ways out here. Peace and quiet."

Reisil finished her meal and then stood. "I had better get going. Thank you for the tea and food."

Nurema waved off her thanks with a knobby, arthritic hand. "You'll be back tomorrow to look in on Teemart?"

"I'll come midmorning before I make my rounds in Kallas. I won't be late."

Nurema sniffed. "See that you aren't."

Reisil bade farewell and made her way back up the path to the road. Her eyes felt thick and her pack unbearably heavy. The events of the day seemed far away, as if behind a window of thick, wavy glass. She was too wrung out to feel anything but a creeping numbness, which she welcomed.

She trudged up the hill with wooden steps. The sun had begun to set and already fireflies flittered brilliantly in the dusky air. Purple bindweed closed its petals against the night and a woodpecker pounded away on a birch glowing gold in the setting rays of the sun. Despite her exhaustion, Reisil couldn't resist stopping to smell a wild cattleberry, the sprays of tiny white blossoms smelling of vanilla and bergamot. She sighed and picked some. The flowers made a lovely flavoring for sweet breads. She would bake some in the morning and bring it back with her to Nurema and Teemart. It would help tempt his appetite and Nurema's too. She had little doubt that the bread and cheese they just had together was all the other woman had eaten in the last day.

She reached the road and turned back toward Kallas, then veered off along the path to her cottage. She ambled along the crown of the hill into the copse of trees through which she'd sprinted that morning. She stopped for a drink at the stream and then jumped over, this time not splashing herself.

Whoever had built her cottage had been a fine craftsman. It had two rooms and a loft, and was entirely made of smooth round stones hauled from the river. All but the back wall. The builder had set the cottage against the base of a finger of white- and yellow-streaked rock that towered over the trees around. Reisil liked it because few could get lost trying to find her. Her greenhouse was connected to the cottage on this wall, and in the winter the sun-heated stone reflected back warmth to her plants. The kitchen fire did the rest, as the chimney wall joined the two buildings together. Her garden spread out from the greenhouse and was bounded by a wood fence overgrown with gooseberry vines. Fruit trees clustered between the finger spire and the bluff.

When she'd returned to Kallas six months before, the council had offered her Kolleegtark's house. But though she remembered her times there fondly, his home had proved too small and didn't at all suit her needs. The townspeople had been so pleased at her appearance that they had not objected to her living so far outside the walls, and refurbished the cottage and built the greenhouse according to her specifications, donating materials and home comforts. Though no formal acceptance of her had been made, their generosity promised a future here, that they would provide for her needs as she would provide for theirs.

"I belong here," she told the twilight. "I am a tark. Nothing else."

Kek-kek-kek-kek.

The cry came like an answering challenge.

Reisil jerked out of her reverie, the strident sound reminding her of the barking wails of wild mountain dogs. She stared woodenly at the goshawk, who settled on the peak of her roof.

"Go away," she said at last in a low, adamantine voice. "I don't want you."

~Stay.

Chills like fingers of ice danced over Reisil's flesh. That voice in her mind. It had the feel of steel, of fingernails scraping across slate. It no longer held any of the qualities that had seemed so dangerously enticing at their first encounter.

"You cannot stay. I don't want you. I don't want

you!" Reisil shouted the words like a child shouts at a monster in a nightmare.

The bird's head swiveled, eyes glowing orange in the sunset.

~Stay.

This time the word stabbed into Reisil like a jagged blade. Saljane bent down and snapped her beak at Reisil as if to tear her flesh from her bones.

Reisil flinched and stepped back. Dismay and frustration balled in her stomach. Tears slid down her cheeks.

After a moment the bird straightened, mantled and shook herself from head to tail.

Reisil pressed a hand to her lips, her breath shaking in her chest.

She flung herself into the cottage beneath Saljane's shadow and slammed the door. She pulled the shutters closed and latched them, as if by doing so she could get rid of Saljane and all she represented. Without lighting a lamp, she crawled into bed and huddled wakefully there all night.

Reisil stumbled from her cottage at dawn, eyes deep-set and bloodshot in her pale face. Palpable relief coursed through her when she realized Saljane was gone.

For good, she hoped.

But she knew better. The goshawk had made herself clear the night before. Now it would be a contest of wills. Reisil squared her shoulders. It was a contest she would win. During the long night she'd gained control of her fears and uncertainties. Her refusal of Saljane, of the Lady's gift, had been swift and instinctive. But none of the doubts that rose like phantoms in the night could tear from her the certainty that she had made the right decision. Her will was fixed.

She prepared herself a breakfast of oatcakes with butter and honey and a compote of dried fruit stewed with red winter wine and walnuts. She washed the dishes in the hot water left over from her tea and then set off for Nurema's, her attention fixed on the ground in front of her.

Nurema greeted her with a wave as she scattered corn for her chickens.

"How is he today?" Reisil called from the fence. Nurema upended her bowl and patted the bottom for the last grains before joining Reisil.

"Better. He drove me outside with his chattering. Like a squirrel, nothing to say and yet he keeps barking and barking." Her fingers opened and closed in an imitation of Teemart's jaws.

Nurema led Reisil into the cottage, where she went to Teemart's bedside and fussed at his blankets. Reisil was glad to see her patient was propped up slightly against his pillows and that his face had lost that angry redness.

"How do you feel?" Reisil asked him.

"Better," he croaked, ducking his head bashfully.

"Throat still sore?"

He nodded, toying with the ragged edge of the blanket.

"We can do something for that." Reisil dug in her pack for the lozenges she'd brought. "Suck on one of these. It'll dull the pain and reduce the swelling. I'm going to make some more of that brew for you as well. Don't talk anymore. Rest your throat."

She proceeded to make the brew while Nurema went to collect eggs from her chickens and milk her goats. She returned just as Reisil had given Teemart another dose. He made a face as he handed the cup back to Reisil.

"If it tasted good, everyone would want to be sick," she said, smiling. "Go back to sleep now. You still need a lot of rest. I'll be back tomorrow."

Nurema followed her outside.

"Going into town?" Reisil nodded and Nurema harrumphed. "Good luck. Varitsema's probably got them all turned upside down by now. Stop back by on your way home. I've got some eggs, milk and cheese for you."

"I will, and thank you."

"Hmmph. Well, then. Did I ask for thanks? Get on with you. I've work to do."

Nurema made a shooing motion with her hands and

disappeared into the cottage. Reisil grinned and set off, her heart swelling. It was a good beginning to the day.

In town, Nurema's prophecy proved correct. A whirlwind bustle swept through every nook and cranny. New tiles around the common well. New paving stones to replace broken ones. New whitewash, new paint, new plantings, new railings and steps, new lamps, new flags and banners, new signs. What wasn't new was cleaned, polished, straightened, oiled, squared, tightened, glued, trimmed, washed, swept or pounded. The pace of it was furious. Hurry, hurry, hurry. Varitsema was everywhere, encouraging, preaching, admonishing. The Patversemese would know Kallas's worth and supremacy.

Beneath the fury of activity Reisil sensed a fury of a different kind. The banter she heard was sharp-edged, the laughter bitter as wormwood. The air pulsed with unvoiced malice and hatred. Everyone wore a mask of goodwill, but beneath . . . beneath the people of Kallas snarled and snapped with the helpless rage of caged animals.

Reisil moved among them, offering soothing words and smiles and treating various ills: sunburns and heatstroke, bruises, smashed fingers, cuts and blisters. Everywhere she was in demand and never had a moment to sit. And everywhere the rage seethed.

The medicinal supplies in her pack diminished and were replaced by gifts of bread, wine, dried apricots and apples, cheese, bacon, sausage, new squash, salt and, most generous, nussa spice from Raim.

"I'm in charge of the welcome banquet," the kohvhouse proprietor announced as he handed her a plate heaped with a mouthwatering array. "Varitsema wants it in the plaza for all to attend. He's given me the keys to the coffers. He wants it to be the most spectacular event the Dure Vadonis and his retinue have ever experienced." Raim's eyes glowed with anticipation.

"I'd be pleased to help," Reisil volunteered. "I'm pretty good with a scrubber and a dirty pot."

Raim clasped her hand. "I think I can find something

better than that for you, tark of my heart. Your hands
will be welcome indeed."

Reisil left him to his planning, taking her lunch outside to a table set beneath a blue-and-cream-striped awning. The breeze carried on its back the smells of freshly
mowed hay, manure from someone fertilizing a field,
woodsmoke and roasting meat.

Sudden cries in the street yanked her out of her reverie and she ran to the door. On the corner opposite
the kohv-house, perched on the flagpole jutting from its
foundation above the door, was Saljane. Reisil's face
paled, her jaw hardening.

Kek-kek-kek-kek.

A crowd swelled quickly about the goshawk. Saljane
preened herself and then roused her feathers, shaking
them into place. She swiveled her head, cocking it at the
wondering people below. She then shifted to stare directly at Reisil, who felt the searing accusation like a
brand on her forehead.

Before anyone could notice who had attracted the goshawk's attention, Reisil ducked back inside and gathered
up her pack, her lunch sitting like a lead weight in her
stomach. She retreated out through the courtyard,
hands trembling.

It was more than a contest of wills, this battle between
her and Saljane. Reisil could win and still lose if the
townspeople discovered her secret. And with Saljane
pursuing her, they might.

And so it went for days. Saljane continued to make
appearances wherever Reisil was. Her odd behavior
soon became the favorite topic of conversation as everyone questioned the bird's purpose: Why she hadn't made
her choice? Was this an ill omen?

"Are you sure it's *ahalad-kaaslane*?" asked Pori the
coopersmith of Sodur and Upsakes. Only five days remained until the Patversemese entourage arrived.

The three men stood together near the well in the
square where Reisil was drawing water to replenish her
empty water pouch. Sodur's silver lynx sprawled in the
shade of the well, tongue lolling from his mouth, his

tufted ears flicking back and forth. Upsakes's weirmart shared the lynx's sense of the heat and flopped herself beneath the well house along the well's cool tile ledge, panting.

"Have we not said so already, many times?" demanded Upsakes.

"It can't be aught else. No wild goshawk would behave as this has," replied Sodur with a sharp glance at his companion.

"But then why has it not chosen?" Pori clasped his thick hands around his jutting belly, avoiding looking at the short-tempered Upsakes.

"Who am I to answer for the bird? She will make her choice in her own good time." Upsakes's voice was distinctly dismissive and Reisil felt herself bristling. She liked Pori. He was kind and generous and always singing. His shop was a haven to children. Still he persisted bravely against Upsakes's curtness, his wide forehead creased into a frown.

"But it is unusual, isn't it?"

"The Blessed Lady sends us so few such birds—who can say how such choosings go?" inserted Sodur in a placating way before Upsakes could make a scathing reply. "The goshawk will make a choice sooner or later. Mayhap the one she searches for is not here."

That set Pori thinking. "Of course! That's it!" He turned excitedly to his wife and sister who'd come to stand beside him. "We sent that caravan to Koduteel— they should be back any day. Bird's got to be waiting for them. Young Kaval went on that trip to learn the business. That's just got to be it!"

The rest of those standing about listening caught his enthusiasm as dry tinder catches a spark, and the rumor swept through Kallas like wildfire. Reisil felt a confused mixture of consternation and hope. Smart, handsome, keen-witted and quick to smile, Kaval was a perfect choice. Her heart clenched and she bit back a cry of protest. She could not lose him, lose his tender touch that sizzled across her skin and turned her bones to clay.

The animosity in the stare she turned to Saljane was like a spear thrown from her heart.

~Why are you doing this to me? Why do you keep coming back when you know how I feel? When you know how much it could hurt me? Do you want me to lose everything?

The goshawk preened her chest feathers, making no sign that she heard Reisil's furious questions.

"Afraid she'll make off with your lover? Or wishing she'd pick you?" Juhrnus had come to stand behind Reisil and she started, flushing. She should have known that where Upsakes and Sodur were, Juhrnus could not be far.

She glared at him. The sisalik perched on his shoulder and Juhrnus stroked the lizard's leathery jowls. "What would a goshawk want with you?" Juhrnus pressed. "I doubt even a buzzard would want you."

Somehow, as much as Reisil wanted Saljane to go away, as much as she wanted to be a tark, she could almost have thrown it all away right there, just to see the look on Juhrnus's smug, sneering face.

She opened her mouth and snapped it shut. Without a word she turned and walked away, teeth gritted, knuckles white as she clenched her hands together.

Juhrnus broke into a peal of laughter. Her face flamed, but she remained stiffly straight as she went, never looking back.

Chapter 4

The next day a company of knights clattered over the bridge from Patverseme. Their tall, elegant horses moved with the grace of dancers. The riders wore shining armor with brilliant tabards and shields blazoned with the Dure Vadonis's coat of arms. A black-and-gold diamond pattern circled their chests and trimmed the sleeves and necklines of the indigo cloth. In the center of each man's chest two crimson lions leaped past one another. Beneath them on the blue field was a red three-pronged coronet denoting the Dure's rank.

Upon arrival, they met with Varitsema and several others of the city council. Soon after, all but two returned to Patverseme, the others serving as envoys until the Dure Vadonis's arrival in four days.

The two knights were treated with careful courtesy and given sumptuous lodgings and delectable viands. But everywhere they went, the people of Kallas spat behind them, making signs to ward off evil.

Reisil did her best to soothe the seething emotions, reminding the townspeople of what they had to gain by peace, but she could hardly shake off her own agitation and fury. Beginning the night of the knights' arrival, Saljane had once again begun baiting Reisil at home.

She perched on Reisil's windowsill, shrieking when she lit the lamp. Reisil dropped it, shattering its chimney. The haranguing continued through the night and morning, from the roof, the fruit trees, the fence. Nothing

Reisil did made any difference. She reasoned and cried and even screamed back at the goshawk like a fishwife, but to no avail.

"Are you well?" Roheline asked her on the third day following the knights' arrival, concern drawing her attention away from the mural Varitsema had commissioned her to paint in the town plaza. It was a celebration of Kodu Riik, nearly finished now. Paint splashed her cheeks, her chestnut hair and the smock she wore over her tunic. Her hands were dyed shades of blue, green, red, pink, yellow and orange.

"Tired, like everyone else," Reisil replied with a forced smile.

"You should try to get some rest while you can. The Dure Vadonis and his party arrive tomorrow. Have you met the two knights he sent ahead?"

Reisil shook her head, her heavy dark braid snaking down her back with the movement.

"Well, you are about to." Roheline stood, her usually merry face carefully expressionless as she nodded greeting to Varitsema and the two knights he escorted.

"I believe you have already met the talented Roheline. And this lovely and gifted young woman is Reisiltark." Reisil nodded, feeling herself blush at Varitsema's description.

The two knights gave her and Roheline a short bow. They were both tall and handsome, as the tales said knights ought to be. The first had dirty blond hair and blue eyes, a crooked nose that clearly had been broken, and a chipped front tooth that gave him a boyish look. He grinned and a dimple creased his cheek, adding to the effect. The other was as dark as Reisil. There were creases around his mouth and eyes that showed he knew how to smile, but now there was a look of haughty disdain fixed on his expression, which did not vary. His nose was straight and aquiline, his cheeks high-boned, his jaw firm. He wore his hair long, pulled off his face and held at the nape of his neck with a silver clasp. His eyes flickered across Reisil and Roheline, dismissing them both, then traveled to Roheline's mural. This, too,

he seemed to dismiss, standing there with an air of polite boredom.

"These two gentlemen," Varitsema continued grandly,
ignoring the second man's inattention, "are Sirs Glevs
and Kebonsat. Kebonsat is the eldest son of the Dure
Vadonis."

Ah, so that explains it, thought Reisil. *He's nobleborn,
which has made him rude and self-important.* Then again,
Juhrnus proved that one didn't have to be nobleborn to
be rude and self-important.

"Bright morning to you. And welcome to Kallas," said
Roheline in a restrained voice.

"Your work is quite beautiful," said Glevs in a deeper,
more respectful voice than Reisil expected. "I particularly like the way you've made the Urdzina. It's like a
ribbon of pure silver." He pointed to the portion of the
mural containing an image of Kallas nestled on the bluffs
above the Sadelema. In the opposite corner was Koduteel. The river began at Kallas and wandered through
the mural, connecting the scattered images of people
working, laughing, crying, playing and dancing. It halted
its course with a flourish of drops at the foot of Koduteel. Animals of every sort romped through the mural.
Even Saljane had made an appearance, Reisil suddenly
noted. Roheline had painted her perched in the branches
of a plum tree heavy with ripe fruit, her body melding
with the leaves. Only her brilliant amber eye with its
hint of red was wholly visible.

"Urdzina?" asked Roheline, bringing Reisil back to
the conversation.

"You call the river Sadelema," explained Glevs with
a deprecating little wave.

"We of Patverseme call it Urdzina. It means little rivulet," said Kebonsat in a bored tone that said the river
was hardly worthy of being called such. Reisil bristled.

"How dull. Sadelema means 'sparkle.' I think its pref-
erable, don't you?" Without waiting for an answer, she
picked up her pack and slung it over her shoulder. "I
should be going now. May the Lady smile upon you all,"
she said, flashing an apologetic look at Roheline, whose

paint-spattered hand covered her smile, and set off across the plaza.

She had gone halfway when there was a clattering of hooves and a galloping horse burst into the plaza in front of her. Its rider pulled up. The dappled gray gelding snorted and pawed at the ground, its neck arching as it sidled side to side.

"Kaval!" Reisil exclaimed with glad surprise.

"Bless the Lady for my luck! I've found you first thing." He jumped to the ground and swept Reisil up into an exuberant hug.

"I've missed you sorely, my own tark," he said in an aching voice against her ear as he set her down. He went to his saddlebags and fumbled inside, returning with a small roll of cloth. He handed it to her. "I cannot wait any longer to give this to you. It's been burning a hole in my bag for weeks."

Reisil smiled and unrolled it carefully. It was a silk scarf. It had been dyed in soft shades of twilight, then painted with brilliant wildflowers. Reisil shook it out. "It's beautiful," she breathed. "I can't believe it's for me."

Kaval took and draped the scarf around her shoulders. "Everything's for you," he said. "I thought I made you understand that before I left."

Reisil blushed, dropping her eyes to the ground.

"Who are they?" Kaval's voice turned suddenly hard and suspicious, his hands crushing the silk scarf. Reisil followed his gaze over her shoulder. Varitsema herded the two knights toward them.

"You haven't heard?"

"Heard what?"

"Too much to explain it all now," she said. "There is to be peace with Patverseme and these knights are part of the ambassadorial entourage. The rest of the party arrives tomorrow. If we fail to welcome them properly, the Iisand Samir has promised severe retribution. *Severe,* Kaval," she said, squeezing his arm warningly. It was all the explanation she had time for before Varitsema descended on them.

"Bright day, young Kaval. I hope the Blessed Lady smiled on your journey. Your father is well?" Varitsema clasped Kaval's hand jovially, though his eyes remained watchful and stern in his narrow face.

"Very well. He is seeing to the unloading of the wagons." Kaval eyed the two knights with belligerent antipathy.

"But you could not wait, I see." Varitsema smiled at Reisil, but that measuring expression never left his eyes, and he kept them fixed on Kaval. "I would introduce you to Sirs Glevs and Kebonsat. They are in service to the Dure Vadonis, who arrives tomorrow."

"Welcome to Kallas," Kaval said in a slow, unwilling tone as he reached out to clasp each man's arm in greeting. Gone was the jubilant, carefree man who'd galloped in search of Reisil. In his place was a stiff, guarded stranger, aloof and wary.

"You've just returned to Kallas?" inquired Kebonsat, his face equally hostile.

"Yes. We've been to Koduteel. The roads are dry. Your journey there should be an easy one," he said tightly.

"It is our hope." Kebonsat's gaze flickered to Reisil, who stood frozen in place. He scrutinized her as if seeing her for the first time. Perhaps he was. She doubted he'd bothered to look before.

She knew what he saw—a masculine-looking woman with a face of flat planes and bold features. Beautiful she could never be called, but attractive enough. She was no match for either man in height, but neither was she tiny at a full seven inches over five feet. She was slender but strong: a woman made for work, not pleasure.

Kebonsat's gaze shifted back to Kaval and Reisil bristled, feeling like a goat at auction. Kaval stepped closer and slid a possessive arm about her shoulders. She just barely resisted the urge to shake it off and slap them both. They were making her a trophy in some sort of rivalry that had sprung up the instant they laid eyes on one another. Glad as she was to see Kaval, as good as it felt to be in his arms and feel the warmth of his smile, she would not put up with this sort of posturing.

"I'm afraid I must desert you," she said to Kaval, disentangling herself. "There's much to be done yet. Thank you for the scarf."

"Bide a moment. I must return to help my father anyway. I shall walk with you."

Kaval nodded to the two knights and Varitsema and collected up the reins of his horse. He put his hand on the small of Reisil's back as they walked away.

They had not gone four steps before Kaval began grilling Reisil on the events of the last two weeks.

"How could Iisand Samir agree to this!" he exclaimed. "If you could see what it's like in the rest of Kodu Riik. People are starving, and worse. Men without hands, without eyes, without feet. The Patversemese have no honor; they cannot be trusted to keep any treaty. And what about Mysane Kosk? Can we just forget that? We still don't know all that happened there. Those wizards left no one alive to tell the tale, and no one who goes there now comes out alive."

His bitter vehemence shocked Reisil and she eyed him askance. Her entire acquaintance with Kaval had been one of gentleness and comfort. As a child, she'd followed him about like a lost puppy. Older than she by two years, he'd always been patient and kind, always defending her against Juhrnus, always ready with a joke or a sweet. Grown into a man, he topped her by six inches. Broad-shouldered and athletic, with short-cropped brown hair and blunt features, he always had a ready smile, a contagious laugh. Upon her return to Kallas, he'd welcomed her with a warm embrace and flattering admiration. They were together in every spare moment they could manage.

The ruthless fury on his normally handsome face made him look ugly, and Reisil hardly recognized him. He'd never spoken so of Mysane Kosk to her, had never spoken of it at all.

"To threaten *us*—Iisand Samir must be insane! And for what? For a treaty that those soulless bastards will break as soon as they have the chance. They should all be put to the blade."

Before Reisil could reply, a shadow swooped down at them. She felt the rush of air across her head and flinched away. Saljane's strident *kek-kek-kek-kek* echoed down the street.

"What was that?"

Once again, Reisil's reply was cut off. Pori ran into the street from his shop.

"Kaval!" The excited coopersmith grasped Kaval's hand and began pumping it up and down. "Congratulations, my boy. Knew it had to be you. And here you're back and she comes right for you. Saw the whole thing. Dived right out of the sky like she was going after a rabbit. Magnificent! Never saw anything so wonderful."

"Pori! Pori! Stop. What are you talking about?" A bewildered Kaval pulled his hand out of the other man's grasp.

"Why, the goshawk. She's *ahalad-kaaslane,* come in search. Been here nearly two weeks and hasn't made a choice." Pori had begun to look confused. "Didn't she choose you?"

Kaval shook his head. "If so, she didn't tell me about it."

"Why . . . but why not? Why hasn't she made her choice?" Pori's face had fallen and he looked forlorn. It might have been funny if Reisil didn't know the truth. Because of her, this good man was humiliating himself.

"I don't know." Kaval shrugged regretfully and grasped the other man's shoulder. "Thank you, old friend, for the kind wishes and hopes. It would be a great honor to be chosen by such a bird. I am flattered you would think I could be *ahalad-kaaslane*."

Hearing the reverence in his voice, Reisil bit her cheeks and studied the ground. They left Pori shaking his head and muttering. Reisil was too caught up in her own worries to hear much of Kaval's continuing tirade against the Iisand and the Patversemese. She left him when they reached the wide courtyard hubbing Kaval's father's warehouses.

"I had better be on my way."

He smiled at her, that same lopsided grin that always made her heart race. "I'll see you tomorrow, won't I?"

"I'm going to be helping Raim with the preparations for the feast."

"Oh, right, the feast." His voice hardened again.

"Will you be there?"

"I expect so. If only to see you." He waved at the bustle of activity within the courtyard. "There is much to do here and my father intends me for another trip at the end of the month. He is so pleased with the success of my journey that he has agreed at last to let me take on more of the business. It means a lot more time here, so I won't be able to come visit you very soon." He gave a diffident shrug. "So if you will be at the feast, then there is where I must be as well."

Reisil nodded, feeling a thrill of tingling pleasure and sharp disappointment at his words. Pleasure, disappointment—and relief. Much as she wanted to touch him, to snuggle in his arms, she did not want him to visit her in her cottage. Not with Saljane hanging around.

"Thank you for the scarf," she murmured, stroking it with soft fingers. "It's lovely."

"No more so than you," he replied, taking her hand in his warm grasp and kissing her. "I will see you tomorrow."

Reisil watched him walk away, his stride purposeful, as if he forgot her as soon as he turned away. He approached his father, who was marking figures on a list as the wagons were unloaded. Kaval grasped Rikutud's arm and drew him aside, his hands chopping at the air. She knew he brought the news of the treaty. Rikutud had heard already, of course. He had returned from a short trading trip days after the meeting at Raim's. He grasped Kaval's arm and handed his list to one of his men before drawing his son into the rear of his home. Reisil sighed. All her words to the contrary, she wasn't so sure that the treaty was a good idea either, but the war being over, that was very good. If it meant hosting the Patversemese for a night, then so be it.

She thought about Iisand Samir's threats. Reisil didn't doubt that he would make good on the confiscation of everyone's property, turning the townspeople out. Including her. She'd lose her cottage and become a wandering tark after all.

But no one would be so stupid and reckless as to chance that, she comforted herself. Kaval and Rikutud might be angry now. But it was often said that Rikutud would rather have kohv with the Demonlord than put a penny in the poor plate. No, he would never risk his business. Kallas would do the right thing, and the Dure Vadonis would be duly impressed by the town's hospitality, and then he would travel on to Koduteel and sign the treaty.

As usual, Saljane awaited Reisil at home, perching on the eave above the door. Silhouetted in the shadows, she looked like a malevolent wraith.

Reisil scowled up at her, shivering as the ember eye sparked in the depths of the bird's ebon form. She made a sound like a growl and strode onto her porch, shoving her door open with a bang.

Reisil had taken to closing her shutters during the day so that the bird could not enter while she wasn't home. It made the cottage stuffy and hot. She thrust each of them open, muttering as she banged her forehead on the window's edge.

She lit the lamps and gently draped the scarf Kaval had given her over her bed, caressing the fabric with soft fingers. Then she set about preparing her supper. Behind her she heard a flapping of wings and a thump. Turning, she found Saljane clutching the back of a chair, wings raised for balance. She eyed Reisil defiantly, beak open in a soundless cry.

"This pestering isn't going to work, you know," Reisil said, leaning back against the counter as she peeled a potato, her fingers trembling slightly. "I am what I am and that's just the way it is."

~Belong. With. You.

Reisil started, not expecting the communication, and jabbed herself with the knife.

"No."

Saljane said nothing more, but merely stared. She watched as Reisil ate her hearty supper, as she washed the supper dishes, as she set the cottage to rights, as she took a hip bath, as she crawled into bed, blowing out the lamp and pulling the covers tight around her neck.

Despite her calm demeanor, Reisil did not fall asleep quickly. She could almost taste Saljane's voice, metallic and bitter. Who would want such a bonding? There were songs about the love between the *ahalad-kaaslane*. She couldn't imagine it. She wanted the love of a flesh-and-blood man. Kaval.

Her fingers touched the scarf and she coiled her fingers in its length, her lips curling into a smile.

Reisil woke the next morning with gritty eyes and a gummy mouth. She groaned as she lumbered up out of bed and stretched, her spine cracking. Her head felt thick and her stomach grumbled.

She stirred the fire to life, adding wood until it popped merrily. While she waited for her tea to boil, she combed out her hair and rebraided it. She dressed herself in soft cotton trousers the color of faded violets. The full legs tapered down her leg to a two-inch cuff of a rich, dark purple that she'd embroidered with leaves and flowers. The overtunic was of the same purple as the trouser's cuffs and came down to her knees, with splits up the sides to allow free movement. She tied a ribbon about her neck to match the faded violet color of her trousers, then laced on her sandals. When she was through, she glanced down at herself, pleased. She'd made the dye for the outfit herself by boiling the shells of tiny freshwater clams. It had taken her several years of experimenting before she'd hit on the shells as a source of the pigment, then another year to figure out a proper mordant.

Reisil had thought to bring a gift back to Kallas to repay the town for its care of her. She'd not yet shown anyone the fruits of her labor and smiled to think of Roheline's excitement at obtaining the pigment for her paints. Nor would she be the only one eager to make use of Reisil's discovery.

After a moment's debate, Reisil tucked the scarf Kaval had given her into her pack along with a long apron. She didn't know what Raim had in mind for her today, but she doubted he'd give her a chance to come home and change before the festivities began and she didn't want to get too filthy. Whatever did find its way onto her clothing, she'd be able to hide much of it with the scarf.

The cool morning breeze stroked her cheeks. There a light mist rose from the river and the scent of growing things filled the air. A bubble of happiness burbled up inside Reisil. She thought of Raim's wonderful food, the delight on Roheline's face when she saw the purple of Reisil's clothes, of Kaval's possessive arm curled about her shoulders. She ran a few steps and dropped back to a walk, laughing out loud.

To her surprise, Teemart waited for her outside the gates. He wore heavy boots and a battered straw hat that he tore from his head and crushed in his fist at her approach. He smiled shyly at her and avoided meeting her eyes.

"Bright morning," Reisil said, curiosity coloring her voice.

"Ma sent me to give this to you," he said abruptly, holding out a small object. "She said she'll not take it back. It's for you and only you."

"How are you feeling?" Reisil asked, taking the small, cloth-wrapped package, turning it over in her fingers. It was hard and had a flat shape covered with bumps. A gift of gratitude for her care of Teemart, she supposed.

He lifted one shoulder and kicked at the dirt. "Fit enough. Been mending walls and cutting sod."

"Don't overdo it," Reisil cautioned.

"No, ma'am. I wouldn't do that," Teemart replied, still looking at Reisil's feet.

"Are you coming to the feast?"

"I can't say. Ma will do what she'll do."

"Well, I hope to see you both there," Reisil said. "Tell your mother thank-you. I'll come 'round and thank her myself when the commotion of the Dure Vadonis's visit is over." She turned to leave but Teemart's rough hand on her sleeve stopped her, his face flushing darkly.

"Ma wanted me to tell you something else. She said to say that she knows all about it and that you'd better stop—" He broke off and rubbed a hand across his mouth. His eyes flickered up to hers for a second, then back to her feet.

"Go on."

"You know how Ma is. But she said to tell you, so . . ."

"It's all right." But it wasn't. A fist of foreboding closed around Reisil's throat.

Teemart licked his lips. "Well, she said that she knows all about it and you'd better stop being a fool and take up what's yours. She said you ought to know better and not to be such a coward."

At the last Teemart's voice dropped into a whisper. He didn't wait for Reisil to reply, but jogged off along the road home, his head jerking up and down with his awkward gait.

Reisil stood rooted to the ground, mouth open, Nurema's gift clutched in her hand. The message had to refer to Saljane. But how did the old woman know? Had she seen the goshawk flying over, following Reisil, and made the connection? She was a keen-witted old woman, for certain. But if she knew, then who else?

Her sense of joyous well-being drained away, leaving her trembling. Slowly she unwrapped Nurema's gift. Inside the cloth was a silver talisman of the Blessed Lady.

Reisil gasped.

The workmanship of the pendant was exquisite. It showed a gryphon in flight, a moon and sun clutched in its talons, a streamer of ivy dangling from its beak. The eye of the gryphon burned red, reminding her uncomfortably of Saljane's eyes. Reisil could see every feather on the gryphon, every hair of its fur. Where had Nurema gotten it? It was too fine a thing to have come from Kallas. Too expensive for her to just give away.

Reisil turned the pendant over in her hand. The back was as finely worked as the front. That Nurema meant

the pendant as a reinforcement of her message, Reisil
did not doubt. But she was no more inclined to be
pushed into becoming *ahalad-kaaslane* by the old woman
than by Saljane. She'd return the thing in the morning
and that would be the end of it.

To keep it safe until then Reisil slipped the talisman
onto the ribbon about her neck and retied it so that the
cold metal fell between her breasts, hidden from sight.

She passed through the gates with an absent wave at
the gatekeeper and made her way to Raim's kohv-house.
The pendant lay chill and heavy against her breast, its
rough edges chafing her tender skin. It never seemed to
warm with the heat of her skin, but remained a cold
reminder of Nurema's admonishment.

Raim greeted her with a cheery wave as she entered
his kohv-house, hardly glancing up from his sheaf of lists.

"Bright morning! Sit down. Have some breakfast.
You're going to need a good meal for what I've in mind
for you. Something better than porridge and dried fruit."
A boy brought her a plate of eggs, smoked fish, crisp
buttercakes and grilled squash, and a cup of creamy hot
kohv with a dash of nussa spice. As Reisil began her
meal, Raim glanced up, noticing her at last.

"Ah! What beautiful color!" He clapped his hands
together in his extravagant way. "My Roheline will be
envious. You will get no rest until she has some of this
wonderful purple."

Reisil smiled at him, sipping at the hot brew.

"I will gladly give her some of my dye, and hope she
takes pity on my poor cottage. It's so dark and dreary."

Raim chuckled.

"It is no hard bargain," he said. "You could charge
much more and she would pay. But now I must return
to my kitchen. The Dure Vadonis will arrive today and
all must be ready. Varitsema is like a nervous mother.
He will not forgive me if the food is undone." He
pushed through the swinging doors, calling over his
shoulder, "When you are through, let me know and I
will set you to work."

So busy did Raim keep her that Reisil missed the ar-

rival of the Dure Vadonis and his entourage. So busy
did he keep her that she almost could forget Nurema's
message and the talisman around her neck.

Almost.

She began her morning overseeing the arrangement
of the tables and seating arrangements. Roheline, who
was making lavish decorations with candles, blown-glass
lamps, cartloads of flowers, ribbons, banners, silver-
toned chimes and gleaming metal ornaments, went into
raptures over her outfit. Reisil promised her some of the
dye, for which Roheline pledged to come begin painting
in the cottage as soon as she was able.

She stroked the sleeve of Reisil's tunic with covetous
fingers. "Don't give out the formula too quickly," she
cautioned Reisil after a moment. "It will make anyone's fortune."

"I am here to serve Kallas, not make a profit," Reisil protested.

"As is correct for any tark. But trust in me, there are
those who will see nothing but profit in your dye. Rikutud, for instance. He's a wily one, and eats and breathes
money. He will not wish to share with all of Kallas. But
all could benefit from the dye if you arrange it so."

Reisil grinned wickedly.

"All right. I'll give you the formulas for the dye and
the mordant, and you can handle the rest."

"Me! Oh, no! I have much too much to do," Roheline
exclaimed. "I could not do such a thing." But her eyes
sparkled.

"But it's your idea. And I know just the woman who
could help you." During this season of spring cleaning
and sprucing up, Reisil had been able to find odd jobs
for Shorin, the starving mother who'd accosted her in
the street. But those jobs would dry up quickly now. A
dye works would set her up permanently. Though the
ahalad-kaaslane had already begun moving the squatters
to a new village along the river twelve leagues to the
north, Shorin would have an easier time in Kallas. And
Roheline already liked Shorin, admired her dry humor,
hard work and devotion to her children.

Grinning with satisfaction, Reisil gave Roheline a

wink. "I'd better get on with preparations. I can't have
Raim angry with me." Reisil gave the other woman a
sunny wave and departed. As she left, she could see
Roheline's mind clicking away at the problem. The dye
could become an enormous business, Reisil knew. In
taking it on, Roheline might not have time to paint. Yet
despite her words to the contrary, she seemed willing to
make that sacrifice, at least for now. *But what happens
later?* Reisil asked herself. *What happens when she wants
her life back?*

She scanned the nearby rooftops and sky for the ever-
present Saljane. She was nowhere to be seen.

The bird wanted Reisil to sacrifice her life for a new
one, a new challenge. But she wasn't like Roheline. She
wasn't interested in that new challenge. She wanted to
be Kallas's tark. She wanted to explore her burgeoning
feelings for Kaval. *Ahalad-kaaslane* were forbidden such
attachments. They must keep free of all biases, which
meant constant travel and few true friends. She did not
want to be *ahalad-kaaslane* with the goshawk, with a
lynx, with a bear or a mouse. She did not want to be
ahalad-kaaslane at all.

With the serving arrangements well under way, she
returned to Raim. He sent her on a flurry of errands.
When the city bells rang, signaling the arrival of the
Dure Vadonis and his entourage, Reisil was outside the
walls in the woods, where pits had been dug days before.
Inside them roasted two steers, four pigs, six goats and
a bevy of chickens.

"So it begins," muttered Taimeoli, whom Raim had
put in charge of overseeing the roasting pits. Reisil eyed
him, wondering if he felt as Kaval did.

"Do you know," Taimeoli continued, "that my
brother and two cousins went to fight in the war? Killed
they were. All three together at Mysane Kosk. Or at
least we haven't seen them since." He sighed, his square
face set in hard lines. His lame foot explained why he
had not gone with his brother and cousins to fight.

"I didn't know," Reisil said. "It is a great loss."

Taimeoli frowned. "I didn't care for my cousins much.

But I do miss Aare. He was one of the Lady's bright lights. The Patversemese have a lot to answer for." At Reisil's sharp look Taimeoli held up his hands. "I'm not the one to ask for such answers. But don't look for me tonight. I'll not welcome them to Kallas. My family died to keep them out. Where's the justice of it?"

Reisil thought of Roheline, Shorin and Saljane.

Changing lives. No choices. New challenges.

The Iisand Samir had given Kallas no choice but to welcome the entourage from Patverseme. Taimeoli had had no choice but to let his brother and cousins go off without him. They had had no choice but to die at Mysane Kosk. She wasn't giving Roheline much choice with the dye. Shorin had had no choice but to leave her home and beg. The challenge in all of it was to keep going, to keep building their lives.

And then there was Saljane.

"They'll be gone in two days," Reisil said. "It's not long."

"No. The wizards razed Mysane Kosk in two days. It's not long at all."

Feeling unsettled, Reisil returned to Raim to report the progress of the roasting meat. Flour dusted his hair and colorful spatters patterned his long apron. He waved her inside, nodding as she reported.

"Ah, good! I need you. Come here and ice these tarts. Like so." He showed her how to squeeze the thin honeycream icing onto the trays of fruit-filled tarts that lined the tables of the kohv-house. "Good. Exactly. There is plenty more when you run out," he said, pointing to an enormous copper bowl at the end of the board. He washed the sticky icing from his hands, watching her critically. "There are meat rolls, wine and fruit here when you are hungry."

With that he trotted off into the kitchen, leaving Reisil in the relative peace of the kohv-house dining room. She donned a smock and apron and set to work. She had completed nearly half the trays when a man and woman wandered through the courtyard, under the blue-and-

white-striped awning. They stopped, uncertain, eyeing
the trays of tarts lining every flat surface in sight.

"Is there no service today?"

Reisil started at the sound of Kebonsat's voice, turning around warily. With the back of her hand, she
brushed a stray hair from her face.

"Not to speak of, no. But there is plain fare, if you'd
like. I can get that for you."

Kebonsat exchanged a look with the girl who'd accompanied him. Though not as tall, she bore an uncanny
resemblance to him. She shared the same high cheek-
bones, aquiline nose and firm jaw. Her dark hair was
caught up in a series of braids and combs to create a
tousled, cascading effect that was quite striking. She
wore a light summer gown that swept the floor in soft,
delicate folds. Sapphires twinkled in her ears. She nodded at Kebonsat. He turned back to Reisil.

"Thank you. We would be grateful." He said the
words formally, but the coolness of the tone contradicted
completely the meaning of the words.

Reisil gave him a sharp look and then waved to the
tile-topped tables beneath the awning. "You'll have to
sit out there. I'll get you something. No choices, I'm
afraid."

The words continued to ring in Reisil's ears as the two
Patversemese went to sit.

No choices.

I'm afraid.

No choices. I'm afraid.

I'm afraid. No choices.

She piled a platter with cold meat rolls, apples, pears
and plums. She added a bowl of radishes, plates, napkins
and forks, and a jug of lightly spiced wine.

"Can I help?"

Reisil jumped at the girl's musical voice close behind
her.

"The gruff Kebonsat is my brother. My name is Ceriba. Can I carry anything?"

"I am Reisil," she answered, handing Ceriba the jug
of wine and two cups. "I can manage the rest." She

followed Ceriba back to the table where Kebonsat sat
stiffly, frowning at his sister with undisguised disapproval.

Reisil waited for Ceriba to sit before setting down
the platter.

"I've heard this kohv-house serves the best food in
Kallas," Ceriba said, breaking the silence.

Kebonsat picked up a meat roll and turned it over in
his hand. "Doesn't look like much." Ceriba gave him a
Look and Reisil thought she might have kicked him beneath the table.

"You'll get a better taste of it tonight. Raim's preparing the feast in honor of your arrival."

"So you don't own the kohv-house?"

Kebonsat laughed. "She is a tark, Ceriba."

Again that Look.

"Won't you join us for a few minutes?" she asked
Reisil. Reisil was tempted, just to annoy her brother,
who sat there looking absolutely aghast at the prospect.
But she shook her head.

"There's a lot of work yet to be done. But I thank
you. Enjoy your meal."

Reisil returned to glazing the tarts, keeping her back
turned to the two young Patversemese. Her stomach
grumbled and she thought longingly of the meat rolls
and fruit, but she did not want to have to share a meal
with Kebonsat. His rudeness would sour the food in
her stomach.

The two finished their meal about the same time that
Reisil completed the tarts. She wiped her hands on her
apron and turned around, only to bump into Kebonsat
standing behind her. Ceriba was stacking the dishes on
the platter and returning them to the board.

"How much do we owe you?" Kebonsat queried
abruptly. Reisil bridled at his curtness.

"I'll tell you what. I wouldn't want you to have to pay
for bad food, so why don't you just leave Raim whatever
you think his food is worth, if anything at all." He had
the grace to look embarrassed, but Reisil didn't bend.
She lifted her eyebrows and crossed her arms.

"It was passable," Kebonsat said grudgingly. Ceriba came to stand beside him.

"Nonsense. The food was delicious. I don't know what your cook did to give the meat such wonderful flavor, but you, my brother, ate them so fast I feared for my fingers."

"I was hungry," he said stiffly.

"Hunger will make a body eat anything," Reisil agreed, her green eyes narrowing as her temper heated. "Slugs, bugs, carrion. Myself, I'm fond of Raim's cooking, even just plain meat rolls. But I'm just a common tark with common tastes. What do I know about good food like noble folks eat? Now if you will excuse me, I really must be going. There is yet a great deal to be done before tonight's festivities. Though I wouldn't hold out much hope for the food," she said tartly.

With that she gathered up her glazing utensils and returned them to the kitchen, adding them to the piles of dishes waiting their turn to be washed, mumbling angrily beneath her breath.

Behind her, Ceriba laughed. Caught by the richness and joy in the sound, Reisil stopped just inside the kitchen door to listen.

"I don't think you've made a good impression on her at all, my brother."

"I wasn't trying to." Reisil could almost smile at the truculence in his tone.

"I noticed. She noticed. Don't you think you ought to try harder to get along with the Kodu Riikian people? After all, Father has told us again and again how important this treaty is. Patverseme can't afford a war here anymore, not with Scallas arming."

"You can say that? After losing our uncle? After they murdered our cousin Keris and his sons?"

"You are so young sometimes, Kebonsat. It wasn't murder. It was war. They've lost a lot of friends and family too. I'm not going to forget our uncle or cousins, but I want peace. I'm tired of war. I pray Scallas will rethink its interest in us once this treaty is signed. If our attention is not divided between two enemies, they may decide we're too difficult a nut to crack. So stop acting like such a prig and try to get along. Father is trusting you not to sabotage his efforts."

Reisil peeked out through the crack between the swinging doors.

Kebonsat gazed down at his sister. Affection softened his exasperated expression. Ceriba returned his look, hands on her hips.

"I'll make a better effort," he said finally.

"Good. See that you do. Have you paid for our meal?"

He shook his head and dug in his purse. Reisil started and pushed back inside. With a quick gesture she untied her apron and lifted it over head, followed by the smock. She glanced up at last, effecting surprise to see the two of them still there.

Ceriba gasped and clapped her hands.

"What lovely colors! Wherever did you get such cloth?"

Relieved that they had not noticed her eavesdropping, Reisil smiled and smoothed her tunic. "It's a new dye."

"It's beautiful. I must tell Mother about it. She has long desired a true purple dye."

"I believe we still owe for our meal," Kebonsat interrupted, returning to his curt manner. "This should cover it." He dropped some coins into Reisil's hand. She closed her fingers without looking at them.

"I'm sure it's fair," she said, challenge threading through her voice. His lips tightened, but he did not respond to the dig.

"Will we see you this evening?" asked Ceriba.

"I shall attend."

"Then we shall see you there."

"If we get back before Mother finds I've taken you wandering. Otherwise she may chain you to your bed." Kebonsat flashed a quick grin at his sister. It was an infectious grin, relieving his face of that stiff, superior expression. Reisil found herself smiling with them. She returned Ceriba's merry wave as the two Patversemese departed.

The rest of the afternoon flew by and by dusk Reisil was exhausted, but all was in readiness. Fireflies sparkled in the evening air as if conjured. Roheline had turned the square into a magical bower of flowers, light, crystal, color and melody. Musicians sang with lutes and lyres in one corner. The serving tables groaned beneath the weight of Raim's preparations. The delectable aromas of roasted meats, sweet puddings, fresh breads, broiled fish, herbed vegetables, and so much more drifted enticingly through the air. Varitsema and the city council escorted the Patversemese entourage to the square, followed by the townspeople. There was room and food for all.

Reisil watched them arrive from a corner table. The Dure Vadonis and his wife looked regal and smiling. She had unexpected ginger hair, while he had the same dark looks as Kebonsat and Ceriba. Those two followed after, seating themselves to the left of their mother. To the Dure Vadonis's right sat another man. This one had a foul, cunning look. He wore long robes of scarlet, and a queer, twisted piece of silver with three points pinned to his collar. His hair and beard hung long and silky black. He stooped somewhat, giving an impression of fragility. Reisil didn't believe it. There was something steel-like about him, something sinister and hungry, like hunting eyes in the night.

The rest of the Dure Vadonis's retinue were seated at other tables, while Varitsema and the council took up the rest of the head table. Reisil noted that a group of ten *ahalad-kaaslane* took up one table, their animals close by. They had filtered into Kallas over the last weeks, aiding with preparations and helping to situate the squatters in their new village. Among them was Juhrnus, his sisalik sprawled across his shoulders. It blinked slowly at the furor of activity.

Varitsema waited until the townspeople had filled out the rest of the tables and there were no more seats to be had. At the last moment Kaval arrived, squeezing in beside his father.

The mayor of Kallas was in his element. He began his speech with an extravagant welcome to the assembled crowd and the Dure Vadonis. He praised the treaty. He then went into raptures about the beauties and wonders of Kodu Riik, finishing with a dissertation on Kallas. He spun on for fifteen minutes and then turned the floor over to the Dure Vadonis with a flourish and a bow. The Dure waited for the applause following Varitsema's speech to end, then stood, looking to Reisil like an older Kebonsat. Silver dusted his temples and his close-cropped beard.

"Many thanks for your warm welcome," he began. "Our countries have long been at war and it lightens my heart to be given such a reception. I have great hopes for a future of amity and friendship between Patverseme and Kodu Riik. It will not be an easy task for either side. We have all lost much in this war."

He looked over the silent crowd gravely. Reisil found herself nodding. So he, at least, recognized the obstacles to peace. He hadn't said forgive or forget. Just put it aside. Too much blood under the bridge to do more. She thought of Taimeoli and his dead brother and cousins.

"It is my hope that today we begin to build a trust. A trust that will carry Kodu Riik and Patverseme into a long lasting peace. That we can find ways to build a trust so that our children will have to worry only about raising crops, fishing, building homes and living their lives in harmony and tranquillity."

A spattering of clapping met his last words and he appeared satisfied as he sat down. He might not have hoped for any applause at all, Reisil thought. And no one threw anything or heckled him or tried to cast him out on his ear. It probably counted as a successful speech.

With the conclusion of the speeches came the food. Boys and girls from most every family in town had been conscripted into service and now carried platter after platter down the table rows. Others followed with pitchers of ale and flagons of wine. Raim scurried back and forth in a frenzy of command. Reisil soon found herself with a plate piled so high she hardly knew where to begin. She hadn't eaten half when her stomach began to protest and yet the food was so good, she could not convince herself to stop.

Covertly she eyed Kebonsat and took smug pleasure in his obvious appreciation of Raim's food. *Passable* indeed. Ceriba kept up a running patter, her smile quick and ready. Reisil couldn't help but like her. The other man beside the Dure Vadonis said little except to mutter occasionally at the Dure. He had been introduced as Kvepi Buris—one of Patverseme's wizards. More than one person had hissed at him, to which he responded with a mocking smile.

He glanced up, his yellow gaze snaring hers. The rest of the world faded. Sound, color, smell, touch, taste: Reisil felt as if she were in a hollow vastness, floating, a fist closing around her, squeezing the air from her lungs. Her mouth fell open; her ribs compressed. She heard them creak, could feel them rubbing against each other, but she could do nothing. She could not draw a breath. Panic made her scrabble at the tablecloth and overturn her trencher and cup.

Unbidden, her hand rose with leaden speed to grasp the talisman at her throat, which had worked itself out of her tunic sometime during the day. She clutched at it, feeling the edges biting into her palm. Heat flared in her fist and suddenly the invisible pressure exploded and she felt the hard bench below her, the chattering of the townspeople, the aroma of Raim's food. A red haze blotched her vision and her blood thundered in her ears.

Reisil gasped, her breath coming in raw sobs. Someone pounded on her back, thinking she had choked. At last she waved her helper off. Her eyes shot over to Kvepi Buris, whose face was flushed, his lips shining red. He tipped his glass to her and drank, his expression wintry as arctic ice.

Reisil turned away, tucking the pendant back down into her shirt. The metal had lost its heat and hung cool between her breasts. Her hand ached and she touched the bloody welts where the edges had cut into her palm.

She stared dumbly down at the table as hands cleaned her place and put down more food and a full cup of ale.

Her mind drifted, torpid with shock. Fear scuttled along her nerves on twitching spider legs. The wizard had attacked her. Why? And how? Sodur had said wizard magic wasn't supposed to work in Kodu Riik. Except it had in Mysane Kosk, she reminded herself. She looked at her palm. The Lady's talisman had stopped the attack. She had no doubt of it. But it hadn't prevented it. And if the wizard could work his magic in Kallas, what could he do farther inside Kodu Riik?

Reisil gave a startled cry and nearly spilled her ale again when an arm reached across her for a basket of bread. Someone patted her shoulder.

The rest of the feast passed in a blur. She smiled at jokes and pretended to listen to stories, picking at the delicious food. But her mind spun, losing its lethargy, tangling in unanswerable questions. Why did the wizard attack her? What was he planning next? How did the talisman protect her? What should she do now?

Reisil hardly remembered anything of the next two hours. It wasn't until the tables were being cleared that she came to herself, dragging herself from the depths of fear and confusion.

She gathered her dinner dishes and carried them to the makeshift scullery, where scullions attacked the towers of dirty crockery with vigor. The angry tension that had continued to twist Kallas tighter over the last days seemed to have relaxed as the townspeople enjoyed the fruits of their labors. It helped that the Dure Vadonis spoke quietly and gave obvious deference to Varitsema and the members of the city council. What would they do if she told them what the Kvepi Buris had done?

Reisil's stomach churned. What had he done? Nothing that anyone could see. She bit her lips. She couldn't say anything. The treaty was too important. She wouldn't be responsible for having the Iisand turn the townspeople out of their homes. And the wizard had attacked only her—maybe for spite. Maybe for entertainment. Maybe he wanted someone here to know that he was not cowed, any more than Kallas was.

Reisil had forgotten the fruit tarts and could not even

eat half of one, so knotted was her stomach. After these were served along with hot wine and kohv, the entertainment commenced. Jugglers, singers, acrobats and musicians romped into the square with shouts and laughter. Tables were cleared from the center of the square to give them a stage. They performed well into the night, further relaxing the tension.

Reisil remained out of the way at her corner table, Raim having refused her offer of help.

"You've done enough for me today, my lovely tark. Time for you to enjoy."

Kaval dropped down beside her and put an arm around her shoulders, nuzzling her neck as she snuggled fervently against him, wrapping herself in his warmth.

"I've wanted to see you all day," he said in a low, intense voice. "My father's kept me hopping. Not only that, but he's decided I need to take on more responsibility. He wants me to go through the journey ledgers with him tonight."

"Tonight?" Reisil asked, keen disappointment flooding through her. After the wizard's attack, she wanted nothing more than to be held.

"He's got to make payments to the other merchants he represented on this trip tomorrow." Kaval shrugged. "He's never allowed me into the books before. So I'm going to have to do without you for one more night." He fingered the scarf she'd wrapped around her shoulders. "That looks beautiful on you. I knew it would." He squeezed her hand. "Promise me you won't run off with one of these Patversemese knights while I'm gone."

He said it lightly, but Reisil could hear the blade of cold rage beneath.

"They'll be gone tomorrow," she placated, closing his hand in both of hers.

"Meanwhile we fawn at their feet like dogs hoping for a stroke on the belly. Look at us, making a spectacle, and for what? So that our enemies will feel comfortable and welcome." Kaval pulled away and stood up. "I won't be a part of it anymore, and I won't watch. You shouldn't either. You should go home."

He swept off on a tide of anger, leaving Reisil feeling cold. She wanted to go home. But somehow she was unwilling to let the wizard see how much he'd shaken her. Not that he had paid her any attention after that last, long look. She'd watched him surreptitiously, but he'd never again looked her way.

"I don't understand. Why has the bird not chosen?" Upsakes said quietly to Sodur at the foot of the table where Reisil sat. "I have never heard of anything like this before. It worries me."

"You think something is interfering?"

"Such a thought has crossed my mind. But how could that be? Unless—" Upsakes trailed off. Reisil saw him turning to look up at the wizard.

"Surely not," Sodur objected. "If the wizards could do such a thing, they would have long ago. The war would have gone much better for them."

"Maybe it's something new." Upsakes looked up into the starlit night. "But I feel something is wrong. Very wrong indeed."

The cold that had wrapped Reisil at Kaval's departure deepened. She wanted to tell them about the wizard's attack, but the Iisand's threat stopped her. Instead she left the gathering, dodging Juhrnus when he would have intercepted her. She felt a moment's pang of guilt. What if he was ill? Or his sisalik? But his expression said he merely wanted to bait her.

She hadn't gone more than a few steps beyond the city gates when a shadow detached itself from the wall. Reisil jerked and spun about.

"Ho, m'girl. A bit jumpy tonight? Rightfully so. I came to warn you. Something's brewing. Feel it in m'bones."

"Nurema, you startled me."

"You need a good scare. And you might just get more than you asked for. You got my message." Reisil couldn't see the other woman's face in the shadows of the gate.

"I did," she said. She felt her legs beginning to shake. A scare? The wizard had nearly killed her in full view of the town. And if he'd succeeded, it would have looked like she had choked to death. And the only person who could have argued otherwise would have been dead. She shuddered, realizing this was exactly why he had chosen her. He would have been able to test his powers without anyone being the wiser.

"Hmph. Well, I came to tell you myself. Don't trifle with the Blessed Lady. You've a destiny. It may not be the one you wanted, but it's the one you got. Better tote the load now or you'll be regretting it later. That's all I have to say."

Nurema trotted past and down the road. Reisil ran after her.

"Wait!" She fumbled at her neck for the pendant. "I can't keep this. It's too expensive, too fine."

The old woman shook her grizzled head. "It's yours. Ask me about it someday and maybe I'll tell you. You're not ready now, though. Don't want to hear it. Remember, you are what you are, no matter what path you put your feet to."

With that cryptic remark, she sped off, leaving Reisil with the gryphon talisman dangling from her hand. She retied it about her neck, not entirely ungrateful to have it after the wizard's attack, making her way home slowly, hardly noticing the sweet symphony of crickets and night birds or the creamy scent of early-blooming moonflowers.

She stopped on her stoop and stared at the goshawk perched above her door. She waited a moment, wanting oddly to tell Saljane about the wizard's attack. But she gave a slight shake of her head. Inside, she opened up the shutters and lit her rosemary candle. Saljane followed her in, strutting around her table, wings half-unfurled, pecking at the wood. Reisil ignored her and crawled into bed. Her head spun. Memories of the wizard's attack, Nurema's words and Kaval's deep-seated hatred battered into each other and spun awry like ninepins.

She lay sleeplessly in bed wishing for Kaval. She wanted the comfort of his body hard against hers, his warmth and deft touch. When at last she fell asleep, her dreams were an unsettling combination of foreboding and aching yearning.

She woke the next morning with the sun streaming in her windows. It was midmorning, far later than she generally slept.

She sat up. Saljane perched on her footboard, staring at Reisil with unblinking eyes.

Reisil returned her regard for a few moments, then climbed out of bed. Saljane's unrelenting stare discomfited her, but she forced herself to endure it. One day the bird would understand that Reisil could not be moved.

Her ribs ached, but the sharp edge of fear had dulled. The Dure Vadonis and his pet wizard would be moving on to Koduteel today. The wizard would have to behave where there were so many *ahalad-kaaslane*. There was no point risking Kallas by telling, especially without any proof.

Making that decision, Reisil dressed and loaded her pack, adding extra tonics for bellyaches. After last night, there would be plenty of people in need. She added a length of purple ribbon at the last moment. Ceriba had been friendly and kind. It wasn't Ceriba's fault that her brother had all the manners of a blue jay. The ribbon would make a good gift for her. But she wouldn't tell Kaval about it. Reisil shook her head. He would not understand.

She set off into the humid morning, leaving the shutters wide open. Saljane followed after her, flying from tree to tree, keeping pace. When Reisil left the trees, Saljane winged away. Reisil breathed a quiet sigh of relief.

When she approached the gates of Kallas, she found them closed. A gravid silence hung over the city like a pall. Reisil stood before the gates, turning about in confusion. Seeing no gatekeeper or guards, she banged on the gatehouse door and called out. For a long time no one answered. Then a guard appeared above her on the battlements. He stared at her unsmiling.

"Kallas is closed."

Reisil blinked, mouth hanging open. It took her a moment to collect herself enough to respond.

"Closed? What do you mean?"

"By order of the mayor and council. The gates of

Kallas are sealed until further notice. No one leaves, no one enters.''

Just then bells began to toll from the four drum towers that cornered the walls of the town. Deep and sonorous, their tones resonated through her bones.

"What is it?" she demanded. "What's happening?"

The guard disappeared and a moment later another took his place. This one Reisil recognized.

"Leidiik! What is happening? Why are the gates closed?"

"Best go home, Reisiltark. Someone stole the Dure Vadonis's daughter last night."

Chapter 5

The color drained from Reisil's face.

"Stole her? Ceriba? I don't understand. Leidiik, please! What's happened?"

He looked over his shoulder and leaned farther over the parapet, his voice dropping.

"She vanished from her rooms sometime last night. Her guards had their throats slit and there's bloodstains on her bedding. *Ahalad-kaaslane* are searching Kallas now, hoping she's still here somewhere, alive."

For a moment Reisil was struck dumb. Then her tark instincts surged to the fore and she stood on tiptoe.

"Let me in, Leidiik. Maybe I can help."

"Can't do that. Safer outside anyhow. Patversemese are making all kinds of threats. With that wizard of theirs—remember Mysane Kosk." His voice dropped and he made one of the old signs against evil.

"But you know me," Reisil persisted, feeling the urgency like a hand pushing on her back. "And I'm needed in there."

"Sorry, Reisiltark. Orders is orders."

He disappeared then, returning to his watch. Reisil continued to stare up at the empty battlements for a long minute. Her mind spun furiously. Who would kidnap Ceriba? What could they gain from it? Ransom? Certainly the Dure Vadonis would not continue on to Koduteel to sign the treaty. Was that it? Did someone in Kallas hate the Patversemese so much that they would do such a thing? But that made no sense either. The

Iisand Samir would certainly not hesitate to make good
on his threat. Reisil couldn't think of anyone who would
risk that. It had to be someone else, someone not of
Kallas.

Her mind flittered to the wizard in his scarlet robes,
then dismissed him. He was evil, she had no doubt. His
spiteful attack on her proved that. But he had nothing
to gain by kidnapping Ceriba. If he wanted to keep the
war going, there were better ways to make it happen
than kidnapping the daughter of his liege lord. The cost
of the Dure Vadonis's discovering such treachery would
be very high—the wizard would lose too much by that.

Reisil sighed. What did she know of politics? There
were so many other possibilities she couldn't even begin
to guess at. What if this had nothing to do with Kallas
or the treaty at all? If someone wanted to get at the
Dure Vadonis's family, this trip was a perfect opportunity. He could only bring a small honor guard. Anything
else would look hostile or fearful. For all anyone knew,
this could be an attack by one of his Patversemese
enemies.

She retreated down the road. Instead of turning on
the path to take her home, she continued past, going to
Nurema and Teemart's croft.

Nurema stood outside, one hand clutching the back of
the bench where she and Reisil had sat two weeks ago.
Her gaze was turned toward Kallas, as though she could
see the town through the dense trees. The bells continued their sonorous tolling. Teemart knelt on the roof of
the cottage, stolidly hammering at a loose shingle.

"What's the racket about?"

"Kallas is closed. Ceriba cas Vadonis was kidnapped
in the night."

"Dure Vadonis's daughter? Who do they think did
it?"

"I don't know." Reisil repeated her conversation with
Leidiik. "No one in Kallas would do such a thing, I'm sure
of that. Not with what the Iisand Samir threatened."

Nurema's bark of laughter startled her.

"You are a child, aren't you? Listen, girl. You're

thinking about people all wrong. The people of Kallas are patriotic. Never forget that. They love Kodu Riik and hate her enemies. For most, Patverseme is still an enemy. Oh, Rikutud's thinking of the profits of new trade, but the rest—they don't forgive or forget so easy. They aren't so greedy. Maybe there's someone in Kallas who thinks Iisand Samir is making a mistake. Maybe someone thinks any sacrifice made for his country is worth it. Maybe someone is willing to see every one of us turned out of house and home just so that Kodu Riik won't have to get in bed with Patverseme. It's not a question of good or evil, black or white. If someone from Kallas did it, he did it to be a patriot. He's thinking he's fighting evil.

"Now the real question is, what are you going to do about this mess?"

"Me?" Reisil's voice squeaked and she swallowed her fear. Looming before her was the path she'd avoided for two weeks, the end of her life. She kept her voice steady with effort. "There's nothing I can do. I can't even get in the gates."

"You're certain of that?"

Reisil gave Nurema a blank stare. The other woman shook her head and sucked her teeth, then sat on the bench, gesturing for Reisil to sit also. Nurema scratched her head.

"You surprise me, girl. You go around, cool as anything, acting twice your years. Then in a heartbeat, you turn green as a cucumber. How can you be a tark if you don't understand the world you live in? Oh, you know your herbs and plants and brews and medicines, but that isn't all there is to being a tark. You don't know the history, the values. Or maybe you do and you just don't want to know. I told you, girl, you've got a destiny, and the Blessed Lady's going to see you put your feet on her path, one way or another.

"Don't argue now." She held up a brown-spotted hand. "I'm going to tell you what you don't want to know. The only folks can get in or out of Kallas right now are the *ahalad-kaaslane*. They don't answer to Iisand Samir; they serve the Blessed Lady and Kodu Riik itself. Law of the land. They aren't subject to anybody else's rule. They come and go as they please. Oh, sure, the Iisands like to pretend they have governance of the *ahalad-kaaslane,* but it just isn't so."

Nurema stood up abruptly, her expression tightly closed. "I'm going to go weed my garden. Time for you to go weed yours."

Reisil found herself at home and hardly knew how she'd gotten there. Nurema's words wheeled around her mind, chasing and chasing until they cornered Reisil. She knew what she had to do. The tark in her wanted it, too. There wasn't any choice anymore, if ever there was.

She confronted her cottage, examining every stone as if to implant it in her memory. Then she went inside, touching the walls, the bedstead, the shelves and windowsills. She went into the greenhouse and did the same, watering a drooping corbano plant. She returned to her cottage and stood in the doorway for long minutes, hardly seeing her carefully planned garden, the sprawling vines or the softly rustling trees.

There were no tears.

She went to her closet and rifled through, finding at last a winter vest of supple doeskin. She donned it, pulling the laces tight. Next she scrounged an old boot with holes in the toe that she had intended to patch. She cut off the shaft and slit it down the seam, tying it around her arm with strips of leather. Satisfied that it was secure, she turned to the door. As a quick afterthought, she grabbed up the scarf Kaval had given her, wadded it into a ball and shoved it in her pocket with Ceriba's purple ribbon.

Last she unpinned her tark's brooch from her shoulder and set it on her kitchen table, her fingers trembling as she drew her hand away.

Today, to be a tark, she had to become *ahalad-kaaslane.* The irony of it burned in her throat and her stomach tightened.

She turned without a backward glance and went outside to the copse of fruit trees lining the edge of the bluff. Far below she could see the river sparkling like a silver gypsy ribbon. She loved the view, found it soothing on many occasions. But she had no head for heights and took her pleasure well away from the edge.

She closed her eyes and reached out with her mind.

Saljane did not come right away, and Reisil wasn't sure the bird had even heard her call.

She called again.

A black speck appeared in the sky, circling. It grew bigger as it descended. Then suddenly it stooped, dropping like a stone. Saljane's wings belled out at the last moment and caught the bird with a loud pop. The goshawk winged once around Reisil and settled onto the limb of the buckthorn. Her entire posture radiated challenge.

Silence swelled between them. Reisil did not know what to say and Saljane gave her no help, only stared, cocking her head back and forth as if trying to make up her mind about something.

"I need you." The words burst out before Reisil knew what she wanted to say.

Fury. The goshawk mantled. *Kek-kek-kek-kek.*

Reisil tried again, wondering how much the bird could understand. The bird. Saljane.

"I am called Reisil. And you are called Saljane."

~Yes. The goshawk inserted the word into her mind on the edge of a white-hot knife. Reisil flinched from the contact, but forced herself to continue.

"That means secret. Does that mean you have a secret? You are a secret?" *My secret,* thought Reisil guiltily. Then shrugged aside the thought, focusing on Saljane. "Why me?" She asked the question that had gnawed at her for weeks.

This time, instead of a word response, as she was becoming accustomed to with the goshawk, an image formed in her mind. Saljane perched on the arm of a woman. Reisil couldn't make out the misty lines of her face. She had honey-blond hair. It cascaded to her feet in a thick wave, and was woven with chains of nuts and flowers. A circlet of silver oak leaves curved around her forehead. She wore a tunic and trews of green, patterned like the foliage of the forest. She held Saljane close to her and whispered something, then flung out her arm. Saljane launched into the air like a shot from a cannon.

The picture faded and Reisil found herself staring deeply into Saljane's amber eyes.

"The Blessed Lady," she breathed. "And then?"

The image this time was nothing Reisil could make out. A blur of colors and patterns; then suddenly she cried out and staggered. She was falling, falling, falling. The sickening drop seemed to go on forever; then she was brought up sharply. Now she was circling. Below her was a woman—no, not a woman. It was herself, watering her garden, the day Saljane had erupted into her life.

The image faded before those moments could be replayed, but Reisil could feel the bird's fury whirling hotter.

She blinked and climbed to her feet. Her throat was still in her mouth and her whole body trembled. She hated heights. Why would the Blessed Lady pair her with a bird—any bird?

Reisil bent and put her hands on her knees, closed her eyes and took several deep breaths, telling her stomach to get back down out of her throat.

"I suppose I deserve that. Are you going to keep doing that the rest of our lives together?"

The rest of our lives together.

Reisil shifted so that she could no longer see her cottage, greenhouse and garden. She'd said good-bye to those already. She was going to accept the Blessed Lady's gift and begin her new life dry-eyed and square-shouldered.

"The *ahalad-kaaslane* serve the Blessed Lady and Kodu Riik. I thought I could serve better as a tark. But there's trouble here and I need you. There's going to be war again with Patverseme if we can't get Ceriba back and find out who kidnapped her." She shook her head, face set. "Kodu Riik needs peace. As just a tark, I can do nothing. But maybe that's why the Blessed Lady sent you to me now. Maybe this is what she wants us to do."

Reisil looked at Saljane. The bird dipped her head as if nodding. Reisil took a breath to steady herself, hoping she'd have the courage to carry it through. "All right then. Let's go."

She lifted up her leather-wrapped arm and Saljane dropped heavily onto it. Her talons closed around Reisil's arm and the girl gasped as she staggered under the weight and pressure. She lifted her arm, using her other hand to brace it, letting Saljane climb onto her shoulder. Sweat ran down her back and between her breasts as the morning warmed, but she was glad of the padding and protection the winter vest provided her shoulder as her companion's talons clamped down.

It would have been easier to let Saljane fly, but Reisil thought she ought to make some effort to show her repentance and commitment. She hoped her new companion recognized what she was trying to say in leaving the cottage with nothing but the clothes she wore and her *ahalad-kaaslane* on her shoulder.

Saljane sat quietly, her feathers rustling in Reisil's ear. As they turned onto the road, the goshawk stretched her head down and rubbed her beak gently on Reisil's cheek. Reisil felt sudden tears rise in response to the caress and dashed at her eyes. Ahalad-kaaslane *don't go around crying like children,* she told herself sternly. But her heart lightened. She wasn't alone.

"Does that mean you forgive me?" she asked, turning her head to peer up into Saljane's brilliant eyes.

~I am yours. You are mine.

The words retained that sharp, steely tang, though they no longer cut with fury.

"I guess that's yes. Or as close to as I'm going to get for now. Maybe I'll ask again later, when you learn to trust me a little more." She was silent a moment, thinking.

~Can you understand me? she asked Saljane in her mind.

~Yes.

~Do you know what I'm thinking?

Curiosity. *~What?*

~*No. Do you know what I think when I think it? Or do I have to tell you?*

~*We are young together. We will fledge together.*

"I take it that means no for now, maybe later after we bond more closely. That's probably a good thing. I don't know that you'd like to be inside my head that much, but I know being in yours is going to take some getting used to."

By the time she reached Kallas's gates, her shoulder and neck ached from the unfamiliar strain of carrying Saljane's weight. The bells had ceased to ring and she heard only eerie silence from the other side of the walls. No one greeted Reisil. She stood for a moment, heart pounding. She wiped her palms against her thighs, squared her shoulders and took a deep breath.

"This is it. Are you ready?" she asked Saljane. The goshawk roused her feathers and gave herself a little shake. "All right then."

Reisil once again pounded on the gatehouse and called out. A guard appeared.

"Let me in," she demanded.

"Town's sealed. No one goes in. Go away." He vanished with a clink of arms and Reisil felt her temper rising. She banged again but got no response. They thought they'd ignore her.

"We'll see about that," she muttered. "Saljane, can you fly up there? There's at least one guard who knows me. I want you to find him."

Agreement.

"I'll need to see through your eyes. Can you do that?"

Suddenly Reisil felt Saljane in her mind. Again that sharp tang of alien thinking. Reisil's sight shifted and doubled. Her stomach lurched as she fumbled to make sense of the images coming simultaneously from two sets of eyes.

Reisil shut her eyes and still saw, but this time from just Saljane's point of view. Everything stood out with a clarity and sharpness she had never before experienced. She could see ants crawling along the wall fifty feet away. Across the fields she could see each leaf on the trees as if she stood right before them.

"Let's do it then."

Reisil put her arm up so that Saljane could climb onto it, then, remembering the vision of the Blessed Lady tossing Saljane into the air, Reisil did her best to emulate her. The goshawk gave a tremendous leap as Reisil swung her arm up. Massive wings beat the air and the wind of it buffeted Reisil.

The walls rushed past as she streaked with Saljane into the air. Keeping her eyes closed, she sank cross-legged to the ground. Blue sky, bright sun, up and up. Wheeling around, skimming the air, Kallas far below, streets empty. Reisil marveled at the view, seeing all of the town at once. Almost she could forget how high up Saljane was.

Her stomach lurched again. Almost.

She put her hands flat against the road, feeling the dust and grit beneath her palms. She remained safely on the ground, she told herself, teeth grinding together. Saljane was born to fly. No danger, no danger.

Saljane circled, hovering over the gate. Reisil could see herself on the ground, head bowed as though in prayer. Needles prickled all over her skin. She felt herself panicking, struggling against Saljane's hold on her mind. The bird clamped down, pinning her as though she were a fat rabbit. On the ground, Reisil retched, her body trembling with racking effort.

Saljane continued to make lazy circles, waiting for her *ahalad-kaaslane* to find equilibrium. Reisil gulped air, unable to close off their shared vision, unable to withdraw from Saljane's steel-taloned grip on her mind. Fear clawed at her and she battled it back.

"You'd have had help with this if you hadn't been so stubborn," she chastised herself sourly. "And you wouldn't have had to do it in the middle of a road in the middle of a crisis. So get a hold on yourself and get on with it. Saljane's waiting. So's Ceriba."

Reisil forced herself to sit back up, breathing slow, measured breaths. The earth wheeled around her and she fought her sense of vertigo. She concentrated on feeling the ground beneath her. Slowly she settled back into Saljane's mind, hands clenching with effort.

~All right, ahalad-kaaslane. *Let's get on with it.*
Approval.

Then Saljane dropped down, scanning the battlements. Men called out and pointed as Saljane swooped past, searching. Finally Reisil saw Leidiik. He was talking to a sentry a quarter of the way down the wall. His square, seamed face was bleak. He nodded to the sentry and moved past, heading away from Reisil and the gates.

~Turn him back, Saljane.

The goshawk stooped and Reisil's stomach rushed into her mouth. She clamped her jaws shut.

"You can be sick later, when there's time," she promised herself.

Saljane swooped in front of Leidiik, who stopped, surprised. She came at him again, flapping her wings in his face and nearly gouging him with her talons. He took a step back. She landed on the parapet.

Kek-kek-kek-kek.

Leidiik took a step forward and she leaped at him, shrieking, wings battering his head and shoulders. He fell back again and Saljane perched back on the wall. He took another step back and Reisil could see him putting the pieces together.

Good. He wasn't a stupid man.

Saljane crooned approval and fluttered closer. He retreated further and Saljane followed, driving him back to the gates.

Reisil heard the sounds of running feet and surprised voices as the other guards witnessed the spectacle of Leidiik backing along the wall, pursued by Saljane, her wings wide as she snapped her beak.

~Very good, Saljane. Reisil felt a startling rush of affection, pride and elation for the bird. Saljane felt it too. She radiated pleasure at Reisil, who found herself smiling a lopsided grin. In those shared moments, there had been an echo of that belonging from their initial meeting. It wasn't perfect, but it was a start.

~Let me go now. It's my turn.

Saljane released her mind and Reisil snapped back to herself. Carefully she opened her eyes and blinked. She wiped her mouth on her arm, wrinkling her nose at the smell of her vomit. She clambered to her feet and dusted herself off.

"Leidiik!" she shouted. "Leidiik!"

He appeared above the battlements, face bemused. Saljane came to perch a few feet away, preening beneath her wing.

"Reisil? What do you want?"

"I want in, Leidiik. Open the gates."

"I told you, no one—"

"That was before," Reisil said. "Things have changed." She pointed to Saljane. "I have the right to come and go as I please now. And I please to come."

She forced herself to speak loudly and imperiously, feeling herself cringe inside.

"I have my orders," he began again, but Reisil stopped him.

"Your orders don't apply to *ahalad-kaaslane*. And I am *ahalad-kaaslane*." She lifted her arm and called to Saljane, who hopped off the wall and floated down to settle on Reisil's stiff wrist. She waited, staring up at the bemused Leidiik, her arm cramping as she fought to hold Saljane steady. Like everyone else, he'd participated in the endless speculation about the goshawk's choice. Confronted with Reisil, he hardly knew what to do. He rubbed a thick hand over his chin.

"All right. But you're going to go directly to Varitsema and I'm sending an escort with you." He signaled to open the gates.

Reisil nodded and transferred Saljane to her shoulder. The inset pedestrian gate swung open a bare crack and she scraped through. Guards met her, closing around her in a loose circle. She stopped, waiting. Leidiik descended the zigzagging stairway.

"I'll take you myself," he announced. Reisil nodded and followed.

The streets of Kallas were eerily empty. Woodsmoke curling from chimneys gave the only evidence that the town was inhabited.

"Inside, by order of the mayor and council," Leidiik

said, when Reisil asked where everyone was. "And they're making house-to-house searches. If the Vadonis girl is here, they'll find her."

"Who could have taken her?" Reisil wondered aloud, curious about Leidiik's opinion. He was an experienced soldier. He'd fought the Patversemese in the early years of the war, returning to Kallas with a pike wound through his shoulder. He'd recovered eventually, and gone into service to the town. He had a lot of reason to hate the Patversemese, Reisil mused. It would be useful for kidnappers to have someone at the gate. *Was* Ceriba still in Kallas?

"I'll tell you what I think," Leidiik said after a moment, weighing his words. "I think that this kidnapping was well planned. Which means no matter what the council wants to believe, the girl isn't likely to still be in Kallas. Unless she's dead, which isn't likely. More leverage if she's alive. Kidnappers would've had an escape route well established, and that means a way out of Kallas." Which meant at least one guard was in on the plot. Leidiik sucked his teeth and spat and Reisil knew that the idea that one of his fellow guards might have betrayed the town left a bad taste in his mouth.

"My guess is they put her on the river and she's leagues away by now and getting farther away by the moment. That kind of execution requires a lot of people—from both Kallas and Patverseme." He glanced at Reisil, blue eyes grave. "People you wouldn't ordinarily suspect. But there's a lot of folks in Kallas that don't want to see Kodu Riik get into bed with Patverseme. I doubt the Patversemese are happy about it either. The Dure Vadonis has a lot of enemies at home and in Kodu Riik he's got a lot more. Remember the saying: The enemy of my enemy is my friend. I think that there's been another, temporary treaty, one written in blood. I think you're about to step into a nest of vipers and you're not going to know who your friends are. If I were going to give a raw *ahalad-kaaslane* a piece of advice, I'd tell her to walk softly and trust no one until they can prove to you that they had nothing to do with taking the girl."

"Not even you?"

He shook his head. "I know what I've been up to, but you don't. You know I was in the war, you know I have a reason to hate the Patversemese. But I don't truck with cowards who steal girls. If I'm going to pick a fight, I'm going to do it face-to-face. But I could be lying. Don't let your emotions for me or anyone else cloud your judgment. That's the reason why the *ahalad-kaaslane* don't get to call any place home. Can't afford to get too attached to anyone—or to hate anyone too deeply."

"At least I can trust the other *ahalad-kaaslane*," Reisil said confidently, though she thought of Juhrnus and wondered.

"Can you? If you thought that this treaty was a horrible mistake for Kodu Riik, wouldn't you do something to stop it? Wouldn't you be obligated to? I'm not saying that any were involved, but I wouldn't rule it out."

Reisil fell silent, a cold knot settling in the pit of her stomach. Leidiik's argument made sense. Too much sense.

"What makes you think they've taken her out of Kallas?" Reisil asked him finally.

"Isn't any reason to keep her here, and a lot more to get out. They have to buy time to get the war going again. Messages have to be sent to Koduteel and Vitne Ozols. Then councils have to be called, and armies have to be mobilized. It all takes time. That's the good news: You've got a little maneuvering room to find her before everything falls apart. They'll keep her alive for now, trying to figure out how best to use her. But sooner or later they'll have to kill her. She knows who they are and getting caught is sure death. That's the bad news: You've got time to find her, but you're already running out of time. No dispatches have been sent yet, but when they've turned Kallas upside down, you can bet your teeth it's going to get ugly."

They had arrived outside Varitsema's villa. Patversemese and Kallas guards surrounded the place. Leidiik ignored them all and walked straight up to the door. One of the Patversemese soldiers stepped in front of him, face belligerent.

"This house is off-limits."

Leidiik straightened, his bull neck tightening. "The *ahalad-kaaslane* go where they please in Kodu Riik. And she wants to go inside."

The guard eyed Reisil over Leidiik's shoulder and spat. Saljane mantled and gave her strident cry. It echoed along the deserted street.

"My orders are that no unauthorized personnel are allowed." Reisil sidled past Leidiik before he could respond. She stood toe-to-toe with the Patversemese guardsman.

"Quite right. But I *am* authorized. I am *ahalad-kaaslane* and I am in Kodu Riik. So I go where I please. I please to go inside. I suggest you step aside, or there's going to° be a brawl." Reisil met his sneering gaze squarely. Inside she trembled. It was though she had donned a mask. If he pushed any more, tore it aside— they would all know she was faking this bravado. A brawl? She'd be bowled over in a matter of seconds. Fight? Never in her life had she so much as slapped anyone. Not even Juhrnus.

The Kallas guardsmen had begun to gather around, eyeing their Patversemese counterparts with patent loathing. Reisil clutched her shaking hands together. She glared at the guardsman, praying to the Lady that he'd back down. At last he stepped back and pounded on the door with his fist. Reisil felt weak at the knees with relief.

"You can go in," he said to her. "But not him."

Reisil turned to Leidiik. "I'll remember what you said."

He nodded and gave her a salute. "Good luck, *ahalad-kaaslane*. May the Blessed Lady smile on you and Kodu Riik." He marched off, returning to his post. Reisil entered Varitsema's villa. The door swung shut behind her with a thump. Patversemese guards in the lobby eyed her coldly, but said nothing. Varitsema's steward, a thin, harried-looking man, gave her a short bow, staring at Saljane with wide eyes.

"Follow me. This way." He led her up a flight of stairs

and down a corridor. It was a very plain house, Reisil
noted, though peaceful and cool. Moss-green tiles lined
the floors, and the walls were painted creamy white
above a honey-colored wainscoting. She caught a
glimpse of bright-colored paintings and tapestries before
the steward stopped at a set of double doors and
knocked softly. The door opened and he spoke to someone within. The door closed and they waited for a few
moments. The steward shifted back and forth, running a
finger around the top of the wainscoting, *tsk*ing to himself. He brushed the dust from his hands and flashed a
nervous look at Reisil. Saljane ruffled her feathers and
the little man started. The door opened again and the
steward motioned for Reisil to enter.

~*Here we go. Are you ready for this?*

Saljane's reply broke over Reisil like a drowning
wave. No words, just animal ferocity, hunger for the
enemy, willingness to rend, tear and kill.

Reisil faltered in the threshold, caught herself and
continued on. The door closed behind with the echo of
a tomb. She resisted the urge to turn and hammer on it.
Ceriba, she reminded herself. *And war. You are* ahalad-
kaaslane. *However much you fought it, you must behave
as such now.* She heard Elutark's voice in her mind. *You
are what you pretend to be.*

Silence met her. Stares of wonder, of cold shock and
antagonism. Reisil scanned the room. It was Varitsema's
library. Books lined the walls. Comfortably cushioned
chairs upholstered in his own colorful weavings and
climbing plants filled one end of the room. His desk
stood at the other, framed behind by a window looking
out over his garden courtyard. Varitsema stood behind
the desk, frowning. Across from him stood the Dure
Vadonis, grief and rage lining his haggard face. In a
cloistered nook behind him, his wife sat still, face closed,
lips set in a flat line, a dark veil covering her hair. Desperation flickered in her eyes. Kebonsat held her hand,
his expression a match for his father's.

Next came the town leaders, Rikutud, Imeilus, Taktitu, Raim, Roheline, a few others. Then Upsakes with

his weirmart snuggled around his neck. Four of the Dure Vadonis's knights clustered together, wearing chain mail and looking like hounds slavering to be after their quarry. Finally there was the Kvepi Buris in his scarlet robes. He alone appeared unruffled, either by the kidnapping or Reisil's sudden entrance. Still, his gaze on her felt like a white-hot poker thrusting between her ribs. She flinched and turned away, but not before she saw him smirk.

The silence continued and the anxiety knotting in Reisil's stomach grew until she thought she might throw up on Varitsema's wild-rose carpet. *Remember what you are.* Ahalad-kaaslane *do not throw up because they are scared,* she told herself for the second time in an hour. Upsakes moved first.

"Greetings, Reisil," he said, coming forward. Reisil couldn't read his feelings in his face or tone of voice, but she noticed the removal of *tark* from the end of her name. "I see your *ahalad-kaaslane* has found you."

Greetings, but no welcome. Acknowledgment, but no congratulations. Fair enough. She'd flouted her fate and fought bonding with Saljane, succumbing only under duress. If she wanted more than cool civility, she'd have to earn it.

"The other *ahalad-kaaslane* are helping in the search for the Dure's daughter," he continued. Reisil knew what was coming next. She should go help them, make herself useful, get out of the way.

"I serve better here," she said in a low voice that brooked no argument. Upsakes's nostrils flared, a white line bracketing his lips. He glanced past her to the watching room. He nodded curtly, gesturing for her to take a place next to him.

An important skill for tarks was the ability to watch and listen, to make sense of disorder and confusion. So Reisil watched, remembering Leidiik's caution to trust no one.

The quiet produced by her entrance came to a crashing end as the Dure Vadonis pounded Varitsema's desk. "I want my daughter returned," he demanded. "Now. Or I'll take this town apart and raze it to the ground."

Varitsema raised his hands placatingly. "We all sympathize with your pain. And we are searching for her. We will find her. The city is sealed—no one can come or go." His eyes flickered to Reisil and back. "It is difficult to wait, I know, but if you have patience, we will find her."

Reisil frowned. Was the entire search predicated on the assumption that Ceriba was still in Kallas? She thought of Leidiik's words. He'd made sense. She glanced around at the worried faces. One of these people, all of these people, could be involved. It would suit their purposes to keep the search inside of Kallas until Ceriba was long out of reach.

Her glance shifted to Raim and Roheline, whose linked hands were white knuckled. She couldn't believe that they could have any part in this. Trust no one, Leidiik told her. But she had to trust *someone*.

Her gaze snagged on Kebonsat. He stared at her, eyes blistering. Behind his hatred she could see a terrible, leaching pain. She remembered how his face had softened when he'd smiled at his sister in the kohv-house.

She felt time slipping past and thought of the swift-flowing waters of the Sadelema. A boat could go leagues in a very short space. Already the sun was sinking. No substantive search outside the walls could begin until the morning. By then the kidnappers could have Ceriba so far out of reach that any search would be fruitless.

~Saljane, how far can you fly and still hear me?

~Far.

Far enough? Reisil wondered if Saljane's short responses were characteristic of the bird's personality, or if they stemmed from her earlier rejection of their bond. *Time will tell,* she thought.

She slipped from Upsakes's side and went over to the tall glass doors leading out onto a balcony. Varitsema broke off what he'd been saying and everyone turned to watch. Reisil lifted Saljane down from her aching shoulder.

~Follow the river.

She brought an image of Ceriba into her mind and projected it at Saljane.

~Seek Ceriba.
Eagerness. The Hunt.

Reisil swung her arm and Saljane leaped into the air,
her wings pumping powerfully. She sped upward until
she was nothing more than a speck, then nothing at all.
Reisil watched the sky for a long moment, then returned
to the library, color burning high in her cheeks.

"Just in case you're wrong," she said to Varitsema.
"Just in case her kidnappers found a way out past the
guards last night. Saljane will find her."

Chapter 6

The silence that met her statement was like an indrawn breath, pregnant, apprehensive. Reisil felt her face burning and her stomach clenched. Varitsema's gaze thrust through her like knives. Still she held her ground, chin outthrust, arms straight at her sides.

"What do you know? Why do you think she's been taken outside the walls?" demanded Ceriba's father. "Speak, girl!" He lunged at Reisil and snatched her shoulders in a hard, pincer grip, shaking her.

Upsakes leaped forward, as did Kebonsat. Upsakes's arm hatcheted down between Reisil and the Dure Vadonis, breaking the Patversemese's grip. Reisil stumbled back, landing with a hard thump on the floor.

"This is Kodu Riik. No one attacks *ahalad-kaaslane,*" Upsakes ground out, nearly nose-to-nose with Ceriba's father. Kebonsat pulled his father away, sneering down at Upsakes.

"Yes, this is Kodu Riik," he spat. "Where young women are stolen out of their beds and those who call themselves men stand about doing nothing but gossiping like old women." He stood four inches taller than Upsakes, though the shorter man outweighed him by a good three stone. The weirmart snarled and crouched down as if to spring at Kebonsat's eyes.

"Careful how you go, puppy," Upsakes warned, his teeth biting off each word, his square face flushed dark red. "You are not safe at home anymore."

"Do you threaten my son? Now, when you have sto-

len my daughter?" The Dure Vadonis wrenched from
his son's grasp and whirled on Upsakes. "I want her
returned now. Or you will all regret it. Remember Mysane Kosk."

The temperature in the room dropped until Reisil expected her breath to turn white. No one moved, the
Dure Vadonis's words ringing in the still air. In the sliv-
ered gap between Upsakes and the Dure Vadonis, Reisil
could see the wizard's thin lips curved, his yellow eyes
gleaming. Frozen on the floor, she remembered the way
he'd crushed the breath from her with no more than
a look.

"Please. Gentlemen. Let us not quarrel. It will not aid
us to find the young lady." Varitsema stood between the
two infuriated men, hands on their shoulders, pushing
them apart. His face had paled and he looked like a
ghost. Reisil clambered to her feet and retreated back
to the balcony doors.

The Dure Vadonis shook off Varitsema's hand and
went to stand beside his wife, while his son remained
opposite Upsakes, his feet planted wide, one hand hovering near the hilt of his sword.

"What *will* help us find my sister?" Kebonsat demanded, never taking his eyes from Upsakes. "You've
searched the town all day and found nothing. Someone
might think you are deliberately stalling a search outside Kallas."

"It is very unlikely that she could be spirited out of
Kallas. There was not enough time and the gates are
closed at night. If we thought it a real possibility that
they smuggled her past the guards, we would not hesitate a moment to send every last man after her. But if
she is still within the walls, as we surmise, opening the
gates might allow the kidnappers to escape with her."
Varitsema spoke quickly, but with careful, placating reason. "We must take the search methodically. Such care
takes time. We must look in every attic and basement.
We must examine every inch of every wall, floor and
ceiling for hidden compartments and tunnels. We have
only limited manpower to do this. Please, Kaj and

Dajam Vadonis, Kaj Kebonsat, we are doing everything in our power to find the Dajam Ceriba. Even your wizard has agreed that we can do no more."

"Indeed," Kvepi Buris said in a low, sorrowful voice, which Reisil found incongruously melodious as he nodded sage agreement to Varitsema. He spread his hands, his long fingers limp and weakly curling. "My powers avail us little." He paused. "However, with the help of some of my Guild brethren, it is possible I could do more."

Reisil bit back a protest. He'd nearly squashed the life out of her with hardly a look in her direction. Invite more wizards here? Was this the plan? To open a door for the wizards into Kodu Riik? She crossed her arms, hugging herself against the chills running over her skin.

Reisil saw Kebonsat flash a look of bitter dislike at the wizard. Lady Vadonis looked hopeful, grasping her husband's hand and staring up into his face pleadingly. He bent and whispered in her ear and she collapsed in on herself, pulling her hand away. The Dure Vadonis shot a look of warning at the wizard, who shrugged and shook his head as though expecting just such a response. Still, Reisil thought he did not appear at all surprised by the decision. And she wondered about Kebonsat's reaction.

In an effort to distract and break the tension, Varitsema sent for refreshments. The assembly broke into small clusters, each talking in hushed tones. Reisil stood by herself, watching the darkening sky through the window, wondering when Saljane would speak to her.

"You have presented us with quite a surprise," Upsakes said close to her ear. Reisil started and turned around, smelling the mustiness of the weirmart on his clothes, the cloying odor of laudanum on his breath. "I wonder what took the goshawk so long to choose?"

Reisil felt herself coloring, but could not look away, struck still by his heavy lidded gaze, glittery and hypnotic as an asp's.

"Strange she should choose a tark, of all things. But then I guess it takes all kinds." He paused and, when she didn't rise to the bait, went on. "There are many facets of being *ahalad-kaaslane* which you must now learn. Your—inexperience—has made this affair more difficult. You must learn to be more politically savvy, my dear. It is why all *ahalad-kaaslane* undergo mentoring with someone more experienced. Mistakes, even a wrong word at the wrong time, can be quite disastrous."

The implication that she had nearly precipitated a disaster was not lost on Reisil. She bristled, but forced herself to remain silent. Another rule for being a tark: Silence gains answers. He leaned closer and Reisil held her breath against the odor of the drug, the weirmart, and sour ale. His rough cheek brushed her forehead. If she tilted her head just a finger-width, they'd be kissing. She took a half step back, repulsed.

"You have an opportunity now, to slip away and join the search. You could learn a lot, and, of course, the faster we locate the girl, the better for everyone. Remember the Iisand's threat to Kallas. Your goshawk could do a lot to help."

"I will be pleased to do so," Reisil said. "As soon as Saljane returns."

"Call her back," Upsakes suggested.

"Have you injured yourself?" she asked, shifting the subject. "Laudanum can have an addictive effect. Nor does it mix well with ale. I know of other treatments that could soothe any pain and not have those effects."

"My injuries and illness are none of your business. You are no longer a tark," Upsakes said sharply as he jerked upright. "It would be best if you remembered your place. Now call back your bird and take up your duty to Kodu Riik."

"I will *always* be a tark, whether you choose to listen to my recommendations or not," Reisil contradicted, her backbone stiffening at his superior manner. "And Saljane and I will aid in the search of Kallas *after* she has completed her current search."

"Did you not hear? They threaten us with another Mysane Kosk! Do you want that on your conscience, little girl? Do you want to be responsible for such a thing? I've been there—it's a bloated, black sore on the earth. Nothing grows there that isn't twisted and evil. Nightmares and disease creep out from its edges. You say you're a tark, but you invite this horror to your own home, to the people who befriended you, who raised you after your parents left you. Did they know something we should? What kind of foul-hearted bitch are you that you would invite a Mysane Kosk here?"

Reisil stared at him in shock. Spittle clung to his lips and his hands were fisted. He looked a little mad. From his shoulder his weirmart bared her needlelike teeth. Reisel quailed from his ferocity, but she couldn't give in. Somehow she *knew* Ceriba wasn't in Kallas anymore. She knew it the way she knew that fire and rattlesnakes were dangerous. It didn't matter that it wasn't the most logical explanation. Every instinct said it was true. And because of it, she couldn't succumb to Upsakes's fury.

"I am doing what I think best. Whatever comes, I won't be held responsible for anything the wizard does. I did not kidnap Ceriba. Whoever did that tempted such a disaster, not me."

She moved away, coming up short as she found herself face-to-face with the Dure Vadonis, Lady Vadonis and Kebonsat. She swallowed, her throat dry. They stared at her, saying nothing. Reisil licked her lips and felt in her pocket for the ribbon she'd meant to give Ceriba. She drew it out and held it out to Ceriba's mother.

"I had planned to give this to Ceriba today. She liked the color so much."

Lady Vadonis took it from Reisil, unrolling it and running her fingers over its soft length.

"She told me about this purple," she murmured, her voice low and rough. Reisil's heart contracted at the pain in it. "She went on and on about it." She looked up at Reisil. "She spoke well of you. It's very good of you to think of her."

"We're going to find her."

"I pray so." The Lady Vadonis looked away, her voice cracking. Kebonsat gripped her shoulders and Reisil moved away, giving the family privacy.

"So, tark of my heart. You are the one for whom the goshawk has been searching." Raim and Roheline stood together, holding hands as they surveyed Reisil up and down. Reisil's heart thumped and she ached at the distrust clouding their expressions.

"It would appear so," she said, her voice low.

"Strange she did not know you when she first saw you," Roheline said in her rich contralto voice. She did not smile, and Reisil felt the loss of her usual sunny affability. "Or that you did not know her."

"I know her now. That's all that counts."

"I wonder. But you are to be congratulated. A new *ahalad-kaaslane*. We are fortunate that your choosing came at such a time."

Reisil smiled weakly, disliking the stiff formality between them. She had begun to count Raim and Roheline as good friends. Sadness welled up inside her. *But* ahalad-kaaslane *are permitted no friends, nothing to color judgment or distract from their duty.* Leidiik had deliberately reminded her of that fact.

A knock at the door and the steward entered. He spoke to Varitsema, then slipped out. Varitsema's frown increased. He returned to his desk and waited until silence fell.

"There is no news yet," he announced with an apologetic look at Ceriba's family. "They have thoroughly searched fully half of Kallas and will continue through the night."

"This is preposterous!" shouted the Dure Vadonis. "Half my men are standing about doing nothing. Set them to the search and we will have Ceriba back—if, as you say, she is still in Kallas."

The mayor was already shaking his head regretfully. "The citizens of Kallas will submit to a search by the *ahalad-kaaslane*, but they will not open their homes to Patversemese soldiers. It is almost too much that a contingent of your men accompany the search."

The Dure Vadonis riposted angrily, but Reisil returned to the balcony. The sun hung like a golden ball in the western sky.

~Saljane, can you hear me? What do you see?
Silence.
~Saljane!
Reisil gripped the stone balustrade, leaning over it and looking into the sky.
~Saljane!
Reisil took a breath. Two breaths.
~Ahalad-kaaslane.
Reisil sagged against the stone railing upon hearing Saljane's flat, chill voice.
~Where are you? What have you seen?
Without warning Saljane caught her mind. Reisil clutched for balance, closing her eyes to block out her own sight as Saljane's overwhelmed hers. She had no sense of what she saw. Black and gray shapes on a wide panorama, fuzzy, lumpy edges limned in orange and gold. Lines and blotches, sharp squares and a shining ribbon of gold. The Sadelema!
~Have you found her, Saljane?
Before she could consider how high Saljane might be flying or where, the bird stooped and Reisil's vision blurred. Saljane plunged and Reisil's stomach leaped into her throat. The goshawk crashed to the ground, snatching a blue grouse in her talons.
Without pausing, she flipped the bird to her beak, beating her wings with heavy thrusts. She rose to a tree branch and stripped the feathers before tearing into the fat carcass. Bones snapped and Saljane bolted chunks of meat, lifting her beak to the sky to aid her swallowing. Reisil's gorge rose. She tasted hot blood and raw flesh. They assuaged a desperate hunger not her own. Her stomach lurched again and she fought it down, aware of the people just inside. She was not going to let them see her on the floor, retching like a dog.
Sweat beaded on her forehead and dampened her hair. Her knuckles whitened as she clutched the stone railing. Quickly and efficiently the goshawk finished her meal, scrubbing her beak against the pale, furrowed bark of the tree.
~Dark. Cannot fly.

Reisil blinked. Goshawks couldn't fly in the dark?
~Did you find Ceriba?

Another image flashed in her mind, this time earlier.
The sinking sun bleeding into the sky as she floated
above a tree canopy. Off to the right and left there were
squares of green and gold, separated by hedgerows. Far
off, she could see mountains. Now they were gliding low
over the canopy. Saljane found an opening and dropped
through. She skimmed between the branches, weaving
in and out, flipping on a wing tip. Reisil's stomach
heaved. Grimly she tightened her jaw, biting her tongue.

Finally Saljane found a path, following its sinuous
curves with silent grace. Reisil breathed deeply through
her nose. She felt herself sinking to the chill paving
stones, legs too rubbery to hold. Saljane's mad flight
slowed and now she made gliding hops from one branch
to another, a hundred feet above the ground. Below,
Reisil could see a line of shapes moving through the
dappled shadows. Despite the goshawk's sharp sight, she
could see little through the clutter of trees. Saljane
dropped lower, perching at the edge of a clearing. Leaf
mold lay thick on the forest floor and wildflowers
bloomed in scattered clumps.

The line of riders pulled up inside the clearing next
to a stream. Amongst them was a trussed figure, head
wrapped in a bag, hands tied to the pommel, feet roped
together beneath the horse's belly. She, for Reisil knew
without a doubt it must be Ceriba, wore men's trousers,
the too-large waist belted with a length of twine, and a
heavy wool shirt. Heavy socks covered her feet and a
cloak wrapped around her.

Six men accompanied her, but Reisil couldn't make
out their faces. They did not have cause to look up and
wore their hoods pulled up. They put Ceriba next to the
newly kindled fire, laughing and slapping shoulders.
They pulled Ceriba's hood off and fury blistered through
Reisil. Even so far above, Saljane could see the bruises
around one eye and her swollen lips.

Suddenly, like a snuffed candle, the vision winked off.
Reisil shuddered, blinking. She found herself staring at

a dozen feet. She followed a pair of polished black boots up a pair of finely woven trousers, past a long, embroidered vest over an orange silk blouse, up the fierce face to a pair of staring gray eyes. The Dure Vadonis.

"What do you know? Tell me at once!"

Reisil raised a quashing hand.

~Saljane. Where are you?

~Trees. I wait for morning. They wait for morning.

Good. They would go nowhere without Saljane following.

~Which way? North or south of Kallas?

Saljane jerked her *ahalad-kaaslane* back into her mind. Reisil had an impression of lazy spirals, then sudden thrust as the quarry came in sight. A boat pulled up high on the bank, a trail into the trees where horses had waited. More spirals. A low dive over the river. She could see it tumbling over rocks in shallows. South. The river ran south. Saljane rose in the air again and circled. Reisil searched for landmarks, something to say how far Ceriba's captors had taken her before departing the river. The Sadelema snaked away in a series of twists and turns and narrow rapids. A small wooded island hardly larger than an oxcart thrust itself up into the tumbling white current. She saw nothing else to distinguish that portion of the river.

She came back to herself, still on her hands and knees, breath coming between her lips in short pants. The Dure Vadonis knelt beside her. She looked at him. She opened her mouth to speak, but a storm of coughing racked her. He called for a drink and thrust a cup of wine into her hand. Reisil sipped, letting the cool liquid moisten her parched tongue and throat.

"Saljane's found her. They took her downriver and then west." She remembered the boat pulled out of sight behind a screen of trees on the right riverbank. West into Patverseme.

The Dure Vadonis made a strangled sound.

"She is . . . alive?"

Reisil nodded. "A bit worse for wear, but alive."

She began to push to her feet and found his hands

helping her. Another pair gripped her other arm gently
and she flicked a startled look at Kebonsat. The two
men helped her inside and settled her in a cushioned
chair. Reisil was grateful for the assistance. Her body
ached and shook. Sweat drenched her clothing and made
her hair cling to her scalp.

"Tell us what you know."

Ceriba's father had pulled up a chair opposite. Someone thrust a roughly made sandwich into her hand and
replaced the wine with cool, sweet tea. The scent of mint
and lemon quickened her taste buds. She glanced up and
smiled gratefully at Raim, who nodded and stepped back
to give Upsakes room.

Reisil described what she had seen through Saljane's
eyes. At the description of Ceriba's bruises, the Dure
Vadonis's eyes blazed and Kebonsat let out a string of
curses.

"We must go immediately. We've wasted enough time
already. Send for Koijots," Dure Vadonis instructed his
son. He paused a moment to take Reisil's hand, squeezing it fervently. "Thank you." He turned to leave, settling his arm about his wife, but Upsakes detained him
with a blocky paw on his forearm.

"Listen to counsel. Is it wise to act so precipitously?"

"Precipitously? They've got a full day's lead. Who
knows what they'll do to her. We've delayed long
enough." He tried again to leave, but Upsakes blocked
his passage.

"Consider, just for a moment. First, do you know
where they left the river by Reisil's description? No, and
neither do I. Does anyone here?" Silence, a dozen heads
shaken no. "But we may be able to find out. Second,
who do you trust? Who stole your daughter? What's
their purpose? To draw you within reach and murder
you? To ruin the treaty between Patverseme and Kodu
Riik? It might be that those you trust most are party to
this abduction. You might be providing them an opportunity to kill you easily without any witnesses. Finally, a
party as large as yours will move too slowly to overtake
the kidnappers. And if you succeeded, might they not
kill her just to aid their escape?

"A smaller party is more prudent. One which consists of both Patversemese and *ahalad-kaaslane*. Such a party could move swiftly and stealthily. It would have a better chance of rescuing your daughter. At the same time, if you stayed here in Kallas or proceeded on to Koduteel, you would undermine any efforts to ruin the treaty, if that is the intent of this kidnapping. There may also come communications from the kidnappers—ransom demands. You should be here to answer those."

"Stay here? While ruffians have my daughter? Unthinkable!"

Despite his words, Reisil could read the doubt in his eyes. Upsakes had hit several sore points. Points she agreed with. The Dure Vadonis did not want to sit and wait for his daughter to be rescued, but neither did he want to give way to those who had stolen her. Inside the rage and frustration she saw ruthless implacability. The only reward he had in mind for them was bloody and agonizing.

She shivered. Someone was going to pay for this. Pay dearly. Was it too late for Kallas to rectify the situation? To prevent the Iisand Samir from making good on his threats to cast every soul out?

"The people of Kallas have every encouragement to help find Ceriba," Varitsema chimed in, his face pale. "The Iisand Samir has vowed that we will lose our homes and lands if we should disrupt the treaty process. Even if we did not share your contempt for those who would kidnap a helpless young woman, we would have ample selfish reasons to see her brought back safely."

"You have already seen what aid the *ahalad-kaaslane* can be in rescuing the young lady," Upsakes pushed.

"You would go?" the Lady Vadonis asked Reisil in a constricted voice. "You would help find my Ceriba and bring her back? She might be ill or hurt. You could tend her. If she's—" Her voice broke. "If she needs it."

Reisil met the other woman's pleading gaze. She nodded. "Of course. Even now Saljane watches over her."

The Lady Vadonis closed her eyes, her lips compressing into a flat white line. Then she visibly collected herself and nodded to her husband.

"It will be so. I will send my son in my place and remain here in Kallas until she is returned. But do not take overlong. I must send word to Vitne Ozols very soon. Three, maybe four days at most. The envoy from Koduteel will arrive tomorrow, I believe. I will have no authority over their actions. If they send to Koduteel, then I must to Vitne Ozols. After that, we won't have many choices. You must get my daughter back quickly."

And if she is returned? Reisil thought about the treaty. If Ceriba's kidnapping had been an effort to ruin the peace between Kodu Riik and Patverseme, would those behind it escalate their efforts? She reached out to Saljane. The sleepy bird responded with reassurance. All was quiet; the girl was asleep.

A river trader rousted from his bed recognized the twisting curves of the river and the island that Reisil described. Called Voli, Reisil doubted he'd washed for a week at least.

"A fair distance. That island is past Priede. Maybe two or three leagues. Ripping quick current there."

"How far to Priede?"

Voli rubbed bloodshot eyes, his breath smelling of vinegar, ale and onions. He burped and eyed Kebonsat uneasily. Ceriba's brother stood silently, arms crossed over his chest, watchful as a starving bear. Their party crowded the taproom of the Vesi Inn, where the trader had taken a room. Reisil sat with her back to Kebonsat at the end of the table, while Upsakes sat across from Voli. The innkeeper hovered behind the bar, his clothing rumpled and unevenly buttoned.

Voli scraped thick fingers through thinning brown hair, his face and scalp burned dark by the sun. "River's running high with spring melt, even with the drought. By boat, maybe ten or twelve hours. Lotta logs, debris, rapids. Need a good crew and have to go with a flat bottom. Gets shallow near Priede, but fast."

"Good horses available in Priede?"

The trader shrugged. "Good enough. Not much to look at, but sturdy. Don't eat much, but work like dogs."

Upsakes looked at Kebonsat. "That's it then. We go to Priede, buy horses, then pick up the trail. We can leave at first light."

"We can leave now," Kebonsat objected. "We could cut their lead in half."

Voli laughed. "Forget it, boy. No one runs the Sadelema at night. Not when she's high. Not when they're logging. You'll get yourself dead if you try. I don't know anyone who's fool enough to take that kind of job. Not for love or money."

"Let us collect our gear and get what rest we may," Upsakes said, standing. "Voli, we require your services. Gather your crew and make sure they are ready to go at dawn." His tone brooked no argument and he turned to leave, motioning for Reisil to join him.

"Return to your cottage and get your things. Bring along a blanket, sturdy clothing, a good cloak, waterbag, foodstuffs, a pot and bowl, and whatever weapons you may have. At least a belt knife, I hope." He eyed her narrowly, wide face hard. His weirmart had disappeared from his shoulder. Reisil wondered where she had gone. "I suggest also that you bring a leather kit to make jesses for your *ahalad-kaaslane*. They are handy in securing messages, if it becomes needful. Paper would also be useful. Do not overweigh yourself. You are *ahalad-kaaslane* now. You must travel lightly. I would not expect to return."

"I had not thought to," Reisil murmured.

Upsakes made a disgusted noise. "You had not thought to be *ahalad-kaaslane* at all." His lip curled, as if talking to her left a bad taste in his mouth. "Be at the dock at first light. We will not wait for you." He stalked off without another word, leaving Reisil alone in the velvet darkness of the deserted street.

Reisil returned to her cottage and packed her things swiftly. To Upsakes's list, she added string, needles, thread, a pouch of oil, flint, whetstone, fish hooks, comb, extra socks, a cake of soap, four candles, and a thin pouch of coins. Her medicine kit went into an oilskin bag. Her cloak had been a leavetaking gift from Elutark. It hung to her heels in long, billowy folds. Made of doe hide, it had been dyed forest green, then well rubbed with oil to make it waterproof. Green for growing; green for healing. Inside it was lined with soft, curly sheep fleece like that of the vest she wore. Deep pockets edged its inner sweep. She added an extra blanket to her kit, as well as an extra shirt and trousers for Ceriba and a pair of boots. She hoped they wore a similar size.

When she'd completed her packing, Reisil dressed herself in the heavy clothing she always wore when she went scouring the hills and mountains for plants. She ate the half a chicken pie in her larder and filled her pockets with plums. Exhaustion netted her limbs, but the notion of staying the night in the cottage was untenable. Slinging her kit over her shoulder, she departed, her hand lingering on the door handle as she pulled it shut.

The dock was set in a natural cove below the bridge a quarter of a league. A short jetty protected the harbor area from logs and other debris. Most coming to Kallas were flat-bottomed, from the south, but occasionally a steeper-hulled boat floated down from the north where the Sadelema ran black and deep and wide. There was a flurry of activity and lights around Voli's boat, one of three trading crafts in residence.

She sat on a knoll to watch the bobbing lights a moment, hearing the curses and laughter of the crew as they readied for launch. Crickets chirped to the night birds and an owl hooted while the Sadelema murmured softly. Reisil smelled the comforting scent of damp earth, wild mint and woodsmoke. Sleep came at last and she slept heavily.

A clanging bell startled Reisil awake just before dawn. She struggled upright, wincing at the ache in her shoulders and arms from carrying Saljane and sleeping on the ground. She rolled her head on her neck to loosen her muscles, rubbing the grit from her eyes and making a face at the sticky taste in her mouth. She picked a few leaves from a patch of wild mint, relishing the crisp, cool flavor.

~Saljane, how fare things with you?

An image of gray logs spread out in pinwheel fashion came to Reisil.

~Sleeping.

Saljane's mental voice was swift and hard, like a talon striking, and Reisil winced. The contact was almost painful. She wondered if it were purposeful, or Saljane's natural habit.

She gathered her things and ambled down to the dock, eating one of the yellow-fleshed plums from her pocket. The clanging was Voli rousting his small crew from their beds. He flashed her a grin and jerked the chain on the dull brass bell hanging from the rail.

"Bright morning," Voli called. "And bright fortune. Be a fine day." He nodded toward a wooden box fastened down to the aft deck, its lid thrown wide. "Throw your kit in there. Careful with those traps there. Break a leg falling through. Latch 'em down when we cast off. Here come your companions."

Down the road came Kebonsat with two men. One was Glevs, the knight who'd accompanied him through the square when Kaval had come home.

Reisil swallowed and an ache filled her chest.

Kaval. She had been trying not to think about him. She had daydreamed of a future with him. But now . . . Tears burned her eyes and she retreated to the other side of the deck so that no one would see. Her fingers found the scarf he'd given her in her pocket and she caressed the smooth material between rigid fingers. She hadn't had a chance to say good-bye, but as much as she missed him already, she couldn't regret it. She didn't want to see his face when he discovered she was *ahalad-kaaslane*. When he learned she'd deceived him and the town both, that she'd refused the Lady's gift.

Biting her lips and swallowing her pain, she forced her mind from Kaval. Later she would grieve.

She turned around and examined the other man accompanying Kebonsat. He had red hair with streaks of gray fastened at the base of his neck. His close-cropped beard bristled gray with streaks of red along his chin.

He had wide shoulders and a thickened waist, though he moved with a kind of innate stealth. He was shorter than Kebonsat by half a head and his pale blue eyes darted back and forth, seeing everything. He wore well-seasoned leathers, a sword and knife on his left hip and a wickedly hooked lohar, like a tiny scythe, fastened on his right, a longbow over his shoulder.

"Well met," Voli hailed with a flourishing bow. Reisil smiled. Sober and on the water, the man was a rogue. "Come aboard. Stow your gear. Keep out of the way, if y'please. Managed a bit of a cargo in the wee hours. That Rikutud is a hard bargainer. M'boys are getting it settled. Businessman, you know. Have to find a profit in every venture. Ah! The stragglers." He glanced at the brilliantly lit dawn sky. "Punctual." He said the word as if it offended him, as if punctuality meant idleness and sloth.

Voli greeted Upsakes gaily. Upsakes wore a new cloak of heavy wool, the weirmart back in its usual place on his shoulder. Behind him came Sodur, who, in contrast to Upsakes, looked already travel-worn. He wore an oft-patched cloak, its ragged hem hardly reaching his knees. His boots were scuffed, the heels worn low. As usual he looked hungry, his thin, crooked nose dripping in the chilly morning.

"By midday it will be sweltering and we'll make a holiday feast for the mosquitoes," declared Voli. Sodur eyed him darkly, his lynx twining against his legs. Voli was uncowed.

"This all of us then? I'll cast off then, shall I?"

"There's one more. He'll be along shortly."

"We don't have time to wait," Kebonsat declared.

"Just a few moments," Upsakes said. "That won't make much difference. Ah, here he comes now." He waved his arm and the trotting figure began to run in earnest.

Reisil's stomach sank. Juhrnus. Puffs of dust rose with every pounding step and he hardly paused as he leaped aboard, out of breath, his sisalik nearly strangling him with its tail as it clung to him for balance. He slung his kit into the waiting box and nodded greeting to Upsakes.

"My apologies, Kaj Kebonsat." Upsakes said. "It occurred to me in the last moment that Juhrnus might be an important addition to our mission. His sisalik can move quietly and quickly in water and sees in the dark. I did not want to lose any advantage in rescuing the Dajam Ceriba."

Juhrnus stroked his fingers over the sisalik's head and glanced around. He did not seem surprised to see Reisil, but for once said nothing derogatory. Instead he gave her a cold look and turned his back. That suited her fine. Maybe now that she was *ahalad-kaaslane,* he would cease to torment her. Or she'd have Saljane eat that sisalik for breakfast.

She turned to face the river, feeling it catch the trading barge in its grip as the crew cast off. The wooded bank opposite retreated behind them. Her throat knotted as they floated away from her home, her life as a tark.

"Bright morning." Kebonsat settled in beside her, forearms on the railing. He had tanned, callused hands with long fingers and a sprinkling of dark hair. He stared at the water. "What news of my sister?" he asked urgently, his hands curling into fists.

~*Saljane.*

~*Ahalad-kaaslane.*

~*What chances?*

The bird swept her away. She gripped the railing, closing her eyes against the doubled vision. Saljane remained in the tree. Below, the kidnappers broke camp. One prodded Ceriba to mount. She fought him, jerking out of his hands. He grappled her and shoved her to the ground. She kicked out but he dodged and his boot thudded into her ribs. Reisil cried out in shock. Another man approached and pulled the first one away, lofting Ceriba into the saddle like a sack of onions. He tied her hands and feet, though she listed to the side, obviously in great pain.

The forest floor was so gloomy that Reisil couldn't make out more than blurry gray patches for faces, hard as she tried to pick them out. Without warning, Saljane leaped from her perch with a stomach-churning lurch and Reisil retched over the rail. Saljane glided between the boles, coming to a rest on the opposite edge of the clearing. Now Reisil could see better and hear. Ceriba's captors were mostly silent and the morning stillness was broken only by Ceriba's sobs, the sounds of jingling bridles and the snorting and sneezing of the horses. Her six captors mounted, leading Ceriba toward Saljane's perch.

Reisil did not recognize the first man. He was middle-aged, with a hard-bitten face. A scar twisted from his left eye up into his hairline. Behind him . . . Reisil knew him, though not by name. Only a handful of years older than she, he was a journeyman wheelwright from Kallas. He was also the man who'd kicked Ceriba. Behind him came a stranger leading Ceriba's horse, then Ceriba. The next man had a thick paunch, red cheeks and steel-gray hair. Reisil didn't see who came after. Saljane skipped past to the last, snapping her beak. A black pit gaped in Reisil's chest and she willed it not to be.

But it was.

Kaval.

Chapter 7

Reisil gave a sharp cry and staggered back from the railing, fist pressed to her lips. The connection with Saljane ruptured as her mind ricocheted from Kaval's treachery. *What has he done?* Bile crawled up onto her tongue and she swallowed it down, feeling hands grasping her.

"What's happened?" demanded Upsakes, and Reisil heard venom threading his voice. Justified, she thought. Because she refused the Lady's gift.

She opened her mouth, not knowing what to say. Upsakes held one arm while Kebonsat steadied her with the other. The two men glared at each other and Reisil could feel their animosity like heat from tall-burning flames. She forced herself to give a dry chuckle, a sound that tore at her constricted throat.

"It's nothing, Upsakes. I should not bond with Saljane when she's flying and I am rocking on a boat. Makes me green."

She felt Kebonsat's fingers tightening on her elbow and she glared at him meaningfully, not wanting to reveal what she'd seen to Upsakes. Kebonsat was the only one she could really trust. He loved his sister and could not be involved in her kidnapping. The others— She bit her tongue, tasting blood. If Kaval could have done it, then any one of them could have too.

Much to her relief, Kebonsat did not challenge her story. He merely helped settle her onto the deck, offering her a flask of water, which she gulped.

"Proper training would benefit you," Upsakes declared, standing above her. The sun blazed brilliantly behind him and she could not see his face in the shadow. "One does not learn to be *ahalad-kaaslane* overnight."

Heat flooded Reisil's cheeks and she bent her head down. Overnight. If she'd accepted Saljane from the first, she'd have had two weeks to acquaint herself with being *ahalad-kaaslane*. If she hadn't fought her fate, would she have such debilitating reactions to Saljane's flights?

"At least she found my sister instead of wasting time on a useless search," Kebonsat retorted.

"Yes. We are grateful that she did that much," Upsakes said, stroking his weirmart's head. "As the only *ahalad-kaaslane* in Kallas with a bird companion, it was lucky she decided to help."

Reisil cringed from the acid in his voice. Upsakes waited another moment, then retreated back along the deck to where Juhrnus watched with a sneer. Kebonsat crouched down beside her. The sun was growing hot and sweat dampened her tunic. She pulled off her cloak, letting it puddle around her hips.

"What does he mean, *lucky* you decided to help?"

Reisil licked her lips, avoiding Kebonsat's brooding stare, trying to decide what to tell him. Somehow she didn't want him to know how much of a coward she had been—continued to be, she thought, scornful of herself. Right now, she wanted nothing more than to be home, tending her raspberries, pulling weeds out of her carrots and stewing pungent magga root against winter need. Not here, with these grim-faced men with blood in their eyes and hate on their tongues.

"He thinks that I was hiding being *ahalad-kaaslane*," she said finally in a tissue-thin voice.

"Hiding? Why? To aid in the kidnapping?"

Reisil stiffened, meeting the sudden cruelty in his voice with shocked horror.

"No! Never! Any brute who would do such a thing—" She broke off, remembering Kaval.

"What?" prodded Kebonsat, suspicion still coloring his voice.

Reisil swallowed. What had Nurema and Leidiik told her? Patriotism. Kaval thought of himself as a patriot. Her throat burned. He might call it that. But he had stolen an innocent girl from her family, bloodied and bruised her, maybe even planned to kill her, if Leidiik was right. That wasn't patriotism, wasn't love for Kodu Riik. That was not justifiable. Not forgivable. So why did her mind and heart keep crying out for him to hold her, to smile that lopsided grin and reassure her that everything was all right, that he hadn't really done it, that there was a reasonable explanation?

She remembered his reaction when she told him of the treaty and felt a tearing grief building in her chest. She caught her breath against the pain. *This must be akin to what Kebonsat feels,* she thought. She gripped his hand, tears slipping down her cheeks.

"I am so sorry. He's right. If I'd accepted Saljane, if I hadn't fought so hard not to be *ahalad-kaaslane,* I would have been able to help sooner."

Kebonsat looked startled, his strong, callused hand clenching on hers.

"I don't understand."

Reisil's breath jerked in her chest and she pressed her other hand to her lips and closed her eyes. Finally she pulled it away and gave Kebonsat an unsteady smile. She glanced past Kebonsat and saw Upsakes glowering at them. She dropped his hand. "Now isn't really a good time to talk about it. I do have to talk to you, but—" She broke off.

"But?"

"You love Ceriba. I know you wouldn't have done this to her."

Kebonsat's eyes turned flat black and Reisil heard his teeth grind together.

"What are you saying?"

Reisil licked her lips. "Just that I am sure you didn't have anything to do with this."

"And you think someone here might have?" Rage kindled in his expression.

"I'm new to being *ahalad-kaaslane.* And I don't understand much about what I am supposed to be," she said. "And neither do I know much about intrigue or politics. I am just a tark." Her voice cracked. She swallowed. "But even so, I can't believe the men in the forest are working alone. Not that you can trust me." She thought about Leidiik's words to her and found them on her tongue. "I know what I've been up to, but you don't. I could always be lying."

Something that she could only call fear rippled over his face and was gone. Somewhere, men were taking his sister farther away.

"I'm sorry," she said. "I should have told you she was all right. Though she keeps fighting back and they don't like it."

Kebonsat's face went red, then white, and he swore low, bitter, sharp-edged curses.

"She's never had the sense to know when to be still," he said.

"She's brave," Reisil replied. "I wish I had such courage."

"I wish she had less."

"No, you don't. She must know you'll come for her, and she'll start planning for it. She'll stop antagonizing them and start making a strategy." Reisil spoke confidently, sure of Ceriba. She hardly knew the other woman, but tarks were taught to read people, to know them.

So why didn't you know about Kaval? a niggling voice accused her. She remembered what Leidiik had said: *That's the reason why the* ahalad-kaaslane *don't get to call any place home. Can't afford to get too attached to anyone.* Had her feelings for Kaval so colored her judgment that she could not see the traitor lurking within?

"Your pardon, but may I speak to Reisil a moment?"

Despite his pinched, hungry appearance, Sodur wore an expression of quiet comfort, and Reisil found herself nodding. Kebonsat rose and returned to the company of Glevs and the other Patversemese man.

Sodur sat cross-legged beside Reisil, turning to watch the flow of the water, his lynx curling up with his square head on his *ahalad-kaaslane*'s knee, tufted ears swiveling. A low purr rumbled from deep in his silvery belly.

"Bright morning," Sodur said, wiping the drip from his nose with a dirty handkerchief. Reisil returned the greeting, unable to read much from his profile.

"You pose something of a problem on this journey," he began without preamble. "We will depend on you to be our guide, but you have not had any training, and the bond with your *ahalad-kaaslane* is weak yet—I suspect even damaged." He paused and Reisil swallowed heavily. He stroked the lynx's ears and the purr intensified. "Such a crisis is not the best way to solidify the *ahalad-kaaslane* connection. How does your Saljane respond to you?"

"I don't know," Reisil mumbled. "How is she supposed to?"

Sodur chuckled and patted her leg, speaking in his quiet, kind way. "Indeed. Most *ahalad-kaaslane* animals live as long as their human counterparts. I've heard of rare occasions when the animal dies, the Blessed Lady sends another in its place. But most often not. I could not imagine losing my Lume. I would not survive his loss, I think. If I did, I would not wish a replacement. But that is not of importance now. I have no experience with any but Lume. I cannot tell you how Saljane is supposed to respond. Do you think it is a good bond?"

"I didn't want it," Reisil confessed, needing to explain herself to someone. Sodur's calm, companionable voice warmed her and she felt herself wanting to open up to him. "I told her to go away. More than once. Told her to choose someone else. I am—I was—a tark. She was angry."

Sodur nodded. "She seemed so, hanging about Kallas. It was confusing."

"Then the kidnapping happened and I didn't have any choice anymore. Maybe I never did."

"When the Lady chooses us, everything else disappears," he said. "No matter how much we resist."

Reisil looked at him, surprised, and he chuckled again. "Oh, no. You are not the first to try to escape the

Blessed Lady's net. Nor will you be the last. The life of the *ahalad-kaaslane* is difficult, the road narrow and steep, with few opportunities to rest. Though the bards' tales and songs glorify us, a wise person sees past the stories to the difficult reality. Unfortunately, the road is made more difficult by resistance. Under ordinary circumstances, we would have prepared you for *Randaja*—the spirit journey to the Vale of the Blessed Lady. She would have spoken to you and helped you understand Her purpose for you. But now, even if we had time, it's no longer possible. Before She will see you now, you must prove yourself worthy, committed." He smiled, a bittersweet smile, his attention turned inward as if he remembered something.

"Until then, you must fumble your way with Saljane on your own." He patted her leg again and stood. Lume sat up with a groan and a yawn, pink tongue curling. "When the god Vaprus first gave Senjoor fire, Senjoor found the gift precious and dangerous. He held in his hands the means to save countless lives in that dreadful, unending winter, or kill many more. In the end he died by fire, though it saved his people. I don't think he ever regretted the gift, however much it cost him personally."

"I could do a lot of good as a tark," Reisil said rebelliously.

"You could. You *will* do a great deal of good as *ahalad-kaaslane*. Your tark training will not go to waste."

Reisil leaned back and stared up at the blue sky, hearing Sodur's steps fading along the deck. The river smelled of fish and weeping willows. The sound of waves lapping at the hull lulled her and the sun warmed her face.

~Saljane?

~Ahalad-kaaslane.

Again that knife-blade edge to their contact. Reisil hesitated.

~How fares Ceriba? she asked finally.

~They ride.

No pictures, nothing.

Reisil hesitated again and she could feel Saljane's impatience.

~*How fare you?*

Silence. Reisil waited, but there was no reply. She pushed again.

~*Do you . . . do you remember my name?*

~Ahalad-kaaslane.

Was that reproach?

~*No, my name.*

Silence. Then, ~Ahalad-kaaslane.

Flat. Denial.

Did that mean Saljane would not use her name? Was she reminding her of their bond and Reisil's repudiation of it? Reisil blinked at the sky, feeling a stone growing in her chest. There was a closeness between Upsakes and his weirmart, Sodur and Lume, even Juhrnus and his sisalik. An aura of love and sharing. Would that ever happen with Saljane? Or had she destroyed it?

The river flowed and Reisil's head pounded. She dozed, her dreams filled with images of Kaval and Saljane. Of Ceriba, on the ground, being kicked. Only this time Kaval kicked her and Saljane screamed and screamed.

She woke with a jerk, rubbing her gritty eyes, her mouth dry and tasting of copper. Her stomach grumbled and she fumbled in the pocket of her cloak for a plum. It had been squashed, but tasted sunny and sweet. The juice ran down her chin and she caught it on her fingers, licking them clean.

She became aware that the boat was no longer moving along the river, but swung in a half circle, so that the prow was facing upstream. She stood and saw Voli with her companions clustered around him. She approached, hanging back at the edge to hear.

"Most times," Voli was saying, "they sort themselves out in a few days. Water's high and the current's fast. Breaks 'em apart. Can't hold. Or folks from downriver come and tear 'em loose, get them going again."

"We don't have a few days," Upsakes declared, his blocky forehead shiny.

Voli shook his head and shrugged. "Nothing else to do. Tie up to the bank so's we don't get bashed against the jam and wait. Can't port around, not enough of us and too many trees. Wouldn't get through." Several of his crew nodded vigorously.

Reisil looked out onto the river and saw what it was they were talking about. A tangle of logs blocked their passage on the river. Constructed mostly from cut logs with the limbs stripped off, mixed with a few snags—trees tumbled into the river from storm or weakened roots—the logjam formed an impassible barrier across the river.

"Be a storm in a day or so up in the mountains. Flood surge should wash it out. It won't hold long," Voli determined.

"How far to Priede?" Upsakes asked. "We'll go ashore here and go by foot."

Voli shook his head with a grimace. "Can't. Closer to the Kodu Riik side; have to put the boat up there. No bridges or towns for leagues either. Right bank's steep. Too dangerous to swim across even if you could get yourselves out—bad currents."

"Then we'll cross on the logjam itself. It looks sturdy enough."

Voli scratched his jaw. "Wouldn't recommend it. Could go at any moment. Slippery too, and always shifting—end up bilged on your own anchor. Be as doomed as if Squire Ketch himself had aholt of you."

Upsakes looked defeated and Kebonsat furious.

Reisil wondered if Voli's excuses were true, or just a means to slow them down. Could he be working with the kidnappers? She looked at the logjam. It cracked and snapped together, rising up and down on the water like a breathing thing. She shivered. To get a hand or leg caught between any of them— Bones would be crushed. A four-foot-diameter log broke free and the current battered it back against the pile. One end caught and the water drove it under, flipping the other end high in the air. It held for a long moment, dripping, ponderous; then the sunken end was released. The log shot up

into the air and fell whistling, splashing into the river
and sending waves washing over Reisil's feet.

Voli raised his hands. "See? Time of year for it. Have
to wait."

"They didn't come down more than a day ahead of us.
How did their boat get through?" Kebonsat demanded.

"Magic?" Juhrnus suggested.

Upsakes made a guttural sound, his eyes bulging, his
hands reaching and straining as if he wanted to stran-
gle something.

Before he could say anything, Voli spoke. "Could be.
Likely not. Fact is, it happens. Loggers cut as fast as they
can this time of year. Take advantage of the snowmelt.
Drought will make more of these as the river drops.
Less profit."

He began giving orders to his crew, who poled the
boat closer to the Kodu Riik bank. One crewman stood
on the upstream rail and made a high, arcing dive into
the water. He carried a line tied about his waist, and
when he rose to the surface, already the current had
swept him to the middle of the boat. He kicked hard,
his powerful strokes drawing him to the bank. He jerked
as the line caught him just before the jam. He was forced
to swim upstream, tracing the span of the rope. At last
he clambered up the rocky edge, deep panting breaths
moving his ribs like bellows. He untied the rope around
his waist and secured it to a tree. Thick welts circled his
waist, following the grip of the rope, and blood ran down
his legs and arms where he'd kicked and scraped against
the rocks along the bank.

The towline secure, the anchor was hauled up and
Voli and his men hauled the boat closer to the bank. A
second line was thrown to the waiting man and he secured it to another tree ten paces downstream from the
first. The two lines held the boat away from the rocks
on the shore with the aid of the hungry current and the
anchor, which once again had been dropped, this time
tossed as far as possible toward the opposite bank.

"You've done this before," commented Sodur.

"Hardest part now is to keep from getting hit. Best

to pull her out of the water, but too many rocks and too steep. Pikemen on the stern will shove off stray logs. Won't be long, though. River's rising—natural dam. Get a few more logs hitting—you can figure on tomorrow evening. Be in Priede before you know it."

Sodur gave Upsakes a frowning look and Reisil knew he was thinking of the Dure Vadonis. Ceriba's father had said at best he could hold off three or four days before notifying Karalis Vasalis and Iisand Samir of Ceriba's kidnapping—if the envoy from Koduteel cooperated. If the logjam held until the next evening, two days would be gone. And Ceriba would be two days farther away. Reisil's mouth went dry. War. There would be more war. More death and more lost friends, lost brothers, lost hands and feet and legs and eyes. Another Mysane Kosk. What was Kaval thinking? There was no patriotism in this. None at all.

The man who'd braved the currents to secure the mooring lines to the trees came back aboard, kicking his legs in the water as he drew himself hand over hand along a taut line. Reisil applied a salve to the rock abrasions and the rope welts around his waist and ribs, giving him willow bark to chew.

"No need for all this trouble," he said, brown eyes cast down as she gently rubbed the salve into his bruised and broken skin. "It'll heal up good. Don't need to bother *ahalad-kaaslane* with it."

"I want to be bothered," she replied with asperity. "Besides, why shouldn't I see to your injuries? It was a brave thing you did for us."

Color seeped into his gaunt brown cheeks and he twisted his ragged hair, burying his chin in his hunched shoulders. "Just my turn is all."

"Well, you served us well and we are grateful."

Reisil left him there to sleep in the narrow shade of the long storage box that housed the pikes. At the stern of the boat the crewmen laughed and shouted as a log barreled past and rammed the jam with a thundering crack. The tangle shuddered and held, the newest arrival rasping sideways to nudge and thump against its brethren.

Upsakes, Sodur and Juhrnus ate lunch from their stores, and Reisil realized that her own stomach was grumbling again. She drew bread and cheese from her pack and sat apart from her fellow *ahalad-kaaslane*. Sodur had been kind and she appreciated his amity, but she did not relish the company of Juhrnus or Upsakes. The latter man was clearly angry with her and resented her inclusion on this journey.

She shrugged and found a spot at the bow of the boat, dangling her feet off the edge below the rail. She wanted to be making this journey as little as Upsakes wanted her to be. But that did not change her obligation to Ceriba. To the Lady. Despite her reluctance to accept becoming *ahalad-kaaslane*, when at last Reisil had shouldered the burden, she had done so willingly. Just as she had taken up the burden of finding Ceriba—a more personal mission now that she knew Kaval had a hand in the kidnapping. She would not lay those burdens down for anyone.

She ate slowly, her back to her companions, watching the waters of the river slide by, sending bits of flotsam and jetsam into the harbors of the rock teeth, pushed there on waves of foam. That was her, she thought. Torn from her home, carried on a current not of her own making, bouncing against rocks, searching for a safe haven.

Kebonsat knelt beside her. His face was a polite mask. Not even the muscles in his jaws clenched to give away the fury and frustration he must feel. Somewhere in his young life he'd been taught unrelenting control. But Reisil saw it in his eyes. That and desperation. She remembered the smile he'd exchanged with Ceriba, the affection and joy they had shared together. She had no doubt that there was no limit to what he'd do to regain his sister.

"I have need," he said. "If you are willing."

His peculiar emphasis on *if* made her cautious.

"What can I do?"

"Call back your bird."

She stared at him in surprise. He made a sound low in his throat and thumped a fist against the rail, his control

cracking. "Damn it! I don't want to leave her alone with
those bastards. But with your bird's help, we can break
the jam. We can't afford to lose days. Even with your
bird showing us the way, they could decide to kill her
anytime. Or worse."

Reisil didn't want to think about "or worse."

"What do you want of Saljane?"

Kebonsat hesitated. "Koijots is not a wizard."

Reisil frowned. Not a wizard. Why would Kebonsat
bother to tell her that? She waited for him to continue.

"He is not a wizard," he repeated, "but he does have
some magical abilities. He might actually have become
quite powerful, but he would have had to join the
Guild—" Kebonsat paused again as if choosing his
words. "He would have suicided before that. So instead
my father made him a tracker. His loyalty and skills have
served my family well. What he does now . . . it's a risk
for him if it's revealed to the Guild." He waved a hand
at the crew and *ahalad-kaaslane*. "But he's willing to
risk it, for Ceriba's sake."

"What would you need of Saljane?" Reisil asked. Except for Kvepi Buris, she'd never been close to the making of magic. And now Kebonsat wanted her, wanted
Saljane, to aid in a spell. She gripped her hands together
to keep them from trembling.

"Nothing dangerous," he said reassuringly. "Koijots's
spell won't work unless it's carried over to the logjam.
She'll have to place it where he says and that's all."

Reisil nodded, deciding. Time was running out. "I'll
ask her."

Reisil closed her eyes, feeling a crawling along her
spine. They were watching her, the other *ahalad-
kaaslane,* curious about what Kebonsat was up to with
her.

~Saljane?

Presence.

~How fare you, Saljane?

Hunger. Hunt.

Reisil tried again, hoping for something more tangible. Words.

~We need you here.

Curiosity.

~There's a logjam. A spell could break it up, but they need your help in placing it.

She put her palms over her eyes, curling her fingers into her hair, and tried to create a picture in her mind. Instead she found herself unable to focus, fragments of the last weeks intruding, chief among them Kaval. Tears squeezed from her tightly shut eyes and she pressed harder with her palms. She wasn't ready to think of him yet. Slowly she built the image of the tangle of logs damming their path. She willed Saljane to see, wishing she had the power to bring the bird into her mind as Saljane did her.

Her vision canted suddenly and her mindscape was full of whirling green. Then it settled and she realized that Saljane perched at the top of the tree canopy. The whirling green was Saljane's swift-moving gaze sweeping across the panorama of wind-tossed trees. In the near distance, Reisil saw the thrust of gray mountains rising above the forest. The Dumu Griste mountains.

Saljane's hunger twisted in Reisil's own gut. The goshawk hadn't eaten since the blue grouse the previous day and it had hardly been enough to dull the gnawing in her belly then. Reisil said nothing. She would not ask Saljane to do more than she would, not on the fragile link that held them together. It was possible that Saljane would hunt swiftly and wing her way back before nightfall. They could be in Priede early in the morning, if no logs bashed them in the night.

Suddenly Saljane launched, up and up. Reisil gasped and rocked back and forth, her stomach bounding into her throat and then dropping to her toes.

"What is it? Are you all right?" Kebonsat put his hand on her rigid shoulder.

"Flying," she said through clenched teeth. "High."

"Is she coming?"

Reisil shuddered as Saljane flipped almost sideways, buffeted by winds. A storm was moving in over the mountains. *There's no danger,* she told herself. *You're back on the boat. Only your mind is with Saljane.*

The wind sang along the edges of her wings as the

goshawk coasted on a current. Saljane could feel her *ahalad-kaaslane* struggling against her rising panic. The bird crooned soundlessly. Reisil felt the croon vibrate in the marrow of her bones, and with it a flower of delight bloomed inside her at this sign of concern.

"Fish," she said to Kebonsat, her hands still over her eyes. "She'll be hungry." Then she gave herself up to the flight.

By the time Saljane returned, Reisil had managed to relax enough to enjoy the sensation of flying without feeling as if she were going to throw up. The landscape spread out against her inner eye in odd shapes intermixed with carefully tended fields and cots. As Saljane approached the silver ribbon of the Sadelema, Reisil stood, extending her arm. Saljane circled, then plummeted down, snapping her wings wide and landing gently on the outstretched arm, her talons closing convulsively on the leather gauntlet.

Reisil pulled her around to stroke shaking fingers over the bird's smooth head. She grinned with the wonder she felt sharing their flight and landing. The goshawk dipped her beak and again Reisil felt that croon and the flower inside bloomed larger.

~There's fish for you.

Saljane flapped to the deck, where Kebonsat tossed one of a dozen trout he and Glevs had caught during Saljane's return flight. The silver and rainbow-hued fish flopped on the polished wood. Saljane snatched it in her talons and flew to the rail, where she proceeded to tear and bolt the flesh. She ate three more in quick succession before Reisil stopped her.

~You'll not be able to fly if you eat all of them at once.

Saljane dropped the head of the fish she'd just finished and scraped her beak against the rail to clean it.

~Are you ready?

Reisil glanced at the sun. An hour or two of daylight left. If the spell worked quickly, they'd be in Priede by nightfall.

"What's going on?" Upsakes stood with his feet

braced wide, hands on his hips. A dose of laudanum taken with his lunch had put him to sleep, and Reisil had been glad that he had not observed her rapport with Saljane or Koijots's preparations for the spell. Looking at the elder *ahalad-kaaslane* now, his eyelids drooped over bloodshot eyes. "What is your *ahalad-kaaslane* doing here, girl?" he demanded.

Reisil glanced at Kebonsat and back.

"I called her."

"Why?"

"I needed her."

Upsakes's face twisted. Reisil took a step back. Was this the same man who had been so congenial, if superior and haughty, these last weeks in Kallas? Sodur laid a hand on Upsakes's shoulder and gave Reisil a sober, questioning look.

"My tracker has a means to destroy the logjam, with the bird's help," Kebonsat said, shifting to stand between Reisil and Upsakes. "It's a minor spell and should do the trick, if it's placed correctly."

With his explanation, Upsakes's fury increased, his eyes bulging, veins standing out on his neck and forehead. Sodur's hand tightened, but Upsakes pulled free, shoving the other man aside. Lume snarled as his *ahalad-kaaslane* stumbled and fell. Juhrnus helped Sodur up, his sisalik hissing. Upsakes's weirmart reared up and bared her teeth, gathering herself to launch at Kebonsat's face. Before she could, Saljane flung herself into the air and beat at the *ahalad-kaaslane* pair with her wings. Upsakes swung at her but she flipped aside, avoiding the blow. He fell heavily on one knee, unable to recover his balance after his lunging swing. Before he could do more, Sodur and Juhrnus took him by the arms. He struggled against their grip, swearing viciously. When he realized he couldn't free himself, he turned on Reisil.

"Wizardry! Here? After what they did at Mysane Kosk! And you—helping them with it. Traitor to Kodu Riik! Traitor to the Blessed Amiya!" He fairly shrieked his accusations, his pupils so that dilated his eyes appeared black. Spittle ran down his chin and he nearly wrenched free of Sodur's and Jurhnus's restraining grips. Reisil blanched and her stomach churned. Still she refused to back down, refused to look away. She reached out mentally for Saljane's support, needing the strength of her steel-edged mind.

"I am *ahalad-kaaslane*," she found herself saying, and wished immediately that she hadn't. She might have Saljane, but she'd not come to this willingly. It seemed wrong to claim it when she hadn't yet earned it. Did she want to earn it? The question startled her and she surprised herself with the answer. Yes. Yes, she did. But on her terms. She would do what she knew was necessary and right, no less.

"I am *ahalad-kaaslane*," she repeated more clearly. "I serve Kodu Riik and the Blessed Lady in the fashion I believe best."

Reisil turned to Koijots, who remained a silent observer, his eyes blue as deep water. "What do you need Saljane to do?"

He held out his palm. On it rested a thin piece of leather. A complex construction of thread, leaves, hair and sticks stuck up stiffly from the leather base. Reisil frowned at it and then back up at him.

"That's it?"

"It's enough, placed properly," he replied in an unexpectedly soft voice. But then he was a tracker and silence was his way.

"Where?"

"There. See in the middle near the bottom where the three logs have splintered? See that smaller branch, shaped like a half moon, the bark still green and white? There."

Reisil repeated the instructions to Saljane, though the goshawk made it impatiently clear she already understood.

~*Be careful. Those logs could shift and catch you. Be swift,* ahalad-kaaslane.

Reisil's mind caught on the last word in a flash of revelation. Earlier in the day she'd asked Saljane if she remembered her name, and the reply had been *ahalad-*

kaaslane. Suddenly Reisil understood that Saljane had intended no insult, a refusal to know her. It was an endearment. It meant someone close to the heart, soul-kin. Reisil stroked Saljane's chest, a lump in her throat at the rush of emotion she felt for her.

~I have been stupid, haven't I? I will try to be better.

The response from Saljane was both impatience to begin, and the emotional equivalent of the tolerant smile adults give to children who have just realized an important lesson.

Reisil placed the leather loop handle Koijots had attached to his spell in Saljane's beak. The goshawk fluttered into the air and flew to the logs. Reisil held her breath. For the first time she became aware of the creaking shift of the massive pile, fully twenty feet high, and how loud the river sounded, pounding against the logs.

Chapter 8

Saljane clambered to the correct spot in fluttering hops, talons gripping the slick, wet wood with splintering strength.

"Gently, gently," Koijots whispered, drumming his fingers on the rail. Reisil was surprised. When first she'd met him, he'd had the self-contained air of a hunting cat, relentlessly patient.

Upsakes continued to mutter epithets and Sodur and Juhrnus retained their sharp hold on him. The weirmart wound around to reach her *ahalad-kaaslane*'s face, licking his cheeks with worried absorption. Upsakes shook the little animal off with a bull-like bellow and the weirmart ducked down, clinging with all her might to his surging shoulders.

Reisil clutched the rail, unable to do anything more than watch. Suddenly the pikemen at the bow of the boat shouted. Thunder sounded and the boat jerked and leaped like a child's toy on the end of a string. The group at the stern stumbled together and Upsakes tore free to scrabble over the rail. Sodur caught him, Lume's mouth closing around the powerful man's ankle. Upsakes hardly noticed. Juhrnus and Glevs closed to help, and between them they wrestled the angry man to the deck. His weirmart squalled and yowled from beneath the tangle of bodies, but never loosed her companion.

The boat dipped. Reisil felt the deck below her shudder as logs hit it one after another. Nine thunderous bangs in all. The squeal of wood scraping along the hull echoed in the air, and Reisil felt the deck twist and buck as if a sea serpent roiled beneath. Voli shouted orders and the pikemen shoved on the great, tumbling tree stems.

Forgetting her mindlink to Saljane, she screamed warning to the bird.

"Saljane! Look out!"

The horde of logs crashed into the jam with a deafening sound. Jets of foaming spray exploded upward, drenching the deck. Like thrown matchsticks they tumbled, end over end, careening wildly. One shot straight up like a giant's arrow, falling in a long, graceful arc to smash down on top of the jam with a crack of thunder, only to tumble free on the other side. Reisil gripped the rail with white fingers. There was no sign of Saljane in the maelstrom.

At last there was calm. Not silence. The swollen river continued to rush, the logs thumped and rubbed, waves and foam washing over them. The crew cheered for themselves, that they had kept the boat from capsizing, that the logs had struck glancing blows and not holed the hull. Reisil would have cheered too, but she still didn't see Saljane. Koijots stood shoulder-to-shoulder with her, searching the wreckage. Reisil searched the sky.

~Ahalad-kaaslane.

Tears sprang into Reisil's eyes and she whirled around, eyes raking the air.

~Where are you?

~Here.

She heard a whistling and Saljane winged past, the spell still dangling from her beak.

Koijots muttered something and turned to Reisil.

"It can still be done. I think. There as before, lower now, but quickly, before these new logs set. It'll take more than I've got if that happens."

Koijots pointed out the spot he wanted and Reisil communicated it to Saljane. Once again the bird perched on the top of the wood tangle, talons gouging into the slick wood, wings unfurled for balance. With fluttering hops, she journeyed down to the spot Koijots had indicated. The tangled mass creaked and shivered beneath her. The recent additions to the pile groaned and cracked together, rolling and pitching on the river's angry current.

Finally Saljane hung the spell on the stump of a branch, as big around as Reisil's wrist, and broken off less than a foot from the trunk. The goshawk launched herself up with heavy flapping of her wings, but did not gain much altitude. A log beneath her canted and rolled, shoving upward what appeared to be little more than a sapling. Reisil screamed as the wood whipped into Saljane. Feathers exploded like dandelion puff and Saljane screeched. She fell into the water at the edge of the boat, just out of Reisil's reach.

The young *ahalad-kaaslane* didn't think. She vaulted over the rail into the frigid, boiling current. She sank, sodden boots and clothes pulling her down. The current grabbed her, drove her forward toward the battering logs. Reisil kicked furiously upward and back, against that angry pull. The cold cut through her chest, and when she broke the surface her lips were already blue. She kicked hard against the current, searching for Saljane.

There! Too near the tumbling logs. The goshawk's head was above water, her beak open, her eyes impossibly wide. Her wings opened and closed in the water, but the saturated feathers were too heavy to be of any use, even if she could have dragged herself from the water, even if the blow had not broken something.

The current whirled Saljane around and batted her toward the churning logs. Reisil kicked hard, flinging herself up and over, letting the driving current help her. Her arms closed around Saljane and she pulled them both under. The bird struggled against her grip. Reisil broke the surface again, kicking backward, the knobby bark of redwood log not eight inches from her face. Saljane's talons raked her stomach in panicking fury, but Reisil refused to let the bird go. The vicious beak bit deeply into her cheeks and neck as the terrified, pain-stricken bird fought for freedom. Blood ran down her face in thick ribbons, but Reisil was so cold she hardly felt the injuries.

Somewhere in a detached part of her mind, she found humor.

~*Oh,* ahalad-kaaslane, *what have we done to each other in our short bonding? If we survive this, may we both be better friends.*

The current dragged at her and she found herself between two spinning logs, larger in diameter than she could put her arms around. When they came together, they would crush her. Reisil sucked in a breath and flung herself sideways, under the water, under the log. She pumped her legs, but they hardly seemed to move. Her lungs screamed from the pain and cold. She could see nothing but a glimmer of blurry light above. Where was the boat? Where was safety? She could not stay under any longer, could hardly resist the demands of the current. And Saljane—could Reisil be drowning her *ahalad-kaaslane*? She thrust herself up toward the light.

Her hair clogged her eyes. She could see nothing. Reisil gulped air, her lungs burning. She couldn't feel her fingers, couldn't feel her feet. Logs rumbled together—where? How close? Saljane twitched in her arms but no longer struggled, no longer pecked and scratched.

Sudden hands closed around her.

"Steady, now," Kebonsat said, his voice strained. "We've got you."

Reisil wasn't even capable of relief. She let herself go slack as two sets of hands tied a rope around her waist, beneath her arms where she clutched Saljane to chest.

The rope grew taut and she felt herself pulled through the water, then up out of it like a lead weight. She dangled over the steel current, inching upward in jolting tugs. More hands grappled her and pulled her to the deck, where she lay in a frigid puddle.

"How is she?"

"Blessed Lady! She's blue. Is she breathing?"

"Get something for these wounds. At least they're clean. She won't have lost much blood either. Cold as she is, the blood's sluggish."

"Gonna scar bad, 'less you get them treated right.

Need to get to Priede to the tark there. Best play that spell if you still can."

The voices whirled around Reisil. Kebonsat. Sodur. Glevs. Voli.

"So cold," Reisil whispered.

"Gotta get her dry. What about the bird?"

Gentle hands settled on hers still clutching Saljane.

"Let her go, Reisil. You got her out; let us do the rest." The voice was soft and comforting. Sodur. She relaxed her arms. "Good girl. I'll get her warm and dry. Concentrate on yourself now."

~Saljane?

~Saljane?

Weak. Safe. Worry. Pain.

They were pressing a cloth to her face and neck and she felt someone tugging on her boots, then her trousers. They lifted her and carried her to a pallet out of the rising wind. They cut her shredded jerkin from her and all movement stilled about her a moment. Then muttering. Kebonsat? They bound her ribs and stomach and swaddled her in blankets. She shivered, her body shaking like an aspen leaf in a gale. Fiery agony spread questing fingers along her stomach and up her face. Despite the chill, sweat beaded on her forehead and her body twisted, seeking escape from the pain.

"Give her some of this."

Reisil found a cup on her lips and sipped. Then spat. She struggled, tearing herself from Kebonsat's bracing arm. Sodur brought her up short, pressing her back down. This time his voice was less gentle, more commanding.

"You've no choice. Saljane lives in your mind, hears your thoughts, especially now when you're in so much pain. You may not want the laudanum, but she needs you to have it, or I can't help her. You jumped in the river to save her. Would you let her die now for your aversion to the drug? Wouldn't hurt you either. Can't do a lot more for you until we get to Priede. Do you *want* to suffer the entire way there?"

Again Kebonsat held the cup to her lips. She looked

at Sodur through her agony, lips compressed. Then with
a sigh she drank. It tasted bitter and sweet and foul,
despite mixing it with wine. She drained the cup with a
grimace and lay back. Sodur patted her shoulder and
left.

"Upsakes?" Reisil couldn't help but ask. Kebonsat
seemed to understand the question.

"No harm from him. Sodur gave him a dose of that
stuff as well. He ought to sleep until Priede."

"Good." Reisil sank back, pain fading already. She
still felt cold and grateful to Kebonsat, who cuddled her
beside him. It wasn't personal, she knew. He was a
fighting man and knew that she could yet succumb to
hypothermia and shock. A weight settled on her right
side. Lume. The yellow-green eyes glowed at her and
his heavy head settled on her hip with a rumbling purr.
Reisil gave him a dreamy smile, then dropped into darkness without dreams.

She woke, a comfortable weight across her thighs,
something like a collar around her neck—but not unpleasant. The ground rumbled beneath her. Every
jounce gave her a lash of pain. She blinked. The sky
above was black—no stars. Storm clouds. She remembered seeing the storm moving across the Dume Griste
mountains when Saljane was flying. Wind fingered into
the wagon bed and plucked at her hair—dry now. She
craned her neck and saw nothing but the painted
wooden sides of the wagon and the back of the driver,
his hat pulled low, the neck of his blue woolen coat
pulled high. The wheels made a dry, scuffing sound on
the road. Were they in Priede? Where were the sounds
of the town?

They rumbled over a rough patch and her head
bounced. She moaned. The collar on her neck wriggled
and she stiffened. Upsakes's weirmart peered up at her,
yellow topaz eyes gleaming.

"What are you doing here?" she wondered in a
husky voice.

The little animal nosed her chin and squirmed down

beneath the blankets. Reisil blinked at the matte-black sky. Why wasn't the little creature with Upsakes? Still, her animal warmth around Reisil's neck was welcome and she snuggled into it, drifting off again.

She woke when she was being lifted out of the wagon. She struggled against the hands that held her.

"Easy now. The tark's inside. Sodur's already taken Saljane in."

Reisil forced herself to relax. Kebonsat held her gently. She looked at him blearily, her head on his chest. A beam of yellow light fell across them and they entered a cottage high on a hillside above Priede. *That's why no city noises,* she thought.

The scents of the room nearly broke her heart, smelling so much like her own little house. Not hers anymore, she reminded herself, the knot in her throat swelling. Herbs hung drying in bunches from hooks on the beamed ceiling. Tansy and chamomile, rosemary, coltsfoot, dragon's blood. A stew bubbled in a pot hung on a tripod in the spacious fireplace, the yeasty smell of fresh-baked bread making Reisil's mouth water.

"Ah, what have we here? Lay her down on the table. Better light than at the bed. That's right, stay there, keep her from rolling off. Laudanum, eh? Can smell it. Wearing off, though, eh?"

Reisil understood the last to be directed at her and nodded to the man with short, bristling gray hair around the sides of his round head, his bald pate shining rosy gold in the candlelight.

"Righto. They tell me you went into the Urdzina." He *tsk*ed, pulling the blankets off her carefully. "Not wise, m'dear. Cold, cold, cold. This time of year especially. Running high on snowmelt, despite the drought. Little irony of the gods. Ah. And these from the bird?" He glanced across her to Kebonsat, who nodded confirmation. Glevs stood beside him. Where were Sodur and Saljane? She began to struggle up, her gaze darting to the door. The tark pressed down on her shoulders as Kebonsat and Glevs seized her arms and legs.

"Gently now."

"Saljane."

The tark looked at the other two men with raised eyebrows, his red pug nose twitching.

"The goshawk," Kebonsat said by way of explanation.

"Ah. Well, worry no more. I'm not the only tark in town tonight. There's a visitor—my sister—who is also a tark. She's got the care of your *ahalad-kaaslane*. She's very good and has a way with animals. Now I'm going to have to give you something to put you to sleep again. No, no. I know best right now. You need stitching, and I can't do it if you're thrashing about. Nor will my sister manage that bird of yours. Hear it? She knows you're awake now and it's setting her off."

Reisil could hear Saljane's loud cries in the next room and a soothing voice. A woman, somehow familiar . . .

"None of that foul potion again. Try this. Tastes better too, if I do say so."

Reisil swallowed the liquid held to her lips, eyes widening in surprise. She knew this drink. She'd learned it from Elutark, one of her mentor's own recipes.

"Good, good. Now, before you fade away, do reassure that bird of yours."

~*Saljane*. Ahalad-kaaslane.

Red worry. Sparks. Pain.

Reisil felt the concoction the tark had given her beginning to take hold. She didn't have any words to give the bird, so she tried to show her feelings instead. Pride. Affection. Something deeper, something to fill the loneliness she kept buried deep in her heart, loneliness rooted in her parents' abandonment. Tears leaked from the corners of her eyes and trickled down to dampen her hair. A sob hunched in her throat and she swallowed hard on it.

Had she made Saljane feel so in refusing her? Could the bird forgive that sort of pain? Could she?

Reisil woke again to flickering shadows. A smoky scent mingled with the herbs, and a duskier, masculine smell rose from the pillow and sheets. She wriggled and realized she was in the tark's bed, with Lume lying lengthwise beside her.

She lay still for a moment. There was a sound of a

sleepy fire, the creak of the roof and a rattle of a shutter. In the stillness she could hear Lume's even breathing and her own racing heart.

The day's events rose up and flooded her mind and she knew her dreams had woken her. She felt the same urgency she had standing at the gates of Kallas—an invisible hand pushing against her back. Every moment took Ceriba farther away; every moment brought disaster closer.

She struggled up on her elbows, sucking a silent breath against the ache in her side and face. Lume stretched a paw across her stomach in protest, his claws delicately extended on the quilt. Candles glowed on the mantel and the table. The tark slept in an overstuffed chair opposite the bed, his feet propped up on a wood block. The chair was covered with a geometric-patterned orange and brown brocade, threadbare along the arms and shredded completely along the bottom. He must have a cat, Reisil decided. One who'd decided to retreat while Lume invaded its home. In the window burned a rosemary candle, flame tall and straight.

Her stomach growled as she sat up further. Her head spun. She gasped, feeling the wounds along her stomach as she moved. It was enough to wake the tark.

He yawned, looking at her. She was wearing a man's shirt and nothing else. Lume rolled over and snuggled into the warmth she'd left behind.

"I thought you'd wake soon. You *ahalad-kaaslane* never do things properly when it comes to healing yourselves. I expect you'll be rambling off with the rest of them in the morning. No sense at all. No sense." He was shaking his head, bustling through his cabinets for a bowl, half a loaf of bread and a crock of butter. "That bird of yours, though. She won't be flying for a week or more. Nothing broken, thank the Blessed Lady. But bad bruising. Elu's done what she can—my sister is very good, you know. The best. But still, be a week, and then short flights. Up to you to see her fed, but then that's what having an *ahalad-kaaslane* is for."

Reisil clutched her fingers on the quilt over legs. *Elu? "Elutark?"* She gasped.

The tark turned around, eyebrows raised.

"That's my sister. Lives in Kodu Riik still. Down visiting me. I'm Odiltark, by the way. Always good to know the names of the people who've had their hands in your blood. How do you feel?"

Reisil was still reeling. Elutark *here*, in Priede. "Where is she? Elutark."

"With your bird." He nodded toward the next room. "Asleep, I should think. If she has any sense."

The door opened on silent hinges and Reisil's teacher and mentor slipped into the room, shutting the door behind her.

"She never did have much sense either." Odiltark sniffed, laying out another two bowls. "I suppose you're hungry too? I could use a bite, since I'm awake. Let's see what else I can find." He went back to rummaging in his cupboards.

Reisil turned her stricken gaze on Elutark. She was just as Reisil remembered. Silvered chestnut hair in a long braid wound around her head, bright blue eyes in a round face, small, birdlike hands, deft and gentle. She reached out and touched the bandages on Reisil's face.

"What have you done to yourself, Reisiltark?"

Tears ran down Reisil's cheeks.

"Just Reisil, now. I've become *ahalad-kaaslane*."

Elutark frowned and sat on the edge of the bed, brushing the tears away.

"Oh, no, my child. *Ahalad-kaaslane* you may have become, but you will always be a tark. The Blessed Lady has extended both hands to you. You have been chosen for great things."

Reisil blinked. Great things? Her? She shook her head and then winced.

"Just so. Though you shall find it an uncomfortable burden. Being either is difficult in any case, but both—" Elutark smiled and stroked Reisil's hair from her face. "You will manage. You were my brightest student. And you have always understood what being a tark means. How to serve. Your life has been hard, growing up without parents or family, passed off from hand to hand. Lonely and terrible as that was, it has made you staunch, capable and self-reliant. You will realize how much one day. But for now, just know that our Blessed Amiya could not choose anyone better."

"They are two different things, tark and *ahalad-kaaslane*. One heals, the other—"

"They are different, but not so opposite as you imagine. The *ahalad-kaaslane* preserve and heal Kodu Riik as the tark does its people. Both come from the Lady's hand."

Odiltark lit more candles, setting the table with dried fruits, jellies, pickled vegetables and the leftover stew he'd been cooking when Reisil arrived.

"There now. Let's get you up to the table, shall we?"

Reisil looked at Elutark. "Saljane?"

"Asleep. With a bit of that sleep nectar. She'll be very sore for several days. She won't be able to hunt for herself, nor fly. If she were in the wild, I wouldn't count much on her chances. You must be careful also. I don't want you tearing out those stitches or letting them go septic. Lady knows I'd rather have you here for a week to mend, but I suspect you won't tarry."

Reisil shook her head, feeling that silent push at her back.

The brother and sister tarks helped Reisil to the table. For a while silence reigned as the three fell to with purpose and determination. Soon crumbs, drippings and scraped bowls were all the evidence left of their meal.

Reisil sat back, feeling sleepy again. She yawned.

"Where are my friends?" she asked. Not quite the right word for them. She didn't really count any among them friends. She wished she could trust Sodur. She liked his dry warmth, like a cozy hearth on a stormy night. Kebonsat had been kind to her, but that didn't make him a friend. Though she knew she was drawn to him. He was like the safety of a stone wall at her back when shining eyes threatened from the dark.

"There is an inn not far from here. It is quite comfortable. They shall return for you in the morning. The two who had dunkings I gave a concoction of my own.

They'll be lucky not to have come down with chest colds, the both of them."

Both of them? Reisil rubbed her head. She remembered Kebonsat's voice in the water, but someone else had helped him tie the rope around her. Who?

"Time for you to get back in bed. I told them not to bother us until well after dawn, so you still have a few hours' sleep yet. Drink some more of this. Don't argue— I want you to sleep. Tomorrow is soon enough to start abusing yourself again. There you go; that's a good girl."

They tucked Reisil back in, Odiltark patting her shoulder before settling back into his armchair. Elutark stayed beside her, perching on the edge of the bed.

"I'm so glad to have seen you," Reisil murmured, her hand in the other woman's. "I have missed you."

"I too, sweetling. I have missed you in my home, prattling on about this and that." She smiled, taking the sting out of her words. "It sent me down here to my brother for company. He's a cantankerous old man, but he's done well with your wounds. Go to sleep now. I'll sit here with you."

Reisil closed her eyes, her hand warm in Elutark's, Lume's feline whiskers tickling her ear.

She woke to the clatter of crockery and the mouthwatering smell of scrambling eggs, frying ham and baking biscuits. She sat up, feeling the tightness beneath her bandages where her skin pulled at the stitches. The ache of her wounds gnawed, but she felt no heat of infection. Reisil set her teeth against the pain. She must learn to be harder, stronger. The road from here would be difficult and painful and she must bear it.

She thought of Ceriba and the way the man had kicked her. Her spine stiffened. Did Kaval plan to kill Ceriba as Leidiik said the kidnappers must? Her hands balled in the quilt. She thought of the night of Ceriba's kidnapping, the way she'd lain in her bed longing for Kaval. But he had not been thinking of her at all. He had been in Ceriba's bedroom committing a crime that could not be forgiven.

Reisil ground her teeth together, fighting the tears that burned in her eyes. She would not cry for Kaval. He deserved no tears. Ceriba needed her now.

Kebonsat sat at the table with Sodur. Lume curled in a ball at the foot of Reisil's bed. He pushed against her hand and she rubbed his ears.

~Saljane?

Sleepy. Red. Hunger. Red.

~I'll get you something to eat, something for the pain.

She swung her legs over the edge of the bed. The shirt she wore hung to her thighs. She glanced around for her clothing and saw it on a line by the fire where Odiltark had hung it to dry. She blushed and pulled the quilt from beneath Lume, who clung to the fabric for a moment, then stood and turned about on the sheets before curling back into a ball. Fingers of pain made her breathless and she gentled her movements, wrapping the quilt around her. Elutark was nowhere to be seen. Odiltark muttered and bobbed back and forth, stirring, flipping, salting, tasting.

"Reisil! Bright morning. How are you feeling?" Sodur swung his leg over the table bench and came to Reisil's side, accompanied by Odiltark. She smiled and murmured something, clutching the quilt, feeling silly with the bandages swathing her face.

How bad would they scar? she wondered suddenly. She'd never been one to spend time in front of the mirror, but she had always considered herself attractive. Kaval had certainly thought so, anyhow. For a moment she remembered him in her cottage, hands cupping her face— She shied from the memory, her mouth twisting. As *ahalad-kaaslane,* she must expect a solitary, wandering life. Scars would make no difference in such a case.

"Here are your clothes. One of my old jerkins—yours was too torn to fix. You may dress in the next room, but be swift. Breakfast is ready and these men are bottomless stomachs. Off with you now!"

Odiltark let her into the next room, which contained two beds. A breeze ballooned in the dandelion-yellow curtains. Candles burned on the low table along the same wall, sending scents of meadowsweet and lemon thyme swirling through the room. For aid in sleeping. Reisil approached Saljane, who nested on one bed in a circle of flannel sheets and soft wool. The bird blinked at her.

Red. Hungry. Red.

"I know. Me too. I'll get dressed and see what I can find."

Reisil dropped the quilt and tugged off the shirt, unable to smother two or three small moans when she pulled too hard against her stitches, or brushed too closely against her face. Saljane watched her, clicking her beak once or twice. Bending to lace up her boots was almost more than Reisil could manage. She quailed. How was she going to manage riding a horse?

She gave herself a mental shake.

"I will have to manage, won't I? I promised Ceriba's mother, and I've seen what those men have done to her. She'll need me when we find her, even if Koijots can track them without your help, which he'll have to do until you can fly. I'll ask Odiltark for some supplies. A couple of bottles of Elutark's sleep nectar would be nice. And a tincture for pain. We'll want some horsetail. The way that man kicked Ceriba, I can't imagine she doesn't have broken ribs. And we'll ask Odiltark for some catmint, if he's got some fresh. That'll help Kebonsat and whoever else jumped in the river, if they do end up with chest colds."

Reisil caught herself.

"I'm sounding like a tark, aren't I? First we have to find her, and before that, I'd better get you something to eat and something to ease your pain."

She ran her fingers over Saljane's sleek, feathered head. The bird nipped lightly at her fingers.

Red. Hunger. Remorse.

"And I'm sorry I refused you when you came for me. If I hadn't, maybe you wouldn't have fought me in the water."

~We are learning, ahalad-kaaslane, Reisil said to Saljane, forming the words carefully in her mind. *~I shall not fail you again, and you shall learn you can trust me.*

Reisil gave Saljane's head another stroke and then returned to the main room of Odiltark's home. Sodur had brought with him a salmon for Saljane, which he'd fished out of the Sadelema that morning. Reisil smiled thanks and carved it into strips on a trencher and carried to Saljane, who gulped the pink flesh ravenously. Using a wooden straw with one end fashioned into a bowl, Reisil gave her *ahalad-kaaslane* a dose of Odiltark's pain reliever.

"That should hold you for a while."

Reisil then tucked into her own breakfast, having also taken a dose of the pain-relieving tincture.

"Glevs, Juhrnus, and Upsakes are purchasing horses, picking up supplies, and nosing around to find out what they can about Ceriba's captors," Sodur explained.

"And Koijots is scouting their trail. We should be able to leave within the hour—if you are able?"

Reisil nodded affirmative to Kebonsat's question, trying to appear confident. She had seen Ceriba's captors taking her to the Dume Griste mountains. To catch up, they would need to ride hard. She hoped she would indeed be able.

"How is Upsakes this morning?" she asked delicately, spooning chokecherry preserves on a flaky, hot biscuit.

"Back to his old self," came Sodur's dry reply.

Reisil glanced at him sharply, but said nothing more. Back to his old self. The one who disliked her so much? Who resented how she'd become *ahalad-kaaslane*? The way she'd thrust herself into the middle of things, without "proper" training? Not to mention giving aid to a wizard, or whatever Koijots was.

Or was it something more? She caught her breath as another possibility struck her. Did he hate her for ruining the perfection of the kidnapping plot? She thought about his weirmart cuddled around her neck in the wagon, keeping her warm. Had that been at Upsakes's behest? A way to spy on her? Or a friendly gesture?

Reisil sighed, shoving her plate away and resolving to keep out of Upsakes's way as much as possible.

"Right, then. Well, I'd better have a look at your bandages. Come along now."

Odiltark herded her into the back room, sitting her down on one bed.

"Elu has gone to see about a boy with a fever. She wanted to be here to see you off, but she's better with children than I am. Boy's been beaten. I'm sure of that. Idiocy. Spare the rod, spoil the child. Now his body's too weak to fight off the fever. I'd like to bring him back here, but the parents are stubborn. So Elu's going to stay there, if I know her at all.

"Ah, these are looking very nice. Let's just smear a little of this ointment on there, gently now." His touch was deft but light. "You'll need to clean these cuts once a day and change the bandages for clean ones. Now don't give me that look. I know you're a tark, but tarks are infamous for neglecting themselves while looking after everyone else. Put yourself first for a few days. I've told those two behemoths out there the same thing. Slather on more of this ointment with every change of bandages until you run out. Should last about five days. By then things will be well on their way to healing. You'll scar, no getting around that. The ointment will do a lot for that, though, if you use it, and keep the wounds clean."

Odiltark gave Reisil all the supplies she asked for, waving off her gratitude.

"When you're out tramping around, think of me when you run across something special. Seeds, flowers, leaves—what doesn't grow in these parts. Bring it by when you're through again."

"I shall miss this place," Reisil said, stopping in the doorway to glance around. "It's a cozy cottage. It reminds me of . . . my old one," she said. Not home, as she almost had said. That place wasn't home anymore. Kallas wasn't home anymore. The ache of grief swept through her.

She lifted her chin. No more self-pity. Every moment that passed, Kaval and his cohorts took Ceriba farther away. Pity *her*. Save *her*.

"One last thing," Odiltark said. "Elu wanted you to have this. She said you'd misplaced yours." He held up

Elu's silver tree-and-circle tark's brooch. Light flickered over the branches of the tree and lit the candle flame in its heart. Reisil's lips fell open and she stared. Odiltark chuckled, taking her hand and placing the brooch on her palm and closing her fingers about it. "Now don't go ruining the gift with protests. Elu wants you to have it and *I'll* not be the one to gainsay her. I know better. Off with you now, and take care of those wounds."

The edges of the brooch dug into Reisil's tightly fisted palm and she felt a silly grin spread across her face.

Kebonsat and Sodur waited outside, having been joined by Upsakes, Juhrnus and Glevs with a string of sturdy mountain horses. None were more than fifteen hands high, with steep croups and narrow chests. Hers was a dun gelding with a dark stripe from his black mane to his black tail. He nuzzled her arm softly, whiffling her pockets hopefully. She patted him, rubbing his forehead and ears. He snorted, stretching out his head and closing his eyes in delight.

Her packs were already tied behind the cantle. A basket containing a nest of sheepskin and carded wool for Saljane had been fixed to the hornless pommel. Kebonsat gave Reisil a leg up. She bit back on a yelp when she swung her right leg over. He helped her find her stirrups, frowning at her.

"Are you going to manage?"

"I'm not going to be left behind," she replied in a harsh tone.

He flashed her a sharp look that she could not answer, not in front of everyone else. Soon she'd have to find a way to tell Kebonsat what she'd last seen while Saljane was watching Ceriba.

Odiltark lifted Saljane up to her and she settled the groggy bird into the nest with gentle fingers.

~*Comfortable? Things will get a bit bumpy. The wool should help cushion you from the worst of it.*

~*It will do.*

Reisil blinked, startled. She hadn't expected an answer and felt warmed by it. She'd seen the loving connection between Lume and Sodur, had seen how their eyes met in understanding, how Sodur reached out to the lynx as a chosen friend. Had she and Saljane finally begun down such a path? She thought of the long years yawning ahead of her. She feared loneliness, feared the rootless wandering being *ahalad-kaaslane* entailed. But Saljane would be a constant companion, a friend to share joys and sorrows, fears and discoveries.

Buoyed by the thought, Reisil straightened in the saddle and pinned the brooch on her collar, uncowed by Upsakes's glowering looks or Juhrnus's expression of disgust. *We will fledge together.* And she was still a tark.

She said good-bye to Odiltark, thanking him effusively.

"And tell Elutark I will see her again. Soon as I am able. Nor will I forget to bring you something from my travels."

"Bright journey to you. And we will see you when we see you. Sooner rather than later, I hope."

Chapter 9

Odiltark's cottage nestled on a hillside north of Priede. Ceriba's trail went south along the river before turning deeper into Patverseme. Between lay the sprawling trading town. It had long ago been a frontier fort in Patverseme's expansion northward. Now its gates hung open, intermittently guarded by a mix of militiamen in ragged uniforms and guardsmen too decrepit for any other work.

The group of rescuers passed through the gates with Kebonsat in the lead. Nothing the knights wore revealed their identities. All marks of heraldry had been left behind or packed away. In tall boots, leather breeches, heavy cotton shirts, oilskin cloaks, and plain scabbards, they looked like any other blank shields.

The streets threaded through a mazelike warren of disreputable shops and apartments boasting furtive doors and sly shutters. Sewage ran in trickles down the sides, dammed here and there in stinking lakes and putrid puddles. Reisil found herself gagging on the stench and pressed her hand over her mouth and nose. Saljane mantled, her head swiveling back and forth. A high, aching sound came from deep in her chest. Reisil laid a reassuring hand along her *ahalad-kaaslane*'s back.

The small group proceeded in silence through the warehousing district, an industrial area where the cartwrights, carpenters and smiths plied their trades, on down along the docks where they'd landed the night before and out through an unmanned postern gate, though the gate itself had gone missing. Reisil scanned the river for Voli's flat-bottomed boat, but he'd already unloaded his cargo and found another. She stroked her fingers over Saljane's smooth head. Likely she wouldn't see Voli again.

A strange, bittersweet smile curved her lips. Her new life was a trade-off. If she hadn't become *ahalad-kaaslane*, she might never have met him, and she was glad she had. But her life would also bring too many good-byes.

She glanced down at Saljane, who returned her regard, white brow appearing arched as if asking a question.

~How fare you? Reisil queried.

There was a feeling of disgruntled frustration.

~You'll not fly for a week or more, and then not far. You were brave. Did I tell you so? I am proud of you.

Reisil found herself grinning at Saljane's radiating pleasure, that her *ahalad-kaaslane* recognized her courage, that Reisel took pride in her. She nipped Reisil's fingers affectionately.

Beyond Priede was a chessboard of farm and forestland, filled with the soothing twitter of birds and crickets. Reisil found herself relaxing, despite the knotty gait of her mountain horse. She breathed deeply of the mist-dampened air, redolent with mustard and nettle and pine.

Koijots met them half a league along, stepping out of the bushes. He leaped with liquid grace onto the spare chestnut Glevs had been leading. He reported to Kebonsat in a low voice. Upsakes urged his mount forward, his face a study of concentration, but Kebonsat did nothing to include him. Koijots soon concluded and nudged his mount forward, Kebonsat falling into frowning silence.

Koijots had tracked the kidnappers' trail from the river, and by early afternoon they arrived at the place where the captors had cached their horses. The cropped grass, horse droppings and firepit indicated they had waited for several days. The kidnapping had been planned well in advance.

Sodur helped Reisil down, steadying her. She could hardly stand. Her wounds burned and her legs wobbled. She forced herself to walk off her stiffness, eating the soft cheese and nutty flatbread from Odiltark's oven standing up.

"The trail leads west, as expected," Kebonsat was telling Upsakes, who had his arms crossed over his barrel chest and his blocky chin thrust out.

"Your pet wizard tells you this, eh?" he sneered.

"Koijots is no wizard. He does not have any affiliation with the Guild. He is a tracker. " Kebonsat kept his voice carefully neutral, but Reisil saw the muscles of his jaws knot.

"Hmmph. Doesn't make what he did with that logjam anything else but wizardry. Can't trust 'em. Minions of Pahe Kurjus," he said, naming the Demonlord.

Reisil gasped and glanced furtively over her shoulder. Others did the same. To name the Dark Lord out loud was to call him forth from his netherworld of fire and night, torment and suffering. The wizards were said to worship him, that he was the source of their magic. Reisil thought of Mysane Kosk and believed it.

Kebonsat turned first white, then red. His fingers flicked toward his sword hilt. He flexed his hand, forcing his hand away with effort.

"Koijots is my sworn man," he said in an icy, flat voice. "If he serves the Dark One, then so do I."

Upsakes didn't look away from the unyielding challenge on Kebonsat's face, his jaw working as if he'd say more. Reisil tensed. At last the square-faced *ahalad-kaaslane* muttered something and looked away. Kebonsat gave a jerky nod and pivoted on his heel, striding over to check his saddle. Resil let go the breath she'd been holding. Glevs glowered at his friend's back, gripping his own sword with a white-knuckled hand. After a moment he pulled his hand away, then spat, nearly hitting Upsakes's foot. The *ahalad-kaaslane* glanced sharply at the Patversemese knight, then deliberately turned his back. Glevs took a step after him, but Koijots caught his arm and led him into the trees.

Reisil fed Saljane another dose of the sleeping nectar before mounting again. Kebonsat kept the pace slow, for her sake, she knew. But though his face remained expressionless, his bay gelding caught his mood and worked himself into a lather, jolting forward in eager leaps and bursting hops. Yet even with the slow pace, by evening Reisil had rubbed the inside of her knees raw on the saddle. The wounds on her face made it nearly impossible to chew her supper, and the wounds on her ribs allowed only shallow breaths.

The next morning her companions gave her all the rest they could, saddling the horses and packing the camp while she slept. She ate her cold sausage sandwich breakfast in a blurry haze, her body screaming protest at being back in the saddle.

~Are you hungry? she asked Saljane, inwardly scolding herself for not thinking of her needs sooner.

~I ate.

Reisil caught an image of Sodur with a skinned rabbit, slicing off strips for an eager Saljane.

~That was kind. It should have been me.

Reisil projected a feeling of apology and remorse.

~You are hurt. He is not.

~I am your ahalad-kaaslane.

~I hurt you.

Now Reisil felt Saljane's emotions rush over her in thick, black waves. A torrent of grief, guilt and self-doubt. Saljane was young, Reisil realized, trying to hold herself still in the buffeting torrent. Young and inexperienced, despite her raptor confidence and metallic resolve. She thought bitterly of those first moments together, those first wildly loving moments. If only she'd accepted Saljane then . . . She drew a breath and sighed. Water under the bridge. Regrets would not help now. Now she must look to the future. They *would* fledge together in many ways. They would teach each other and care for each other.

~We hurt each other. We didn't mean to. We won't again.

~We are ahalad-kaaslane.

Reisil heard the tentativeness in Saljane's mindvoice even as the bird affirmed their pairing. She winced. She knew she was at the root of this alien uncertainty. Saljane could not yet trust Reisil, could not believe she would not suddenly change her mind. Time. It would take time, and remembering to feed her when she was sick and hungry.

~*We are* ahalad-kaaslane, she repeated, resolving to stop regretting what was irretrievably lost.

Saljane burrowed down into the basket, tucking her head under her wing. Like a child, Reisil thought. Trusting in her parent to protect her in the dangerous, helpless night. She swallowed around the hard lump that rose in her throat. A gift indeed. She sent the Blessed Lady a quick and heartfelt prayer of gratitude.

The morning passed uneventfully, if slowly and painfully. The muscles of her legs knotted and twisted. The sores inside her knees broke and bled and dried, then cracked open again. Adding to her misery was Juhrnus, who had unaccountably come to ride beside or behind her as the trail permitted. He aided her dismount at the nooning, bringing her bread and cheese with yellow slices of sweet onion and tender watercress.

She leaned against the trunk of a paper-skinned white birch, eyeing him over her lunch, making no effort to disguise her suspicion. He sat stiffly, dropping heavily to a log. His sisalik hissed and gouged his claws into Juhrnus's wrist to steady himself. Reisil smiled as Juhrnus yelped and dropped his food onto the forest mat. But the loving expression on his face as he soothed his *ahalad-kaaslane* with a low croon astounded her.

Reisil polished off her lunch, then fumbled in her pack for a disinfectant salve and cheesecloth. She eyed the ointment and bandages Odiltark had given her. She could wait to change her bandages until the evening, she decided, suppressing the voice in her mind that told her to change them immediately.

"Where do you think you're going?" demanded Juhrnus, blocking her passage as she retreated into the privacy of the undergrowth.

"Is that your business?"

He crossed his arms smugly across his chest. "Upsakes assigned me to you. So you *are* my business, little sister."

"Assigned you to me?"

"Since you're so new to being *ahalad-kaaslane* and all. And he and Sodur have better things to do than shepherd you. So do I. Course, if you'd bonded with your goshawk when she first came to you . . ." His sneer made Reisil want to kick him.

"Well then, if you're going to insist on tagging along after me like a little puppy, come on. I have saddle sores and I mean to take care of them. In fact, I can use your help, if you've got the stomach."

He frowned and opened his mouth, but Reisil marched off as best she could on her sore, shaking legs. A watchdog. To keep her from making mistakes? Or to keep her from finding Ceriba?

She shook her head. Upsakes had made certain this rescue effort was well outfitted, and he'd reasoned the Dure Vadonis away from haring off after his daughter. Would a man who wanted to see an end to the treaty argue for the safety of the Dure Vadonis?

Reisil sighed. Upsakes was not at all likely to be a traitor. More likely, in fact pretty plainly, he just didn't like her. He knew she'd refused Saljane's first overtures, that she had not wanted to be *ahalad-kaaslane*. That alone would be enough to make him hate her. And then for her to help Koijots with that spell! No, if Upsakes didn't like her, it wasn't because she upset any plans to kidnap Ceriba and end the treaty between Kodu Riik and Patverseme.

She found a fallen tree and sat on it, setting her supplies beside her. Juhrnus halted a few feet away, watching her pull her trousers down. Reisil concentrated on the sores, determined not to let him bother her. She gasped as she bent and the wounds on her ribs pulsed fire.

Her trousers stuck to the sores and a whimper escaped her lips as she pulled the material free, her eyes watering.

"Those are pretty ugly. Like the ones on your face," Juhrnus commented unhelpfully. "You're going to scar bad, you know. Good thing you're *ahalad-kaaslane* after all. Now you won't be expected to get a man."

Reisil gave him a disbelieving look. What he said was probably true. Brutally true. His lack of tact—or was it malice?—should not have surprised her, not after years of it. But somehow it did. As *ahalad-kaaslane,* shouldn't he have been nobler? More mannerly? Not for the first time did Reisil wonder about Juhrnus's choosing as *ahalad-kaaslane.*

Then the moment struck her and she began to giggle, and then laugh. Soon tears rolled down her cheeks and she grasped her stomach, the laughter jerking her stitched wounds.

The rest of her companions came running and now the situation seemed even more ridiculous. There was Juhrnus, looking dumbstruck, like a smug cow struck by lightning on a clear blue day. And she with her trousers around her ankles, blood seeping down her legs from her saddle sores, laughing hysterically.

Sodur rushed forward, alarm in his dark eyes. Upsakes eyed her with cold disapproval, while Kebonsat and Glevs looked askance from her to Juhrnus and then to the blood on her legs. Finally she gained control, taking deep breaths. She felt good. Oh, indeed, sometimes laughter was the best medicine!

"My apologies," she said, hiccuping a little. "I have just been informed that my scars now make me so ugly I shall never attract a man again." She looked at Juhrnus, who had the grace to blush and stammer something about not really meaning it. "Lucky for me, I am not particularly interested in attracting a man." She thought of Kaval. "In fact, I'm completely and heartily not interested, so no need for anyone to feel sorry for me—if indeed you were inclined to do so." The look she cast at Juhrnus was meaningful. "Of course, it calls into question why you might be trailing about after me. Perhaps you like ugly women?" Now she looked at Upsakes. "Or is it something else entirely?"

Ho! That made him mad. He hadn't wanted her to know. She smiled again, a kind of joy running through her. This was almost fun.

"We had better dress these," Sodur said, kneeling beside her.

"That's what I had in mind. I've got some things here, though I would certainly appreciate help binding them. I seem to have lost my helper." Juhrnus had disappeared, and Reisil giggled.

"You have a wicked streak, you know that?" Sodur said as he took the cloth and salve from her and dabbed at her sores.

Kebonsat joined them, washing the blood from her lower legs with water from his flask. His face was tight with anger.

"He is an ass. You are a strong, capable, wise woman. It is those things that give your face beauty and character. Those scars will not mar your kind of beauty," he muttered.

Reisil blinked at him. "What a lovely, gallant thing to say. You are a knight indeed."

"I wouldn't have thought you would find much humor in Juhrnus's mockery," Sodur said.

"I rarely have before. But it seems so petty now. And really, he'd do more to remind me of the hurt I've caused Saljane." Reisil's voice turned serious, her mouth compressing. "I've done little to be proud of there."

Sodur finished with the leg he was working with and changed sides with Kebonsat. "You are doing fine. You and Saljane had a rocky beginning, but you're progressing well now. Don't think I haven't seen her affection for you. Animals are not like humans. They have no ability for human intrigue or machinations. What she feels, she feels. And she cares for you. She would not do so if she didn't sense your affection for her.

"Now, it would be best if you could rest these wounds until they closed, but I see you will not be left behind, so like any *ahalad-kaaslane,* you will ride through in pain and suffering. Stubborn and willful—you are indeed one of us."

•

A wide smile broke across Reisil's face, and her heart thumped.

"Though you will not have to endure the pain of that whelp's company," Kebonsat growled. "You can ride with me."

"Good idea, though you may ride that horse of yours off its legs before tomorrow. This journey of ours is proving a lengthier proposition than we hoped. It would be best if you could preserve the energies of your mount," Sodur advised as he helped Reisil to stand. "Otherwise he will fail you when you need him most." She fastened her trousers, waiting for Kebonsat's blistering reply. Instead, his words came almost apologetically.

"You are right. I must curb myself."

"It is no easy task, but necessary. You will better serve your sister."

"I know. But every time I think of her—"

"Concentrate on the next footstep, not the length of the road," Sodur said. "And you shall arrive at your destination in time."

"You sound so certain." Under the mocking tone, Reisil could hear the terrible need for reassurance, for the certainty that Ceriba *would* be rescued, alive and well. Sodur heard it too.

"If signs have any meaning, then we have the Lady's own blessing in the shape of Saljane and Reisiltark." Reisil started and Sodur opened his hands in a gesture of surrender. "We cannot overlook her gifts. You *are* a tark, as you are *ahalad-kaaslane*. And you have set us on the path of truth in the Lady's name. We cannot ask you to be less than you are."

Tears pricked Reisil's eyes and she gripped Sodur's hand in wordless gratitude.

Midafternoon and Kebonsat sat stiffly silent, his eyes darting and flickering, his body like marble. His horse no longer pranced and lunged, but walked stiff-legged, sweat streaking his haunches. Every snorting breath sounded like a drumbeat.

They followed Koijots, the trail easy enough even for Reisil to read. The kidnappers did not care about pursuit. Reisil recognized the camp where Ceriba and her captors had spent the night. She recognized the tree where Saljane had perched. She said nothing.

By now, heralds would have been sent to Vitne Ozols and Koduteel. Armies would be rousing like beehives stirred with hot sticks. Then they would surge into one another like red-eyed bulls. The ground would shake with the might of their clashing, the air would howl with voices of hate and vengeance. More bones, more blood, more orphans and widows, more crippled warriors.

But it might all be prevented if Ceriba could be found and returned, if the traitors could be discovered and eliminated. Which meant they could no longer dawdle along at the pace of a wounded woman and her bird.

Reisil spent the rest of the afternoon gathering her strength. It felt like a frayed and tattered cloak, made too thin and fine, inadequate for the weather in which she wore it. But it was all she had. Tomorrow she would belt it around her and stride out quickly and with purpose. She wouldn't be the reason they didn't reach Ceriba in time.

Night drew a curtain across the forest and forced them to halt. Sodur dressed Reisil's wounds and served her supper. Kebonsat took the first watch. Reisil rolled herself into her cloak, pretending to sleep. She could no longer put off telling Kebonsat what she'd seen.

Exhaustion weighted her and it was all she could do to fight off oblivion's sweet lure. She waited until she heard the deepened breathing of her companions. The sound came blessedly quickly, for they were tired as well. She rolled to her knees and saw the shining discs of Lume's eyes watching her from where he curled up against Sodur's back. Reisil nodded to him and clambered to her feet, edging out of the circle of slumbering bodies, going in search of Kebonsat.

He crouched along the path, head cocked. He lunged up at Reisil's approach.

"It is only me," she whispered.

"You should be asleep. You need your rest." Rest to make her faster, rest to hurry them closer to Ceriba.

"Yes. But I also need to speak with you."

Reisil looked over her shoulder, then edged farther away from the camp, drawing Kebonsat with her.

"What is it?" he asked almost gently, and she was grateful for the kindness.

"Remember when we got on the boat, when you asked me for news of your sister?"

His voice was puzzled. "Of course. The uneasy bond with you and your bird made you ill."

"I said that. I meant for you to believe it. But it wasn't true."

"Not true? What do you mean? What are you hiding?" he demanded.

Reisil licked her lips, retreating farther down the path. She did not want the others to know what she'd seen. She wanted to trust them, but she had been wrong about Kaval. She reached for Kebonsat's hand. It was rough and tense and it resisted her warmth. She let it go.

"I trust you, amongst us. And though I am *ahalad-kaaslane* and should feel confident of my fellow *ahalad-kaaslane*, I don't. I can't. Maybe I'm too new, too untrained. I don't know. And if I can't trust them, neither can I put any faith in your men. Do you understand?"

In the darkness she saw Kebonsat shake his head, shadow within the darkness.

"I will swear to both Glevs and Koijots," he said. "They are bound to my family. Glevs's father and grandfather served my family. They could not do this to Ceriba."

"Couldn't they?" Reisil asked. "Couldn't either one be so loyal to Patverseme that he'd kidnap your sister to prevent a treaty he thought would destroy his country? But that's of no matter. I will tell none of them now what I tell you. If you choose to share it, then you may. She is your sister, after all."

"What? What about her?"

And she told him of all she'd seen. Of Ceriba's rebellion. Of her punishment. The way the green-cloaked man had kicked her. Of the scar-faced man and the journeyman wheelwright from Kallas. Of Kaval.

Crickets chirped and a vole scuttled through the dried

pine needles layering the forest path. Kebonsat stood
still as one of the black-trunked trees. Reisil heard his
breath like a winter wind, tearing and rough.

"Bastards."

Cold as a stone dropped into a deep well. The word
was a curse, a promise, a declaration of war.

"I wanted to tell you sooner," Reisil said. "But there's
been no chance to speak with you alone. If I cannot
trust someone I—" Her voice broke. "If I cannot trust
my own judgment of Kaval, then I cannot say that any
of our companions is not a traitor. By refusing the
Lady's gift, I gave up the benefit of Her wisdom, of Her
guidance. I must rely upon my own, and it is faulty
indeed."

"Kaval was your lover."

Reisil could not see his face or read in his voice
whether his statement was an accusation. She flushed,
keeping her voice steady with effort. "Yes." Silence
thickened between them and Reisil didn't know what
else to do or say. In the darkness she could not tell if
his silence grew from fury, thoughtfulness or something
else. Finally she turned around and walked back to the
camp. He did not follow or call after her.

She woke with heavy eyes and a foul taste in her
mouth. Her hand was sticky with pine sap where she'd
slept in it. She fed Saljane from a rabbit Koijots brought
her, thanking the tracker gratefully. Sodur checked her
bandages. The wounds were healing well, no signs of
infection. Still it would not take much to tear them open
again. So be it.

~*How fare you?* she asked Saljane.

Sated. Irritable. Sore.

The goshawk tried to mantle but the wool of the basket foiled her wings.

~*You must rest or you won't get well.*

~*You do not rest.*

~*I don't want to fly.*

Saljane swiveled her head and gave Reisil a burning
look.

~*But I do want to go faster. It's going to be a long,
painful day. I would like to give you more of the sleep
nectar so that you may sleep through it.*

Saljane tipped her head, the white brow making her
look rakish.

~*I am strong.*

Reisil smiled.

~*I am not. If you were to sleep, I would feel better. To
know you were comfortable.*

She waited while Saljane considered, smiling in relief
at her *ahalad-kaaslane*'s reply.

~*I have eaten. I have pain. I will sleep.*

With that Saljane succumbed to Reisil's ministrations,
and even before Sodur had tied the basket to the pommel of Reisil's saddle, the goshawk was asleep. Reisil
took a draft of the pain reliever. It would not make her
sleepy. She mounted without aid, though she bit the inside of her cheeks raw.

She looked down the path. How far had they taken
Ceriba? How long before the war between Patverseme
and Kodu Riik flared again to life? Reisil squared her
shoulders. Today she would force Kebonsat to pick up
the pace, if she had to lead the way herself. And they
would ride into the night and break camp before dawn.
They would earn back the leagues that had grown between them and the kidnappers.

He did not look at her when she pulled up beside
him and then past, urging her mount into a jolting,
ground-eating jog. She gritted her teeth against the
pain, thanking the Blessed Lady that Saljane did not
have to bear it.

"What do you think you're doing?" Kebonsat cantered up beside her. Reisil nudged her dun gelding to
go faster.

"I can either ride or talk. Which do you prefer?"

He glared at her, his mouth half-open. Then it
snapped shut and he settled in beside her.

"You must not make yourself ill. It will serve no
good purpose."

Reisil waited until she could catch sufficient breath.

"In our hands we hold the fates of our two countries." *If it's not too late.* "We must regain Ceriba, and we must expose the traitors. For that I will die if I have to."

She kept her eyes firmly on the path ahead, not wanting to see his response, especially if it was amusement at her rather extravagant statement. But he said nothing more, maintaining her pace exactly, letting her decide what she could do.

Soon, however, Reisil's concentration turned inward. She was forced to trust Kebonsat to make sure that her dun gelding stuck to the path. It was all she could do to keep herself in the saddle, clutching a two-fisted grip on her pommel.

At the nooning stop, Sodur helped her down, but said nothing, merely checking her wounds. They had not broken open. Odiltark did very good work indeed. Reisil ate and drank standing, though her legs trembled and she could hardly hold her food. If she sat, she'd be too stiff to get on her horse again. She hardly noticed Sodur herd Upsakes and Juhrnus away from her, or Kebonsat and Koijots plant themselves around her as if she were a castle to be guarded. Then Kebonsat helped her mount and they were off again.

So engrossed was Reisil in handling her pain, in managing not to fall of her horse or slow their pace, that she did not notice when the attack came.

Suddenly it was as if she had woken up from a dreamless sleep into a waking nightmare. She heard screams, she heard cracking and whirring, she heard thunder and something like a rushing wind, though the air was calm. She saw nothing, not even her hands clenched around her reins, not even Saljane in her basket. Only blank darkness. Her throat closed and sweat sprang up all over her body.

The gelding lurched, flinging himself forward, and then they were galloping into blank darkness. She heard the air rushing in her ears, and screams, felt underbrush slapping her legs, crackling and crashing as they charged through the forest. She clutched at her saddle, yanking on the reins. But the gelding had the bit and terror spurred him on. Reisil seesawed back and forth on the reins furiously, the leather growing slick with sweat.

At last the gelding ground to a sudden halt, his haunches dropping, his forelegs thrusting out straight. Reisil was flung up against the pommel, which gouged into her stomach. Her breath left her in a coughing whoosh and for long moments she could not breathe. Pain raveled through her. She listed to the side, her breath coming in gasping whoops as her mount staggered for balance.

When at last she caught her breath, she heard only silence, but for the panting of her horse. He stood trembling, his skin twitching as though pricked all over by a swarm of stinging flies. His ribs swelled in and out between Reisil's legs. His head dangled to the ground.

Fear wrapped Reisil in a cloak of clammy shadow. She reached down with one hand and stroked the gelding's neck, taking comfort in his warmth.

"Easy, boy," she whispered. "Easy. We're going to be all right." His skin shuddered and his head shot up, banging into her forehead and nearly knocking her senseless. He jumped into a half rear, settling down as she continued to soothe him, clutching at the saddle for balance. When he stood still again, Reisil stroked her fingers over Saljane, her head pounding from the impact with the horse's bony head. The goshawk stirred beneath her touch, but did not wake. Relief ran over her like a warm shower. Saljane was still alive.

Reisil tried to see, but the darkness was complete and irrevocable, as if she stood in a cave of coal. Where was she? Where was the trail? Where were her companions? Why couldn't she see?

"Kebonsat?" Reisil called. "Sodur?"

There was no answer.

Chapter 10

Reisil sat thinking, her mouth dry. That she had some-how lost power of sight, she doubted. Aside from the throbbing where she and the horse had cracked heads, there was no pain. Nor would the dun be so frightened if he could see.

She held up her hand to her face. Nothing. The blanketing darkness was complete. Panic exploded inside her and she fought it. Minutes skipped by, Reisil too stricken to move. Then, slowly, her mind battled back the swamping fear and she came to a decision. Sitting here would do no good.

Slowly she swung down. She leaned into the gelding's shoulder, waiting for the pain and dizziness to pass. She felt gently over her forehead with her fingertips and found a lump on her temple. Already her right eye had begun to swell shut.

"Well, at least seeing isn't a priority right now," she muttered, startling the gelding, who let out a groaning neigh. When she felt confident of her equilibrium, she knelt down, keeping a firm grip on the reins. Rocks scraped and rolled beneath her fingers. Gone was the dense leafmeal carpeting that had marked the forest trail. She stood, keeping one hand on the dun and edging around him in a circle, reaching her other arm out to feel for trees or anything to tell her where she might be. Nothing. Only open air, chill, as if the sun had gone down. Or been blown out like a candle, she thought grimly.

With a certainty she could not justify, she knew that this was wizardry. But what exactly this wizardry might be, she did not know, nor how to counter it. Deep inside she shuddered, The dark filled her mouth and nose, clogging her throat. She struggled for breath.

"Lady," she gasped.

The air seemed to warm and Reisil thought she smelled a hint of green grass and honeysuckle. She breathed slowly, relaxing. But the darkness did not lift.

Reisil trembled. The power of the *ahalad-kaaslane* came directly from the Lady. They prayed for aid and she sent it. Reisil was *ahalad-kaaslane* now. Should not the Lady answer? Or was this a test? Were her companions even now free of this dreadful night, while she must demonstrate her faithfulness? Her worth? Or was it infinitely worse? Was the Lady helpless to respond?

She swallowed, waiting for an answer. None came. She straightened her shoulders. Test or not, she couldn't stand there forever.

"We'll have to go forward and hope we don't blunder into a hole or fall off a mountain," she said, needing the sound of her own voice in the unwavering darkness. "With any luck we'll find the others and get out of here."

The dun started at her voice and reared again before thrusting a trembling nose into Reisil's outstretched hands. She rubbed the hollows above his eyes and behind his ears. He leaned into her with a sigh that was more a gust of fear. A sudden smile flashed across Reisil's face. He seemed more like a child in need of comfort than a beast that outweighed her by ten times.

"It's going to be all right," she reassured him, trying to sound like she believed it herself. "I'll lead the way and you follow behind. Careful how you go. Feel each step before you put your weight down." The last was for herself, but it still felt better to hear the words out loud.

Reisil tied the reins to her belt, wanting both hands free. She stretched them out in front of her like a sleepwalker, reaching out her toe like a dancer to feel the way. The gelding hovered close behind, his nose against her ear. The sound of his breath and the musty warmth of it on her neck comforted Reisil. She reached back to pat his head now and then for reassurance.

She had no idea which direction to take—or which direction was which. She remembered the sounds of the screams as her flight began, but now only the crack and scrape of the gelding's hooves across stone broke the silence. Once she thought she heard shouts and tried to follow them, but they seemed to jump about—first ahead of her, then behind, then left. At last she stopped.

"This is getting us nowhere. Better to see if we can't walk a straight line out of this cursed night," she told the horse in as brisk a voice as she could manage. *You are what you pretend to be. Be not afraid.*

"The straight line is the problem, though. Without landmarks or the sun or the moon, how are we going to keep from going in circles?" She paused for a moment, thinking.

"We're on a slope of some sort. We could try following it up or across. Keep the downslope to the right. That would mean if we went around in a circle, we'd have to go around the mountains." Reisil was certain that the horse had made a mad dash out of the forest, or that the attack had come upon their arriving at the Dume Griste foothills. If only she had not been so dazed! But she could remember nothing.

"Going uphill might be better. It might be that the darkness is only so deep—like a lake. We'd better hope the footing stays solid. I don't like the thought of ending up in a rockslide. I wish Saljane could fly. She might be able to get above it. But no, she might run into a tree or mountainside on the way. And what if she couldn't get above it? How would she find us? How would she land?" Reisil shivered at the last.

Thinking about Saljane made Reisil pause. Concerned that Saljane would panic and try something foolish like flying, Reisil had not woken the bird. But now it occurred to her that Saljane was her *ahalad-kaaslane* and had a right to know of their trouble. Perhaps she might help. At least she could hear better than Reisil. The sleep nectar should be wearing off soon anyhow.

She felt her way along the gelding's neck and shoulder, then reached up to touch Saljane's warm body.

~*Saljane.* Ahalad-kaaslane. *I need you.*

The goshawk woke up slowly, groggily. Confusion, then full-fledged panic coursed through her like a mountain avalanche. Reisil could hardly bear the contact. Pain radiated down to the soles of her feet. She clutched the edges of the basket, trying to reach Saljane with comfort and reassurance.

~*Saljane! Please! I am here. Listen to me. Saljane!* Ahalad-kaaslane!

The last word seemed to reach the frantic bird.

~Ahalad-kaaslane!

~*Yes. I am here. You are not alone. You are not blind. At least, you can't see, but that's because there's no light. Some sort of wizardry, I think. An attack.*

Reisil kept her mental voice soothing and matter-of-fact. She laid her hand on Saljane's back and felt her *ahalad-kaaslane*'s heart racing, pulsing against her hand like a war drum. She sent her the calm she had managed to carve out of the last hours—how many? How long had they been stumbling around in the dark? She refused to consider it. Refused to consider what might have happened to her companions. When she and Saljane managed to get out of this blinding nothingness, then they'd look for them. Until then, they must not worry about what they couldn't help.

They. Reisil sent Saljane her relief and joy in her company. Someone she could talk to, and who could talk back.

Saljane sent back her own pleasure that she had Reisil to share her fears, that Reisil wanted and needed her.

~*I am learning how much.*

~*Carry me.*

Saljane began to struggle up in the basket and Reisil helped balance her bruised companion as she climbed up Reisil's outstretched arm and onto the thick padding of her shoulder. Sodur had sewn a patch of leather onto her cloak so that Saljane's talons would not shred it while she was bedridden in Odiltark's cottage. He had also provided her with a gauntlet of supple buckskin. It stretched from her right hand to her neck, with straps that ran under both arms and buckled over her chest. It was well padded on the shoulder, with thick oak strips forming a ladder-grip underneath a boiled-hide plate. The same strips also underlay the stiffened and reinforced hide along her forearm, giving Saljane a place to grip and balance without poking holes in her *ahalad-kaaslane*.

When Sodur had presented it to her the nooning after leaving Priede, Reisil had been speechless, turning it over in her hands, admiring the craftsmanship.

"Wherever did you get it?"

Sodur had given her a satisfied little grin.

"Odiltark directed me to a falconer who fashions these himself. They are quite unique. Most do not contain the wood—which is replaceable. See how the pockets are fastened? Makes for a better gauntlet, more comfortable for you both, especially since Saljane can really dig in. You could carry her at a full gallop, I should think."

"This is marvelous—how much did it cost?" she asked suddenly, thinking that in Kodu Riik, people provided gladly for the *ahalad-kaaslane* without charge. In Patverseme, however, the *ahalad-kaaslane* were more likely to be considered enemies.

"That is no concern of yours," Sodur said, patting her leg. "You could not continue with that makeshift bit on your arm, and I had the means to help you."

Now Reisil lifted her arm so that Saljane could step to her shoulder. Her talons dug in fiercely and for a moment the pressure on Reisil's shoulder was so intense she gasped. But Saljane relaxed her grip, bending her head to nudge Reisil's cheek with her beak.

"I thought we'd try to go up and across," Reisil said. Her voice sounded tinny and dull. For a moment terror threatened to smother her. She could not convince herself to keep her eyes closed and just pretend the light had not gone out of the world. She felt the darkness like bat wings brushing against her face. Reisil fought for breath, drawing a sobbing gasp of air into her paralyzed lungs, counting to five with every breath in and every breath out. She stroked the gelding's ears, feeling her fingers shake. She cleared her throat, once, twice.

"That might get us out of this mess in two directions. Unless you have another idea. Can you tell anything about where we are?" To her ears she sounded almost normal, confident, calm. Thank the Lady for small blessings. Reisil did not want her companions to be infected by her fear. *As if it were a cold that I could pass on to them by sneezing,* she mocked. But as a tark she'd learned fear could be catching, and right now Saljane and the gelding needed her strength. For if they could catch her fear, then perhaps the same was true for the opposite.

Saljane swiveled her head.

~I see nothing.

Her tone lacked inflection, but Reisil could feel the tension in her companion; she could still hear her heartbeat racing.

"Then let us go and see if we can find an end to this mess." She kept her voice determined. Elutark's admonishing voice rang in her head: *You are what you pretend to be.* Reisil lifted her chin. All right then. She was going to pretend to be strong, fearless and confident, and Blessed Lady willing, they would find their way out of this blinding night.

Reisil had to feel for each step with care. The ground grew rockier and more uneven. Brush and thistles grappled her legs, snagging on her leggings and leaving behind prickly burrs. She had no sense of time. She stopped and drank out of her water bottle, trying not to do more than sip. She didn't know how long she would need her supply to last. She wasn't hungry, but she forced herself to eat a hard journeycake from the bottom of her bag. Twice more she stopped to drink, then again finally to rest when she stumbled over a tangle of low-growing weeds and fell heavily onto her shoulder. Saljane screeched and leaped clear, but for a long moment Reisil could neither catch her breath nor move. More than one stitch had popped open and she felt blood seeping beneath her shirt.

~Ahalad-kaaslane?

The worry and verging panic in Saljane's mindvoice spurred Reisil and she rolled over gingerly, feeling the ground with her hand so that she did not sit on either Saljane or a prickly pear.

~*I am here, though a bit bruised up,* she told Saljane.

"I think it might be time to rest for a bit," she said out loud for the gelding's benefit. She had not lost her grip on the reins in her fall, but he had pulled to the end and no doubt stood splay-footed and white-eyed. She stood up and slipped his bit out, leaving his bridle over his head so he could graze. She returned to her seat on the ground, groaning when a rock bit into her backside. She felt around for the offending rock and tossed it aside, startling both Saljane and the gelding when it rattled loudly in the black stillness.

"Sorry. We'll rest here a bit and then keep going." She reached out and found Saljane by touch and drew the bird closer before lying down. She hoped the bleeding along her side would stop with just the pressure of lying on the wound. Reisil didn't think she'd sleep, but exhaustion subdued pain and soon she dropped into uneasy slumber.

She woke with a start, a jet of panic racing up her spine. Then she caught herself, remembering, and forced herself to relax and breathe. When she had convinced her hands to unclench and calmed her pounding heart, she sat up. Saljane made a protesting sound and spread her wings.

~*How do you feel?* Reisil asked her. Before the wizard night had fallen, they had been three days out of Priede. Odiltark had thought Saljane could make short flights in a week.

~*Stiff. Not as sore.*

Saljane's mindvoice held a distinct tone of determination.

~*Very good. But don't try to fly before you're ready. It could damage you so much that you might never be able to fly properly again.*

She put the warning as baldly as she knew how. Saljane wasn't given to human emotions, though she indeed could feel anger, pleasure and irritation, all of which Reisil had experienced with her. But Saljane had suffered several days of being grounded and Reisil knew how much her *ahalad-kaaslane* hated it. Not that she could do much right now anyway, Reisil thought. Not without being able to see. So something good was coming out of the wizard night.

Reisil got up and stretched, her legs and back aching from the brisk pace she'd set during the previous day—a whole day? two? more? less?—the headlong gallop, and then the steady climb up the slope. Her right eye would not open and she expected she looked as if she'd been in a tavern brawl.

Reisil breakfasted on another journeycake. It was like sawdust in her dry mouth, and she dared not drink more than a swallow of her meager water supply. Saljane, though hungry, was not yet ravenous. Reisil cupped her hands and gave the thirsty gelding a sip of water—not enough. They'd have to find a spring or creek soon. Saljane refused the pain tincture Reisil offered, wanting to be alert.

"I'm not having any either," Reisil told her. "Maybe when we're clear of this mess . . ."

Clear of this mess. And when would that be? Not until Ceriba was found, not until the war was averted. And it would be. This wizard's trick wasn't going to stop her, and it certainly wasn't going to stop Kebonsat.

Reisil completed her preparations and then felt gingerly under her shirt. She found her bandages stiff with dried blood.

"The bleeding has stopped." Reisil said aloud. "All right then. If we're all ready, I think we should get moving."

She lifted Saljane to her shoulder and gave the gelding a pat on the neck before beginning again the arduous process of feeling her way over the rocky slope.

The temperature dropped steadily, though Reisil found herself sweating as she inched her way along. She racked her shins against an outcropping of rock, yelping with pain. Her voice echoed back at her and she froze in place.

A breeze threaded ghostly fingers through her hair. It gusted hard, keening mournfully like an unbound wraith. There were no other sounds but for the breathing of the gelding and the scraping of his hoof on stone as he pawed at the ground.

In that moment, Reisil felt how alone, how lost they were. She had continued on, natural optimism telling her that they *must* come out of the wizard night eventually. But now, hearing the wind's bleak voice, she began to doubt. Hopelessness rose up in her throat and she opened her mouth in a wordless cry.

Before panic could take her, she felt Saljane in her mind, solid as the slope beneath her feet. There was the image she'd shown Reisil once before. She saw the Blessed Lady with her honey-colored hair bound around in leaves, vines and flowers, a silver leaf circlet around her brow. She whispered to Saljane, then flung her up into flight. For a moment as Reisil watched, the Lady seemed to look straight at her, the moss-green filling Her knowing eyes from corner to corner. She seemed to measure Reisil. One eyebrow flicked up as if in challenge. Then there came a smile. It invited Reisil to be daring, to be bold.

Reisil blinked and shook her head as she abruptly returned to the present, to the dense darkness. The warmth and glow of the Lady's glade still held her like an embrace and that smile taunted her fears. She straightened her shoulders.

"Best keep going," she said. "Standing here won't see us free of this wizard trick."

And so she began again and minutes slipped away, puddling into hours. Reisil kept going, slowly, cautiously, relentless, obstinate.

In that lifted brow had been a gentle rebuke, a reminder of who she was, what she'd become.

Ahalad-kaaslane. Reisiltark.

Elutark said they were blessings from both hands of the Lady. She would not turn her back again on those gifts.

You are what you pretend to be. Then so be it. I am tired and hungry and I am going to find a way out of this cursed darkness.

*   *   *

All at once the unending ocean of unnatural night ended and she stepped into blinding light.

Reisil stood still as the stone mountains facing her in the brilliant sunshine, her hair clinging damply to her forehead and neck. She blinked her unswollen eye. Tears rolled down her cheeks. Saljane gave a scream of triumph. The gelding neighed his own relief and shook himself from head to toe like a wet dog.

They stood on the shoulder of a bluff. A few yards away the edge dropped away into a steep-sided canyon. A sparkling blue river trimmed with green trees and red willows snaked along its bottom. Beyond, the Dume Griste mountains towered, snowy peaks wreathed around by wispy white clouds.

"Thank the Lady," Reisil whispered. A few steps more and she might have led them right over the precipice. She shuddered, her mouth dry as she looked down into the canyon. Brown specks moved across one of the meadows. Reisil drew a deep, steadying breath, curling her shaking fingers around her thumbs. Those brown specks were wapati—red mountain deer.

Reisil spun around, turning her back on the spectacular view and that sickening drop into yawning space. Behind her the curtain of night had vanished. The bluff rolled away in a long, brushy slope broken by brown and white outcroppings. The forest below looked like a shadowy ocean lapping up against a mountain shore. A gust of wind swept across the bluff, keening through the clumps of sage and thornapple. Reisil shivered as her sweat turned icy with the wind's breath.

"We can't stay up here. We have to find water. And then the others."

Reisil took a tentative step forward, half expecting the wizard night to close about them again.

But the sun continued to shine brilliantly. A determined smile curved her lips. "Well, then, let's see if we can find our way down to the river."

She didn't mount the gelding. His head drooped and his eyes looked dull. He twitched his tail listlessly at the deerflies that bit at his flanks and belly. Reisil brushed them away.

"It's going to be all right. We'll find you some water and good grass and you'll feel better." He lifted his head and nipped at Reisil's sleeve. She laughed and patted his withers. Her blood felt fizzy with being alive and free, with the joy of the sun's caress, with the sounds and smells that rushed back with the light. The clacking sounds of grasshoppers, the sough of the wind, the twittering of larks and sparrows twined together into a symphony, brilliant as the sunshine.

They ambled their way down the slope, the gelding pausing here and there to crop at a sparse bit of grass fringing a boulder. Reisil did not push him, knowing that the toll on his mind and spirits had been heavy, made worse by hunger and thirst. She wondered what had broken the spell, and hoped it had broken for the others as it had for her, if indeed they had been caught up in the spell.

Finding the entrance to the river canyon was more difficult than Reisil expected. It took a sharp twist and snaked away at a right angle from the bluff, forcing them to drop down into the valley and circle the steep mountain slopes.

Reisil feared that in turning south to search for the river, she was putting a greater distance between herself and her missing companions. But in all truth, she had no idea where she'd left them or how far away, and the need for water was a more pressing concern.

More than once exhaustion and growing weakness made her stumble over the hummocks of stone and weeds. Saljane was heavy on her shoulder and the sun hot on her head. She wished for her floppy straw hat, left behind in her cottage. Her cloak with its deep hood was too heavy to wear and she tied it behind her cantle. If this kept up much longer, she'd have to ask Saljane to perch on the saddle instead. But Reisil rebelled against the thought. Saljane was hers to care for. Putting her on the saddle smacked of surrender, of cowardice. She kept walking.

At last the mountains' smoky blue shadows lengthened, extending their cooling protection over the weary
trio. But those same shadows signaled the fast-
approaching dusk. Reisil increased their pace. Before
long the gelding's head came up and his ears pricked
forward. He whinnied, dragging against the reins. Reisil
jogged to keep up, chewing her lips against the streaking
pain in her neck and side. Saljane clutched deeper on
the padded wooden perch on Reisil's shoulder, raising
her wings for balance.

The gelding led them up a wash through a notch between the folds of the hills. They followed a game track
packed dry and hard, picking their way around the litter
of tumbled rocks and scrub. Reisil's legs and ankles
ached with the strain of the climb as they scrabbled up
a steep incline. They came to the top and entered a
narrow passage like a corridor through the crest of the
hill. Reisil could not fit beside the gelding and instead
led the way, hearing her saddle scraping the gray rock
walls. The passage ended abruptly after forty paces and
they stepped out onto a gentle slope that rolled down
to the river. The gelding let out an eager neigh and
tugged at the reins. Reisil hurried, unwilling to turn him
loose, fearing he'd wander off.

She set up her small camp in a grassy space bounded
by trees on three sides with the river on the fourth. After
the gelding had drunk his fill, she picketed him out in
the tall grass and set about catching her dinner. She
caught two trout, each the length of her forearm. These
she cleaned, stuffing them with watercress, wild onions
and mushrooms she found growing along the bank. She
packed them in a coating of mud and moss before setting
them in the coals of her crackling fire. She then returned
to her line, catching four more fish in quick order.

~Eat what you like, she told Saljane when she tossed
the first flopping trout to the bank. *Catching fish has
never been so easy. I could probably pull them out with
my hands.*

Like the gelding, Saljane set to eating with gusto. Reisil marveled at the clean, economical way the bird ate.

Finally Saljane was sated and Reisil told her to go to sleep in the basket.

Reisil washed herself in the frigid shallows of the river, her body blue with goose bumps. Her fingers touched the pendant hanging around her neck, low between her breasts. In all that had happened, she'd forgotten it. She ran her fingers over it, feeling its weight, wondering why Nurema had given it to her, and how it had stopped the wizard's attack the night of Ceriba's kidnapping. The amber eyes of the gryphon glowed in the dying sunlight like rich, dark honey. They seemed knowing, watchful. Reisil looked away, dropping the pendant and resuming her chilly bath.

She carefully pulled free the bandages on her side, yelping when they stuck. She washed her wounds, pleased to see that they were closing nicely despite her fall. She rubbed on some of Odiltark's ointment and rebound them.

By this time her supper was ready and she cracked open the mud cocoon on her first fish. She gobbled greedily, burning her fingers, lips and tongue. She ate both, then filleted the remaining fish and laid them over a rack of twigs she bound together with tough blades of the green grass. She raked out the coals into a little trench she dug beside the fire and set the rack carefully over them. She built up the fire again and then sat back, enjoying the crisp mountain night, her mind wandering over the past days like fingers over harpstrings, thinking ahead to finding her companions and resuming the search for Ceriba.

Saljane would soon be able to take short flights, which would aid their search greatly. Koijots was a good tracker, but with Saljane they could look much farther, faster. Not only that, she might be able to warn them of traps or ambushes.

Reisil's mind scudded on to Ceriba. How was she? What had they done to her?

Kaval's face rose up in her mind's eye and grief squeezed her heart. For a moment she could almost feel his urgent grip on her hips, his lips pressing against hers.

Tears rolled down her cheeks. She shivered. She wasn't naïve or stupid. She knew what men could do to a woman, especially if they planned to kill her anyway. Did Kaval even now grip Ceriba's waist with the same urgency he'd gripped Reisil's? Did he press his lips to Ceriba's, choking off her cries? Reisil bit back a sob.

She didn't want to think Kaval capable of such a thing. She didn't want to think she could have cared so for such a man. But still a knot turned tighter in her stomach and she remembered the bruises on Ceriba's beautiful face. *Oh, Lady, what has Kaval done?*

Reisil stumbled down the riverbank away from the camp as her sobs broke loose and tore open her throat. She sank down under a cottonwood, head on her knees, her tears coming in guttural, choking cries.

~What grieves you?

Reisil started and sat up, her chest heaving as she wiped away her tears. Saljane stood awkwardly on the ground, her talons curling into the black river soil.

~I'll be fine.

~You grieve, Saljane insisted.

Reisil said nothing and Saljane hopped forward, her amber eyes sparking red in the light of the setting sun. Reisil thought of the talisman around her neck.

~We are ahalad-kaaslane.

~I know.

~You think telling me of your grief will hurt me?

~Yes.

Saljane tilted her head, thinking, and Reisil marveled at how easy this silent speaking had become. As if she were born to it. The smile that touched her lips was bittersweet.

~We are ahalad-kaaslane, Saljane finally said in her mind. *We cannot hide from each other. Strength together, weak apart. The Lady wills it.*

Reisil hesitated, then nodded. Only by sharing themselves—bad or good—could they strengthen their bond. Keeping secrets would only weaken the goshawk's faith in Reisil. Saljane would know she was not trusted.

Reisil reached out her arm and Saljane climbed onto

its unprotected length, careful not to dig her talons into Reisil's flesh. Bracing her arm across her knees, Reisil brought Saljane up so that she could look into the goshawk's eyes, her throat knotting as she searched for the right words.

~It's complicated for me. I have chosen to follow the path the Lady has set for me, and I don't want to turn back. I don't. But I miss my home, and I miss being a tark. I dread seeing Kaval. I cared so much for him—I still do. What kind of person does that make me, knowing what he's done?

Reisil felt Saljane's steel touch in her mind. She forced herself to relax, to let her *ahalad-kaaslane* see her memories and feel her emotions. Would Saljane understand the knotted guilt, betrayal, joy and loss she felt?

Finally the bird withdrew.

~This does not hurt me. You grieve for what is past. But we are ahalad-kaaslane *now.*

~And Kaval?

~Sometimes the egg rots in the nest, though it looks the same as the others, was Saljane's terse reply.

In that Reisil understood that whatever confusion and grief she felt for what she'd lost, for how stupid she'd been, for how easy she'd been to deceive, Saljane understood and forgave—even though Reisil could not yet forgive herself. Her tears began again, this time healing tears. That someone *knew* and forgave—it lent her peace. And more.

The tie forged between them would be lifelong, and whatever she'd lost—or rather, whatever she had left behind—she had gained something greater. Without her bond with Saljane, Reisil would not be here searching for Ceriba. No one would. The kidnappers would have spirited her away without hardly a trace. Sodur was right. As a tark Reisil could make a difference to a few, to Kallas. But as an *ahalad-kaaslane* and a tark, she could prevent a war. Blessed Lady willing.

Reisil sniffed and wiped her eyes, touching the gryphon pendant through the material of her shirt. Its essence was the fierce life of the animal world, Saljane's indomitable will and strength, the heartbeat of the mountains and trees, the rivers and oceans. Blessed Amiya herself.

"Lady, lead me straight and true," she murmured. "I will follow whatever path you set for me with all my strength and heart. And I'll not let my feelings for Kaval stop me from what I must do." She looked at the bird.

~Let's get some sleep. We've had a difficult journey, and tomorrow we begin again.

Chapter 11

"Koijots is dead."

Reisil blinked at Glevs, unable to grasp the meaning of his blunt declaration. She glanced at Upsakes, who had sat down on a rock to tighten the laces of his boots. His weirmart crouched on her belly in the thin grass. Both men were streaked with dirt, their clothes torn, hands and faces crosshatched with scores from thorns and thistles. Upsakes had lost his horse, and Glevs's mare hopped awkwardly along on three legs, carrying her left forefoot off the ground.

"How?" Reisil asked finally.

She had encountered Upsakes and Glevs shortly before noon, having returned to the forest and trailed around its edge. After several hours she had ridden up onto a slope, hoping that Saljane might spy something from that advantage.

The two men emerged out of the trees into the brilliant mountain sunshine a league away. She yelled and waved, but they did not see her, and instead turned away and began picking their way north. She rode after them as fast as she dared, but the pain tincture she'd swallowed that morning was swiftly wearing off and she could not bear too much jostling. Nor did she want to risk the gelding losing his footing on the rocky slope.

She overtook them as the shadows lengthened to fill the rolling space between the foothills and the forest. Glevs called a greeting to her in a glad voice, then delivered his bad news.

"Koijots is dead."

"How?"

"Tumbled into a ravine," Upsakes answered. "Right when that foul darkness let up. Startled him, maybe. He'd wandered up to the edge of it—he was leading us along—and then the light came back and he went down. Lucky we didn't follow him in. Broke his back. Nothing we could do for him."

Upsakes spoke matter-of-factly, as if discussing what to eat for breakfast. The tone chilled Reisil. She'd have felt better with a hint of the hatred she knew he felt for wizards.

"We're without a tracker or horses. Ellini help us, for if she doesn't, I don't know how we'll find Ceriba now." Glevs sounded weary and bleak as he called upon the Patversemese deity of luck and war. Though he did not voice the words, Reisil knew what he was thinking: that they might not find Ceriba in time.

"We will find her without your wizard," Upsakes declared with a haughty wave of his hand. "We likely have a better chance without him. My guess is that his spell on the boat warned them, led them right to us. So to my mind, the bastard got what he deserved. You can bet good money I won't be stopped by tawdry wizard tricks. I am *ahalad-kaaslane* and it will take more than a bit of darkness to put *me* off the trail."

Upsakes had stood up and his face turned a mottled red, his lips twisting. He looked as he had on the boat when he'd attacked her, Reisil realized uneasily. And he was spoiling for a fight.

He got one in Glevs. The Patversemese knight moved more quickly than Reisil could have expected in his condition. In a blink he'd closed on Upsakes and slammed his fist into the other man's jaw, knocking him back. The crack of the blow echoed against the hills. Glevs drove his other fist into Upsakes's gut. The other man doubled over, then charged into the knight, driving his shoulder into his gut with the bellowing grunt of a bull.

Then they were rolling on the ground, pummeling each other as Upsakes's weirmart chirped her distress, racing back and forth in the grass.

Reisil could do nothing to stop them. Shouting did no good. She doubted they even heard her. The dun snorted and tossed his head, edging away from the scrabbling men, and she let him. She wasn't going to try to break them up. She wasn't going to get knocked about, tearing open her stitches for such schoolboy nonsense.

She examined the surroundings, debating whether to ride on and leave them to sort themselves out. Riding alone did not worry her, though she carried no weapons and wouldn't know how to use them if she did. She didn't fear attacks from bandits. She had more to fear from Upsakes, she thought. He didn't like her and was clearly capable of rabid violence. She pitied his poor weirmart, whose plaintive cries had grown more forlorn and desperate as the pounding brawl progressed. She gritted her teeth, annoyed. If she left them, she would only have to find them again later. Time was too much a factor.

So she stood at a distance, watching. After a while their movements grew ponderous, their blows inflicting less damage. Both were blood-soaked and bruised, with swollen lips, eyes and knuckles. Glevs had broken his nose. They drew apart, eyeing each other, then closed again with grunts and curses. All this Reisil cataloged through narrowed eyes, her mouth pinched tight, her nostrils flaring. She supposed Upsakes would be wanting a tark after this. Well, he could bloody well do without!

"Let them look after themselves," she said aloud.

"Seems they are doing just that."

Reisil gave a glad cry and twisted about. Kebonsat, Sodur and Juhrnus had come out of the forest, no doubt drawn by the noise of the fight.

"What's this all about?" Sodur asked, pulling his horse up beside her as he eyed the two combatants.

"Pissing contest," Reisil said.

"Ah. Just so."

"You are well?" Kebonsat asked, crossing his wrists over his pommel, his face ominous as he glanced from her black eye to the spectacle before them. "You have been with these rogues?"

Reisil shook her head. "I got separated." She reached

up and touched her eye. The swelling had gone down with a compress of cold river water and witch hazel. "This was just a bump in the night."

"You wandered about alone through that mess?" Juhrnus sounded surprised and a little bit impressed. Pride surged in Reisil.

"Not alone. I had Saljane and the horse." She patted the gelding's golden shoulder. "The company could have been worse."

"Indeed," Sodur said meaningfully.

Glevs at last noticed that their audience had grown. He disentangled himself from Upsakes and turned a glad face to Kebonsat.

"Bright heavens! I am pleased to see you." His nose angled strangely in the middle.

"So I see."

Glevs had the grace to look shamefaced as he wiped a trickle of blood from his cheek.

"What's this all about?" Flames tipped in blue ice burned in Kebonsat's eyes.

"Just settling an argument," Upsakes said, brushing dirt and grass off his clothing. Like Glevs, his knuckles and hands were bloody and bruised. His left eye was swollen shut while the other was merely a slit. He ignored his weirmart, who clung to his boot, whimpering piteously. "Nothing to trouble anyone else about."

"Then you won't mind if we get started after my sister?" Kebonsat said in a frigid voice. "Has anyone seen Koijots?"

Glevs explained what had happened. Kebonsat's knuckles whitened as he clenched his reins, but he gave no other outward sign of his reaction. But Reisil knew that the two had been close, that Kebonsat had depended on the other man's counsel and friendship. This was a hard blow, made worse by the fact that with every passing moment, Ceriba was slipping farther away.

"Lume will pick up their scent," Sodur reassured him. "Shouldn't be hard. They left a pretty clear trail through the forest. No reason to start hiding it here."

"I've lost my horse," Upsakes said.

"And mine isn't worth a damn. She can't put weight on that foreleg," Glevs added, sounding as though he were talking through wool, an effect of his broken nose.

"Koijot's horse?" Juhrnus asked. Reisil glanced at him in surprise. He was thinking.

"Ran off when we sprang the wizard trap," Upsakes answered. "Probably halfway to Priede by now."

"Then we'll have to switch off," Kebonsat said decisively. "Turn your mare loose, Glevs. She'll find her way back. Pair up and spread out. Give a shout if you find the trail. Reisiltark, ride with me."

He turned his mount in the direction of the river canyon and Reisil followed. Sodur and Juhrnus turned the opposite way, leaving Glevs and Upsakes to sort themselves out.

Kebonsat kicked his horse into an easy jog, scanning the ground as they went. He rode in silence for a while, then said, "I had hoped you were not alone in the darkness. Tell me what happened."

So Reisil related her story to him, pausing here and there to pat the gelding's shoulder or stroke Saljane, who had moved down to perch on the pommel of the saddle. When she was through, silence descended again, and Reisil was glad not to have to say more, concentrating instead on keeping her seat. Her wounds continued to ache.

"You are a remarkably brave woman," Kebonsat said suddenly. Reisil experienced a thrill of pleasure at his praise. There were expectations for the *ahalad-kaaslane*: that they would be resourceful, courageous, capable and wise—otherwise why would the Blessed Lady choose them? She felt none of those things. She could cook and mend a broken arm, she could counsel a mother through the grief of losing a child, but she was not rugged, she was not at home in the field or forest, under the stars in mountains or deserts. She was useless in a fight. Still, she *had* kept going in that dreadful darkness when she might have given up; she *had* found a campsite with food and water; she *had* retraced her trail back to her companions. All but Koijots. She shivered. She had nearly walked off the edge of the bluff. A few steps more— She shivered again.

Suddenly Kebonsat pulled up and dismounted, crouching on the ground, his fingers playing over the earth.

"Got you," he muttered.

He stood and took the hunting horn from his saddle and blew three notes to call the other four searchers back. The sound echoed down the valley. He said nothing as he put up the horn, staring up at the mountains as if demanding they draw aside and reveal his sister. His lips were pressed into a flat line.

"I'm sorry about Koijots," Reisil said into the silence ranging from him like ripples in a deep, dark pool. He glanced at her and she saw that the flames in his eyes continued to burn with that curious blending of white-hot flames and glacial-blue ice.

"He shouldn't have died. It's all wrong."

"It was an accident," Reisil said comfortingly. "I very nearly did the same thing."

Kebonsat made an angry chopping gesture in the air and turned to face her. She felt the intensity of his gaze like a blow and recoiled.

"You are not understanding me. He would not have walked over a cliff into a ravine because he would not have been blind in that darkness. He had wizard-sight."

"I don't understand. What is that—wizard-sight?"

"Wizards can see in the dark without any light at all. It's the basic hallmark of wizardry. Supposedly a gift of the Demonlord. Even the least talented magic-wielder can see in the dark."

"All of them?"

Kebonsat drew a breath and let it out. "It's the way the Guild sorts out people with power from those who don't. Every Sanctuary has a testing gate. It always leads into a lightless maze that ends somewhere in the inner sanctums. The mazes change constantly. Parents bring their children, vagrants come—" He broke off, grimacing. "Anyway, when he was a boy, Koijots was made to walk one of them. He used his sight to escape. So no, he would not have just fallen into a ravine in the dark. Something else happened."

Reisil stared at him, jumping quickly to the obvious conclusion.

"You're saying that Glevs or Upsakes—"

"Or both of them," he broke in, his voice bleak as an empty well.

"Killed Koijots."

"Handy, too, that Glevs's horse has come up lame, and the two belonging to Koijots and Upsakes have gone missing."

"Oh, my Lady," Reisil breathed. "But they must know you'll suspect them!"

"Maybe. Koijots was a cagey one. He might have pretended that he couldn't see. Maybe he even suspected them."

"He never said anything to you?"

Kebonsat shook his head. "But he was like you. He didn't trust any one of us but me, and I think you."

"Me?"

Kebonsat smiled at her surprise. "You found Ceriba with Saljane. Both you and your bird nearly died in the river. And you stood up to the others to do it. As I said, you are a remarkable woman and Koijots was no fool."

Reisil blushed, trying to think of something to say to turn his attention away from her embarrassment. "He didn't trust even Glevs? Even though you did? Hasn't he been with you awhile?"

"Yes. I have always trusted Glevs without question." Reisil read unfamiliar doubt and self-recrimination on his face. "His family has long supported House Vadonis. His grandfather died saving mine. I would have trusted him with my life. With Ceriba's life. It is lucky I have not yet had the opportunity to tell him the information you confided to me the other night."

"So what do we do now?"

"They'll try to delay us more. That fight was likely a way to throw off the scent of collaboration, as well as to slow your search for the rest of us. I don't like to think about what would have happened if you had stepped in to stop them—you wouldn't have stood much of a chance, even with Saljane's help."

Reisil stared at him, dry-mouthed and wide-eyed. Certainly Upsakes didn't like her. But Glevs had treated her with utmost thoughtfulness and courtesy. Would they really have tried to kill her? That Kebonsat believed it with granite certainty made her insides tremble.

She thought of Kaval. He had said he loved her, had defended her from the other children growing up. And yet look what he'd done to Ceriba. Why should she not believe that Upsakes and Glevs could be capable of murder? If Kebonsat spoke true, and she thought it likely, then they'd already killed once. It would have been nothing to add another body to their total.

She inhaled deeply, refusing to give in to the panic that swept through her. She'd been close to death three times now on this journey—in the river, on the bluff, and now with Glevs and Upsakes.

And there would be more.

This was what it meant to be *ahalad-kaaslane*. To confront evil in the Lady's name. Just as tarks healed in Her name.

"So what do we do?" Her voice was low but steady. Kebonsat looked at her and on his face she read approval tinged with relief. She realized suddenly that he needed her to be strong, that his world had been tilted and shaken up and he felt no more on solid ground than she did. Instead of frightening her, the realization calmed her. *You are what you pretend to be. Be calm. Be confident.*

"I'd like to get rid of them, but I don't see how—not without proof. And we still don't know about Sodur and Juhrnus. We must be very, very careful. Let's hope we can speed our journey without springing any more booby traps." And hope Ceriba would be alive when they got to her. He didn't say it, but it hung between them all the same.

"I can't believe Upsakes's weirmart would let him . . ."

Reisil paused, remembering the little creature's pitiful cries in the grass as the two men fought. And what could she do to stop him? She thought of the way Saljane could enter her mind, take it over at need like a steel trap snapping. But Reisil opened herself to Saljane, allowing it to happen, and she never lost control of her mind doing so. Maybe the Blessed Lady would intervene. In kidnapping Ceriba, Upsakes had renounced his duty to Her and to Kodu Riik. But maybe he didn't see it that way.

She remembered Nurema's caution. Kaval and Upsakes and Glevs—they might all think of themselves as patriots, saving their countries from evil. And if the job of the *ahalad-kaaslane* was to confront and defeat evil, was not Upsakes doing just that? At least in his own mind? He'd be obligated to, she remembered Leidiik telling her, if he believed the treaty was a horrible mistake for Kodu Riik.

And who was Reisil to say otherwise? He'd been *ahalad-kaaslane* far longer than she. He knew more, had seen more. Should she be helping him?

Reisil thought of Ceriba, the way her captor had kicked her, her sobs. No. The Blessed Lady could not countenance that. She would not have sent Saljane if She did not want Reisil to try to stop them.

Reisil met Kebonsat's gaze squarely.

"We'll have to watch our backs and get proof. In the meantime, we must not let them know of our suspicions. Can you do that?" he asked.

"What's the choice? I will do what I have to," Reisil replied, hearing something larger in her words. Would she do what she had to do? Even if it meant killing? Could she do such a thing?

Yes. Her stomach twisted and heaved and she fought it back. Yes, because she was *ahalad-kaaslane.* Yes, because she was a tark and if she did not, if she hesitated in a crucial moment, then Mysane Kosk might happen again. Many people would die on both sides. She could not let that happen, not if it was in her power to prevent it.

"Ho! We heard the horn. Have you found the trail?" Upsakes called as he and Glevs mounted the hillside. Their bruises had begun to worsen. Reisil didn't know how Upsakes could even see anymore, so swollen were

his eyes. Just then Sodur and Juhrnus cantered up from
the opposite direction.

"Trail goes straight into the mountains. Lucky that
storm was all wind and flash. Not enough rain to wash
away the tracks."

"Lucky," Juhrnus repeated.

Kebonsat shot him a look. "Very lucky."

"Let's see how far we can get then, shall we? Lume
should be able to keep us on the right track," Sodur
said in his desultory way, which Reisil found calming.
"We've got about three hours of light." He surveyed the
group. "We'll double up. Juhrnus, you ride behind
Reisiltark."

Reisil started and looked askance, Juhrnus no less so.
Sodur gave him a hard, warning look before turning to
the others.

"Upsakes, you're bigger than Glevs. Take Juhrnus's
horse. Glevs, up here behind me."

The changes were quickly made, though both Upsakes
and Glevs groaned pitifully as they struggled to mount.
Juhrnus said nothing as he hooked his toe into the stirrup Reisil freed for him and swung up behind her. His
chest was warm against her back, though she held herself stiffly apart. His sisalik rode on his shoulder, the thick,
fleshy black tongue thrusting slowly in and out as he
tasted the air.

They followed the tracks up into the mountains, and
promptly lost them. Lume kept the scent, however, and
they continued on in silence, the pace as fast as could
be managed with the overloaded horses. At dusk they
began a long, curving descent into the river canyon, far
above Reisil's campsite. Conversation turned quickly to
the wizard night.

"Had to be the spell on the boat. Warned them we
were following," Upsakes insisted. "Or that tracker did
it himself. Was one of the kidnappers."

Reisil tensed, waiting for Kebonsat's explosive response. But he didn't hear. He was prowling the edges
of the camp.

"I doubt that. If he wanted to delay us, he wouldn't

have broken the logjam. More likely it was some sort of magical trip line. Precautionary," Sodur said.

"Will they know we've triggered it?" Reisil wondered.

"It's hard to say. By getting Ceriba out of Kallas at night with the gates closed, they'll assume we spent our time searching the town thoroughly before turning our attention outside. As we would have, if Saljane hadn't found her trail," he said with a slight tip of his head toward Reisil. "With any luck, they'll believe themselves safely away. My guess is that the wizard night was just an added safeguard. With any luck, the wizard who set it won't want to be bothered with keeping track of it, especially since they shouldn't be expecting pursuit so quickly."

His logic seemed unimpeachable and the conversation turned to the trail ahead.

Soon after, Kebonsat set the watch, flicking a meaningful glance at Reisil. They could not afford to sleep through any of the others' watches. Covertly they would have to maintain an extra watch of their own. Seeing his look, Reisil dipped her chin toward Saljane.

During the ride she and her *ahalad-kaaslane* had had a silent discussion about Kebonsat's suspicions. Saljane had agreed that Upsakes might have participated in Ceriba's kidnapping, surprising Reisil with her calm acceptance of the possibility.

~You don't think it's unlikely that he might have done this? Reisil pressed. *He is, after all,* ahalad-kaaslane.

~He must do as he believes the Lady would wish. He must protect Kodu Riik and all Her people.

~But if She disagreed, wouldn't She stop him?

~The Lady does what is best. And we are here.

~But this will lead us to war again. This will kill many, many people in Kodu Riik and Patverseme both!

~Then we must stop him.

~How can he think this is right?

Even in her mind Reisil wailed the question like a child who had been betrayed. All her life the *ahalad-kaaslane* had represented justice and right in Kodu Riik. Their presence meant evil could not hide, and the weak and powerless would be safe. Saljane's answer, though correct, gave her no real satisfaction.

~He must believe or he would do otherwise.

Now, as the fire flickered and popped, Saljane blinked her shining amber eyes at Reisil.

~I will watch. I have rested much and will sleep tomorrow.

Exhaustion embraced Reisil and she fell into a heavy sleep, as Kebonsat rolled out his blankets near hers.

Juhrnus wakened her the next morning and she sat up groggily, her eyes dry and scratchy. He was curiously restrained, saying no more than a word or two to her. He saddled the dun gelding in the shadowy predawn and loaded up her saddle packs. Reisil quickly ate her breakfast of stale bread and cold fish, washing the dusty, dry crumbs down with cold river water.

~Did anything happen last night? she asked Saljane.

~They snored, the bird replied, with an image of Upsakes and Glevs. Reisil smiled around her food. They *would* snore, one with a broken nose and the other with all that swelling. She'd straightened Glevs's nose, but could do little else for it. Kebonsat and Sodur had frowned on her trying to ameliorate the swelling or pain. So long as the other two could function, they deserved the consequences of their nonsense. Was it the *ahalad-kaaslane* coming out in her that she heartily agreed? Reisil wondered. But it was more than that. Their pain might help make the two men off balance, distract them from any plots they might be hatching.

~And when they watched?

~Nothing. Stirred the fire. Walked in circles. No threat.

~What about Juhrnus and Sodur?

Those two had taken the last two watches, leaving Reisil to sleep through the night. She still had a great deal of healing to do, Sodur told her. And sleep was the best cure.

~Stirred the fire. Walked in circles.

The wounds on Reisil's ribs felt remarkably better this morning, and the gouges on her face had closed so well that she no longer felt the need to go bandaged, though she slathered her healing ointment over them liberally. Kebonsat and Sodur both smiled encouragingly at her, though both were taken aback by the livid scars spreading like winter-stripped willows over her cheek and jaw and down to disappear into her collar.

Juhrnus treated her no differently and somehow Reisil felt better for that. He didn't like her, true, but to him, she remained who she was, no need for pity. Kebonsat had said that the scars would not mar her kind of beauty, but that was before he'd seen them.

They set out again, following the trail that now ran parallel to the river, following the sinuous twists as the canyon gave way to a steep-sided gorge. The grasses made a whithying sound as they brushed through them, sending up tangy green scents of summer.

Saljane gave her *kek-kek-kek-kek* cry, raising her wings so that Reisil had to lean out of the way. She bumped Juhrnus's chest and he put his hands on her shoulders to steady her.

~Stop that!

~Feel good. Fly?

~Not yet. This evening, and only for a short while.

They had decided the wizard night had lasted two days, which meant Saljane should be healed enough to try flying. Saljane subsided and Reisil could feel her impatience, almost sulking, if a goshawk could be capable of such a human emotion. But Saljane remained quiescent the rest of the day. Reisil didn't look forward to the goshawk's flight. Just the thought of that dizzying height made Reisil's gorge rise. She swallowed and breathed deeply, trying to relax, doing her best to keep her reaction well hidden from her *ahalad-kaaslane*. She remembered that first day, asking if Saljane could read her thoughts. Maybe someday it would happen, but for now she was glad to be able to keep a few secrets.

They paused for only a few minutes at the noon hour to stretch and relieve themselves while giving the animals a chance to snatch a few mouthfuls of the lush grass. The way grew steeper shortly after, and Reisil's dun and Sodur's sorrel began to show signs of strain, slowing their pace even more. Kebonsat took Glevs on his horse and Upsakes took Juhrnus on his, increasing their speed for the moment. But Reisil knew it couldn't last. Something would have to be done.

"The Lady will provide," Sodur reassured her, bringing his horse up alongside.

"I hope so," Reisil said dubiously, looking at Upsakes. He had lost his laudanum when he lost his horse. As a result, his temper seemed to grow sharper and more erratic with every passing moment. She said nothing of the small vial she carried in her healer's pack.

"Do not be hard on him," Sodur said, following her gaze. "He may not appear so at the moment, but he has been one of the Blessed Lady's brightest stars." At Reisil's look of astonishment Sodur chuckled. "You have not seen him at his best. He was chosen quite young, long before my Lume found me. We were friends in Koduteel. Young ruffians, the lot of us, running about making mischief. Then one day Kasepu, his weirmart, appeared out of nowhere, crawled up his trouser leg, chittering away furiously at him. I think he'd been in the midst of playing a practical joke on his mother. He was only eleven years old. Youngest *ahalad-kaaslane* ever.

"Everyone seemed to think it was a sign of greatness to come. And he has done some remarkable things, especially in the war with Patverseme. He rescued an entire village by himself, and he's spied out many of the enemy's secrets." Sodur sighed. "But he failed at Mysane Kosk. There was misinformation. On his word, many troops and supplies were directed elsewhere and he sent refugees into Mysane Kosk." Sodur fell silent, the clopping of the horses' hooves measuring the minutes. After a while he roused himself and spoke again.

"So you understand him a bit. The massacre was a blow to all of Kodu Riik, but he took it worst of all. He's always been so sure of himself as *ahalad-kaaslane*. Everyone, including Upsakes and myself, has always believed the Lady chose him so young for a great purpose, a great destiny. Then Mysane Kosk happened. He's felt responsible for it. It drives him."

*Drives him to help kidnap Ceriba? To keep the war
going until he can get vengeance?* Reisil wondered.

"What's it like in Koduteel?" Reisil asked, changing
the subject. "Upsakes said I should have gone there
for training."

"There are very few *ahalad-kaaslane* with birds, and
even fewer with birds of prey. They—you—are a special
resource that the Iisand uses heavily, which is why you
will need to go there."

"What does he need us for that others can't do?"

"So many things, but the predator birds can fly higher
and farther than any other. And they need not have
the supervision that sillier songbirds need. They carry
messages, spy out enemies—they are also responsible for
the deaths of not a few wizards."

"How?"

"The birds stoop so quickly and from so far, the wizards don't realize they are under attack until too late. A
stooping hawk can break an unsuspecting man's neck,
or gouge through his eyes into his brainpan. I don't need
to tell you, a tark, how easy it could be to kill someone
that way. If the bird hits during the casting of a spell
when a wizard's shields are down, the blow need not be
fatal—the magic rebounds on the wielder. We've lost a
few birds that way, but have won battles also."

"And Saljane would be taught to do these things in
Koduteel?"

"Those and many more. Your training will include
everything from surviving in the wilds to courtly behav-
iors. The *ahalad-kaaslane* have free reign in Kodu Riik,
coming and going as we choose. We have no rankings,
though generally experience gains the respect it deserves. There are those who spend more time in the
court, acting as liaisons between the *ahalad-kaaslane* and
Iisand Samir. But any one of us can go anywhere at any
time, right into the Iisand's bath chamber if you like—
though he might have something to say about it. You
must remember that we serve Kodu Riik and her people.
Though we often accommodate the requests of the Iisand, we are not bound to him; the Lady's law is always higher."

"So why did Iisand Samir threaten Kallas?" Reisil demanded, surprising herself with how angry she was at the idea. Sodur shook his head, frowning.

"I do not know. I wanted to ask the herald—Upsakes and I know a good number of them. They travel Kodu Riik as we do, gathering information and bringing messages from Koduteel." He paused and his head shot up.

"What is it?"

He looked at Reisil, for a moment not seeing her. He paled and swallowed, his throat bobbing jerkily.

"Sodur, what's the matter?"

He started and blinked at her.

"What? Oh, nothing. Just something struck me . . ." He said nothing more, turning his head forward, his brow furrowed.

They rode well into the dusk, making their camp by firelight. With Lume's help, Sodur had brought down a doe earlier in the day and so they feasted on roasted venison.

Reisil allowed Saljane a short flight up the gorge as the evening approached.

~Don't hunt, she advised. *You may strain those muscles if you stoop. And no acrobatics, either.*

She felt Saljane's joy in being airborne, though she didn't have to suffer the view from above, Saljane not insisting that her *ahalad-kaaslane* link minds.

Sodur took the first watch and Kebonsat followed Reisil to the river, where she rinsed the pot in which she made tea from her precious supply.

"Will Saljane be able to scout ahead for us tomorrow?" he asked.

"I think so. She didn't feel much pain today, though it would be easy for her to overextend herself. She'll have to rest often—if I can convince her to do so."

"Good. We need horses—maybe we can find a croft or village."

The next morning Reisil tossed Saljane into the air before clambering aboard the gelding. Once again Juhrnus rode behind her and Glevs behind Sodur. The morning was cool, with a promise of heat for the afternoon.

A breeze twirled the loose tendrils of her hair and sped away across the grasses.

Before she could mount again after the noontime halt, Saljane grabbed her mind. Reisil clutched the saddle and gasped, closing her eyes against the confusion of their shared sight.

Saljane skimmed above the gorge, which wormed away into the sly hollows of the mountain's shoulders. In a crook of the river below was a stockaded village. Cultivated fields made geometric patterns in greens and golds along the river in both directions.

~Good girl, Reisil told Saljane, who radiated triumph back. *How do you feel? Can you keep going?*

~Rest, eat, fly again.

~Good, but don't overdo it. See if you can find any traces of Ceriba, if the trail keeps following the gorge.

Saljane let go and Reisil swallowed down her lunch, which had crept back up her throat as she swooped over the river gorge. Juhrnus steadied her as she straightened and released her grip on the dun gelding's mane.

"There's a village ahead," she announced to the others.

"Lady be praised," said Sodur. "We'll buy replacement horses for Upsakes and Glevs and fresh mounts for the rest of us."

"Any idea how far?" Kebonsat asked Reisil. She shook her head. "Let's go then, and see if we can get there before nightfall."

They came at last to a place where the river gorge narrowed into a bottleneck and they could go no farther following the river's path.

"The village must be beyond," Reisil said, looking up at the rocky cliffs through which the river boiled in white, frothy fury.

"Here! There's a path," Sodur called. Glevs rode behind Kebonsat again. Sodur and Lume had picked their way along the brushy base of the cliffs and now waved them over.

Red sand lined the zigzagging path upward. Manmade, Reisil thought.

They mounted the trail, leading their horses up the

steep incline. Reisil was panting as she reached the top. She paused in the fading sunlight to gaze into the valley below.

The path flung itself up over the cliffs in savage, steep jumps, and then dropped down more gradually, following a gentle curve into a long valley. Horses, goats and cattle grazed below, guarded by herders and dogs. The village lay another half league beyond the point where the path melded with the valley floor. A swampy low patch spread out from the river in between, dividing the pasturelands from the village. Cattails, butterbur and comfrey rooted in the marshy ground, and swarms of mosquitoes hummed above.

"Do you think it wise for all of us to approach at this hour?" asked Glevs as they reached flat ground. "I'm looking a bit disreputable, as is my friend here," he said, jerking his thumb at Upsakes.

Kebonsat glanced over his shoulder. "You're right. I will go and make the purchase."

"Not alone," Upsakes protested. "Take Sodur with you. While you're trading, he can find out about your sister—how long since they passed through and where they said they were going."

Kebonsat nodded, eyes narrowed, unable to fight the logic, though Reisil could see the suspicion dancing in his eyes. Glevs swung to the ground.

"We'll set up camp by the river."

Kebonsat and Sodur departed into the golden dusk leading the other two horses. Juhrnus and Glevs fetched wood while Reisil dug in her pack for fishing line. She sat on a tussock of grass over a six-foot drop where the water had gnawed away the underside of the bank, untangling her line and slapping at mosquitoes.

She heard Upsakes digging a firepit behind her. After a few moments, his footsteps crunched on the gravel behind her. He stopped, watching over her left shoulder. Her skin prickled. Reisil kept working at the tangle, tugging too sharply and reknotting what she'd just worked free. Upsakes made a disapproving sound and bent to pick up a smooth river rock for lining the fire pit. His breath steamed hot against her neck as he stooped. He straightened, laying his free hand on her shoulder and squeezing gently, like a lover.

"You've no idea how long I've been wanting to do this," he said in a swollen, gloating voice.

Then pain exploded behind Reisil's ear and she collapsed unconscious to the ground.

Chapter 12

Reisil's head throbbed and her mouth tasted of grit. She lay twisted on the ground. Groaning, she turned to lie flat—or as flat as she could with her bound hands gouging into her back. She flexed her fingers and found she could hardly feel them, so tight were the bindings. Nor could she feel her feet.

"She's awake." Glevs squatted beside her, roughly shoving her onto her stomach to check her bindings. He ran his fingers over her swollen flesh and yanked to see if they were loose. Reisil whimpered at the pain. "Good job. She'll not get those undone soon."

"Not soon enough, anyway," Upsakes said, his voice juicy with satisfaction.

"You don't like her much, do you?" Glevs stood and walked away, leaving Reisil facedown.

"She's poison. She refused the Blessed Lady's gift, and now she's corrupted the bond. Her assistance to that wizard is clear proof."

"How's that different from you? We've got wizards on our side," Glevs pointed out.

"Necessary evil, and I know the difference. She doesn't. I accept my *ahalad-kaaslane* and she doesn't. I am acting as the Lady wishes, and in hindering me, she does not."

"If you say so. What about the whelp?"

"No telling where he stands and no time to find out. They're getting too close to ruining the plan. Besides, he's *ahalad-kaaslane*. If he is truly faithful to the Lady, then he will be grateful to aid in our success in any way he can."

Upsakes planned to kill her and Juhrnus too. She knew it as if he'd danced through the clearing shouting it.

A creeping stiffness invaded Reisil and she began to tremble like a bowstring pulled too taut. A moan in the shadows beside her made her realize that Juhrnus lay inches away, his head at her feet.

"Aid?" Glevs laughed, a brassy, booming sound. "I don't know that he'd call getting dead aid, but why not? It will certainly keep him out of trouble." He laughed again, a greasy, sinister sound. "I'll miss you, you varlet, when this is all over and we go back to trying to kill one another."

"As you say, but we're not through yet. Once we take care of our present company, we'll have to fan the flames. Let the others finish the Vadonis girl, then take the body to Vitne Ozols. If her father hasn't committed to a new war by then, that should do it. He's got enough influence in court to convince your Karalis to revoke the treaty. With the wretched evidence of his daughter's ill-used body, he won't think twice."

"You play dirty," Glevs said in an admiring voice. "I wouldn't have thought any *ahalad-kaaslane* would treat with the Wizard Guild, or kill your own."

"Couldn't have managed it without the Guild, nor they without me," Upsakes replied smugly. "As for Sodur and Juhrnus, I put the blame on that bastard-get, Reisil. If she'd taken the Blessed Lady's gift when it first came to her, then I'd have sent her with Sodur and the other newly chosen to Koduteel, where they'd have been well out of danger. As it is, we're only here because of her. I ought to be in Kallas right now, planning our war strategy. But you must take some credit as well. It cannot have been easy to let us have the daughter of your employer, and now to kill his son. You grew up together, no? And your family has long served House Vadonis."

"As you say, I regret the steps I've had to take. But this treaty cannot be allowed." Glevs sounded unrepentant. Reisil growled in her throat, remembering Kebon-sat's adamant defense of his boyhood companion.

"Hsst! They're coming back. Kasepu says they are crossing the wetlands now," Upsakes declared.

"Then let's get these out of the way."

Glevs and Upsakes bent over the two captives. Reisil choked on the handful of dirt Upsakes shoved in her mouth before he tied on a gag. Fear and fury vied for dominance as he pinched her cheek, his lips shining with saliva. He grinned, the tip of his tongue running along the edges of his teeth.

"There you go, girly. Not a good time to make noise now." He stood up, rolling her over to the steep edge of the bank with his feet. "Call your bird, girly. See what good it does you. She'll not come in time. Maybe if you'd done like I told you, you wouldn't be in this mess." Then he shoved her hard and she pitched down the bank, plunging down into soft mud and shallow, sucking water.

Reisil wrenched away from the water's frigid tongue and banged up against Juhrnus, who had fallen between her and the bank. He wriggled away, his body making wet, slurping sounds as he inched along. He was making a moaning, keening sound behind his gag, a sound of unrelenting grief. Reisil followed, her nostrils flaring as she struggled for air, her tongue straining to push out the dirt and gag that choked her.

~*Saljane!* she called.

~*I am here.*

~*Come back! Come back to me now.* Reisil's head and side throbbed and she couldn't feel her hands. Her mind felt shattered and unfocused, so much so that she could hardly maintain the contact.

~*What has happened?*

Worry. Fear. Fury.

~*Come back. Hurry.*

The connection broke, snapped by a wash of pain and fear. Reisil lay supine in the water. It was futile to call Saljane. Upsakes knew the goshawk was not a night bird. Hot tears seeped from Reisil's eyes. What had she done?

There was nothing Saljane could do, even if she didn't get lost or run into a mountainside.

Reisil clenched her jaw, feeling dirt and grit grinding between her teeth. She wasn't going to die easily, whatever Upsakes planned. She squirmed furiously, forcing herself up out of the water. She and Juhrnus lay together on a narrow edge above the eddying river shallows. Downstream they could hear the thundering bellow where the gorge narrowed and the river plunged madly through the notch in the rock.

She struggled against her bonds until pain forced her to rest. The dirt on her tongue was turning to mud and she swallowed some, then set up coughing behind her gag. She wanted to scream; she wanted to pound her hands and feet in the fury of frustration. But when the spell of coughing subsided, it was all she could do to catch her breath, and so she lay there pliantly against Juhrnus, the pain and fear swelling like a tide within her. Her heart pounded like galloping hooves over cobblestones. Reisil breathed deeply, closing her eyes against the moon-dappled darkness and forcing her body to quietness so that she could listen.

For a long while she heard nothing but the lapping of the river and Juhrnus's faint keening. She dared not think about the cause of that grief.

Then faintly she heard the jangle of bridles and hoof sounds, then voices, questioning. A deep one—Sodur. And a lighter baritone—Kebonsat. Then Glevs with his voice like a sweet horn, and Upsakes's rough bray.

Reisil tensed. She could make no noise that her friends could hear, though she would be ready if Sodur or Kebonsat should come close enough for her feeble grunts to signal warning.

Kebonsat's voice grew louder and now she heard the sudden, sliding chime of a drawn sword. Glevs, placating, then a roar like a bull and the battle was met.

Reisil lay still as stone, her head raised as she sought to sort sound from sound. Metal clanged amongst threats and shouts, guttural words of hate and loathing and a silence—Sodur who said nothing.

She was so intent on the struggle above that when something touched her cheek in the darkness Reisil jerked and wrenched away, her throat filling with a scream that had no place to vent. Then the touch came again, a soft twitching nose, a stroking paw. Upsakes's weirmart—Kasepu!

The little animal scuttled over Reisil and down her back to gnaw at the bindings on her arms. One by one they gave way.

At last the creature wriggled off to chew at Juhrnus's bonds while Reisil rubbed ungainly, swollen fingers over her forearms, deeply indented from wrist to elbow by the tight leather. Fire ran in rivulets over her skin to her fingertips.

She realized then that she could remove her gag and she hooked at it with clawed fingers. Three times she grappled at the muddy cloth until her fingers hooked beneath it. She twisted it off, her fingers dumb and clumsy. She spat the mud from her mouth and wiped her lips on her sleeve.

Juhrnus sat up beside her and she let out a yelp of surprise. Then she reached over and tugged the gag from his head. He too spat and for a moment his keening stopped, then began again as he rubbed at his arms.

Above, the sounds of battle grew louder. There were shouts and a sudden crescendo of clanging swords, over and over again as the fighters pounded against one another.

Then silence.

Reisil didn't wait. She yanked the bindings from her ankles and struggled up the embankment, sliding back down on the slippery mud and weeds, tearing her fingernails as she grappled at roots and branches.

Her breath rasped in her throat, her ribs aching from her stitches and Upsakes's kick, making it difficult to get a lungful of air. Still she scrabbled upward, determined to stop Glevs and Upsakes, afraid of what she'd find. On her stomach she squirmed over the edge of the bank, face, arms and body slick with mud, her mouth a red snarl of animal rage.

Kebonsat braced his foot against Glevs's chest and twisted his sword free. Sodur knelt on the ground beside Upsakes, tying his hands and feet. The clearing had been churned into mud as if a herd of cattle had stampeded through.

Reisil clambered to her feet, unseen by the two men. She staggered a few steps into the clearing, stopping when her foot bumped into something. She looked down.

"Reisiltark!"

Kebonsat spun around at Sodur's shout and leaped across the clearing, catching her by the shoulders.

"Are you all right? Where's Juhrnus?"

"I am well enough. He's down there." She pointed back to the bank without taking her eyes off the small body on the ground. She pulled herself from Kebonsat's grasp and knelt beside Juhrnus's sisalik. The lizard lay like a sodden rag, his slitted eyes open and staring. She stroked her fingers down his yellow-and-green-striped length.

"Is he—?"

"Dead? No. But close. Very close." Reisil answered Sodur absently, her mind seeking down another path, seeking after an elusive memory, almost instinct.

Her fingers kept stroking.

She felt a faint tremor beneath her fingertips as the little beast drew breath. Then Juhrnus was there, his hands flat on the ground beside his *ahalad-kaaslane,* tears runneling through the dirt on his face.

"Wake up, Esper," he begged through swollen lips, his breath rasping in his throat. "Please! Please! It's too soon to leave me!"

Another time Reisil might have found some amusement in seeing Juhrnus the bully and her longtime tormentor on his hands and knees, tears and snot running together down his chin. Now, however, she felt only pity and the urge to help, to *do something* to save Esper, to retrieve something back from the abyss of loss drawing blackly from the center of her soul.

But without Saljane, she could do nothing.

A scream pierced the air and the whistle of speed as Saljane plummeted into the clearing, clutching furrows from the dirt as she landed.

Wondering joy suffused Reisil. Saljane was safe and here. She had flown blindly through the night for her. For her.

She looked again at Juhrnus and Esper and her heart twinged with hope.

~Saljane! I need you.

With another scream, Saljane launched herself at Reisil, landing heavily on her unprotected shoulder, the gauntlet having been stripped away by Upsakes before he'd trussed her up.

~Ahalad-kaaslane.

The steel-edged mindwords carried with them a wealth of relief mixed with the dregs of panic shot through with rage.

~Ahalad-kaaslane, Reisil returned, her own emotional welter matching Saljane's. *We have work to do. You must help me.*

Saljane looked at Esper and the sobbing Juhrnus.

Then from Saljane came the image of the Lady's talisman dangling around Reisil's neck.

Reisil unlaced the throat of her shirt and pulled it free. Sometime in their journey it had ceased to lie cold against her skin.

Sodur made a sound and she glanced at him questioningly. He reached out a tentative hand, but did not touch the exquisitely detailed pendant.

"Where did you get that?" he asked in a reverent voice.

"It was a gift."

He rubbed a hand over his cheeks and mouth.

"Aye, it would have to be, wouldn't it." He looked at her intently, as if to see past some barrier, as if to look at her for the first time.

Reisil waited for him to say more, but when he didn't, she turned back to the task at hand.

~What do I do?

~Blood calls to blood. You are the Lady's children.

Reisil licked her lips, scowling at the talisman. She glanced back at Saljane and nodded, understanding coming to her.

"May I have your knife?" she asked, holding her hand out to Kebonsat. He hesitated, then put his belt knife in her hand, hilt first.

Reisil looked at the silver moonlight playing over the blade. She knew what to do, as if she'd known all along, as if the knowledge had lain dormant for just this moment.

"Blood calls to blood," she said aloud, and reached her hand to Sodur, who extended his without comment. She drew the blade across his thumb until the blood flowed easily. She then held the pendant out to him and he let his blood flow over the metal. For a moment heat flared and it glowed like a coal. Reisil nodded as if her expectations were correct and turned to Juhrnus, repeating the process, though he hardly noticed, still whispering frantic encouragement to Esper.

Finally Reisil drew the blade across her own thumb, first rubbing the dirt away on her trouser leg. She drove the blade hilt-deep into the ground before her, then dripped her blood onto the hot metal. As she did, the amulet flared like a sun, filling the clearing with blinding, brilliant light.

~Help me, Saljane!

She felt her *ahalad-kaaslane's* mind join with hers, melding together, then thrusting outward on fiery wings, flying, flying, seeking.

~Hear me, Blessed Lady! I have need. I plead your aid for one of Your own, who will certainly die too young. Help him!

Reisil sent her prayer arrowing out before her as she and Saljane soared together into that grayness between worlds, between the death of night and the birth of day, between the real and the imaginary, between fact and fancy, between knowing and faith.

What time passed, Reisil could not say. Doggedly she repeated her prayer until the words lost meaning, burned away by the fury of her need. Saljane supported her like the bones of the earth and Reisil cast herself farther and farther. The tark in her was willing to let her body go altogether and let her spirit fly free, untethered, unanchored.

"Such is not necessary, child." The honey-pepper voice streaked through Reisil like ice and fire together. She felt it resonate through her so that her spirit trembled like a plucked bowstring. The world suddenly seemed to spin and distort and she felt herself tumbling like a dandelion seed caught in a whirlwind. Before panic could overwhelm her, she came to an abrupt halt. Dazedly she stared about, goggling.

They were in a glade—she and Saljane, Juhrnus and Esper, Sodur and Lume. She knelt on a bed of grass lush as emeralds, thick as a bear fur rug, each blade appearing to have been cut to a height by fairy hands. Around the edges of the glade moonlight and sunbeams twined together in columns of heart-swelling beauty. Wisteria and honeysuckle clung to the columns. Birds trilled and bees swarmed over the sweet-smelling flowers. Between two of the columns a figure moved and stepped into the glade. The Blessed Lady.

Reisil stared, mouth open. The Lady appeared much as She had in Saljane's vision. Her honey-blond hair fell to Her feet, bound around by leaves and flowers, Her silver oak-leaf circlet crowning Her brow. She had a martial appearance, more like a warrior than a mother, more like death than life. She waited for Reisil to collect herself, watching with unworldly eyes. They were a solid green from corner to corner, though not a constant green. They smoldered with shifting colors—now the red-gold of autumn maples, now the purple of flowering vetch, now the blue of a mountain tarn under a clear sky. She tilted Her head, a smile curving Her red lips.

"You have called for my aid, daughter. Ask your boon."

Reisil felt herself stiffen as a welter of emotions washed over her. Fury, foremost—at Upsakes, at her sense of helplessness as Esper's life slipped away, at her satisfaction, even pleasure, in seeing Kebonsat twist his sword from Glevs's gut, at the Lady for making her into a being with such divided instincts, to kill and to save. Then loss and fear, uncertain hope and running through it all, the singing joy of having Saljane.

She laid her hand on Esper, his ribs shuddering beneath her touch, his skin dry and hot. The sisalik was nearing the end of his life, laboring fiercely for every fevered breath. His eyes were fixed on Juhrnus now, the two lost in a communion beyond any comprehension, deeper than love, deeper than the blood ties of family.

Reisil felt herself swaying on the edge of the black abyss at the center of her soul.

"I ask your aid in saving the life of this *ahalad-kaaslane*," she said, her voice uninflected, as if all the color and emotion had washed away to drip into that abyss, to vanish forever, with every other thing lost.

"Why?"

Reisil paused, feeling a lump in her throat. Yes, why? She looked at Sodur, but could read nothing on his face. It was as if he held his breath, waiting for something. Something from Reisil?

She felt Saljane's hard beak against her cheek and reached up to stroke the short feathers along the top of her *ahalad-kaaslane*'s head.

"Because—" She stopped. What reason was good enough? Love? Loss? Hope? Fear? She looked into the Lady's watching eyes, colors brightening and melding, then fading as new colors surged. Realization struck.

This was a test. A test of who she'd become and what she learned, as a tark and *ahalad-kaaslane*. Sodur had said she would not come before the Lady before she proved herself. Now she had forced her way, and must still prove herself.

"Because you can," she answered finally, speaking clearly, quivering chin held high. She felt the truth of her words into the marrow of her bones, and her voice rang with it. "And you love life and you love Kodu Riik. When infection sets in, the tark tries to cure the body. Sometimes you must cut away pieces; sometimes the body dies for all you try to do. But the goal is still to make it healthy, to keep the people healthy. Kodu Riik is sick right now. Patverseme too. And Esper and Juhrnus are part of the cure. They'll both die, if you will it, to serve Kodu Riik. But now Esper's death is pointless. It doesn't serve. And without them, we might not succeed." *We might not succeed with them.* Reisil clamped down on that stray thought, hoping the Lady had not read it.

A slow smile broke across the Lady's face and she nodded.

"You have learned well, child." She stretched out one hand, holding it up for Reisil to see. She gasped. The Lady's fingers were hooked like talons and the nails were shards of crystal limned with silver and gold. She rotated her hand that Reisil might see fully. For a moment Reisil didn't understand; then she saw the patterns on the Lady's skin—green like a field of hay, gold like ripe barley, red as autumn willows—patterns of leaves and vines appeared on the Lady's white skin like translucent tattoos, shifting, changing, like wind over water.

"I am the land, I am its life and its protector. You are my children and I do not like to see you hurt. But sometimes the old bull elk makes food for the wolves; sometimes the young leopard starves for lack of hunting skills. These things happen, and must happen, for it is life and the balance must be maintained or there will be chaos and horror."

Reisil froze, hearing in those words an implacable refusal. She looked at Esper and Reisil felt that abyss of loss opening wider, spinning like a whirlpool, tearing bits of her off and sucking them down into a void of nothingness. Her head bowed, heavy with a weight she could not bear.

"But you are right. This death serves no purpose." Reisil took a breath, uncertain that she'd heard what she heard. She cast a wild look at the Lady, who still watched her, assessing. Then the Lady nodded and came to stand behind her, putting one clawed hand on her shoulder, soft as a falling snowflake, heavy as a mountain avalanche. Reisil felt Esper's chest jerk beneath her fingers. Power filled her like a current of liquid sunlight. It traveled through every part of her, down to her fingers and toes, warming the frigid cold in her heart, spinning light into the abyss at the center of her soul. She drew deep, sobbing breaths, each one filled with light and joy.

Then the power ran down her arm and into Esper and she watched as the color flared bright in his hide and his eyes blinked with the glow of returning vitality. Inside, his broken back knitted, his burst veins reached out to one another and connected. His tail twitched and curled up around Juhrnus's arm. Her childhood nemesis gave a shout of joy and tears pricked Reisil's eyes.

"That's enough."

Reisil took her hand away, and watched in amazement as gold drops formed on her fingers and dripped over the emerald grass. Where they fell, flowers sprang up in a riot of color.

Suddenly Juhrnus and Sodur and their *ahalad-kaaslane* began to ripple. They faded from sight. The Lady removed her hand and came around to face Reisil, who continued to kneel, awe written in every plane of her face.

"Thank you," she whispered, clutching her hands together.

The Blessed Lady smiled and brushed Her fingers over Reisil's mud-caked hair.

"You have done well."

"You are not angry at me? Because I refused Saljane for so long?"

"You, more than any other, understand what it means to be *ahalad-kaaslane*. Because you hold both of my gifts—tark and *ahalad-kaaslane*. You, more than any other, are a true *ahalad-kaaslane*. The first one of my children, Talis, was like you."

She reached out and scraped a crystal talon over the pendant. "I made this for him. To accept both gifts is a difficult burden, requiring great strength and courage. The gift was offered and you have come to your choice with an open heart. Could I be angry at your care? To fulfill both is hardest of all. Wise are you in recognizing this. Luckily it is not often necessary to ask one of my children to take on such a task. Since Talis, there has been only one other who has worn both mantles.

"But now there is great need. Kodu Riik will not survive a continued war. The land will become barren and so will her people. I had hoped Upsakes would recognize this and aid in the peace. . . ." The Lady bent and picked up a small animal—Kasepu. The little weirmart shivered and clutched at the Lady, mewling and crying. Reisil recognized the sound. It was the same one Juhrnus had been making. A sound of profound grief and loss. Her heart ached for the poor animal. The Lady stroked the distraught weirmart, turning a sad face to Reisil.

"She has been betrayed, more than I. Upsakes lost his way. He became arrogant, thinking of the glory of Kodu Riik rather than its health and safety. This is why you are needed. He has corrupted many with words of alarm and promises of vengeance. Iisand Samir remains steadfast to me. He did not threaten Kallas. Those were lies to create dissent and support for Upsakes's plan."

She sighed, a strangely human and unexpected behavior. "You must stop this war. You must decide what flesh must be cut away, what cure must be wrought to save Kodu Riik. And you must see that it is done. It will not be easy. It will be bloody with a great deal of death. But if you fail, the cost will be far higher."

She stopped, her gaze resting on Reisil with an unsettling intensity. Reisil swallowed. She had already thought of these things—of having to kill in order to save others. She nodded, agreeing, knowing she was committing herself to horrors she could not yet comprehend, but also that it was necessary and that in doing so, she served the callings of both tark and *ahalad-kaaslane*.

"Good. Then I have one more gift to give you." The Lady bent so that She was eye-to-eye with Reisil.

"Your journey has taken you into the realm of Pahe Kurjus, the one you call Demonlord. I have little influence in his lands, as he has little in mine. But he permits magic in his realm, and therefore you may benefit from this."

She reached out her hand so that the razor-edged talons of Her thumb and forefinger hovered before Reisil, filling her vision. Then they shot forward, stabbing into Reisil's eyes.

Reisil screamed as hot pain exploded and tongues of fire swept through her head. Then as fast as it had come, it was gone.

She blinked and could see. The Lady stood upright, stroking the weirmart as if She'd never moved.

"You know of the wizard-sight—to see in utter darkness without light. Now you have such sight also. You will find also that your skill with healing will be greater than before. Focus your mind on what you want to accomplish, and it will happen. But I warn you, use what I have given you sparingly. It will drain you even to the point of death. There will always be more illness than you can heal. Remember you are both tark and *ahalad-kaaslane,* and that you must allow the cycle of life to happen." She looked at Saljane for a long moment and Reisil could sense a conversation between them.

She looked back at Reisil. "Serve me well in this, for I depend upon you to choose the right path."

Reisil nodded dumbly, overwhelmed, and once again the silvery-gold light suffused the glade, closing around Reisil like a cloak of cedar-scented feathers, warm and comforting. The light faded and Reisil found herself back in the clearing, the scent of cedar filling her lungs.

"Reisil! At last you have come back. Are you well?" Sodur aided her to stand, careful not to jar Saljane. Reisil smiled at him, feeling a spurt of amazement that she could see him so clearly in the dim firelight. She glanced around, seeing Juhrnus sitting with Esper, the two communing together, nose-to-nose. Kebonsat had been caring for the horses, and now approached her, a look of frowning thunder on his face.

She saw everything with crystal clarity, as if the moon shone like the sun.

"I am well, though Saljane is poking holes in me, and I wouldn't refuse a bath." Sodur fetched her gauntlet and slid it up over her arm. Saljane shifted so that he could maneuver it beneath her and then he buckled it in place. Reisil flexed her arm and stroked Saljane's head, the bird ducking down so that her *ahalad-kaaslane* could reach better, crooning deep in her throat.

~I am glad you are here. I didn't think I was going to see you again after Upsakes dumped me down the bank.

~I would fly through fire for you.

~I know. We are ahalad-kaaslane. *I am understanding what that means. I know you have half my heart, my soul. Together we are one.*

~Yes. Saljane bumped her head harder into Reisil's hand, radiating pleasure and joy.

"What happened to you?" Kebonsat stood opposite her, hands on his hips, his feet splayed, looking like a bull trembling on the edge of rage. Reisil knew his rage stemmed from concern. To fight and kill one of the men he trusted most in the world, then to have his companions evaporate into thin air—he was off balance, and only in anger did he find comfort and control.

Reisil gave a gentle smile and reached out for him. She caught her breath. The welts on her arms were gone! And for the first time she realized the pain in her ribs and face was gone as well. Her smile widened, dazzling in the firelight gloom.

"I have been with the Blessed Amiya. And look what She has done!" She held her arms out so that he could see.

"Saljane—how do you feel?"

~Strong. Can fly high and far.

Reisil laughed. "She is well. Now we will be able to ride fast and Saljane will spy out the way."

She put her arm around Kebonsat's shoulders, feeling the tension in him. "The Lady wills that we shall find Ceriba and prevent the war. I have much to tell you all, but first I would wash and then eat." She glanced at Juhrnus and then to Sodur. "You might try to get him cleaned up as well."

With that she retreated down to a shallow scooped-out cove along the river where the water chuckled merrily over its stone bed. When she returned, she found Kebonsat turning a pair of fat grouse on a spit. Sodur and Juhrnus were nowhere to be seen.

"Bathing, downstream," Kebonsat told her when she asked.

Reisil nestled close to the warmth of the fire, studiously ignoring Upsakes, who lay hunched on the ground where Sodur had left him. No matter that his feet and hands were bound, that he could neither see nor speak through the blindfold and gag. Reisil felt his presence like a sucking vortex of hate and rage in the evening stillness.

She concentrated on pulling her comb through the tangles in her hair, letting the repetitive motion smooth her jangled emotions even as she smoothed the wild mess of her hair. Saljane perched on the stack of firewood nearby.

"If this wandering about is going to be my life from now on, I think I ought to just cut it all off," she complained with a yelp when she tore out a knot.

"I have often thought the same thing," Kebonsat said with an unexpected lightness. He came to sit behind her, taking the comb and sliding it through her hair. "It's a tradition that nobility in Patverseme keep their hair long, but damned inconvenient, especially when traveling across country."

"Don't you usually have squires or someone to help?"

"Aye, and tents and armor and cooks and furniture. Not on this journey, however. And I have never been a good housekeeper or valet."

"Must be a terrible hardship for you," Reisil teased.

"Terrible. Ah, what wouldn't I do for a bubble bath, a hot brandy and someone to clip my toenails." Reisil glanced over her shoulder at him. He looked perfectly earnest and she giggled.

"You know when I first met you I thought you were an ass," she said. "Arrogant and puffed up, staring down your nose at everybody. You surprised me, though. You let Ceriba badger you in the kohv-house, and the way you smiled at each other—pure mischief."

"Thank you, I think." A shadow crossed over his face and his smile leached away.

"We're going to get her back. She'll be all right."

The look on his face was haunted, his eyes full of inexpressible pain. "I'll not forgive myself if—"

"There are no ifs. We *are* going to get her back and she *is* going to be all right. Now give me back my comb and get to turning that spit. If you burn our dinner I'll tell your father you simply cannot be sent out into the wilderness without a full entourage, including your own personal nail-clipping, brandy-warming bath maid."

Kebonsat began to laugh and Reisil smiled. This she knew how to do—to break the tension, to help someone deal with fears and pain. She prayed to the Blessed Lady that she was right, that they would find Ceriba safe and rescue her.

And then prevent a war.

Simple.

Reisil sighed and yanked on her hair. It was time to tell Juhrnus and Sodur about Kaval, and Upsakes's lies. And then make a plan.

Chapter 13

After supper, expectant silence fell as Reisil settled beside the fire with a cup of mint tea, resting her elbows on her knees. Esper coiled in Juhrnus's lap. Juhrnus circled his arms around his *ahalad-kaaslane*, eyes red-rimmed. Lume stretched full-length beside Sodur, his silvery fur gilded by the light of the fire's flames. Kebonsat sat to the side of Reisil, his expression lost in the shadows. The night was chill this high in the mountains, and Reisil hitched herself closer to the fire.

But she must soon speak and tell the others what she'd learned. Seeking assurance, Reisil clasped her pendant. Sodur bent forward.

"May I see that again?"

Reisil opened her hand and held it out to the length of the ribbon around her neck. Sodur stared at it, then nodded, giving Reisil a wondering glance.

"Do you know what you hold there?"

"It belonged to Talis. The Lady told me."

"Aye, Talis first, then Galt two centuries later. It's like seeing the past come alive. Wherever did you get it?"

"It was a gift," Reisil said cryptically, unwilling to say any more, though not certain what made her reticent. How had Nurema come by it?

"Indeed. It could not come to you another way."

"What do you know of it?"

"The Blessed Lady chose Talis—a tark he was! Well, now, how did I forget that?" He scratched his newly shaven jaw and then shrugged. "Anyway, the histories of the time are rather muddled, but legend has it that the lands of Kodu Riik, Patverseme, Scallas and Guelt were all of a piece then. That was long before those we know as Scallacians invaded. The lands were ruled by warlords who were constantly fighting over their little territories, sending the yeomanry into endless battles and leaving the women to work the fields and their babes to grow up without fathers. Sons marched off to war as soon as the first fuzz marked their chins, returning home now and again for a visit and a tumble in a lonely woman's bed before marching off again. Most died before they had twenty-five summers under their belts. Talis served one such warlord. He patched up the boys and sent them back out to hack pieces off one another. The lands grew wild and populations dwindled. Illness and starvation swept through farms and villages and the Lady grew angry, seeing the destruction.

"At that time, most of the gods weren't too interested in humanity except for sport. But the Lady saw great potential in us and offered Her Light to those who would obey Her laws.

"So she sent Kolvrane, a falcon, to Talis. She told him to gather all the people he could and bring them to what was to become Kodu Riik. If they followed him, if they put their faith in Her, then She would give them the *ahalad-kaaslane* and guard them from harm, expelling the warlords from Her borders. As a further mark of Her favor, She gave Talis that pendant, Her talisman. With it and Kolvrane, Talis marched across the lands spreading Her words, and many people followed. Soldiers deserted their warlords, mothers dropped their hoes in the fields, children fled in the night. They escaped to Kodu Riik and the salvation the Lady offered. They say that though not one refugee came with more than the clothes on his back, no one starved and no one died in the exodus. The Lady provided for all.

"Eventually the warlords banded together and sought to retake the land of Kodu Riik. But they were repelled. There are legends of Talis calling down fire from the heavens, of his curdling the earth so that no one might cross. . . ." Sodur paused, stroking Lume with a smile. "Some have argued that the eastern crescent of Kodu Riik, with its fens, quicksand and swamps, happened when the warlords sought to land ships. They say that if you dare go into them a little distance, you can find bits of armor and bones from the warlords trapped by Talis's magic." Sodur shrugged. "I am no scholar, and have only a fitful memory for the tales. If you want to know more, you must needs ask someone else. In Koduteel there are scholars who delight in keeping track of such things. They would know more than I."

"You think the pendant gave Talis such powers?" Reisil asked.

"Who knows?" Sodur spread his hands. "You will find out soon enough, I think."

"That was before the lands divided into countries. Perhaps this Talis had wizard blood in him," Kebonsat offered.

Sodur shrugged and Reisil remembered that wizard magic didn't work in the Lady's demesnes. Mostly.

"What else can you tell me about it?" she asked, shifting the topic back to the talisman.

"That I know of, there are no stories of lightning about Galt, though some legends say he could walk through fire. His *ahalad-kaaslane* was a lava-lizard. Oh, yes, such creatures do indeed exist. It glowed ruby-bright, like lava itself, and it could start fires with its breath. The stories go that Galt was an explorer, traveling far and wide, returning with treasures of rare metals and jewels, wonderful artifacts from faraway places no one had ever heard of. Then one day he returned from one of his adventures with both the talisman and the lava-lizard.

"Galt's return was timely. Hordes of krakmurs had burrowed through the Melhyhir Mountains and began to nest in the highlands. Rotten little creatures—no taller than three or four feet, but with powerful shoulders and legs, and great shoveling hands tipped with fierce claws. They ate whatever meat they could find, including people. Especially people. Galt knew them from his travels and organized an attack. It was a dreadful battle, with many losses. There were so many of the krakmurs—endless numbers, it seemed—and they carried with them pestilence. Eventually Galt prevailed and the krakmur burrows were sealed. But you still hear stories of krakmurs attacking farms and villages."

"The Blessed Lady said he was also a tark," Reisil said.

"Very well might have been." Sodur smiled ruefully. "I have been taught much as an *ahalad-kaaslane*. But I must admit to being an indifferent scholar. The old stories never appealed to me, and I don't remember as much as I ought to. Upsakes—" He broke off, looking at Upsakes's prone body. His fingers curled in Lume's fur. "Some of us learned better. When you go to Koduteel, you may find more answers."

"Answers. That brings us back to me. I have something to tell you. I've told Kebonsat some—I felt I could trust him and I didn't know about anyone else. The Lady told me more."

And with that Reisil plunged in, telling Sodur and Juhrnus of what she'd seen through Saljane's eyes, of Kaval and his companions. She then told them of Upsakes's lies, that he'd influenced the herald to say Iisand Samir had threatened Kallas, that it had been a lie to muster hatred for the Dure Vadonis.

"I wondered as much," Sodur muttered, his head caught between his hands as he stared at the ground. "Yesterday. You asked why Iisand Samir would threaten his own people and I remembered that the herald who brought the news was a good friend of Upsakes's. I did not believe he could do this, kidnap this young woman and push us back into the war. I did not want to believe it." He looked at Kebonsat. "I swear to you on the Lady's name that we will find your sister. After the war, after Mysane Kosk, I have no great love for the Patversemese, but this treaty is good for Kodu Riik. It is good for both countries. And this conspiracy is naught but evil, serving only the Demonlord."

"Thank you for that," Kebonsat said soberly, his face drawn lean and hard.

Ordinarily Reisil would not have been able to see him clearly. But her wizard-sight cut through the shadows and she saw the strain molding his lips into a knife slash, saw the dreadful dying hope in his eyes. He kept up a good front during the day, but now he was beginning to understand the extent of the conspiracy. This had been well planned and executed. What chance did Ceriba have against such plotting?

Reisil pondered out loud. "Kaval was gone for weeks—how could he have been involved? I saw his reaction when he learned of the treaty. He was dumbfounded."

"Must have been Rikutud," Juhrnus said. "Kaval would never have done anything without his father's permission. Tied to him like a girl on her mother's apron strings, that one. Rikutud has to be in this up to his neck."

Sodur looked at Juhrnus, bushy eyebrows drawn low, his thin face stern. "A good observation, my young *ahalad-kaaslane*. You know Kaval well, do you?" The suspicion was evident in his voice and a warning rang in Reisil's head. The *ahalad-kaaslane* were in danger of imploding. They must trust one another, yet with Upsakes's betrayal, could there not be others plotting against the Lady's wishes? Would they now turn on one another, destroying the trust that bound them together?

"No. If you must travel that road, then you should know that Kaval and I shared a bed. Another bad choice I've made." Reisil looked steadily at Sodur. Before he could respond, Juhrnus intervened, stunning her.

"You're not all to blame for that. Kaval liked to play the hero, and if I hadn't picked on you so much, maybe you would have seen through him." He dropped his eyes.

Sodur rubbed his hands over his face in a tired gesture.

"My apologies. I also can't help thinking I should have known about Upsakes. How can I blame either of you for not knowing about Kaval?"

"The Lady would not want us to fail because we lost faith with one another," Reisil said. "It is true that I don't like Juhrnus, and that he does not like me. But we will work together because we are chosen. Is that not so?"

Reisil turned to Juhrnus. A flush had crept up his neck to his cheeks and he looked feverish.

"That is so. I serve the Blessed Lady. She has given me Esper—twice now. And I know She wants peace between Kodu Riik and Patverseme. I will do whatever necessary to make that happen. Both of us will." He clutched Esper closer.

"Good. Then we should sleep, and in the morning Saljane shall search for Ceriba. There is just one more thing I must tell you, though I would not have it go any farther than this fire."

The others looked at her warily and Reisil grinned. "We are not to be so suspicious of one another, remember?" she chided gently. "It is just this. The Lady gave me another gift, there at the end. She gave me wizard-sight. I tell you this now because I believe She has foreseen another attack like that in the forest."

"I would agree," Sodur said, nodding.

"Then we must do all we can to prepare. When I was lost, I did not try a torch—I couldn't find anything to burn, even if I could find my flint. Did anyone try?"

"They cast a small light. We were able to see perhaps a foot in front of us," Sodur answered.

"It was better than being totally blind," Juhrnus said. "Esper sees well in the dark but could see nothing in that foul blackness. With the torch, he saw several yards."

"Then we must prepare torches and each of us carry them," Kebonsat declared. "Keep your flints near to hand as well. They may save us, or prevent our being trapped. We'll at least make ourselves difficult prey." He looked at Reisil. "A precious gift indeed. May it serve us well." He stood and stretched, readying himself for the first watch. "What about him?" Kebonsat jerked his chin at Upsakes. "What do we do with him?"

"Nothing," Sodur said, his voice pitiless and barren as a desert waste. "The Blessed Lady serves Her own justice on the *ahalad-kaaslane*. We will leave him to Her."

*   *   *

The next morning they cut branches and wrapped the
ends in rags. Then they packed up and departed, returning to the village to purchase pine pitch for the
torches and rid themselves of the extra mounts before
pursuing Ceriba's trail. The tavernkeeper had told Sodur
that the party had passed through days before.

They left Upsakes without a word or glance. Reisil
shuddered at the thought of what the Lady might have
in store for him.

Saljane winged her way aloft in triumphant delight
She circled overhead and then arrowed away, her body
strong as ever, thanks to the Lady's healing touch.

Reisil rode her sorrel mare comfortably, missing the
dun gelding. She had come to think of him more as a
companion than beast of burden, and regretted the necessity of exchanging him for a fresh mount.

As she rode, Reisil felt her spirit swell with a sense
of strength and purpose she had never felt before. It ran
through her bones like iron and she wanted to laugh out
loud with the power of it. Even the hardships of travel
ceased to bother her as much. She no longer dreamed
of her cozy cottage and soft bed, her copper bathtub
with steaming water, her garden and fruit trees. She
missed them, but she no longer desired them with the
ferocious want of a winter-starved fox. Instead, she enjoyed the freedom of the open air, the spectacular mountain vistas, the new skills she was learning in the wild.
At their stops, she harvested unique medicinal plants,
delighting in the opportunity to discover them herself,
rather than purchasing them from a trader. She imagined
visiting Odiltark and Elutark, bringing them the bounty
of her travels. The daydream made her smile.

Three days passed before Saljane entered Reisil's
mind with a clarion call.

~She is here! I have found her.

~Show me.

Reisil pulled her horse to a stop and gripped her saddle. Flying with Saljane continued to be a wrenching
experience. The heights continued to chill her blood, and
when caught up in Saljane's mind, she had no capacity

to do anything but close her eyes and sit still. She no
longer felt as embarrassed by this fact and had quit hiding it from her companions. There was no time for foolish pride in this hunt. Though Juhrnus had made a few
mocking remarks, which Reisil had expected and ignored, Sodur and Kebonsat had accepted her weakness
with no comment. Now she counted on them to manage
her horse when she could not.

"Kebonsat! Have care. Saljane calls," she cried with
a gasp. Kebonsat spun his horse and caught up Reisil's
reins while Sodur and Juhrnus came up beside her. But
she was no longer there to notice. Her mind flew high
with Saljane.

They coasted on the thermal currents over a green
valley in the western foothills of the Dume Griste mountains. Beyond were rolling grasslands stretching as far as
the horizon.

A fortress keep nestled against a sheer cliff at the
northern end of the green wedge. A high, thick wall
drawn tight against the steep valley sides formed an
apron around the bailey. The ground in front of the wall
dropped sharply down the motte to the valley floor. A
waterfall cascaded over the cliffs into a sluice that fun-
neled into the keep before draining into a crystal lake
outside the walls.

Reisil described it aloud for her companions.

"Can you see a pennant? A coat of arms? Something
to tell us where you are?" pressed Kebonsat.

"On the tower and over the gates." Saljane swooped
low to give her a better vantage point. The wind blew
in short gusts, fluttering the pennants and then dropping
them like sodden rags. Reisil made a gulping sound and
her fingers whitened on the saddle as the bird rode the
unsteady wind.

"Yes, I see it now. It's quartered—yellow and green,
and there are black symbols in the yellow patches. The
upper one is a star; the other is a pair of crossed swords,
hilts up."

"Mekelsek," Kebonsat said grimly. "His keep is for-
midable. What of Ceriba?"

Saljane skimmed away from the tower, surprising Rei-sil when she flew out over the walls into the valley. Outside the walls along the edge of the wood-fringed lake was the kidnappers' campsite. Reisil sought eagerly for Ceriba and found her huddled near the fire, her clothes filthy and torn, her face bruised and swollen. She leaned hunched and awkward, as if in great pain.

With Saljane's piercing vision, Reisil was able to see that her nose was broken. Dried blood stained her cheeks and hands.

Fury lit sparks in Reisil's blood. She reached out a helpless hand, then forced herself to examine the scene detachedly, refusing to consider what else the kidnappers—what Kaval—might have done to their captive. Nor did she describe Ceriba's appearance, merely giving the layout of the campsite and the disposition of her kidnappers.

"I can see four of them. Kaval, the wheelwright from Kallas in his gray cloak, the man with the thick paunch and steel-gray hair, and a stout, yellow-haired man with a smooth-shaven, round face. I don't recognize him. Wait! Yes, I do. He does odd jobs—hauling wood, delivering coal—mostly for war-widows who need the extra muscle. The scar-faced man and the man with the green cloak aren't there. No. I see them now. Near the gates. I think they must be meeting with the lord of these lands. He's got some soldiers with him. I don't think it's going well. The Kaj—a tall man with salt-and-pepper hair in a braid down his back and a black beard down to his chest—he's shaking his head. He looks angry. He's pointing to the other end of the valley. Now he's mounting his horse. The green-cloaked man is reaching out to him—oh! The Kaj just gave him a cut across the arm with his riding whip! Now he is withdrawing into the keep. But his soldiers are following the two men back to the campsite."

Reisil fell silent, watching the two men. The group of kidnappers spoke together for several moments, then began to mount up. The soldiers continued to trail behind as they departed the valley.

"They're leaving and they are not pleased. Two of the horses are lame. They can barely hobble along. They won't go far, not until they get new mounts."

Reisil turned her focus to Saljane.

~You have done well, my ahalad-kaaslane, she told the goshawk in a deeply affectionate mindvoice. *Keep watch over them and we will come fast as we can.*

~I will watch.

Then Reisil withdrew, finding herself more and more in control of her own mind as she practiced the mental sharing with Saljane.

"I bet they were hoping for replacement horses. That lord wasn't too keen on their business, though," Juhrnus said.

"Mekelsek hates my father, and I doubt very much he favors this treaty with Kodu Riik. But he has honor, of a sort. He would not stoop to kidnapping. But neither did he aid her, the bastard." Kebonsat spat, fury flushing his face. "He'd rather stay out of it altogether. Slippery honor indeed."

"How far is it to his valley?" Sodur asked.

"I don't know. I'm not familiar with this part of the mountains. It lies in the western foothills, only four or five days' hard ride from Vitne Ozols."

"With those horses lame, we've got a chance to catch them before they get there. If that is still where they are going, and if we drive hard," Sodur said.

"They must go there if they wish to make . . . effective . . . use of Ceriba." Kebonsat's voice turned bleak and not one of them didn't understand what he meant. To force the crown and Kebonsat's father to abandon the treaty and take up arms again, the violence to Ceriba would have to be severe.

"It wouldn't be enough, though," Reisil said in sudden comprehension. "That's what Kaval and the others from Kallas are for. To sacrifice themselves. They'll confess to working for Iisand Samir or something like that. With what they plan to do to Ceriba, that would do it." Even as she said it, Reisil began shaking her head, wanting it not to be true. It was too horrible to be true.

But the small group exchanged a look of bitter understanding, the puzzle pieces settling into dreadful place. *They think they're patriots. Heroes. Martyrs.* Icy tentacles wrapped Reisil's spine and she covered her mouth with her hand to catch the scream rising up from her feet.

"It's a good plan," Kebonsat said in a strangled voice, his lips white.

"Not good enough," Juhrnus said, his jaw jutting, his eyes narrowing as he scowled and urged his mount up the trail.

Reisil nodded, feeling her own face hardening with determination.

"Let's not dally then," Sodur said, setting off after Juhrnus.

Reisil fell in behind Kebonsat, seeing Ceriba's face in her mind's eye. She prayed that her fears would be without foundation, but knew, with a ghastly certainty, that they were not.

Two hard day's riding brought them to Mekelsek Keep.

The four searchers rode down to the lake just before sunset, setting up a sketchy camp. Juhrnus set about pulling several fish from the lake. Esper slithered into the water and caught several quick-finned graylings of his own, while Reisil picketed the horses.

They were a grim, silent group, figuring themselves less than two days behind Ceriba's captors. But they, too, were in need of new mounts and food. They'd risen before the sun and traveled well into the night for the last two days, scrabbling over steep, treacherous terrain. Fissures yawned wide beside them on the narrow track and ledges crumbled away beneath their weight. The hardy mountain ponies were exhausted. They still had a good chance to catch up with Ceriba's captors before Vitne Ozols—before her captors killed her—but not without fresh mounts and provisions.

The grim news was that Saljane reported that the kidnappers had found a village that afternoon and had stopped for the night. No doubt they would obtain mounts there and pick up their pace the next day. Each of the four rescuers felt time running away like water out of their hands.

"Will this Mekelsek deal with you?" Sodur asked Kebonsat.

"I don't know. He's got three daughters of his own, though. That may help."

"Shall I come with you?"

Kebonsat considered the other man, then shook his head. "I think it best I go alone. But if there is trouble, I ask that you see to my sister."

Sodur nodded and watched the other man unroll the tabard he had not worn since departing Kallas. Kebonsat pulled it over his dusty clothing and buckled his sword-belt over it. A black-and-gold diamond pattern circled his chest and trimmed the sleeves and neckline of the indigo cloth. In the center of the diamond pattern two crimson lions leaped at one another. Centered beneath them on the blue field was a three-pronged coronet, also in red. Over his heart was embroidered a sword, point down, indicating Kebonsat's position as heir to the title.

"Do you think that's wise?" Sodur asked.

"Mekelsek is unpredictable, with doubtful honor, but he might do for the House Vadonis what he wouldn't do for me." Kebonsat shrugged. "It's a slim chance. But it can't hurt to remind him of my father's position. Allying with us could give him prestige in court. I can't offer any trade settlements or negotiations in my father's name; I don't have the authority. But he might choose to hedge his bets against the hope of a reward." Kebonsat's lips twisted bitterly. "As if rescuing my sister weren't sufficient reason for honor."

"It's been my experience that politicians neither love nor hate. Interest, not sentiment, directs them," Sodur observed quietly.

"True. But Mekelsek is no politician. And therein lies my hope. He is a fourth son and a rogue, never expecting to inherit and uninterested in rounds of service, until those standing in the way of his title died—all aboveboard. Illness, the war, a hunting accident. Though

if it weren't for our need, I'd bypass him altogether. He's
volatile and cunning."

"He drove them off without aid. Perhaps that bodes
well for us."

"Perhaps. But he could have just as easily kept them
here." Kebonsat mounted his horse. "Best to get up
there and find out. If I'm not back by morning, go on
without me. Be prepared to run in any case. He might
not be as accommodating to us as he was to Ceriba's
captors." The bitter expression he cast at the fortress
spoke volumes, but he didn't spare another look for
his companions.

Sodur watched him ride up the road to the gates of
the keep, where guards met him. He dismounted and
they led away his horse. It was nearly an hour later
before he was let inside, the gates clanging shut behind
him.

"I don't like the look of that," Sodur murmured. "I
suggest we do as our noble friend recommends and
ready the horses to ride."

Reisil nodded at him over her shoulder. She'd discovered the Lady had spoken true of her ability to heal.
Through just a touch, she sensed illness and pain. If she
concentrated, focusing her attention on the animal's particular problem, the wound seemed to mend itself. But
healing leached her of energy. After each session she
could hardly move, the drain was so great. More than
once she'd fallen asleep in her saddle. She'd resorted to
using the herbal stimulant she carried in her pack, but
she could not continue much longer in that vein. Her
hands trembled constantly and her legs felt like taffy.
Darkness gnawed at the edges of her vision and bright
spots of color danced always in front of her.

She finished with the last horse, soothing a bruise in
his frog, then saddled her mare with fumbling fingers,
leaving the cinch loose. She could tighten it in an instant.
Then she collapsed next to the fire, pillowing her head
on her cloak and falling instantly asleep.

Juhrnus woke her with a rough shake of her shoulder.
"Get up. Someone's coming."

She scrambled up at once, shaking her head to clear the grogginess. Since Esper's illness, Juhrnus had become more thoughtful, less critical. What he thought about in his long silences on the trail, Reisil didn't know, but he'd stopped his habitual caviling, and had begun acting more civilly. He was by no means friendly, but he no longer tormented her with childish, insolent remarks.

He'd grown up, Reisil thought as she watched him check his weapons—sword, knife and a cudgel, which he took a couple of practice swings with. If committing to her bonding with Saljane had changed the path of her life, then nearly losing his *ahalad-kaaslane* had made Juhrnus mature suddenly into a man. That inner core the Blessed Lady had discerned when she sent him Esper had come shining to the surface.

Inexperienced and young he still might be, but he'd begun to learn compassion, and he'd begun to realize his importance as *ahalad-kaaslane* to the Lady, to Kodu Riik. The knowledge both humbled and strengthened him. He no longer wasted himself on personal insult. Though Reisil didn't like him much more than she had before, she was learning to respect him. She would have never thought she'd do that.

She heard jingling and the echoing clop of many horses' hooves on the hard-packed dirt road.

"I don't like the sound of that," Sodur said. "Are they sending a troop to foist us out, or maybe take us prisoner?"

"Looks like," Reisil said, peering into the darkness, hearing Juhrnus slipping the bit back into his gelding's mouth.

Along the moon-brightened road to the fortress came an entire troop of riders, three by three—thirty in all. In the lead rode Mekelsek and another, younger man, and in between they sandwiched Kebonsat. He was too far away to read his expression. Then at the end of the column she caught sight of a string of riderless horses. "Maybe not. They've got spare horses with them. He got through to this Mekelsek after all."

Even so, Juhrnus completed adjusting his gelding's

gear and Sodur and Reisil followed suit, though Reisil was hard-pressed to get her saddle sufficiently tight with her hands shaking as they were. She held them out before her, willing them to be steady. She wasn't going to be any good for anyone if she didn't get some sleep soon.

When the riders arrived, the three *ahalad-kaaslane* waited in a semicircle around the fire. Esper crouched on Juhrnus's shoulder, slitted eyes shining yellow in the firelight, while Lume came to sit beside Sodur. He looked more ragged and unkempt than ever. His thin, stooped figure was unprepossessing, far less so than Upsakes's fiery presence had been. The frayed hem of his bedraggled cloak drooped unevenly about the shanks of his patched boots. He squinted in his peculiar way, his thinning hair needing a haircut. He looked for all the world like a shabby stray dog.

As if hearing Reisil's thoughts, he flashed her a smile and a wink, and Reisil's doubts fled. He might appear hungry and forlorn, but a white flame burned inside him. Upsakes had underestimated him. He hadn't seen Sodur's strength like the quiet, unyielding might of the earth. Now that she had seen it, Reisil wouldn't forget. Would this be what she became? What Juhrnus would become? Reefs against the pounding waves, walls against the howling storms?

The troop pulled up on the road and Kebonsat dismounted.

"Kaj Mekelsek, these are my companions, Juhrnus, Sodur and Reisiltark. This is Kaj Mekelsek and his eldest son, Edelsat."

The other two men dismounted and came forward. With his silky black beard and salt-and-pepper braid, Mekelsek appeared just as Reisil remembered. He towered over her. His son was a match for him in height, though his beard was trimmed close. He had cool gray eyes that stared at her from beneath thick, black brows, his nose thrusting prominently over wide, sensual lips. He must have outweighed Kebonsat by three stone. He carried himself like a young bull—graceful, powerful, quick and fierce. He regarded each of the *ahalad-kaaslane* in turn, his gaze lingering, measuring, before moving on. When he turned to Reisil, she found herself acutely aware of the scars on her face for the first time since the Lady had healed her.

For a moment she thought herself about to blush, but then she lifted her chin boldly. Her scars were a badge of honor, an outward mark of her devotion to Saljane, her loyalty to the Blessed Lady. Some might think her marred, but she thought of herself whole in more than the physical sense. If the Lady had offered to remove them, Reisil would have refused.

In response to the challenge in her look, Edelsat gave her a slight bow, startling her. Her brows angled up.

"Kaj Mekelsek has offered us an escort to find Ceriba," Kebonsat announced. "As well as provisions and fresh horses."

"You are generous, Kaj, and we thank you for your assistance," Sodur said with a slight bow.

Reisil blinked at him, surprised all over again. He sounded like a courtier, his voice gravely soft, his manner upright yet deferential. Was this something he learned as *ahalad-kaaslane*? He had told her that the *ahalad-kaaslane* came and went at will in Koduteel, into the Iisand's own chambers if they so chose. And he had mentioned that she would learn the manners and social niceties in order to get along there. Apparently it served him well in other places, also.

Mekelsek nodded, replying in equally grave tones. "That was well-spoken and I thank you, though this pup does not think as highly of me." He jerked his chin at Kebonsat. "Mayhap he is right and I should have kept those ruffians here. But I had my reasons and I stand by them. Now that you've got here at last, I can do more. There's been a call for troops—the war with Kodu Riik is on again unless you lot can expose the plot against the peace. Toward that end, I've put my men under this whelp's command." He nodded again at Kebonsat. "You'll need the extra help. The news is that there will be some sort of summit between your Iisand

Samir and Karalis Vasalis eight days hence on the Vorshtar plain. Both bring armies. If it goes poorly, then the war will begin right there." He shook his head. "I don't trust this at all. Stinks like a week-gone body. I expect whoever is behind this won't be content to rely solely on your sister to spark action. Something else is in the wind. Nevertheless, if it gets about that you're on your way, they'll try to stop you."

He turned to Kebonsat, snaring his son in his gaze as he did. "I'll send my soldiers with you to rescue your sister. But I want you on that plain when the two powers meet. No one else is going to be looking for treachery from within. You're all that stands between us and war. Remember that. And we can't survive a two-fronted conflict. Scallas perches like a buzzard on our western borders, waiting for the right moment to strike. We'll be squeezed to nothing." Mekelsek paused, his eyes boring into Kebonsat's. "I know you know this already. But you might forget in the next few days. Your sister's been badly treated, and there may be worse for her. Maybe you'll blame me, and if so, you know where to find me. But whatever else you are, you are a knight of Patverseme with a duty to her before all. Remember that too."

Mekelsek turned to his son and clasped his arm in a warrior's grip. "Be well, and don't fail."

Then Edelsat ordered that the spare horses be brought forward. Reisil groaned inwardly when their packs were transferred, realizing that she would be expected to ride into the night. She took a breath and firmed her resolve. She would have time to rest later. She thought of Ceriba, how terrified she must be, how hurt and desperate. Reisil could not falter now.

Edelsat took several packs from his men and offered around hot food and ale, fruit and bread. Reisil ate ravenously, feeling her strength coming back with every bite. It had been days since she'd eaten hot food—since they'd left the village and Upsakes behind.

To her surprise, Mekelsek remained with them, drinking a dram of ale, watching his visitors over the rim.

More than once Reisil found his gaze resting on her as though he could not look away. Meanwhile, Edelsat mounted and led his men off into the darkness. The four companions would overtake them, being able to move more swiftly.

They finished the meal and transferred tack and readied their mounts. Mekelsek looked on wordlessly. To Reisil he appeared nervous and even fretful. Kebonsat turned to him and said a clipped, unwilling thank-you. She knew he felt strongly that Mekelsek should have detained Ceriba's captors. She couldn't help but feel the same, knowing what they had planned for Kebonsat's beautiful, vivacious sister.

Before her mind could follow the path of her thoughts to Kaval, Reisil turned to adjust her cinch one more time. As she lifted her foot into her stirrup, Kaj Mekelsek spoke close behind, startling her.

"If I may, I'd like to have a word with your tark." He spoke to Kebonsat, and a look of stark desperation and pleading shadowed his face. It was out of place on the proud, ruthless features. Kebonsat stiffened, his lips curling into a snarl, an ugly flush staining his neck and cheeks. He stared hard at Mekelsek.

"If you wish."

Mekelsek turned to her and she saw in his eyes a deep-rooted fear, an agony of need. He licked his lips, not looking at Kebonsat, who stood close by, arms crossed, watching with an expression of bitter fury.

"Kebonsat has told me something of your healing gifts," he ventured at last as Reisil looked at him questioningly. "I would ask—nay beg . . . That is, once—if—things are resolved between Patverseme and Kodu Riik, that you might, if you are willing, return here. My lady is gravely ill." He said the last words in a rush, as if the words burned his throat and tongue.

Reisil pitied him, yet she felt a twin to Kebonsat's bitterness stir in her heart. This man had let Ceriba's captors take her away when he could have rescued her. He would have known her pain, her fear, her hope that someone might pull her from the jaws of terror, that someone might stand between her and the oncoming storm. Yet he'd done nothing. And now he wanted Reisil to gift him the life and health of his own wife.

Though she wanted to look to Sodur for advice, Reisil kept her gaze fixed on Mekelsek as she considered. Sodur could not answer this for her. He had not been given two gifts; he could not heal, could not know what compulsions healers felt to relieve the suffering of others.

Refusing wouldn't help Ceriba. And maybe Reisil wouldn't make it back in time to help Mekelsek's wife. What should she do?

"I will," she said finally, and hope flared on Mekelsek's face. She did not look at Kebonsat, but returned to her horse and mounted without another word.

They left Kaj Mekelsek standing there in the clearing, tears sliding down his cheeks as he watched them go. If he could feel so for his wife, Reisil wondered, why couldn't he have felt enough compassion to help Ceriba?

The road rose up over the rim of the valley and dropped over the other side into a land of twisted, buckled rock, barren of trees. As they paused, far away, north and east, they could see the lights of Vitne Ozols. Closer, a firefly light gleamed in the darkness, signaling the village where Ceriba's kidnappers had stopped.

They settled into a swift walk, the road turning into a wagon track, where it would be easy for a horse to turn a fetlock in the dark.

"I feel I should explain why I agreed to return and help with Kaj Mekelsek's wife," Reisil began. Kebonsat, riding beside her, cut her off with a shake of his head.

"No need."

"But I want you to understand."

"I do." He drew a breath and blew it out gustily, raking a hand through his hair. "I really do." Then in a sudden change of subject: "Do you know why he didn't help Ceriba?" He answered without waiting for her response. "Because he feared retaliation by those who had engineered her kidnapping. He's strong here in this valley, but he must trade for a great deal. He must keep

his trading connections open. He won his title by his
deeds in battle, but he keeps it only by political maneuvering. He hasn't got the finesse or subtle mind for deal-
ing with those who've been steeped in the game all their
lives. So he does what he can. In this case, he may well
be right, given the Guild's involvement. I wouldn't want
to be on the left side of the Guild. He waited until we
asked his aid so he was justified in helping. Did I not
say that he had a slippery honor? He didn't even pretend
that he didn't know they were Ceriba's kidnappers,
though the news of her kidnapping has been restricted.
Only the nobles of the land have been made aware
through the demand for troops."

"Why must he wait until asked to help?"

"Because he is then formally obligated," Sodur answered from behind. "He was hedging his bets, expecting someone to turn up soon. If not, I expect he
would have assigned all blame for what might happen to
Ceriba to your family for being lax in your care of her."

"He'd be right," Kebonsat said in a cold and unrelenting voice.

"But that doesn't explain why he waited until you
asked to help Ceriba," Reisil said, confused.

"Because he is a small landowner, and because he did
not know who had taken her," Kebonsat said.

"But why should that matter?"

"It shouldn't, not if he were truly honorable. He
should have rescued her on the principle of her need
alone. But he did not want to risk the safety of his people over Ceriba, not knowing who might retaliate against
him, not knowing if my family would be willing to make
an alliance with his house. Some families would not wish
the return of their daughter. They'd rather see her dead
than have a constant reminder that they had failed to
protect her, and face the embarrassment of her ruined
reputation."

"Ruined reputation?" Reisil repeated, disbelieving.
"What matters her reputation if she can be rescued?"

"A fallen woman—no matter why or how—is not welcomed in Patverseme society," Sodur explained when

Kebonsat remained silent. "And though Ceriba may not have been abused in that way," he said, seeing the stricken look on Kebonsat's face, "it is enough that she was alone with those men through many days, even though not by her choice. Her reputation is ruined. No respectable offers of marriage will be made. She'll never be invited into polite society again. Her friends will refuse to see her. If she foists herself into the social rounds, she will be universally snubbed."

"That's barbarous!" Reisil exclaimed, half turning in her saddle to look at Sodur and Kebonsat to see if they spoke the truth.

Sodur nodded at her while Kebonsat gritted his teeth, his knuckles white on his reins.

"She has been taken and tormented and now you're saying that when we rescue her, she'll face a life of unending loneliness and isolation? That's . . . That's . . ." Reisil fell silent, unable to put into her words her indignation, the sweeping rage that swallowed her.

She thought of Ceriba when she'd met her in the kohv-house, her warm, dancing wit and merry laughter. She couldn't imagine the fate Kebonsat and Sodur described. There must be something else, some other possibility. She couldn't save Ceriba just to let her waste away, isolated from and rejected by all she'd known.

"You see, I do understand your promise to Mekelsek," Kebonsat said softly after a few minutes. "I love my sister dearly, and nothing is going to prevent me from rescuing her. It's more than duty. It's something I must do. When I went into the fortress and Mekelsek first asked about you helping his wife, angry as I was, I knew what your answer must be. You are a healer, and you must respond to his need, just as you are responding to Ceriba's. And though I disagree with what the man has done, I would not see his wife die for my spite."

Reisil felt tears prickle her eyes and swallowed, emotion making her throat ache.

"Thank you for that. It means more to me than you know."

She found herself thinking abruptly of Kaval: his playful, easy manner, his loving touch. She shook her head. She'd thought Kebonsat arrogant and cold in their first meeting. If anyone was capable of kidnapping a young woman, she would have chosen Kebonsat over Kaval. But Kebonsat's haughty manner hid a gentle heart, devoted and passionate, while Kaval's gentleness hid a streak of vicious cruelty. And now, when he must hate Mekelsek, Kebonsat gave her comfort and understanding rather than the blame she expected.

For the first time since she'd discovered that he had helped kidnap Ceriba, Reisil severed Kaval from her heart completely, no longer hoping for some rational explanation, something to say that what he'd done wasn't as horrible as it was. She'd not wanted to believe him capable of such evil, but she had to stop letting their past color her judgment. She had to free herself to do what must be done as *ahalad-kaaslane.*

So she said a silent good-bye to the man she thought he'd been. *When we meet again, I will be* ahalad-kaaslane *and you will be nothing more than a brute, a thief of women, beneath contempt, deserving no mercy. I will give you what you deserve.*

Unbeknownst to her, beneath her tunic, the eyes of her gryphon pendant flared red and subsided.

Chapter 14

They overtook Edelsat and rode on into the early-morning hours, until he at last called a halt. When Reisil would have unsaddled and rubbed down her horse, Edelsat took her reins, signaling for his men to do similarly for her companions.

"You have more need of rest than we."

Reisil nodded gratefully, swimming in a thick haze of exhaustion. She went away a few paces and dropped to the ground, curling up in her cloak and falling instantly into oblivion.

Edelsat woke them in the gray light of dawn, handing them each a cold biscuit with sausage and a hard-boiled egg.

"I sent a couple of scouts on ahead," he reported as they set out. "If the kidnappers have left Praterside, the scouts will pick up their trail."

"They haven't," Reisil said. It was the first time she'd spoken that morning, her head feeling as if it were submerged in mud. "According to Saljane, none of them have stirred out-of-doors since last evening."

"That's strange," Edelsat said. "What are they waiting for?"

Reisil didn't answer. She could think of only one reason. Her hands spasmed on the reins and she did not look at Kebonsat. She hoped they would arrive in time to save Ceriba's life.

They rode hard despite the difficult terrain. By mid-morning, they found themselves dropping quickly out of the foothills onto a flat plain of waving green grasses, stirrup-high, and no trees for miles.

"If we keep our pace, we can be there an hour after noon," Edelsat informed Kebonsat when they paused to water their mounts. Edelsat glanced at Reisil with a question in her eyes. She shook her head.

"Saljane has seen nothing of them. They sleep late."

Her lips didn't want to shape the words, for a dread certainty of what must be happening to Ceriba in that inn made her nauseous.

She at last looked at Kebonsat, and though his face remained stiffly unyielding, she saw in his eyes that he was rapidly drawing the same conclusion. He glanced about to each of them, seeking reassurance that it could not be so. Reisil could only give a little shake of her head. Lying would do no good. Sodur laid a hand on Kebonsat's shoulder.

"Let's get moving," he said in an implacable voice. "We have business with these vermin that will wait no longer."

The ride to Praterside seemed endless, though they rode swiftly: now at a gallop, now at a long trot along the wagon track serving as a road.

A gentle hill carried them upward to a vantage point above the dusty town on the edge of a sluggish brown river. Fields of barley and beans skirted the walls on the eastern side of the river. Across the muddy ribbon, shepherds tended red-brindled dairy cows and squat, black-faced sheep. Clinging to the river's edge, cottonwoods and willows sank thirsty roots into the muddy soil.

The place had the appearance of a quiet comfort and gentle coziness. Yet somewhere inside that aura of domestic sanctuary, vicious men did unspeakable things to a helpless young woman.

Reisil felt a raw blade of ice drive down her spine, and fury hardened her jaw. For the first time in her life she wished she knew how to fight, how to hurt. The feeling made her ill.

Needing comfort, she took advantage of their sudden halt to summon Saljane. The goshawk streaked from her perch in the stand of trees.

Reisil held up her fist and Saljane settled onto it, stretching her neck to rub her beak on Reisil's cheek. Reisil returned the affectionate greeting, scratching the dense feathers on the back of Saljane's head.

They had been separated for days and Reisil was stunned at how much she had missed her *ahaladkaaslane*. It was almost as if she'd hobbled along without her sense of smell and now it came rushing gloriously back. Parts of her that had gone stiff and dry with missing Saljane swelled and Reisil's emotions twitched back into balance. The desire to hurt withered and melded into something else: a desire for justice.

She stared into Saljane's amber eyes, their minds touching in agreement and understanding.

~I have missed you, she said.

Pleasure. Fierceness. Love.

"She's marvelous," admired Edelsat, breaking their communion.

"She is, isn't she."

Reisil asked about Ceriba.

~Men move about. Not in a hurry.

Reisil relayed that to her companions.

"I say we set men on both gates and take a small force inside. They aren't expecting trouble. It would be safer for your sister if we took them out quietly, one by one, rather than make a frontal assault. They'll likely slit her throat if they see us coming."

Edelsat spoke bluntly and Kebonsat made a strangled sound in his throat, but gave a jerky nod of agreement.

"We'll need them alive," Sodur said. "Though we believe at least one must be wizard—we can't let that one use his magic."

"Alive?" Edelsat shook his head, looking at his men, who, Reisil realized for the first time, looked sizzlingly angry. "That may not be possible. My men know what this is about and they want blood."

"Make it possible," Sodur ordered flatly. "Without them to confess and identify their masters, we may not be able to stop the renewal of hostilities."

Edelsat stroked his jaw, rubbing his chin into his palm. After several moments he spoke, his deep voice strained.

"A word, Kebonsat. And you, healer. Privately."

He walked away several paces, out of the hearing of their companions. Reisil exchanged a puzzled look with Sodur before following, transferring Saljane to her shoulder as she did.

Edelsat's expression was grim and faintly uncertain. In that moment Reisil realized how young he must be, only a handful of years older than she, probably close in age to Kebonsat. *And we are going to prevent a war,* she marveled. *A few weeks ago I wouldn't have imagined I could do more than set a bone or settle an argument.*

"My father put me and my men under your direct command for the defense of Patverseme," he said to Kebonsat. "Though he ordered me not to reveal this information, I believe it my duty to you as my superior to report all information that might aid in our success." He eyed Kebonsat as if aware that he was cutting the point too fine, and then looked away. "It will explain my father's recent decisions, beyond what he told you. I am revealing this in your presence," he said to Reisil, "for reasons that will become obvious."

"Slippery honor," Kebonsat muttered, and Edelsat's face flushed as he straightened, baring his teeth.

"Maybe so. But careful how you judge." He swallowed, then continued. "Two weeks ago, riders in official messenger livery appeared at our gates. They claimed to bear messages that could only be communicated to my father in private. Being who they were, my father took them into his study immediately. He met with them for fifteen minutes and then they departed.

"After a while, I went in to see what had passed and found my father collapsed in his chair, white as death, eyes blank as the sun. I shook him, but he did not rouse. I shouted and splashed water in his face. At last he came 'round, though I thought he'd been robbed of his mind. He stared without knowing me, and though his mouth worked and spittle ran down his chin, he made no sounds. So it was for more than a day. I did not leave his side. My sisters and brother, my mother, I refused them all entrance. They could not see my father in such a state.

"Night fell on the day after and I was lighting candles. I did not expect him to speak and so when he did, I dropped my taper. It was as if a ghoul from a child's story had spoken in a voice from beyond the grave, cold, empty, far away. He had not yet recovered his wits, or he would not have told me what I am telling you now. Later he made me promise never to reveal it. But I cannot do that. I cannot!" He ran agitated fingers through his hair, pulling hanks of it free from its braid.

Reisil felt a pang of pity for Edelsat, torn between his father and personal honor. She glanced at Kebonsat to see his reaction. The condemnation for Edelsat had disappeared, and now he appeared both curious and concerned. Not for the first time she found herself admiring him—he was not so proud that he would not hear the other side, that he wouldn't set aside his own concerns and open his heart to another man's troubles.

"Messengers will deliver any message, for a price, and are above reproach in their confidentiality. They never disclose secrets. They would die before that—and many have, killed by their own hands or the torturer's.

"They are too expensive to hire for any but for things of the greatest import, so when one appears on your doorstep, you meet with him without delay. Two mean cataclysm, devastation. Gravest tidings. In this case, the two messengers came straight from the bowels of the Demonlord."

Kebonsat's hand fell instinctively on the pommel of his sword and Reisil touched the amulet beneath her shirt. Edelsat drew a ragged breath and continued, his hands dangling against his thighs.

"They told my father that men would be riding through his lands with a woman—your sister—and that he must provide supplies, shelter and horses for them. They explained that she had been kidnapped, that she might ask for succor, and he must refuse. If he did not cooperate, our people would suffer. My father refused them violently and tried to throw them out. They had other ideas. They forced my father into a chair and held him by arcane force. Then one turned insubstantial—wraithlike is what my father called it. He let out a strange call—like a song of deepest yearning—and it was answered by my mother."

Edelsat paused, breathing hard, his face red, tears tracking down his cheeks as he clenched and unclenched his fists.

"My father watched as the messenger-wraith gave him a malignant smile and drew my mother into his embrace, kissing her like a lover, deep and long. Then he let her go, patting her backside as she departed the room. She never remembered she'd come, never remembered what had happened. Nor did I see her enter or depart, though I never took my eyes from the door. Wizardry." He snarled the word, spitting. "They told my father that his wife would serve as his example. If he did not do as he was told, his children and people would suffer the same fate. Then they departed, leaving him as I found him.

"The next day my mother began to get sick. A slight fever. It grew swiftly worse. The next morning she was burning up. She couldn't walk, tripping and falling over nothing when always she had had the grace of a dancer. Her mouth turned white with red blisters. They spread over her face and down her body."

Edelsat made an agonized sound.

"Then her bones began to break. She broke a finger sewing. She tried to laugh it off as clumsiness, but her teeth began to crumble into powder. Father had her put to bed with nurses to tend her. But even the slightest movement—turning her head—would break something."

Edelsat's voice evened out and he spoke like a stone statue come to life. "The stench of her skin rotting on her flesh was like nothing I've ever smelled, or ever hope to again."

"But even so, your father refused them. I saw," Reisil said softly in the silence.

"Aye. He dared not rescue your sister, but he would not harbor such filth either. When you arrived, he committed himself to your aid, knowing what must happen to my mother, our family. You have never seen a man love a woman as much as he loves her. But whatever you think, he knows his honor.

"You wondered, no doubt, why he met you in the courtyard, not inviting you into the keep," he said to Kebonsat. "My father fears the illness will spread. For days, only a few trusted servants and he himself have been allowed to see my mother. He sent my sisters and brother up into the mountains to our hunting lodge. I have been living in the barracks. He has made many offerings to Ellini, to no avail. She does not answer." He turned to Reisil. "He hopes that Amiya might."

Reisil wiped tears from her face and nodded. "I will do my best to bring healing. I hope it will not be too late."

"Thank you—it is all the hope I have. But I tell you this"—he turned back to Kebonsat—"so that you will understand what we face in this battle, and why my father acted as he did."

Kebonsat reached out and grasped the other man's shoulder. "I have misjudged your father. He could have made no other decision. That he chose to aid us at all is evidence of genuine honor. Let us be about our business so that we may bring relief to your family as soon as may be."

It was swiftly decided that Kebonsat, Edelsat, Sodur, Juhrnus and eight other men would make a sortie on the inn, while the rest of the company would be split in two, guarding both gates.

"I shall come with you," Reisil told her companions when they would have left her in the safety of the soldiers. "I will not be gainsaid in this. I am no fighter—I will not try to pretend otherwise. I leave that all to you, and Saljane shall defend me."

She stroked the goshawk's head as Saljane let out a strident *kek-kek-kek-kek*.

"But Ceriba will need me, sooner rather than later. And she may want a woman." She looked at Kebonsat, who paled. But she could not be gentle for him now, not when she must think of Ceriba's welfare first. "You know what Upsakes said he had in mind for her. That they stayed in Praterside as long as they have likely means that they have been at her, with no intention of keeping her alive. If so, Ceriba may not have time to wait for me."

"She is right," Sodur said in his deep voice. "Not only that, but if they know we are coming, they will kill her. Our odds of saving your sister improve if Reisiltark is with us. Time will be of the essence."

"Fine," Kebonsat snapped, his face gray. "But you stay back and out of the way. I'll not have you on my conscience."

They entered the town quietly, like dusty ghosts. At the sight of armed men in tabards of the Houses Vadonis and Exmoor, not to mention the *ahalad-kaaslane,* with Lume trailing at Sodur's heels and Esper and Saljane staring with unblinking eyes, the townspeople retreated into the safety of their dwellings.

The inn lay at the center of the town at the crossroads of the two main streets. It was a ramshackle place, with gray, weather-beaten boards and a squeaking sign sporting a picture of a black sheep's head. Its yard was dusty, though flowers bloomed in pots along the porch skirting around the front. The windows held no glass, and limp muslin curtains stirred in the afternoon breeze. A fountain fed by springwater tumbled from a divided stone pipe, one side running inside to provide water to the kitchen and bath, the other filling a trough.

Without a word, Edelsat led Juhrnus and four of his men around the back, avoiding windows. Kebonsat waited for them to get in place, then led his team through the front, pointing a finger at the pocket doors between the porch and the common room. Sodur nodded and hooked a finger at two soldiers.

Reisil had described each man in careful detail. Three of them were dining in the common room. They were swarmed and knocked unconscious into their trenchers, never having the opportunity to raise an alert. The rest of the patrons eyed the invaders with frightened eyes, pulling belt knives.

"In the name of my father, the Dure Vadonis, and Kaj Mekelsek of House Exmoor, I name these men trai-

tors to Patverseme," Kebonsat declared in a low voice.
"There are three more. Where are they? Innkeeper, answer me now, if you value your life."

Reisil stood just inside the door, pressed against the
jamb as she watched the proceedings with a trembling
stomach. None of the three men was Kaval. One was
the man with the thick paunch and steel-gray hair; next
to him was the smooth-shaven round-faced man with
yellow hair. Across from him was the wheelwright from
Kallas. Where were the others? Reisil glanced up at the
rough wooden ceiling.

"R-r-room at the t-t-top of the stairs, 'nuther at the
end of the hall. Paid good money, they did. I didn't
know!" The wizened innkeeper wailed the last, stumbling away from Kebonsat, who had caught his shirt in
a hard grip and now thrust him away.

But now came shouts and the sound of running feet.
Kebonsat lunged up the stairs with Edelsat and Sodur
fast on his heels. On the landing, the green-cloaked man
leaped into his way and slashed out with his sword. The
air whistled and Kebonsat ducked, falling to his stomach.
Edelsat leaped past before the green-cloaked man could
recover, smashing him across the back with the flat of
his blade. The green-cloaked man grunted and stumbled,
completing his turn and coming around to do battle.

Finally Kebonsat dove beneath his opponent's guard
and sliced him across the chest. The man made a high-
pitched noise, glancing down at the blood welling
through the slit in his jerkin. Edelsat took advantage of
his distraction to club him on the temple with the hilt
of his sword. The man's sword clattered to the landing as
he twisted and fell onto the stairs, sliding halfway down.

Reisil ran forward up the stairs and stepped over the
unconscious man, the healer in her undisturbed by the
blood.

Kebonsat put a shoulder to the first of the two rooms
the innkeeper had indicated. It was empty but for the
furniture, several packs, and a dozen bottles and tan-
kards buzzing with a swarm of black bloat-flies.

Kebonsat took the scene in with a sharp glance, then

moved down the hall on cat feet, followed closely by Sodur and Edelsat, and trailed by Reisil.

Juhrnus put a hand on her arm to restrain her when she would have pressed closer. She gave him a sharp look as she wrenched her arm free, recalling his attempt at watchdogging her in the forest outside of Priede. But he fixed her in place with an unexpectedly stern look.

"You'll only get in the way," he whispered, and she nodded reluctantly. He was right, but the fact that it came from him grated.

Kebonsat arrived at the last door and pressed his ear to the wood. Suddenly there was a scream—unmistakably feminine—and a crash of pottery. He smashed the door off its hinges and charged inside. Only to stop dead. Edelsat knocked into him and the two men stumbled farther into the room. Sodur slid in behind. A musky animal smell drifted out—smoke, food, sweat and sex. Reisil felt herself snarling.

Though her vision was largely blocked, Reisil could see the scar-faced man standing in the middle of the room holding something in his hand at eye level. He was chanting. Behind him a naked, bloody and badly bruised Ceriba struggled with Kaval. Blood ran from a jagged cut in his forehead, dripping over his eyes and down his chin. He cast a wild-eyed look over his shoulder, then went back to subduing Ceriba. He looked like a minion of the Demonlord, straight from the old tales.

The sound of the scar-faced man's voice was mesmerizing, like honey and song on a moonlit night, and Reisil found herself smiling, wanting to sleep. She yawned and her knees began to buckle. Something inside resisted, trying to keep her upright. Fear scuttled over her flesh as that isolated part of her brain realized she could not stop. Edelsat and Kebonsat both lowered their swords, bodies sagging toward the floor.

~*Do not listen,* ahalad-kaaslane! *He is a wizard. Hear me! Close your ears to his voice.*

Reisil stiffened, shaking her head.

~*Ahalad-kaaslane! He uses magic. Do not listen!*

The steel in Saljane's mindvoice cut through the hypnotizing quality of the man's chanting and now Reisil felt his magic roping over her skin with avid tentacles, spreading up her nose and in her ears, gnawing at her senses. She shuddered and looked desperately at Juhrnus. Esper had broken the spell for him as well. He motioned her back and inched forward, his sword ready. But suddenly Sodur stepped sideways from behind Kebonsat and Edelsat and launched his knife at the wizard. The knife sang past the wizard's hand and through his left eye.

He crumpled to the floor with an expression of shock, mouth still open.

Edelsat and Kebonsat shook themselves. For a second all was still. Then they flung themselves at Kaval, tearing him off Ceriba. She screamed again, kicking and biting.

Reisil moved forward, ignoring the body on the floor and Kaval's whimpering cries as Edelsat pinned him by the throat high against the wall. She reached gentle hands out to Ceriba and put her arms around her, holding her tight despite the other woman's wild paroxysm of animal rage.

"Juhrnus, find me sheets and blankets. Clean ones. Sodur—I want another room, with a bath if possible. And clear out the rest of the inn. No one stays here tonight but us."

Reisil gave the orders like a military commander, her voice ringing. The others moved quickly to obey. Kebonsat clubbed Kaval over the head with a snarl of satisfaction and Edelsat dragged him out to the landing, tossing him down the stairs to join his companions.

Reisil crooned to the still thrashing Ceriba, enduring the blows the other woman cast at her. Saljane had leaped away as Reisil had taken charge, and now perched on the windowsill. Kebonsat sheathed his sword. His arms dangled at his sides, hands twitching as if to reach out to his sister, but afraid to frighten her.

"There's a room downstairs by the kitchen. It has a bath. Everyone is outside, including the innkeeper and his family. Here's a sheet. Juhrnus is getting the room ready." Sodur stood well back so as not to frighten Ceriba, and in the hallway Edelsat turned away, eyes hot with emotion.

"Easy, Ceriba. You're safe now. No one else can hurt you. We're going to take care of you. Remember me? I'm Reisil. We met in Kallas. You're safe now." Reisil repeated the litany in a soothing tone, hugging Ceriba to herself. She'd never had to deal with this kind of trauma. Once, a wife raped by her husband—and that had been difficult. But nothing this horrifying, this despicable. But she had to be strong. Ceriba needed her strength.

The fight drained out of the other woman like water out of a sieve. She went suddenly limp, clinging to Reisil's neck, crying in great, rasping sobs. Reisil reached for the sheet and Kebonsat helped her drape it around his sister's bruised shoulders.

"Let's go downstairs now. Out of this room," Reisil's voice roughened with disgust on the last word. "You can have a bath."

Reisil drew Ceriba into the hallway, talking soothingly all the while.

The room Juhrnus had found was unexpectedly elegant and clearly the inn's best. It contained a broad riverstone fireplace along the northern wall. Facing it was an ornate four-poster bed carved from pale ash and hung with heavy cream brocade. A bearskin rug lay between the bed and the fire, the thick fur shielding bare feet from the cold slate tiles. The window looked onto a kitchen garden, peach and pear trees shading the room from the worst rays of the sun. Beneath it stood a desk of the same ash as the bed. Near the door, a pedestal table draped in linen and topped with two silver candlesticks completed the room's furnishings.

A copper bathtub had been placed before the fire and a heavy kettle hung heating on a tripod in the gaping mouth of the fireplace. An ewer stood beneath a sink beside a spigot at the right of the fireplace, and Reisil remembered the piped springwater running into the inn from the fountain outside.

She eased Ceriba over to the bed. Kebonsat stood

against the closed door, staring at his sister's battered form. Reisil tested the water in the kettle—nearly hot enough. She dumped several ewers of cold water into the tub; then, with Kebonsat's help, she emptied the steaming kettle into it as well. They refilled the kettle and rehung it in the fire; then Kebonsat retreated back to the door.

Reisil sat beside Ceriba. The girl stiffened and held herself away, turning her shoulder to hide her face. Reisil stroked her shoulders and hair, feeling Ceriba tremble.

"Would you like a bath?"

Ceriba didn't answer.

"It will make you feel better. To be clean."

After several moments, Ceriba nodded her head, then glanced over her shoulder at Kebonsat. She looked quickly away.

"I want him to go away. I don't want to see him!" Her voice took on a hysterical edge and Kebonsat paled and made a sound of pain.

"He is your brother. Why don't you want to see him?" Reisil queried gently, feeling her way, not knowing if pressing would do more harm than good. "I thought you loved him."

Ceriba sobbed and bent forward so that her head touched her knees. She rocked back and forth, her cries raw and wrenching. Kebonsat fell to his knees before her, reaching out a shaking hand to grasp Ceriba's clenched fist.

"Don't, oh, please don't! I will leave. Anything you wish I will do!" He waited a moment and began to stand, but Reisil stayed him with a hand on his shoulder. Something told her that if she didn't help Ceriba breach her pain now, the other woman might never be able.

As if the shame were hers and not that of those men who'd used her so cruelly.

Kaval.

His name was wormwood in her mind.

"Ceriba, why don't you want to see your brother?" Reisil asked again, her tone gentle but insistent.

"I am not— It would be—" Ceriba broke off.

Finally she drew a harsh breath and sat up, pulling her hand free from Kebonsat's grip, clenching her arms around her stomach. She stared at the fireplace, her bloodshot eyes remote.

"I am no longer intact as a woman. I would not have my brother see me this way. I am worthless, a disgrace to my family, a stain on their honor." She spoke each word in a toneless voice, biting them off with cold precision, so opposite from her agonized crying of a few moments before.

"No!" She and Reisil both started when Kebonsat lunged to his feet.

He pointed at Ceriba, his finger trembling, now with rage. "How dare you think I would judge you ill because of what those bastards did? Do I blame men in battle because they have been stuck through by a sword or pike? Because they were inflicted with grievous wounds and their bodies gave way?

"You have survived a battle like I will never know and torture of the worst kind. You have demonstrated amazing courage. I thank the gods that you live and have all your capacities intact. I feared—" His voice broke and he swallowed, fury burning like cleansing fire in every line of his face. "I feared that my sister would be lost to me forever. So do not, *do not ever,* say again in my presence that you are worthless, or a disgrace, or a stain on our family honor."

His hand fell on his sword hilt and his nostrils flared as he breathed short, heavy breaths. The air rang with his words and it seemed as if all other sound dimmed. Ceriba stared at him in openmouthed shock, stunned by his vehemence.

"You . . . Can you really mean that?" she asked, the desperation and disbelief mixing with hope and tearing at Reisil's heart.

Kebonsat squatted so that he could look at his sister, not batting an eye at her swollen, misshapen nose, her puffy black eyes, her torn lips.

"How could I not? You did nothing wrong. You survived. I prayed for that. How could I be anything but proud of you? You didn't give up and you fought hard.

You are, and have always been, one of the most wonderful, amazing women I have ever been privileged to know." Kebonsat wiped tears from his cheeks. "If any of our family must bear shame, it is we who failed you, who did not guard you well enough."

Ceriba stared at her brother. She started to shake her head, to deny him, Reisil thought: him and the naked love he offered to her.

Then her face crumpled and she clutched at him. He caught her and held her tight against his chest, rocking her back and forth. "I promise that Mother and Father feel the same. They wish only for your return. Mother told me so herself."

At that, Ceriba broke into fresh sobs. She clung to Kebonsat like a lifeline, and Reisil felt anger flare hotly inside her. Somehow that anger felt right, though the healer part of her was appalled that she could contemplate doing anyone harm. But she remembered what she had told the Lady when she argued for Esper's life. Sometimes you have to cut away the disease to make the body whole.

Justice. It must be found.

~She will have it, Saljane said in her mind, her tone echoing Reisil's searing fury. *~We will find it for her.*

Reisil realized then that though her *ahalad-kaaslane* had not followed them into the room, she hadn't left Reisil's mind since the wizard's attack. Reisil reached out to Saljane and felt the goshawk's touch wrapping her like an embrace. She leaned into it, feeling Saljane's delight at such a welcome.

She stood, touching Kebonsat's shoulder.

"She needs to bathe, and then I must see what I can do to heal her body." Kebonsat had already done much to heal his sister's spirit, and for that Reisil was glad. She did not know if she could have done as much.

Kebonsat lifted Ceriba into the tub, turning his back when Reisil removed her sheet. Ceriba sank down into the water, her exhaustion evident now in her sudden bonelessness, her head tilting sideways to rest against the edge of the tub.

At last she felt safe, Reisil thought. Safe enough to

rest, to trust her friends to watch over and care for her. Good. It would make healing easier.

Suddenly she realized that Ceriba's breath had shallowed. Her breaths came in whimpering pants and her body begain to twitch. Fear rippled through Reisil. Had they rescued Ceriba just to lose her?

She turned to Kebonsat and ordered him to retrieve her pack.

"Don't come back until I say so," Reisil told him. He opened his mouth to object and she held up her hand. "It is your sister's life that hangs in the balance and I tell you now, to interrupt might kill us both. Now go. Time is our enemy."

Kebonsat made no further attempts to argue, but retreated instantly, closing the door firmly behind him.

Reisil knelt down beside the tub. Every instinct told her Ceriba was mortally wounded. Reisil suspected that sometime in the last day, one of her captors' heavy kicks or punches had broken a bone and driven it into one of her lungs. They had meant to abuse her and kill her, leaving the evidence on her body to drive her father to revenge, to reignite the war. And they might yet succeed.

Nothing in her pack would aid Ceriba now. Only that limited power the Lady had given her might have an effect. But would it be enough? If Ceriba died, there would be no stopping the war. It would *have* to be enough.

~Saljane, I need your strength.

Saljane enclosed her in that steel embrace again. Reisil drew her pendant out and clutched it in one hand, placing the other on Ceriba's forehead.

"Lady, hear me in my need. Give me aid to heal this woman."

She said no more, but plunged forward with what she could do herself.

With Saljane, she was stronger than she had been and felt great hope as healing magic unfurled into Ceriba. But the damage within was massive. Reisil poured herself and Saljane into mending bone and tissue, with no regard for their safety or survival.

Ceriba's heart flickered wearily and tried to stop. Reisil rushed there and buttressed it with her magic. But as she did, Ceriba's lungs fluttered and drained like depleted watersacks. Reisil divided strength and forced them to fill. But there was more, so much more. Kidneys, spleen, and splintered bones; blood seeping and puddling where no blood should be.

Reisil refused to give up and pull back. Saljane was no less determined and Reisil felt the bird giving herself wholly over to her *ahalad-kaaslane*. If Reisil could have cried, she would have. Such trust, such utter and complete devotion. What a gift the Lady had given her!

She seized on Saljane's strength and threw herself back into the battle with renewed vigor.

The tide began to turn.

She would win, she saw finally. Ceriba would live. She sent a prayer of thanks to the Lady. Ceriba would live.

Even as she rejoiced in that knowledge, Reisil realized that she and Saljane would not survive; they had given too much. Reisil didn't even consider stopping, didn't even consider saving herself or Saljane.

She pushed, pouring more and more of herself and Saljane into the healing, until darkness fell—so complete she could not see through it. It soaked into her, like ink into a dry sponge.

Reisil no longer felt Ceriba beneath her hand, nor Saljane in her mind. Sorrow washed over her, to have that connection torn from her.

"You are such a healer then, that you would murder yourself and your *ahalad-kaaslane* to save a single patient?" The Blessed Lady's voice sounded gravely disappointed, and Reisil knew that as with Upsakes, the Lady had severed her from her *ahalad-kaaslane*. She had proven herself unworthy.

Pain racked her, loss like a driving sword through her heart. Still, Reisil knew she had done right. Even as Upsakes had known? She gave a mental shudder, but did not repent her actions.

"It is true, I am a healer and I would go far to save a patient." She did not feel her body, did not feel her lips move. Her mind seemed adrift in that smothering darkness, sinking deep into a well of sorrow and despair. But she felt she owed the Lady an explanation of why she'd so recklessly spent Saljane's life and her own. "But healers know enough to preserve themselves. I have been well taught by Elutark to protect myself so that I may better serve. But I am also *ahalad-kaaslane,* and on Ceriba's life depends the fate of Kodu Riik. If she dies, there will be no hope for the treaty. You told me yourself that Kodu Riik would not survive without it. If we must die to save Ceriba, to save Kodu Riik, then that is what we will do."

And suddenly Reisil realized that she was no longer pretending to be *ahalad-kaaslane.* Elutark was right. *You are what you pretend to be.*

Maybe she wasn't always brave, or strong, or capable. But she had finally become *ahalad-kaaslane.* She had told the Blessed Lady no more than the simple truth. She hadn't even considered not saving Ceriba. The cost to herself or Saljane didn't matter. Only saving Kodu Riik.

Golden light blossomed in the darkness and she found herself back in the Lady's glade. She sat on the emerald grass, the silver-dusted pillars glowing gold. The Lady stood opposite, stroking Saljane's throat.

Kek-kek-kek-kek.

Tears streamed down Reisil's cheeks and her lips parted in a silly grin as Saljane raised her wings and sailed down to Reisil. Their minds met, sharing, grasping. The Lady's lips curved.

"You speak well," she told Reisil. "I told you that few are capable of receiving both of my gifts—and truly I have not given into your hands their full potential. I needed you to prove your heart first. Come here."

Reisil stood before the Blessed Lady, her eyes wide as she cradled Saljane in her arms. The Lady laid a hand on Reisil's head, crystal talons curving over the young *ahalad-kaaslane's* head, pricking her scalp.

Reisil closed her eyes and magic filled her. Heat and light raveled around and through her like ivy. It sank roots into her flesh, into her bones and blood.

Reisil drew a deep breath and felt tendrils in her nostrils and mouth, in her throat, stomach and lungs. The sensation was not unpleasant.

At last the Lady lifted her hand and Reisil blinked at her.

"I have given you great power—to heal and more. This is a powerful magic I have given you. I trust you to use it wisely—as *ahalad-kaaslane* and tark.

"Heal my land. Heal my children—human and animal. In Kallas, you have not been exposed to the horrors of the war. I believe they twisted Upsakes from his calling. I hope you will be stronger, for there is much to be done. More than you know."

Reisil opened her mouth, but could not find words. Her heart swelled at the magnitude of the trust the Lady had given her, for she understood that at any time she, like Upsakes, could stray down the gray paths to darkness, and the Lady could not recall her gift of power, though she might take Saljane. She had returned Reisil's demonstration of faith with a demonstration of her own. Reisil would not break it.

"A warning. I give this gift to you, but it will be no easy burden to bear. And I can give you no more than this. You have shown yourself to have judgment, to be capable of making the right choices for Kodu Riik and *all her people.*"

Reisil heard the odd emphasis on the last three words, but quickly forgot about them as the Lady continued. "When you go forth from here now, you may not come again. Not in your lifetime, as long or as difficult as that may prove to be. You will have to find your own way."

The Blessed Lady gave Reisil a long, steady look, waiting. Reisil felt herself nodding, though panic flared inside. To be alone, without aid!

"Not alone," the Lady replied to her thoughts. "You have the *ahalad-kaaslane,* and you will find wisdom and aid in other corners."

Before she could speak again, say farewell or give thanks, Reisil found herself back in the inn on the floor beside the tub, Saljane still cradled in her arms. She looked at the bird and couldn't help herself. She laughed, a merry, ringing sound. She looked at Ceriba.

In the light of the setting sun through the window, she saw that the girl slept. The bruises had gone from her face; her broken bones were once again whole. Reisil touched the water. It was cold. Without thought she called for heat and it warmed beneath her hand. She laughed again and hugged Saljane.

A knock sounded at the door and Kebonsat spoke through it.

"Reisil, are you well? May we enter?"

Reisil lifted Saljane to her shoulder and went to the door.

Kebonsat, Sodur, Edelsat and Juhrnus waited outside. They'd pulled a table and chairs close and had eaten. At the sight of the empty dishes, Reisil heard her stomach growl.

"Your face!" Juhrnus exclaimed.

Reisil frowned, touching her face with her fingers.

"What's wrong with it?"

"Blessed Lady," Sodur breathed, stepping forward peer closely at her scars.

"What?"

Sodur shook his head and grabbed a metal platter from the table. He overturned it and held it up for Reisil to look at herself. Her jaw dropped. Where the livid scars had been, now there were veins of golden ivy, leaves unfurling along her jaw to disappear beneath her collar. Reisil touched them with awe.

"My sister?" Kebonsat asked fearfully.

"Turning into a prune. We must get her out of the tub and into bed," Reisil said.

"She will be well?"

"Thank the Blessed Lady, her wounds are healed. Though her mind will take some time to recover—you have already done much to aid her there."

Ceriba woke enough to stand and be guided to the bed. Reisil managed to get her to drink a cup of broth before she fell into a deep sleep. Kebonsat made a pallet on the floor by her bed, determined to be there if she woke with nightmares.

Reisil did not tell him that she doubted Ceriba would have nightmares. She believed the Lady had granted Ceriba a night of reprieve, of true rest. But she knew Kebonsat would not be torn from his sister's side. He needed the assurance of being with her as much as she would need him in the days to come.

She left the siblings alone and went to eat and wash and then find a bed, feeling a shaking exhaustion running through her muscles. During her meal, Juhrnus eyed her every move with awe, particularly unsettling from him, while Sodur merely smiled and patted her shoulder, and then proceeded to vie with Edelsat in entertaining her dinner with tall tales.

Saljane perched on the back of the chair, grooming herself, and Reisil found herself laughing easily, enjoying the banter, her mind twining like ivy with Saljane's.

Chapter 15

Ceriba slept late the next morning, and Reisil found herself drawn to the macabre business of disposing of the wizard's body. Her breakfast sat like a stone in her stomach as she sat well back, watching the proceedings.

Sodur looked down at the dead wizard lying on the dirt, where they had dropped his body to rest after carrying him down the stairs. Sodur's knife still protruded from the man's left eye socket.

"I'm going to need a new knife. I like the look of that one there," he said.

"Bad throw, if you wanted them all alive," Edelsat observed, coming to stand beside him. He kicked the hand that the wizard had held up before him. Even in death the wizard held it tightly fisted. A round bead the color of a rotten apricot rolled out of it. The wizard's focus. Sodur hesitated a moment and then crushed it under his boot.

"Only good wizard is a dead wizard," he said.

"That is a truth well-spoken," Edelsat agreed.

Sodur raised his eyebrows. "I wouldn't have expected that from one of your country."

Edelsat bent and grabbed the dead wizard by the heels. "Many of us find wizardry not to our liking. This only proves why. They heed only the laws that suit them and damn the rest of us. They claim to serve—giving Patverseme great victories in war. But their true ambition is domination—Patverseme, Kodu Riik, Scallas, the world. The Guild's its own country. And who's going to make them do anything but what they damned well please? Mysane Kosk turned many stomachs here. But we got the point. We knew the Guild wouldn't hesitate to come after us.

"That was before Vasalis took the throne. His uncle was weak and greedy. The Guild bought his soul with their promises. But Vasalis isn't the kind to sit on his hands while his country is stolen out from under him. Hence the treaty: no war, no need for the Guild. I wouldn't be surprised if that's what this kidnapping is about. A way to keep the war going and disgrace Vasalis at the same time. What would the popular Dure Vadonis do, I wonder, if his cousin, the Karalis, refused to avenge his daughter and family honor?"

Sodur took the dead wizard's shoulders and helped Edelsat toss him into the back of a wagon. Edelsat's men had built a pyre outside the gates to burn the body, but had been too uneasy to handle the body.

"Surely there are wizards who are better behaved?"

"What the Guild can't control, it destroys. No free wizards allowed. Oh, it used to be different, when there was a balance between the Nethieche and Whieche." At Sodur's questioning look, Edelsat explained, leading the horses. Reisil followed behind, Juhrnus falling into step beside her.

"Guild used to be a balance of two orders, separate but equal. Then the Nethieche decided they wanted more than just half and set about destroying the Whieche. And they were successful. Now that they have full control of the Guild, they mean to have even more."

The wagon rumbled to a dusty halt beside the pile of wood. Edelsat's men and a handful of townspeople milled around, standing well away, as if the dead wizard might carry an infectious disease.

"Give us hand, Juhrnus. Nothing more we can do here, but I'd like to send this one back to his master." Juhrnus started and stepped up to the wagon, gaze fixed on the dead man. Flies crawled over his slack cheeks and into his nostrils, clustering in his ruined eye. Juhrnus's nose flared and his hands curled into fists.

This was his second death, Reisil thought. But he

hadn't really paid any attention to Glevs. He'd been so caught up in his grief and then joy over Esper. Looking at the wizard's body, she felt only malice, thinking of Ceriba's torment. What did Juhrnus feel? Hate? Horror? Fear?

"The boy's got a taste of it," Edelsat murmured to Sodur. "Might be his making."

"I hope so. He's grown up something of a bully, but if he can be turned around, he'll do all right. He's made a start in this last week. This journey has shaken him up. It's a bitter pill to find out the evil men can do, and how much you have to lose."

Juhrnus looked up at the two men, his voice strained but steady. "Handy trick, throwing a knife like that. Suppose you could teach me?"

Edelsat chuckled, and Sodur grinned, slapping Juhrnus on the back.

"You'll do, my boy. You'll do."

"How much farther?" Sodur asked.

Edelsat pointed to the broken hills thrusting up like knucklebones across the northern horizon.

"Through the Bonelands. The Vorshtar plain lies beyond. It curves like a sickle blade around the top of the Dume Griste mountains, stretching nearly to Kodu Riik. You've seen the edges of it near Kallas, where it turns into swampmire and fens before draining into the Urdzina. If we continue this pace, two days to the plain. After that, another day to the Conclave site."

Reisil remembered that day in Kallas when the herald had brought news of the treaty. She remembered the smell of the white hellebore wafting up from the stagnant swamps of Patverseme. An ominous odor. Almost she could smell it again.

Her fingers tightened on the reins and she glanced at Ceriba riding beside her. Kebonsat's sister looked gaunt and she hugged a shroud of brooding silence around herself. Reisil frowned.

They had left Praterside after the wizard's pyre had burned, three days before. Ceriba, her body returned to health and having the situation explained to her, refused to let them wait any longer on her account.

"I will not be the cause of war," she declared in a low, vehement voice to Reisil and Kebonsat. "I will not let them win." The others held their distance, not wanting to frighten her, but were clearly pleased when Kebonsat reported her response. Reisil was impressed by their reaction, given what Kebonsat had told her of the Patversemese treatment of "fallen" women.

She wondered if Edelsat had spoken to them, for he never wavered in his kindness and consideration for Ceriba, treating her much as he might his own sister. Ceriba hardly seemed to notice. She functioned mechanically, rarely speaking. No one was willing to intrude on her thoughts, isolating her even more. Looking at her now, Reisil resolved to breach that wall of suffering at the evening halt.

Edelsat's men treated Reisil with something akin to reverence, a fact that Reisil found disconcerting and annoying.

"Even Juhrnus has taken to being nauseatingly nice," she complained to Sodur.

"You have been touched by the Blessed Lady Herself," explained Sodur, who treated her as he always had. "It is not often that people see the handiwork of the gods so clearly. But you're right. It is a bit flashy. You could try wearing a hood over your head, if that would make you feel better. But then people would likely still point and stare, though be less kind about it."

Reisil found herself chuckling and her mood lightened. Still, when Juhrnus tried to take over the chore of rubbing down her mount that evening, she lost her temper.

"If I had known, growing up with you bullying me every day, that all it would take to turn you into a gentleman was a pretty picture on my face, I'd have painted it on a long time ago," she fumed. "I am no different today than I was yesterday, and if you didn't like me then, then you shouldn't like me now. So stop it or I swear I'll put snakes in your bedroll and bees in your boots."

She glared at him, hands on her hips. He took a step back, his face turning crimson. Then through gritted teeth he said, "I am trying to be nice."

Reisil smiled. "Juhrnus, from you, nice is just letting me be and not teasing me to death. You do that and I will not shout at you again."

His lips quirked unwillingly and Reisil found herself looking at the real Juhrnus for the first time since Esper's near death. Good. He was growing and learning, but becoming another person entirely wasn't healthy either. She wanted—no, needed—for him to be his infuriating self so that she didn't forget herself. She did not want to succumb to delusions of grandeur as had Upsakes.

The Blessed Lady had blessed her with a gift beyond dreams—she couldn't begin to imagine what she could do, and she had told none of her companions about it. She wasn't ready to bear the burden of *that* yet. *Enormous power to heal and more.* What more? Would she become like the wizards? Everything she knew of them was evil. Was it the power that twisted them? Did none of them do anything good with it? Would she turn into someone like Kvepi Buris, killing just to prove she could? Or would the power consume her so that she felt no guilt in slaughtering an entire town? Reisil trembled, fear prickling the hair on her skin.

If she were not to fall prey to such a trap, she must be reminded of her failings. Who better to do that than Juhrnus, who had, from the time she was a child, done nothing but?

"On second thought, Juhrnus, tease me all you want. Just stop treating me like I'm a shadow of the Lady. I am not. Deal?" She held out her hand and Juhrnus looked at it and then back up at her face. His smile widened and he gripped her hand.

"It's a deal, little sister. Better hurry up about that horse, though, or you'll miss dinner. And with your bones poking out of your skin like a scrawny scarecrow, you can hardly afford it."

Reisil smiled, glad for the first time in her life to hear

him call her little sister. She turned back to her horse, hearing the chuckling of the men around her as they unsaddled and set up camp. Relief swept over her in a wave. Maybe that would put an end to their awestruck deference.

"And you wondered why the Lady would choose such a one as Juhrnus," Sodur said to her as he led his horse past. "You need a thorn in your side to remind you of who you are, of the land and people you serve. In time he will grow into a fine man with a temper and passions, but there will always be others who will remind you, as they remind all of us. It is the Blessed Lady's wisdom."

Ceriba endured the trip in silence. She was not used to hard riding, and each night Reisil went quietly through the camp giving healing where she could, beginning with the horses and ending with Ceriba, Saljane ever present on her shoulder.

"You have done enough for me. Saddle sores and blisters—these are nothing." Ceriba's tone was sullen and resentful. Reisil looked at her a long moment and then stretched out her hand to help her up.

"Come with me. I would speak with you alone."

Kebonsat protested for their safety as they departed, but Reisil gave him a quelling look and he subsided.

The wind whistled among the finger bluffs marking the edge of the long valley. The sound was lonesome and mournful and made Reisil's skin prickle.

She led Ceriba on a winding path, well out of earshot of the camp.

"You have not spoken of your ordeal to me or anyone else," Reisil began in a crisp voice. She knew Ceriba would not respond well to pity or softness. "I believe that you are making a mistake, one that will destroy your life."

"Destroy my life?" Ceriba laughed shrilly. "My life is destroyed. No man will have me, nor will I be received in polite circles. I will be a constant embarrassment to my family."

Ceriba spoke bitterly, and Reisil could feel her impotent rage like heat from a fire.

"So do something different," she suggested. Ceriba stopped and stared at her as if she had gone insane.

"Different? There's nothing different to do. I cannot regain my reputation. I cannot regain my virginity. I must trust your word that I am not with child—for all I know they destroyed my ability to do that, too. Not that it matters."

Reisil sat down on a rock and stroked Saljane, who rode on her shoulder.

"Your life is not over because the path turned from where you thought it would, or should, go. Hear me out," she said when Ceriba would have interrupted her. "I have not experienced what you have. But I have had my life changed drastically. I had a choice to make also: Embrace the new path or don't, and live with the consequences. My consequences were you—if I did not embrace Saljane, you would have died, and Kodu Riik and Patverseme would certainly suffer another long, bloody war, with horrors to the lands and people that I do not even care to imagine. I chose Saljane. It has been painful. But I would not have done it differently.

"You say you have nothing else to do. I have a proposition. You have been roughly used, and though your body has healed, your mind has not. If you go home, I imagine your life will be as you expect and you will become something twisted and bitter, no matter how much your family loves you.

"But you have another option, a path of purpose and hope. I believe that you must take control of your life from those who love you, even as you must from those who kidnapped you. Only in this way will you save yourself, and I think your family. Watching you suffer would be terrible, and might very well destroy them from within." She paused. "You are no delicate flower that you cannot flourish in another place, despite what has happened.

"I suggest you go to my old teacher and mentor—Elutark. She has need of a new student, and what is more, she will help you come to terms with what has happened. In time you will grow strong again. No one turns away a tark; no one snubs or insults a tark. You will walk amongst people with pride again, instead of with your head bowed as you do amongst us. You will help people, and I promise you that it will give you joy. I know it is not the life you would have chosen for yourself, but it is a better choice than the one you foresee, is it not?"

Reisil stopped, her tongue caught between her teeth. She had rehearsed this speech for days, knowing that Kebonsat would rage at her when he found out. But she believed to the soles of her feet that this was a good choice for Ceriba—one that would allow her to heal and to feel capable and in control again. She was gratified to see that the other woman was thinking about it.

Ceriba paced away, her arms folded tightly across her chest. She strode back and forth, tears streaming down her face. Reisil waited, knowing this was a decision only Ceriba could make. The minutes ticked back. The other woman's face contorted and her breath came in short, coughing rasps.

"I will see my family again, won't I?" Ceriba's hands clung together, white knuckled.

"Of course. They may visit you during your training, and you go where you like after. Training is not prison, and Elutark is a gentle taskmaster."

Ceriba licked her lips, scuffing at the dirt with the moccasin-boot Reisil had given her.

"You think I can do it?"

Reisil smiled, saddened by the uncertainty and self-doubt in Ceriba's voice. She remembered such a different woman in Kallas, one who was self-assured and decisive, confident of herself and her world. But that woman had disappeared.

"I do. I would not suggest it otherwise."

"And Elutark will want me?"

"I think so."

Ceriba resumed her pacing, her breath growing steadier. She stopped again in front of Reisil. She licked her lips. She began to speak, but her voice wouldn't come. She cleared her throat, trying again.

"I'll do it." Her voice broke on the last word, and she pressed her hand to her lips, her chin quivering.

"Good. Meet me at the gates of Kallas two weeks from the end of this mess, and I will show you the way."

"You're not— How will I get to Kallas?" Ceriba's voice turned high and frightened. Reisil squeezed her hand.

"I have to return to Edelsat's home at all speeds. There is grave illness there. And you must take the first steps yourself. You must learn your own strength and commit to this wholely. Your family will fight your decision and it must be you, not I, who bids them farewell and walks away. It is you who must take the path. I will help you find the way."

"I don't know. . . ."

Ceriba sank down beside Reisil and Reisil put her arm around the other woman's shoulder. It was a hard thing to ask, so soon after her awful ordeal. But Ceriba must take those steps herself. Between now and then she would be sorely pressed to remain with her family. There was no doubt in Reisil's mind that staying would cripple Ceriba forever. Living with Elutark and learning to be a healer would give her the opportunity to regain her confidence and sense of independence. But only if Ceriba chose that path.

"You think about it. I'll be waiting outside Kallas for you. Now we'd better get back."

They encountered Kebonsat halfway. He cast Reisil an inquiring look and she shrugged.

"I was explaining to your sister that I must heal all hurts—large or small—if we are going to reach Vorshtar in time to do any good. So she will have to put up with my ministrations until then."

As Reisil left them together and returned to the camp, she averted her head from the prisoners, bound to the wheels of a wagon. The first night of their jouney, Kaval had tried to speak to her. Wanting, she supposed, to explain. As if he could. But just hearing his voice conjured the memory of him grappling with Ceriba, his hands smeared with her blood. The recollection turned Reisil's stomach. She could not see him. Not yet, not without wanting to kill him.

Two days later, they emerged from the aptly named Bonelands. Before them spread the Vorshtar plain. It filled the horizon north and east, while the proud reaches of the Dume Griste mountains dwindled away to undulating hills in the west. Green and gold grasses rippled in the summery breeze, making the prairie lands resemble nothing more than a vast, verdant ocean.

"Where to now?" asked Juhrnus.

Edelsat pointed, shading his squinting eyes with the other hand. "Over there, at the old Conclave site, on the banks of the Trieste River. A long time ago, warlords met there to parley. It was sacred. Clerics would mark off a space and whoever entered was guaranteed safe passage. Their conclaves lasted sometimes for months. Good water, grazing and hunting." He glanced at Kebonsat and then back to Juhrnus. "See those smudges? Smoke—a lot of fires."

"Big armies," Sodur commented.

"I didn't know they could gather so fast," Reisil said.

"The troops and horses were well rested from the truce. I doubt much infantry has arrived. These will be cavalry units," Kebonsat said. "Some of those people will be support staff."

"We can't just walk in. By now they'll know something went wrong. They'll be looking for us."

Edelsat glanced at the prisoner wagon, guarded by six of his men.

Reisil followed his gaze and found Kaval staring at her. He'd not tried to speak to her since that first night, but his eyes followed her constantly, pleading. She still carried the scarf he'd given her the day before he left in the bottom of her saddlebags. Every time she touched it, she felt dirty. A reminder that she wasn't yet done with him. Sooner or later she would have to confront Kaval, to quit him face-to-face.

"Let's go closer and get the lay of the land," Edelsat suggested. "As many of us as there are, and armed, we shouldn't stand out."

"What about them?" Kebonsat gestured at the prisoners.

"I'll take care of them. They'll be no trouble," Reisil declared flatly, flexing her fingers on her reins. "We'll just want something to cover them with."

"Or my men could knock them out," Edelsat offered quickly, frowning.

Reisil shook her head, grateful for his concern for her welfare. "If I put them out, they won't wake again until I want them to. If you bash them on the head, we won't be sure." She shrugged, feeling faintly disgusted with herself that she didn't particularly care for the harm that might be done to Kaval and his companions if Edelsat's men cracked their heads. Her only concern was seeing the treaty signed and the war averted.

"You're certain? My men wouldn't mind."

Reisil glanced at the grim-faced men guarding the wagon. They had made no secret of their loathing for their charges. Indeed, they would not mind the opportunity to get some revenge on Ceriba's behalf.

"No, it's better this way."

Edelsat was unabashed and gave her a friendly grin, which she returned. She liked him. He had an easy way about him, though he commanded quick respect from his men. He was thoughtful, clearheaded and compassionate, though she had no doubt that on the battlefield Edelsat would strike fear into the hearts of his opponents. He and Kebonsat had spent many hours over the last days discussing strategies for what to do next. Listening to them, Reisil learned a great deal about strategy and tactics, about how armies worked and about politics.

"It's like a maze—there's so much to know and so much of it seems silly and arbitrary," she had complained to Sodur.

He laughed. "It is why you must go to Koduteel for training. The wheels of power turn on the silly and arbitrary, petty jealousies and bitter grudges."

Now the group dismounted and prepared a simple lunch while Reisil set about the task she'd assigned herself. In an odd way, she looked forward to it. Not just to finishing things with Kaval, but to having an active part in bringing them all to justice.

Before she began, she retrieved the scarf from her pack. When she approached the wagon, Edelsat's men stepped aside with a deference that made her flush. She climbed inside, wrinkling her nose at the smell. She turned to Kebonsat, who waited nearby.

"They need to be washed. I can put them to sleep, but that stench will speak volumes."

He nodded. "I'll speak with Edelsat. Will you be all right?" His glance flicked to Kaval, who stared at Reisil with greedy intensity.

"I will. I have some unfinished business here, and I'd like to get it over with." He gave a knowing look at the scarf bunched in her fist and nodded again, scowling.

"Remember where the blame lies. It is not your burden to bear," he said in a gentle voice that belied his expression. Then he walked away, leaving her alone with the prisoners.

Before any could speak, she laid two fingers on the forehead of the closest man—the cartwright from Kallas. His eyes closed and he sagged over. The other men began to cry out and squirm, but Reisil quickly touched her fingers to each of them and soon they all slumped in unnatural sleep, all but Kaval.

He stared at her, his vivid blue eyes desperate and hopeful. Reisil felt herself harden, even before he spoke, seeing that hope. As if he could charm her, make her overlook what he'd done.

"Reisil, you must let me explain. Please!" His voice was thick and hoarse. Fury kindled inside her as she remembered how wonderful he had made her feel, how special, whispering in her ear in the dark. Her lips flattened. She wanted a bath.

"What could you say, Kaval? Did you like hurting Ceriba? Did you like beating and raping her?" Reisil's lip curled and tears burned her throat. "In all the time

I knew you, I never saw it. Never saw how cruel, how evil you could be. Did you hide it so well? Or was I just stupid, too infatuated, to see the real you?"

He shook his head, groaning softly as he did. "It wasn't like that. I didn't want to. I didn't like it. But it had to be done. It was the only way to stop the treaty. You don't know about the war. Not really. I saw, going to Koduteel—" He swallowed thickly, his lips swollen and bruised from the "care" of Edelsat's men. "The treaty will destroy Kodu Riik. We could still stop it, you and me. That mark on your face—you're *ahalad-kaaslane* now. We could do it." He craned his neck up eagerly.

"Yes. Yes, I am." Reisil took the scarf he'd given her and put it around his neck, tying it securely. "That's why I am here. To put right what you have made wrong. There is no excuse, no reason in the world, that would justify what you've done." She blinked away a tear. "I thought I might love you. I thought you might love me. But I was wrong, about so much."

"And you're wrong about this—the treaty must not happen!" Kaval insisted, the hope in his eyes turning to fear. Reisil shook her head.

"I have learned much on this journey. I trust in and I am guided by the Blessed Amiya, in this and all things." She stopped, an ironic expression on her face. "I don't want to do this, and I don't like it, but it has to be done," she said, in a conscious echo of his words a few moments before. "Now you must go to sleep, and when you wake, you will have the chance to confess and undo some of the harm that you've done before you pay the price. But I don't think you can ever pay what you owe."

Her voice was thick and shaking. She looked away for a moment, and then back. "Think about that, and pray to the Lady for guidance."

With that Reisil put her fingers on his forehead and he slumped, asleep.

By nightfall they had trundled several leagues into the plain, trailing behind them a dark vein of bruised and bent grasses.

"Not much we can do about it. We'll double the watch. We won't have to put guards on the prisoners anymore. That will keep us fresher," Edelsat said to Kebonsat as they considered making camp.

Far ahead, thousands of campfires flared like stars along the horizon as the sun dipped beneath edge of the world.

"I never imagined . . . How many are there?" Juhrnus said softly.

"Between the two armies? At least eight thousand, no doubt with more arriving every day," Kebonsat answered, his voice expressionless.

Reisil shivered, thinking of the death the two massed armies could unleash on each other.

"There's a hut." One of the outriders had returned and spoke to Edelsat. Edelsat looked at Kebonsat, his eyebrows raised. "We've got to wash them somewhere. There's bound to be a creek or spring close by. Couldn't live out here otherwise."

At Kebonsat's nod of assent, Edelsat motioned for the outrider to lead the way.

To call the decrepit shack a hut was generous. It was a windowless box made of grass bound in bunches and tied together. Smoke drifted from a hole cut into the roof. The entire construction kilted sideways on the verge of falling down, held up, it seemed, by a stake of twisted wood that formed a doorpost, to which was fastened a grass door. Alongside the hut was a makeshift chicken coop, and beside it a garden, overgrown with weeds, the tomatoes and beans looking woebegone while the corn appeared stunted.

At the sound of so many riders in the cupped-out hollow, the door opened, revealing a dim orange glow and a cloud of black smoke smelling of burned grass. A sallow, nervous woman stepped forth, closing the door behind her. She stood with arms crossed over her breasts, her eyes wide and staring, her lips flat and bloodless.

Kebonsat dismounted. "Bright evening, madam. We have need of water and a campsite for the night."

Before he could go further, she began to shake her

head, her snaggled teeth biting off every word. "No. You must move on. There's nothing here for you."

But then there was a shout as Edelsat's men found the spring.

"I'm afraid we must insist," Kebonsat said gently, seeing the woman's fear. "We'll not harm you. And we will pay a fee for the use of the land and spring."

The last caught the woman by surprise and she wavered. And no wonder, Reisil thought, as pitifully poor as she obviously was. Then she gave an ungracious nod and withdrew inside, closing the door firmly behind her.

Kebonsat led the way around back to the spring, which lay farther down in the basin of the hollow. Reisil marveled. The Vorshtar plain looked flat, but its tall grasses hid a surprising variety of terrain.

As they set up the camp and prepared dinner, the prisoners were unloaded. The springwater ran in a tiny rivulet down into the grasses and Edelsat had several of his men sluice them clean, not bothering to remove their clothing.

"It'll help some, but when it gets hot, they'll start to cook and smell again," he warned Kebonsat.

"It will be long enough. By noon we should reach the edge of the camps. Father said we had eight days. That means the summit between Iisand Samir and Karalis Vasalis will happen tomorrow or the next day."

"We should split up," Reisil said suddenly. Sodur nodded, his mind jumping ahead of hers. She continued. "Sodur should head directly for Iisand Samir, tell him what's happened. As *ahalad-kaaslane,* no Kodu Riikian will hinder him. And"—she looked first at Kebonsat, then Ceriba—"he should take Ceriba with him. She'll be safer. The Guild will have a harder time getting to her in the Kodu Riik camp. Meantime, we should get the prisoners to your father," she said to Kebonsat. "Juhrnus can go with Sodur—Esper can see farther in the wizard dark with the aid of torches. I can guide the rest of us when the wizard night falls."

"You sound certain it will," Edelsat said, his expression faintly skeptical.

"I am. It will." She did not explain further, but Edelsat accepted her certainty and exchanged a glance with Kebonsat. Kebonsat looked strained.

"I don't like it."

"But she's right," Ceriba said in a low voice. "You know it. Besides, they know their plan failed. They'll be expecting you and will try to stop you. I'll be safer with Sodur—they won't know where to look for me—and you won't have to worry about protecting me."

"And if we should fail, we'll still have a knife in our boot," Edelsat reasoned. "So long as your sister gets to the Iisand before the heavens fall, the war might be prevented. Even if we don't make it."

Kebonsat gritted his teeth, his jaws bunching as he stared at the ground. Then he nodded. "Then so be it."

"We'll leave tonight," Sodur said. "As soon as we have eaten and the horses have rested. The sooner we can get there the better, and if anyone is following, they might not realize you are three less."

Two hours later, Kebonsat hugged his sister and helped her mount.

"Take care of yourself," he told her, holding her hand in both of his. "Don't get into trouble."

She bent and kissed his cheek, saying something in his ear Reisil couldn't hear. Each of the three riders had torches strapped to their saddles. The waning moon cast shabby light, but it was enough to see by and they waded out into the grasses, Sodur in the lead, then Ceriba, and Juhrnus bringing up the rear.

The others bedded down as Edelsat set the watch. Reisil, however, felt edgy and itchy, like ants crawled beneath her skin. She paced into the darkness, starting at the sounds of crickets and the nickering of the horses to one another, her head twisting and turning as if to catch an elusive sound.

"What is it?" Kebonsat stood beside her, his breath warm on her cheek. He sounded tense, pushed to the edge. Ceriba's going had been difficult for him. He was torn between protecting her and preventing the war, between the duties of a brother and the duties of a knight.

The knight won out, but everything he was rebelled at rescuing his sister only to let her go without him into danger.

Reisil shook her head. "I don't know. Something, I—"

She walked away, every sense straining in the darkness. Kebonsat followed, drawing his sword. Reisil headed up the hollow and found herself outside the hut. She circled around it, running her hand over the wall, coming around the corner and startling the chickens into a cackling fervor. She halted at the door.

"What's going on?" Edelsat materialized out of the night, his own sword drawn, his voice low and tense. Kebonsat shook his head and pointed silently at Reisil, Saljane perching quietly on her shoulder.

She ignored them, drawn by something she couldn't understand. It was as if something had taken over her body. Panic roared in her chest and she struggled against the geas on her limbs, to no avail. What demon had taken control of her? She could not even make her *ahalad-kaaslane* hear her.

She reached out to the door.

It resisted a moment; then she felt a tearing as the grass catch gave way. She stepped into the rectangle of dirty orange light. The woman sat up on her pallet and made a choked, frightened sound. Reisil wanted to comfort her, but couldn't. Was the woman right to be afraid? What was Reisil, or the thing controlling her, going to do here?

Kebonsat crowded up behind Reisil and peered past, ready to thrust her aside in case of danger.

A fire made of twisted grass smoked in the center of the dwelling. On either side of it two pallets lay. On one lay a man, staring sightlessly upward, while the woman huddled on the other, grasping two children close. They looked pale and sick, bones thrusting sharply beneath their skin.

But Reisil hardly saw them. Instead she went to stand over the man, who still didn't move. One hand lay over the blankets on his chest; the other . . . The other was gone, as was his arm. There was a rushing sound in Reisil's ears and the feeling beneath her skin increased to an unbearable pitch, as if swarms of insects wiggled and gnawed.

She knelt heavily, as if a hand on her shoulder pushed her down. She put her hands out, curved like claws. A sound tore through her constricted throat as she tried to pull back, but the compulsion was too strong.

The woman made a wrenching motion, then clutched her children closer.

"Don't . . . Don't hurt him! He ain't done nothing to you. War's over—go away!"

Reisil looked at her and the woman gasped. For the first time she saw the mark the Lady had set on Reisil's face. It glowed, and the green of her eyes overflowed into the whites, filling her eyes from corner to corner.

Gold light dropped from her fingers, splashing on the man's face and chest.

He moaned and wheezed, rocking in place. The woman made a keening sound and gave a shriek when Reisil's hands flattened against her husband's chest. The gold from Reisil's hands ran over the man, covering him from head to toe until it wrapped him like a burial shroud. The pattern on her face streamed over her body until every inch of her skin was patterned with glowing, golden ivy. It didn't stop there, but twined upward over Saljane. The bird mantled and gave a shrieking cry.

Then, like a blown candle, the light disappeared.

The woman sobbed piteously, and her children joined her.

Released suddenly, Reisil staggered to her feet and toward the door. Neither Kebonsat nor Edelsat moved, and she realized they couldn't see her. Kebonsat felt her stirring in the air and brought his sword up.

"Reisil?"

"It's me. Let's go."

Reisil pushed between the two men and stumbled out of the hut, gasping for breath. Her lungs felt seared. All of her strength was gone with the Lady. For she had no doubt now that the Blessed Amiya had possessed her. She retreated to the camp and rolled up in her cloak, her mind reeling. Saljane nestled beside her, fierce amber eyes shining in the firelight. Edelsat and Kebonsat followed more slowly, as silent as Reisil.

Reisil fought the exhaustion that dragged at her. What had happened? Why had the Lady thrust Her hand into Reisil like a puppet?

~We serve.

Saljane's mindvoice carried with it a shrug. There was no accounting for the gods.

Comforted by her *ahalad-kaaslane*'s diffident acceptance, Reisil relaxed and fell asleep.

Edelsat roused the camp two hours before dawn.

"Make haste, lads," he called out softly. "Time's wasting." He nudged Kebonsat and jerked his chin toward Reisil. Kebonsat nodded and went to kneel before her as she struggled upright, yawning widely. He watched as she combed out her hair and rebraided it.

"We've got to do something about Saljane. With her, you clearly stick out as *ahalad-kaaslane*. We won't make it far once someone spots her."

Reisil nodded, her brow furrowing. "She can't fly— even if it weren't dark, and she could stay aloft all day, I'll need her with me."

"You could settle her in your lap beneath your cloak," Kebonsat suggested doubtfully. "Won't be comfortable for her and it's going to get hot. You'll have to be careful not to let your cloak fall open. As it is, you're going to get attention for being a woman. Dressed as you are, with that face—you're going to be conspicuous. Patversemese women don't go about in trousers, riding horseback with a troop of soldiers." He paused, thinking. "We could take advantage of that. Put you on the wagon seat. Especially with your face, you'll look like a—" He broke off, his cheeks flushing.

"A whore. Camp follower," Reisil finished with a wry grimace. "Perfectly natural. All right. Let no one say my pride got in the way of stopping the war. Saljane can ride under the seat. Just make sure one of you claims me in case anyone asks."

And ask they did.

With the gold ivy running teasingly from her face down into her tunic, tanned skin, jet hair and snapping green eyes, Reisil looked exotic and mysterious. The past weeks had given her body a lithe quality, as well as a sense of confidence, both of which translated into alluring boldness.

As they entered the sprawling perimeter of the Patverseme army, Edelsat's men formed a protective wedge around the wagon. Otherwise they would have made little headway at all against the eager admirers who sought Reisil's company, some waving pouches of silver, others singing songs and bragging of their physical prowess and stamina. Though some had wives or mistresses amongst the camp followers, most were lonely for companionship. Reisil never responded to their hails, merely smiling enigmatically. But if the interest didn't affect her, the coarse attention infuriated Kebonsat and Edelsat, both of whom grew more and more wrathful.

"I'm fine," Reisil soothed quietly as Kebonsat rode beside her, his face brick red. "They're supposed to think I'm a whore. The plan is working." She was more amused than anything else.

"They are unruly pigs. If they were mine, I'd stake them out for a day." Reisil gave him a startled look, surprised at his vehemence. Then understanding hit her.

"These aren't like the men who had Ceriba. Most of these are harmless. If I said no, I'd be all right."

"It has nothing to do with my sister," Kebonsat said in a contemptuous voice; then he jerked his horse away, spurring him to the front of the line. She stared after him, frowning. Soon he'd increased their pace so that Reisil's would-be lovers were in danger of being run down if they tried to approach.

Traveling through the massive sprawl of soldiers, dogs, horses, camp followers, even families, was like wandering through a small city where the roads changed constantly with no landmarks to guide them. They had concluded that the command and royal tents would be somewhere near the Enclave Point along the Trieste

River, but getting there was no easy task. They snaked through the bustling menagerie at what seemed to Reisil to be an ambling snail's pace. The tension began to show as Edelsat's men exchanged angry words with onlookers. It didn't help that they'd removed any hint of their house connections to avoid detection. And it was good they had, for several times strangers stopped to study their passage with an intent air.

Several were wizards, Reisil realized, after Edelsat pointed out the three-pointed, twisted silver pins they wore on their collars. Kvepi Buris had worn such a pin. None were women. Reisil wondered if women were forbidden power in Patverseme, or if the magic never rooted in them. She hoped so. It made her less like the wizards.

"Won't do any good if we're too late," Kebonsat observed to Edelsat in a frayed voice after they were forced to stop, trapped on either side by tents and campfires, while in front of them on a makeshift parade ground, a squad of men mustered. They ignored the travelers haughtily, while a young knight, wearing chain mail with a tabard of yellow and red and a fox head in blue over his heart, bawled orders. There was no turning around in the cramped space, and it might be hours before the arrogant young lordling was content to let them pass.

"I'm getting very tired of this."

"We'll lose any chance of secrecy," Edelsat warned.

"And if we don't get moving, we'll still be nicely incognito when the war breaks out again. I'll be damned if I let them get away with what they've done to my sister."

"Ceriba will tell them."

"If she made it. If they listen to her. But they stole her credibility when they kidnapped her. You know how they'll treat a virtueless woman." Kebonsat's lips twisted and he spat. "On top of that, she's in the company of *ahalad-kaaslane*, which won't do much for her credibility with the Patverseme court." Kebonsat shook his head. "I don't think we can chance it."

"No choice for it then," Edelsat said, signaling his

men. They dug in their packs and donned their wrinkled tabards, pulling muffling rags from their horses' breast-plates and bridles.

"Guidon!" Edelsat shouted in a hearty voice. A red-headed man, younger than Reisil, detached himself from the formation. He fished a two-inch-wide band out of his hip pouch and worked it up over his right biceps, pulling it tight with his teeth. It bore a divided green-and-yellow background with the star and crossed-swords devices of Edelsat's house. He stopped beside the wagon, giving Reisil a fleeting smile as he drew a pole from its moorings along the wagon's side. He unrolled the attached standards. Edelsat had had Kebonsat's added on top, showing an alliance of the two houses. The red-haired soldier seated the butt of the pole in the pocket of his stirrup designed for that purpose and urged his chestnut gelding out in front. In the meantime, Edelsat and Kebonsat had donned their tabards.

The guidon rode forward into the muster, flanked by two of Edelsat's men. They halted in front of the young lordling, the standards flapping in the breeze. Reisil smiled as she saw the lordling look at the outriders' coat of arms with an expression of disdain. When he glanced up at the standards, however, he blanched, casting a frightened look at Kebonsat, who merely stared, rubbing his thumb along his stubbled jaw.

Quickly the young lordling waved his men out of the way and their procession began again, this time much more quickly as word spread ahead like wildfire. Kebonsat's journey to find his sister had not been kept as secret as it was supposed to be, and now onlookers looked vainly for signs of Ceriba.

Reisil wondered how many hoped he had found her, hoped the war could be averted. She wondered how many desired the opposite. She looked ahead, standing and shading her eyes to see how much farther they had to go.

Too far.

The wizard night swept over them like an ebony blizzard.

Reisil stiffened as pandemonium erupted. She heard

screams and yells, horses neighing, dogs howling. Men and animals scrambled, sightless eyes wide with fright. A nearby tent caught fire, the people inside pulling it down into the flames of the cookfire.

The stench of burned canvas and food swelled in the suddenly still air; then flames swept to another tent and another. The wagon lurched as the team of horses reared and lunged.

Reisil fell sideways, scrabbling at the sides for balance. Seeing the ground rushing up at her, she tucked and rolled. She sat up, rubbing her shoulder with a grimace. It wasn't broken, and neither was her head.

She looked around. Chaos reigned.

Chapter 16

"Torches! Torches!" Kebonsat bellowed, and Edelsat's men responded by lighting those they carried, but still they could see barely a foot before them. The horses could see not at all and shuddered all over, neighing their fright. The driver of the wagon had wrestled his terrified team to a halt, but sat as if frozen, hands clenched on the reins, all senses alert, waiting.

Reisil approached, thanking the Blessed Lady that Edelsat's men had not panicked.

"Dashlor—it's me."

The thick-chested soldier started, head swiveling back and forth.

"Healer?" he whispered.

"Give me a second." Reisil grabbed one of the torches that she'd put in the footbox of the wagon and struck her flint to it. In a few moments the pitch-soaked end flared and she touched another to it. She handed it to Dashlor. He did not see it until it was well within arm's reach. The relief on his sweating face was palpable.

"Stay here. I'm going to get Kebonsat and Edelsat," she said.

~*Come with me, Saljane. There's no use hiding anymore.*

She reached down and freed her *ahalad-kaaslane*. Saljane flexed her talons convulsively on Reisil's shoulder. Even with the gauntlet's padding, Reisil winced.

~*Use my eyes.*

She felt Saljane explode into her mind, though the

disconcerting doubling effect she'd come to expect when she went into Saljane's mind wasn't there.

~How are you doing that? No, never mind. Tell me later.

No longer blind, Saljane relaxed her grip.

The cacophony was growing louder and more discordant as men shouted, crying out to one another, seeking friends and enemies alike in the darkness. More than one shot off random arrows into the melee, or struck blindly with pikes, thinking the camp under attack. Their shocked targets screamed throat-tattering screams. She heard many others cursing the Guild with a ferocity that made her bones shake.

To a man, all of Edelsat's soldiers now held torches. Each sat tensely aboard his horse, faces drawn, waiting for orders. Their discipline astounded Reisil. Though the wizard night had been described to them, none could have imagined such complete, smothering darkness and helplessness. Still they did not break ranks or bumble about foolishly. It was no wonder Mekelsek had managed to carve out a title and holdings for himself, commanding such soldiers.

She made her way to where Kebonsat and Edelsat stood facing off in different directions some twenty feet apart, both pale and quivering on a knife edge, waiting for Reisil. As she approached, Edelsat called for his men to sound off.

"I'm here," Reisil announced, coming to stand between them as the last of Edelsat's men shouted out his name. The two men started at the sound of her voice, peering futilely into the darkness in search of her.

"You can see," Kebonsat affirmed, his mouth pulled into a grimace.

"Yes. But they mean to stall us, perhaps provoke fighting between the two armies," said Edelsat. "If they can get the war started again, we don't matter."

"It's a good tactic. But we're going to do better," Kebonsat pronounced, then swung down off his horse, followed by Edelsat, who looked suddenly unsure.

They reached out their hands and Reisil clasped them. "Let's group up. Reisil, you lead. The rest of us will cluster around the wagon—see if we can put together sufficient torches to light a path for the wagon team," Kebonsat said.

Reisil held each man's strong, callused fingers laced between her own, calling out warning of obstacles. She gathered each of Edelsat's men in turn and soon she had a wake of men and horses trailing behind her in a chain of hands and torches. They gathered at the wagon, deciding quickly to release the riding horses.

"They'll only get in the way. If this cursed night raises, we'll find more," Kebonsat said. "Throw the packs in the wagon. Stretch a couple of ropes out front. Reisil will use them to guide us."

She took point, feeling like the lead goose in a flock flying south for winter. Behind her on either side came Edelsat and Kebonsat, followed by Edelsat's men like beads on a string, each carrying torches low enough to see the ground, if only just a step or two before them.

They pressed forward through the riotous insanity of the encampment. Several times they were forced to stop abruptly to avoid crazed horses and madmen waving swords in blind, berserk fury. Other times they were forced to beat back attacks by terrified soldiers believing the enemy had come among them.

Edelsat's men responded bravely, but their pace was excruciatingly slow, and several men were wounded. One man had to be lifted into the wagon. Reisil dared not stop to heal him, fearing the passing of time, fearing what might be happening at the Enclave. Worse, she didn't know if she were taking them in the right direction.

Edelsat encouraged her, his voice tight, half-strangled in his throat. Kebonsat remained silent and she could feel his stillness like the heart of a tornado. He strained himself at the darkness, seeking any hint of attack, his body taut. Reisil realized that while she might doubt herself and her sense of direction, Kebonsat did not. He trusted her so absolutely that he had turned his attention to watching, obeying her commands with blind obedience.

The cacophony stopped.

All around her, Reisil could see the mad dashing of people, the barking, howling dogs, the squealing horses, burning fires, screaming camp followers, shouting men, men whimpering and cringing on the ground—but she could hear none of it.

A glance over her shoulder at her bewildered companions and her stomach began to curl in dread.

"What's happened?" Kebonsat asked in an undertone.

"Trouble."

All around them space began to grow as if an invisible force pushed outward, thrusting away interlopers, and creating an island dome of black silence.

"I think we've got company," Reisil whispered.

Then instinct grabbed her and she dropped the rope and ducked behind Edelsat, shifting Saljane to her fist. Wizards were coming and she didn't want them to see her. Maybe if they didn't know she was there, didn't know she could see them, she might have an edge. She whispered as much to Edelsat, who nodded, his face bleak as he waited with the patience of helplessness.

"Young Kebonsat. You have returned, and nearly in time. But where, might I ask, is your precious sister? And what have you in that wagon?"

Reisil recognized the smooth contralto voice, rich and cloying as butter sauce. She shivered. Kvepi Buris.

He had stepped out of the melee and into the bubble of black silence followed by another man in a coweled robe of flowing saffron. He was staring at something cupped in his hands, his lips moving in a mumbled chant.

Kvepi Buris looked as Reisil remembered—fragile, with stooped shoulders and long, limp fingers. His long black beard and hair hid much of his face, emphasizing his pale skin and yellow jasper eyes, his large black pupils like infinite wells of malignancy. He smiled scarlet lips, showing teeth that were gray and shiny like poisoned pearls. He wore the long crimson robes she remembered from Kallas.

"Well, young Kebonsat? You have gained new companions, I see. But where are all those delightful *ahalad-kaaslane* who accompanied you on your search?"

Kebonsat ignored the question, facing blindly the place where the wizard's voice came from.

"So it's you, is it, Buris? I thought as much. It's just like you to take the cowardly path, letting others do your dirty work. You pretend loyalty while you stab my father in the back—even now you cannot look me in the face."

"On the contrary. I can. It is *you* who cannot look *me* in the face." The wizard laughed, a sound of genuine humor. Reisil's stomach crawled and she swallowed hard to keep from throwing up. This man was smug with the certainty of his victory.

"But you haven't answered my questions." Kvepi Buris's voice turned stern. "Where is your sister? Where are your companions? What, pray tell, is in the wagon?"

He paced toward the wagon as Kebonsat prevaricated. Reisil tensed, waiting until the wizard was beyond the wagon box. Then she crab-crawled to the edge of the dome barrier and flung herself through, rolling between two tents. She spun about and crouched down, watching Kvepi Buris uncover the prisoners in the back. She couldn't hear him speak, but he would know their sleep wasn't natural.

He marched up the line of men, peering intently at each of the soldiers. Some struck out at him, but he dropped the offenders to the ground with a word and wave of his hand. Reisil recoiled. That they were dead, she had no doubt.

Now he came back around to Kebonsat and used a spell to draw him forward. Kebonsat resisted it with every fiber of himself, but he dropped his torch, taking wooden steps toward Kvepi Buris. The wizard laughed, delighting in the other man's helplessness.

Kvepi Buris touched a finger to his victim's cheek, his eye, his arm, stomach, leg and groin. Kebonsat withered with pain. The wizard was clearly in a hurry to get answers, and did not pause to enjoy his victim's agony, merely inflicted it with swift and brutal force.

Bile washing her tongue, Reisil saw the skin on Kebonsat's face bubble and turn green and black, then, to her horror, bits of flesh dropped to the ground in greasy clots. He opened his mouth and Reisil knew he screamed. The wizard would kill Kebonsat if she did not act. She thought rapidly.

~*Saljane. I have an idea. It will be very dangerous.*

She communicated what she wanted to her *ahalad-kaaslane.*

~*I will do it.*

~*You will only be able to see through my eyes, and I dare not move too close or Kvepi Buris will suspect,* Reisil cautioned. ~*The other wizard is a better target, but I cannot be sure he's making the darkness. He might just be creating the dome barrier. Even though interrupting his spell would likely kill him—if what Sodur told me is true—it wouldn't be nearly enough to stop Kvepi Buris. It would only warn him, and he must not have time to protect himself. You need to fly high and strike Kvepi Buris a heavy blow. Enough to incapacitate him. I'll deal with the other one. He's so engrossed in his magic, he won't know what's happening.*

Reisil stroked a shaking hand over Saljane's back, sending a prayer to the Blessed Lady. Then she tossed the bird up into the unnatural night, staring upward as she did. Saljane winged swiftly upward, blind except for what she could see of herself through her *ahalad-kaaslane's* eyes. Reisil waited until the bird had leveled out, circling slowly in a lopsided, unsteady orbit.

Could Saljane really do this? They had no other options. As she watched, Kebonsat doubled over and dropped to his knees. Kvepi Buris knotted long fingers in his black hair and tugged. The hair came away, attached to clots of bloody, gray skin.

Reisil welcomed the fury that spun through her, driving out the paralyzing repulsion and fear for Kebonsat.

~*Hold on, Saljane. I have to get in place.*

She worked her way around to a place near where Kvepi Buris's saffron-garbed companion stood chanting into his hands at the edge of the dome barrier. The going was slow as she sidestepped brawling soldiers, yapping dogs, plunging horses and all manner of packs, wagons, troughs, buckets, tents, fires, bags of grain, piles of manure and several sprawled bodies.

All the while she kept glancing upward to help keep Saljane centered overhead. She wished she could warn Edelsat of her plan. Kvepi Buris, arrogant of his powers, had not disarmed any of his captives. If Saljane struck the wizard just a glancing blow, Reisil hoped the others would take advantage, though, she pointed out to herself, even if she could warn them, it would be impossible for them to locate the wizard in the darkness.

Reisil kicked something and looked down. A soldier had been trampled and dragged by his terrified horse. He'd lost his helm and a hoof had caved in his skull. She hesitated a moment, then knelt beside him and heaved him over, taking his sword.

"I promise, I don't make a habit of robbing the dead. But I have need and you don't," she said quietly, and then continued on, hefting the unfamiliar weapon in her hand. She was no swordsman, but it would make a good club.

She crouched down behind a barrel, wrinkling her nose as she realized that someone had been using it as a receptacle for midden buckets. She swallowed, breathing through her mouth, barely keeping herself from retching at the stench. Ten feet away with his back to her was the chanting wizard, and beyond him another fifteen paces was Kvepi Buris and Kebonsat.

Her mouth opened on a wordless cry. Areas of blackened, putrefying bone showed through widening patches of gray and green putrescence as more of Kebonsat's flesh rotted and fell away. She didn't even recognize him. How could he still live? Her fingers convulsed around the hilt of the stolen sword.

~Are you ready, Saljane? We have no more time.

For a moment there was no answer.

~Now. Show me the wizard.

Reisil turned her burning gaze on Kvepi Buris and held her breath.

Saljane stooped, dropping like a stone.

Not on target.

The bird was off by several feet. Reisil gasped and Saljane flung her wings wide to halt her fall. With a harsh cry, she flew at the startled Kvepi Buris and raked his face with her talons. Kebonsat slumped to the ground.

Reisil leaped forward, clutching the sword in two hands above her head. She pushed through the circle, though something pushed back at her. Not strong enough. The spell was meant to discourage, but it wasn't a wall. She clubbed the saffron wizard's coweled head.

Once. Twice.

He made a sound like a baby moaning, then crumpled. A black crystal wrapped in red and silver thread rolled from his outstretched palm. Reisil brought the sword down on it and it shattered. Brilliant light flared and she stumbled back, catching herself with one hand on the ground.

The wizard night vanished, and in its place twilight began to fall.

Reisil blinked, spots of white dancing across her vision. Through them she saw Edelsat kneeling beside Kebonsat, a hand over his mouth as he gagged. Kvepi Buris stood surrounded by Edelsat's men. One eye was gone and with it his nose. Blood ribboned down his neck and bubbled where his nose had been. He shrieked, lifting his hands to touch his ruined flesh.

Edelsat's men struggled to finish him, chopping at him with swords that bounced off thin air.

The wizard ignored them, staring at the blood washing his hands. At last he raised his eyes, snarling at Reisil, his teeth and lips smeared crimson.

"This isn't over," he raged, his voice high and pained. "You will pay dearly. When the sun goes down, the treaty will be finished and you will have lost. You—Mekelsek—your mother's dead these past four days. And the disease is chewing up your sisters, your father and brother," he sneered at Edelsat. "By the time you get home, even you won't recognize them, any more than that pompous puppy on the ground there. But you will get to enjoy the pleasure of watching them die. I'll make sure of that.

"And you . . ." He pointed at Reisil as Saljane landed on her upraised fist. "I'll have your poultry for breakfast, and when I'm done with you, you'll beg to die—but you'll live. Years and years. And every single moment of it, you will know this pain. I swear this on my master's soul."

Then he vanished. No chants, no waving hand. He just disappeared from the ring of swords pointed at his heart.

Reisil swallowed the scream that rose involuntarily in her throat, and with effort loosened her grip on the sword she'd used to kill the wizard. She ran to Kebonsat and dropped to the ground beside him, putting a shaking hand on his forehead, the other over his heart.

Healing came swiftly, pouring into him like a golden tide. Again she felt the Lady inside her, guiding her. The golden ivy on her face blazed, wreathing around and over her until she glowed. All around her a pool of radiating quiet formed.

Several minutes passed; then she sat back and the light subsided. Edelsat's awestruck gaze flicked from her to Kebonsat, who took several deep breaths and sat up. He looked around at the stunned onlookers, then at his hands and chest, feeling over his face.

"You're all right," Reisil told him, sitting back on her heels. She felt as if she'd been flattened. Tears prickled in her eyes and her chest hurt. She wanted to scream, to cry, to run far away. But she smiled, so wide it hurt. Joy sluiced through her and she hardly knew how to hold it in.

The joy evaporated as Kebonsat scrambled to his feet, away from her. He looked at Edelsat, his face an expressionless mask.

"Where's Buris?" Kebonsat asked.

"Gone. But wounded. He said that sundown marked the time of the treaty. We don't have much time," Edelsat said after another sidelong glance at Reisil.

"We've got to get a message to my father."

"Saljane can take something. She's seen your father in Kallas, and I have paper and pencil in my pack." Reisil remembered that Upsakes had told her to bring it when they began the journey. She grimaced at the irony.

Kebonsat shook his head, still not looking at her. More than that, Reisil realized, hurt coiling in her chest. He leaned away from her as if he did not want to be too close.

"No time for a note. But . . ." He tore at his sleeve, pulling free a square of gold-and-indigo diamond-marked material. He handed it to Reisil, but did not let his fingers touch hers.

Reisil clenched the material in her fist, trying not to feel as if he'd punched her in the stomach. He'd seen the healing she'd done for Ceriba, seen her mend all the petty cuts and bruises of the last week's journey. There was nothing different, and yet somehow it was all different. She felt his cold withdrawal like a fortress wall, unbreachable.

"My father will know I send this and will do all he can to keep the Iisand and the Karalis at the table. It might give us enough time."

Saljane took the material in her beak and Reisil flung her into the air, putting all the force of her tumbling emotions behind the gesture. The goshawk arrowed away into the twilight and Reisil soon lost sight of her.

"Let's not waste any more time—we need horses. Borison!" Edelsat called. A pug-faced man leaped to attention and soon he and several other soldiers had acquired mounts, some at sword point.

"We'll catch up, sir, soon as we get more," Borison said, handing his new mount's reins to Edelsat.

"What in the Demonlord's domain is going on here?" demanded a sudden, furious voice behind Reisil, and she spun about, wishing for Saljane.

She found herself staring up at a white stallion, its face covered with a brilliantly polished chanfron matching its breast and haunch plates. Upon him sat a golden-haired man wearing full armor. Over it he wore a surcoat in yellow. Emblazoned on the chest was a many-rayed sun in varied shades of green. At the center of the sun was a three-pointed crown picked out in gold thread. Two arrows, points down, crisscrossed inside the crown. Topping his head was a helm in the shape of an eagle, wings flaring back over his head, the visor shaped like an open beak that, closed, would protect his face. Within the shadow of the visor, his eyes glittered like glass. Behind him ranged a company of soldiers wearing his livery.

"Vadonis. You're a sight. Been fighting, have you? And in the illustrious company of House Mekelsek. Slumming these days?"

Every word he spoke was a dart of pure venom. He leaned an arm on his pommel and glanced over the ragged group, his eyes flicking over Reisil, pausing sharply on the golden ivy running along her jaw, then darting away, back to Kebonsat.

"Rumor has it that you misplaced your sister. And what's this?" His spurs jingled as he nudged his horse over to the fallen wizard. "The Guild won't much care for killing one of their own. Karalis Vasalis either. At present, we're in great need of wizards." He smiled, like a spider gloating over a fly struggling in the web. "Perhaps I should take you to him right now. He would be interested to see you, I think. And your father as well, coming home with your tail between your legs. Wherever is your sister?"

Kebonsat lips parted into a matching smile, his body radiating savage loathing. "Indeed, Covail, we would be delighted to have your service. Do escort us. Quickly, if you please," he ordered, as if to a pageboy. Covail snarled, his horse rearing as he dug his spurred bootheels into the soft white flanks.

Kebonsat ignored him, snatching the reins of a tall sorrel gelding from Epiton, a dour, faired-haired soldier. He mounted, spinning his horse around with a sharp jerk of the reins and setting off at a gallop, leaving Covail to catch up. The gleaming blond nobleman could do nothing else but follow.

Edelsat signaled his men to bring the wagon and reached out an arm to Reisil. She swung up behind him and he sent his horse galloping after.

"What was that about?" Reisil shouted in Edelsat's ear, clutching his waist as the horse dodged around a pair of brawling men, then leaped over a mound of sleep rolls.

"They've never liked each other. Both families are in

line for the throne. Blood ties way back when. Covail's ambitious—took on the title two years ago when his father died and has been maneuvering for power since. House Covail has a hoard of money, but bad manners, and a streak of insanity taints the line. House Vadonis has always been a steadfast supporter of the crown, and enjoys higher favor right now. But it hasn't always been that way. Covail'd like to see Kebonsat's family disgraced with a scandal."

Edelsat twisted and yelled "Hold on!" as they cut between two tents, knocking aside a group of men. A moment later Edelsat swung his sword with a resounding clash, blocking the strike of an infuriated soldier whose camp lay in trampled disarray.

They raced through the sprawling encampment, the sun dripping blood as it sank farther beyond the plains. Edelsat's redheaded guidon ran doggedly at Kebonsat's heels, the two standards snapping overhead. Covail followed closely, his own guidon nipping right behind. The rest of the blond noble's men trailed behind in a ragged line, with Reisil and Edelsat bringing up the rear. Far behind, following in the wake of their rampage, Edelsat's men brought the wagon, swords drawn, faces remote and harsh as the peaks of the Dume Griste mountains in winter.

A line of oil lamps ringed the Enclave, and just within, wizards circled like a necklace of brilliant-hued beads, cowls hiding their identities, hands tucked inside their sleeves. Kebonsat ignored them, charging between two wearing pale green robes, only to be thrown backward by an invisible barrier. His gelding gave a shrieking neigh and reared in pain and fright, blood spraying from his nose.

Reisil gasped as he toppled over backward. Kebonsat leaped to the ground, barely pulling his left leg free as the heavy beast crashed to the ground, snapping the saddle tree in two with a loud crack.

"The Summit has begun. No one may enter without leave," a gravelly voice intoned, an old voice. Reisil had no idea which of the wizards had spoken. Kebonsat's face turned a mottled red as he settled his hand on his sword and strode up to one of the pale green-robed wizards.

"I am Kebonsat cas Vadonis and I demand entrance. I have urgent news for Karalis Vasalis."

The figure before him did not move, but Reisil had a sense that the wizard's gaze raked up and down Kebonsat and then dismissed him.

"Are you deaf, man? I am Kebonsat cas Vadonis, heir to the House Vadonis. I bring vital news for the Karalis Vasalis."

Still the wizard did not move, nor did he speak, and Kebonsat went white, fingers tightening on his sword. Then Covail let out a smug laugh and Kebonsat's face flushed pink up to his ears. He turned.

"Something amuses you, Covail?"

"Indeed. It ever amuses me to see House Vadonis groveling in the dirt."

"Don't do it," Edelsat muttered under his breath as Kebonsat stiffened. Reisil sat rooted in place as she watched Kebonsat wrestle with his fury. And win. Or so she thought.

He made a show of studying the ground around him. "Ah, yes. It is unfamiliar territory for me, and I've been quite unsuccessful. Perhaps you will dismount and demonstrate? Given your own familiarity with the terrain and habit."

"That did it," Edelsat muttered again, shaking his head.

Covail burned an ugly vermilion. "You polting midden of guts and garbage!" he spat through the gaping rictus of his mouth. He leaped from his horse, brandishing his sword, pulling his dagger with the other hand. "Defend yourself, you spawn of a whore!"

A crowd of jostling men soon crowded around, offering bets and shouting encouragement, as an equally irate Kebonsat fended off Covail's blistering attack and then followed up with one of his own. Into his off hand appeared his lohar, much like that which Koijots had carried. He put it to good use, twisting it around Covail's dagger and nearly tearing it from his grip.

"They're both damned good. This won't end until one of them drops," Edelsat said in a grim voice, drumming his fingers on his saddle. "I hope it works."

"Works?"

"Kebonsat is not so green or foolhardy as to get goaded into an attack with all of Patverseme hanging in the balance. He's giving the wagon time to get here, and hopes to distract the wizards. If I had to wager, I'd say he's counting on us to do something." Edelsat didn't sound hopeful.

Reisil nodded and looked up at the sky. The setting sun burned orange. There was still time. But she was going to need help. The wizard had said that no one could enter without leave. Well, then, they'd better get leave.

~Saljane, where are you? Have you seen the Dure Vadonis? Have Sodur and Juhrnus brought Ceriba?

~I found him. Gave him the cloth. The wizard returned. They remain in the tent. I watch.

Reisil's stomach clenched and she relayed the information to Edelsat.

"Not good," he said. "Even if Sodur and Juhrnus got Ceriba there, Karalis Vasalis won't sign the treaty without the Dure Vadonis. And Kebonsat's father wouldn't sit on his hands knowing Ceriba was close by. So that means Kvepi Buris has stopped him. I hope to Ellini our friend has not just become the new Dure Vadonis."

"What can we do?"

"Nothing out here."

"What can Saljane do, then?"

Edelsat pursed his lips. "We need in, or they've got to come to us. Iisand Samir and Karalis Vasalis will be in that large pavilion over there."

Reisil looked where he pointed and saw an enormous white tent on a raised platform. Guards stood at attention around its open sides, and inside milled a crowd of people.

"Let's suppose that Sodur and Juhrnus have got Ceriba to the Iisand. Neither he nor Karalis Vasalis wants this war to go on. They're going to be looking for reasons to delay. But the Guild and many of the lords of the two courts will be pushing them hard to declare the truce void, and nullify the treaty agreement. They won't be able to hold off long, not if the wizard night tempted either side into skirmishes. Tensions are very high, and both crowns have reason to hate each other. Luckily, they have put their countries above all that, thus far. So if they want a delay, give them one."

Reisil nodded at his hasty explanation, her mind racing. There was nothing she could do about Kvepi Buris, nothing to help Kebonsat's father. No one within the Enclave knew of the wizard's treachery. He could kill the Dure Vadonis in the privacy of his tent with a wave of his hand and dispose of the body equally effortlessly. There was only one thing she could think of for Saljane to do. If the Iisand and the Karalis wanted a delay, she'd give it to them, and hopefully bring an invitation to enter at the same time.

~Go to the pavilion where they meet, Saljane. I'll be with you.

"I'll see what can be done," Reisil told Edelsat grimly. "But all my attention will be with Saljane. Try to keep me from falling off the horse."

With that, Reisil joined to Saljane's mind as the bird alighted from a cottonwood branch along the Trieste River glowing like a spill of lava in the reflected sunset.

Chapter 17

Air whistled over the edges of Saljane's wings as she circled low over the pavilion. It was a platform the size of a small hayfield, and had been roofed over with white silk. The lofty space was lit by lamps and thick-bodied candles. Through the open sides Reisil could see little more than opulent rugs, a forest of furniture and a milling throng of people richly dressed in satin and velvet. Guards stood at attention every fifteen feet of the perimeter, with more circulating warily through the crowd. She saw no sign of Sodur, Juhrnus and Ceriba.

~*Let's go inside. And be fast, because the Patverseme guards are more likely to shoot than ask questions.*

Fierce determination. Exhilaration. The Hunt.

Saljane spun on a wing tip and dropped in a steep, silent glide toward a space between two guards. So intent was Reisil on trying to see within the pavilion that she did not notice that her stomach did not lurch at the sharp change in direction or the ground rushing up at her.

They swooped under the tent. A wave of shouts erupted in their wake. Saljane wove between the roof supports, well above the pointing courtiers. Reisil was under no illusions that any suspected Saljane to be a wild bird. Both Kodu Riikians and Patversemese alike knew instantly that she was *ahalad-kaaslane*.

Saljane made the most of her speed and agility, searching the vast space of the pavilion from one end to the other. Guards in the royal livery of violet and gold crowded in at the edges, making little headway into the shouting crowd. Reisil saw several bring crossbows to their shoulders. She desperately scanned the huge space.

~*There, Saljane. Near where we came in.*

They had made a circuit of the pavilion, seeing nothing of the two royal parties. Now Reisil knew why. They had entered nearly on top of the great dais where Iisand Samir and Karalis Vasalis met together in the company of their ladies, Mesilasema Tanis and Karaliene Pavadone.

Reisil had seen pictures of the Iisand and Mesilasema. Merchants sold their likenesses during the Nasadh celebrations after the harvest. But the pictures didn't capture the regal aura surrounding the two monarchs. They were young yet, nearing their mid-thirties. The Iisand wore midnight-blue robes edged in a thick band of gold embroidery, and on his head rested a gold crown with a single point in front. Beneath the crown his face was austere, with flinty eyes. The Mesilasema wore a gown of matching midnight blue embroidered over in a pattern of leaves and gryphons to match her husband's crown. A slender filet of gold crowned her golden curls. She appeared demure and girlish in her way, almost frightened.

Karalis Vasalis was some years older than Iisand Samir, and exhibited the dramatic coloring that marked the Patversemese people. He had raven hair and a wide, beaklike nose. His skin was pale like Kebonsat's, and his eyes were a piercing black beneath sweeping black brows. He wore a closely trimmed beard. His face was made unsettlingly savage by the crescent-shaped tattoo in green and black hooking from his left cheekbone to just above his eye.

Behind him, standing at his shoulder, was Karaliene Pavadone. She was as like to Mesilasema Tanis as a hunting cat to a kitten. She matched her consort in coloring, her hair glowing blue-black in the flames of the lamps. Her black eyes were painted heavily with kohl, her lips a slash of red across her alabaster skin. She had a tough, predatory look about her. Most startling was the tattoo in the same green and black, which began just above her left eyebrow and followed its curve, stopping just at the corner of her eye. As with her husband, it suggested a savage, untamed edge.

Attending the monarchs were several wizards in black robes traced in silver arcane symbols from the deep folds of their cowls to the hems at their feet, a dozen lords from each country, a doddering Patverseme cleric in white, and three grim-faced *ahalad-kaaslane*, each looking distinctly out of place in their serviceable leathers.

One was a woman with short chestnut hair accompanied by a black corvet. The tree-cat clung to her shoulders, its sinuous tail flicking back and forth. Next to her sat a blocky man with graying hair, his wolf *ahalad-kaaslane* at his knee. The third man was strikingly handsome with kohv-colored hair worn in a long braid down his back and coming to a dramatic point above his forehead. Rich brown eyes gleamed from a tanned, bearded face. On his shoulder perched a redtail hawk. For the briefest moment Reisil wondered if he was the one who would have trained her in Koduteel.

Then Saljane let out one of her strident *kek-kek-kek-kek* cries and landed in the center of the parchment-strewn table, scattering papers and tipping ink pots as she flapped her wings to steady herself.

"What in the Dark Lord's name is this?" demanded Karalis Vasalis in a low, almost guttural voice, slapping his hand on the tabletop.

"I assure you I don't know. Reikon?" The Iisand's cultured voice was collected and mild, despite the tightness of his lips. The man with the redtail hawk shook his head, eyeing Saljane.

"It's not one I've seen before." He returned Iisand Samir's regard with a piercing look, as if trying to communicate something.

"But it is *ahalad-kaaslane*," one of the wizards said in a nasal voice, his tone accusing.

"Indeed," Reikon answered laconically.

The wizard, bald-pated with a fringe of white around his ears, turned red, his fleshy nose quivering. "Your Grace, I must protest," he said, turning to Karalis Va-

salis. "How can we proceed with this . . . this—" Before
he could find a word sufficient to his outrage, Karaliene
Pavadone forestalled him.

"Kvepi Mastone, I would also like to get to the bottom of this." She gestured at Saljane, who, at Reisil's
suggestion, dipped her beak. Karaliene Pavadone smiled,
a sharp, knowing smile. Did Reisil read approval in her
expression? "I confess surprise at your suggestion that
we delay proceedings until we find an answer, especially
given the passion of your exhortations. I am gratified to
find you so reasonable. Are you not also, dearest?" she
asked her husband, who nodded, his eyes gleaming at
the wizard's stammering discomfort as he tried to
protest.

Deftly Karaliene Pavadone turned to Iisand Samir, ignoring the grumbling of the lords farther down the table.
"Will you consent to look into this matter? We shall
give you two hours. That must be sufficient, I'm afraid,
for we must have swift resolution of this and other matters. In the meantime, we shall seek out our wayward
Kvepi Buris and Dure Vadonis."

At her last words, Saljane mantled and gave a piercing
cry. The four monarchs and three *ahalad-kaaslane* gave
her an intent look, then exchanged furtive glances.
Seeing this through Saljane's eyes, Reisil gave a crow
of triumph.

"They know something! Sodur, Juhrnus and Ceriba
must have made it. They've been waiting for us."

"They'll be waiting a good long while if they don't do
something about these wizards," Edelsat said. "If Sodur,
Juhrnus and Ceriba got there, why hasn't someone
done something?"

"Maybe they are hoping to expose the rest of the traitors. They have to know that the treason runs high—
and now they know there are wizards involved. You
have said that Karalis Vasalis has been at odds with the
wizards since he took the throne. That he's tried to muz-
zle their power. He has to know that at least some of
them are behind this—how else to account for today's
wizard night? And Iisand Samir cannot be certain of his

own people either. The Karaliene has neatly disbanded
the meeting for two hours. Saljane accompanies the
Iisand and the *ahalad-kaaslane*. Maybe they have something planned."

"Let's hope so. Kebonsat's holding his own, but he's
getting tired. He's not fighting to win, but to prolong the
battle. We'll not be permitted to hang about once it's
over. If Kebonsat and Covail weren't ranked as high as
they are, we'd have been cleared out of here much
sooner. As it is, the guards are just waiting for them
to finish."

Reikon, the strikingly handsome *ahalad-kaaslane* with
the redtail hawk, carried Saljane on his gloved fist. He
followed Iisand Samir and Mesilasema Tanis, flanked by
the other two *ahalad-kaaslane,* and trailed behind by an
angry cohort of Kodu Riikian lords and a squad of the
Iisand's personal guard.

They retreated down from the pavilion and into a tent,
ignoring the rumbling of the crowds filling the rest of
the pavilion. At the door of the tent, the lords were
summarily dismissed and the guards left to stand watch
outside.

Inside, Saljane flapped to a perch on the back of a
chair, swiveling her head to watch each of the others in
turn. Reisil gasped as the drapery at the back of the tent
was drawn aside and Sodur, Juhrnus and Ceriba entered
from a small room at the back. Ceriba looked pale and
frightened, but resolute. She clung to Juhrnus's arm, surprising Reisil. Juhrnus had done well, giving the frightened woman support and friendship. Reisil found herself
feeling proud of her childhood nemesis.

"Saljane!" Sodur exclaimed, seeing the goshawk. She
dipped her head at him and he smiled. "Blessed Lady
be praised. They have arrived."

"It seems so, but where are they?" asked the *ahalad-
kaaslane* woman, her corvet leaping to the ground to
touch noses with Lume.

"Outside the wizard circle, or they would be here,"
Reikon said in his low, melodic voice. "But how did this
pretty one get inside? I tried to send my Vesil out, but
the barrier closes over us like a dome."

"She must have come before they put up the barrier. But why?" asked Iisand Samir, tapping his bunched fist against his thigh.

"To bring a message, one would think. But she's not got jesses, and if she carried something, it's gone now."

Saljane gave a cry and flew to Ceriba, landing at her feet.

The Iisand frowned. "She had something for you? Or no, more likely your father. And your father didn't turn up for the summit." The Iisand looked at his wife, then at the gathered *ahalad-kaaslane*. "I don't like this. No one would dare harm the Dure Vadonis unless the blame could be set on us, or the evidence removed."

"Which points to a wizard. Only they can get out of the barrier they've put up," said the other man whose *ahalad-kaaslane* was a wolf. He spoke in a staccato voice. "And that ties our hands. We have no powers to counter them. One or two, maybe. But there must be a thousand of them gathered here and throughout the encampment. This could very well turn into another Mysane Kosk. And Karalis Vasalis won't be able to stop them if that's what they decide to do."

"There must be something we can do!" exclaimed the chestnut-haired woman, slapping her fist into her palm.

Silence answered. Outside the barrier, Reisil sat behind Edelsat, appalled, her stomach lurching. It could not come to this. Surely the Blessed Lady would not allow it.

Her chest burned.

Reisil's mind snapped free of Saljane's and she clutched at her chest. Beneath her tunic she felt the Lady's gryphon amulet. She yanked it out. The eyes of the gryphon blazed red as the rising sun. Reisil cupped it in her hands, her mind scrabbling to understand.

Then it came to her like a beam of moonlight and she knew what to do. Magic to counter magic, a healer to heal Kodu Riik, a warrior to battle evil, a weapon for the Lady's hand. She was all four. The power she'd been given could heal, but it could also be turned to another use. She felt that alien hand inside her, as she had felt it the night before in the grass hut. It gathered itself into a fist.

"Is the wagon here?" she asked Edelsat in a choked voice, never looking up from the amulet.

"Just now. But Kebonsat's come close to killing Covail twice now, and has let himself be nicked up pretty good. Can't go on much longer."

"It doesn't need to." Reisil reached out to Saljane in the royal tent of Iisand Samir.

~Bring them to me, ahalad-kaaslane.

At her behest, Saljane leaped into the air, gliding to land before the tent opening. She impatiently looked over her shoulder at Sodur, giving one of her strident calls.

"By the Lady," Iisand Samir breathed, staring.

"Her eyes! Look at her eyes. Look at her beak. What does it mean?" Mesilasema Tanis put her hand up to cover her pink mouth.

"It means we still have hope. Reisiltark wants us. She must have a plan. I suggest we follow," Sodur said.

"Bethorn, take word to Karalis Vasalis," the Iisand ordered the *ahalad-kaaslane* with the wolf. "Reikon." He nodded for him to open the tent flaps.

Saljane gave another *kek-kek-kek-kek* and hopped through. Bethorn hastened away, and Iisand Samir called for his guards. Saljane leaped into the air, circling low, her piercing cry urging speed.

Reisil broke the connection with Saljane and slipped from the back of the horse. Edelsat jerked around. His mouth fell open and then snapped closed as he jerked back.

"What's happening?" he whispered. "Your eyes . . . they're red as fire."

Reisil looked up at him. Her eyes must be reflecting the burning red of the gryphon amulet. Not for green healing, this power. Not this time.

"Get back. Take Kebonsat with you. Hurry. You don't want to get caught up in this." Reisil's voice sounded remote, like living flame.

She turned away from Edelsat, trusting him to evacuate Kebonsat to a safe distance. She paced toward the ring of wizards. She could see the barrier now, like an overturned bowl the color of stagnant water. The faceless wizards held it before themselves like a shield, held it over themselves like a trap. Fury coiled in Reisil like the winds of a tornado. They felt themselves invulnerable, and they visited their heartless arrogance on their people and the people of Kodu Riik with death and destruction. No more. The Blessed Lady would have it no more.

The air about her crackled silver sparks. She lifted her arms up to the sky and felt power coursing through her like molten metal. She felt herself smiling a death's-head smile—the face of justice. Inside the barrier she saw Saljane. Her *ahalad-kaaslane*'s eyes burned red and her beak streamed gold.

~Come to me, Saljane!

Another step. And another.

She felt the wizards pour more energy into the barrier as they sensed her impending attack. She laughed. Could they stand against lightning unleashed? Against the fist of the Lady as She claimed justice?

Reisil was just an arm's length away from the barrier and Saljane was just beyond, streaking toward her like an arrow of fire. Reisil held out her fist to catch Saljane and took the last step, into the barrier.

There was a wild explosion of silver and black, as if the heavens shot forth a hundred bolts of lightning to shred the night. The sound of it shattered glass and echoed to the Dume Griste mountains.

Reisil stood as if rooted in the soil, Saljane clinging to her fist, the two sharing a single, fierce mind. All around them the earth spun into the air on a tornado of pure energy. Reisil stood within the barrier and felt each of the three hundred wizards circling about the Enclave Point like a living chain. She felt incongruous tears rising in her eyes and mourned for the life that must be pruned away. But pruned it must be.

She reached out her arms and sent blistering shafts of energy through the chain. The power crackled and, one by one, each wizard winked out like a blown candle, until the barrier was gone, until all that was left of the wizards were black, smoking husks like a charred string of pearls.

Reisil stood a moment, power roaring inside her as the alien hand withdrew. She could do more, much much more. She could destroy every one of them, every wizard, every Patversemese soldier. The temptation pulled at her. If there was no Patversemese army, no more wizards, there could be no war.

Sudden horror gripped her throat and she yanked back on the ready power. How could she even think it? Snakes, rats, fleas and leeches each served their purpose in the cycle of life. To annihilate the wizards out of hand would ruin the balance. To kill the army would be entirely evil. These men had families and children.

The power subsided quickly. Reisil felt it draining away into the ground and air. But it wasn't really gone. It would always be there, waiting. Like lightning in a jar. What trust the Lady had put in her!

She glanced at Saljane, whose eyes had returned to the familiar amber, and whose beak no longer glowed, though the tracing of golden ivy remained on her beak, as it did on Reisil's own face.

~We are Her hands. We will never break Her trust.

She felt Saljane in her mind, the pride, the emotion deeper than love, the devotion to the Lady. Reisil nodded, then looked around at what she'd wrought.

The Enclave was now ringed by a border of scorched earth, broken every few paces by the smoking remains of a wizard and melted blobs of iron that had been oil lamps. Reisil stood keystone at the center of the destruction.

Silence reigned, punctured here and there by piteous moans and agonized cries as those who had stood too close found blood running from their noses and ears. Acrid smoke drifted in a dense, ghostly fog, making Reisil tear and blink. She turned. For a hundred-pace radius around her, a hollow gouged into the ground, fully three feet deep. She stood on a narrow island in the center. Beyond that, a fearful crowd assembled—soldiers, lords and ladies. She turned again, looking for Kebonsat and

Edelsat. They stood on the edge of the hollow, faces gray, staring at her, aghast. Blood ran from Kebonsat's forehead and cheek; more soaked his right sleeve. She turned again.

Sodur stood before her on the floor of the hollow, Lume beside him. He smiled gently, holding out a hand to help her down. She transferred Saljane to her shoulder and took his hand gratefully.

"Quite a show," he said in a comfortingly normal voice.

"Let's hope it's enough. I'd rather not do more."

Sodur stopped, looking into her face sharply.

"Could you do more?"

Reisil lifted one shoulder in a half shrug, avoiding his searching gaze.

After a moment he said, "You have come a long way since becoming *ahalad-kaaslane*. It is said that wisdom is not given. We must discover it ourselves, after a journey through the wilderness that no one else can make for us, and that no one can spare us, for wisdom is the point of view from which we come at last to regard the world. I could not imagine that you could have made such a journey to such wisdom and courage in such a short time. But the Lady saw far better than I. You are indeed all that she could have hoped for in her chosen one. I am proud of you."

Reisil felt herself blushing and she squeezed Sodur's hand gratefully.

"I don't feel wise. I feel lucky. Blessed." She stroked Saljane and the goshawk nipped at her fingers.

At the edge of the hollow another hand reached down to help her up. She clasped its callused warmth and found herself face-to-face with Reikon. He smiled at her, as gently as Sodur had done. "Bright evening, Reisiltark. I am Reikon. I am pleased to meet you at last." Reisil had no time to reply as the chestnut-haired woman with the corvet slapped her on the shoulder.

"Well done! I am Fehra."

Juhrnus added his congratulations, and Ceriba touched her hand. Reisil felt warmth from these people, pride.

They did not fear what she'd done, what she was capable of. She smiled gratefully at these strangers who were her family. Then they were interrupted by the Iisand Samir's cultured tones.

"We are indeed pleased to see you, Reisiltark. And amazed. But we must resume our council with Karalis Vasalis if we are not to see the war reborn. Where are your companions?"

"Are you sure you want to?" asked Fehra, her expression as feral as her corvet's.

The Iisand stilled, his face becoming hard and unforgiving.

"What do you propose?" His voice was soft, dangerous, but Fehra pushed on. As *ahalad-kaaslane*, she had no need to fear him.

"We now have power to counter the wizards, so we don't really need this treaty anymore. Especially with Scallas going after Patverseme's other flank. We could beat them."

"We might indeed win, but the cost would be too high. One more death would be too many. You're talking about revenge, and while I certainly don't mind seeing those wizards sent back to the Demonlord, I'm not going to put my people through any more fighting if I can help it. If nothing else, what Reisiltark has done here will help firm Patverseme's commitment to the treaty. They can't afford two battlefronts."

"The Lady told me She wanted peace," Reisil added softly. "Knowing Her will, I could not aid in further war."

That ended the discussion. Fehra looked disappointed, but not angry. Upsakes must have had support among the *ahalad-kaaslane*. Could Fehra have been in on the kidnapping? There was no way to tell. Reisil resolved to keep an eye on the other woman.

Just then Edelsat and Kebonsat arrived with the wagon of prisoners. The group retreated back to the pavilion, where Karalis and Karaliene waited with Bethorn. The two monarchs of Patverseme held themselves stiffly apart, looking pale and suspicious.

Seeing Kebonsat and Edelsat, they thawed slightly. Kebonsat held Ceriba firmly against his side, brushing aside her concerns for his wounds.

Reisil they eyed with chill aversion.

"I wasn't aware that Kodu Riik had any wizards," said Karalis Vasalis to Iisand Samir. "My people will not respond well to this slaughter." His nostrils flared and Reisil could feel his anger waxing hot. He might be at odds with the Wizard Guild, she thought. But Kodu Riik was his enemy.

"As mine did not to Mysane Kosk," retorted Iisand Samir.

"We were at war then. We are not, *now*."

"No, we are not. Do you wish to be?"

A muscle in the Karalis's cheek twitched as the Iisand waited. Finally he gave a short shake of his head.

"No. But I don't know how I'll explain this to my people."

"You can tell them the wizards are traitors," interjected Kebonsat.

"What do you mean?" Karaliene Pavadone skewered Kebonsat with her glittering stare.

"We killed a wizard who was helping the kidnappers, and another plotted with Kvepi Buris to prevent us from getting here." Kebonsat described the attack tersely, leaving nothing out. When he came to his healing by Reisil, his eyes flicked toward her, but once again he avoided her gaze.

He was afraid of her, Reisil realized, and felt a sudden sickening in her stomach. She liked him, had enjoyed his company. Her cheeks flushed in sudden realization of her own feelings. She cared for him more than that. But if the healing had terrified him, she wondered what he'd made of her destruction of the wizards' circle.

She bit her tongue against the grief bubbling up inside her. There wasn't any time for it.

Her eyes flashed to him. She'd almost forgotten Kvepi Buris's angry threats. Was Edelsat's mother really dead? How did his family fare? Her body jerked as if to rush away to help. But she forced herself to be still, knowing the need was greater here. But as soon as she could, she would race to help his family. *May I be in time,* she prayed.

Edelsat caught her eye as if reading her mind. His lips tightened and he gave her a slight nod. Whatever his feelings over what she'd done to the wizards, he clearly did not fear her. But then, in her he saw hope for his family's survival, not just dreadful power. What did Kebonsat see? And could she blame him? Look at what she'd done to those men. The stink of charred flesh hovered over the camp, a constant reminder of the massacre.

She stroked her fingers down Saljane's back, feeling the rumble of the goshawk's soundless croon.

"If Reisiltark had not broken the wizards' circle, we would no doubt be at war right now," Kebonsat said, completing his explanation. He might believe it, Reisil thought. He might even be grateful for it, but she still repulsed him.

The two Patversemese monarchs exchanged a speaking look. Then Karalis Vasalis nodded and Karaliene Pavadone's lips curved slightly in a smile of pure malice. She motioned to a stiffly correct, tall, balding man, the lapels and cuffs of his austere black coat embroidered with the crest of the royal house picked out in violet and gold. He bowed deferentially, his heavy chain of office swinging free from his chest as he fluidly executed the movement.

"Chamberlain Dekot, announce a formal session to convene in two hours. I require full representation by the Guild and the Lords Council, but invite all else who care to listen. And send four of your best scribes to me at once."

The chamberlain nodded, then bowed again and backed away with practiced ease.

"What about my father?" demanded Kebonsat.

Karalis Vasalis frowned. "We will demand that the Guild produce Kvepi Buris and your father, but not until after the session. I don't want to tip our hand." His dark eyes were kind as he gripped Kebonsat's shoulder. "Maksal is my good friend. If I could do more, I would."

During the two hours while they waited, the weary travelers were provided with food. Reisil ate ravenously. Reikon and Sodur sat on either side of her, plying her with questions.

Her Patversemese companions had retired to a different tent to refresh themselves, and Reisil found herself missing Edelsat and Kebonsat equally. Soon she would part from them both, probably forever. The grief she'd stifled came rushing back, and with it came the sickening loss when she realized Kebonsat's fear of her. The savory bread turned to ash on her tongue.

She swallowed convulsively, glancing at Sodur and Reikon, at Fehra and Bethorn. They all seemed easy in her company. Upsakes notwithstanding, the *ahaladkaaslane* were the friends, the family, she'd see again and again.

"Time to go," Bethorn said, peering outside. "Should be quite a show."

"They'll sign the treaty, won't they?" Reisil asked.

"It is as vital to them as it is to us, though that does not always win the day. We shall see," the Iisand answered, emerging from behind the drapery, his arm around his wife. She appeared pallid and weak.

"Is something wrong?" Reisil stood and moved instinctively to the Mesilasema's side, halting when the other woman drew back against her husband with a gasp.

"My wife is expecting our fifth child in five months. Always before she's been strong and healthy. This time . . . I tried to convince her to stay in Koduteel while I dealt with this business here, but she would have none of it."

The Mesilasema lifted her wan face to chide her husband. "You knew better than to ask," she murmured.

"I may be able to help," Reisil offered. Seeing the Mesilasema's fear at the suggestion, Reisil backed away, the blood draining from her face. She swallowed past the hard lump that knotted her throat. "You have only to ask and I will come straightaway," she said in a stiff voice.

The other woman nodded, averting her eyes, and her husband led her away, his face shadowed with concern.

The group of *ahalad-kaaslane* followed, Sodur and Reikon walking beside Reisil. Their presence comforted her as they made their way through the throng of whispering, pointing people, all staring angrily at her.

Patversemese royal guards escorted them up the stairs to the crowded pavilion. The tent had been removed and overhead the moon and stars glittered like ice in the sable sky. They found themselves ordered to a spot near the dais where Karalis Vasalis and Karaliene Pavadone now held court. Gone was the table about which they'd met before. In its stead had been set two high-backed thrones made of black oak carved with twisting symbols that seemed to melt and flow wherever the eye settled for a moment. Reisil rubbed her forehead and averted her eyes from the disquieting carvings.

The glittering nobility formed a waiting, hostile horseshoe in front of the dais. The three black-robed wizards stood on the dais to the right of Karalis Vasalis's throne, the aged white-robed cleric standing farther back. He leaned heavily on the shoulder of his *chela*—a young boy with a black-stubbled head and a predatory face. The Iisand and Mesilasema were escorted to two lower and slightly less imposing thrones to the left of Karaliene Pavadone. These were also made of black oak, but lacked the mystical symbols of the Patversemese thrones.

The Mesilasema wilted into her seat, hands clasped over her stomach, her shoulders hunched. Despite her efforts to seem collected, she appeared weaker and more drawn. Karalis Vasalis nodded to Dekot, who gave a short, sharp gesture. The liveried seneschal struck his staff three times against the hollow floor. The booming sound echoed like a death knell and Reisil swallowed.

"Hear ye, gathered peoples of Patverseme and Kodu Riik. It is with gravest honor that I present the wise and powerful Karalis Vasalis and the radiant and beautiful Karaliene Pavadone, exalted by the stars, anointed by the gods." He turned and gave a low, sweeping bow to the two monarchs, and then backed away.

Several moments of absolute silence passed. Neither Karalis Vasalis nor Karaliene Pavadone seemed inclined to break it, scanning the assembly with brooding deliberation. At last the Karalis signaled to Chamberlain Dekot, who stepped forward, unrolling a hastily scribed scroll. His voice rang loudly out across the gathered crowds, their faces distorted and deformed by the torchlight.

He told the story of Ceriba's kidnapping, of the chase across Patverseme for her, her rescue, and subsequent journey to Vorshtar plain. He described the wizard night in the forest, and then again in the encampment. He told of Koijots's death and Upsakes's and Glevs's betrayal. He described the wizard's death in Praterside and Kvepi Buris's torture of Kebonsat. He described every moment in the lurid detail of a master storyteller, leaving out only Ceriba's violation at the hands of her kidnappers. He finished with Reisil's shattering of the wizard barrier, of which he sketched only the barest bones. The gathered crowd had seen it for themselves and there was no need to supplement their stark and brilliant memories.

When he completed his recital, he surveyed the assembled crowd. Reisil felt the force of his look like a blade across her throat and shivered. This man was dangerous. She wondered how many made a habit of underestimating him. Not many who lived, she thought.

"Such is the testimony recorded in the presence of Karalis Vasalis and Karaliene Pavadone, children of the gods, arbiters of all truth." His mouth snapped shut and he stepped down, rolling up the scroll as he went.

Again silence descended—a waiting silence full of ugly anger and resentment. Not a few people cast threatening looks at the small group of *ahalad-kaaslane,* Reisil in particular, and she was reminded that the truce balanced on a needle and the war could resume at a moment. But still she knew she'd done what had to be done. She didn't know politics or intrigue, but she knew healing, and she knew putrefaction. There was much of this situation to be salvaged, but much that must be cut away to make the body whole and healthy. The wizards in the ring had been the first cut.

"Kvepi Mastone, I should be interested in the Guild's

explanation. I should also like to know where I could
find Kvepi Buris and our good friend, Maksal Vadonis."
The Karalis's voice was all the more frightening because
it lacked inflection, sounding almost casual.

Reisil was not fooled, and found herself holding her
breath. Chamberlain Dekot had called him and his
queen children of the gods. What gods? she wondered.
Those of the old times, when warlords ruled? Before the
Lady had made Kodu Riik? She struggled to remember
names. She often heard Edelsat and Kebonsat swear by
Ellini, the Goddess of luck and war and pain. Reisil
could almost believe the Karalis and Karaliene were the
children of gods, seeing them now. Light and shadow
seemed to radiate from them in thick, pulsing waves,
first choking, then crystal sweet like spring morning mist.

Kvepi Mastone stepped forward, dipping his head in
a shallow bow, then straightened, looking haughty and
dismissive. If she'd been a dog, the hair on her back
would have stood on end. As it was, Saljane mantled, as
did Reikon's hawk. Bethorn's wolf dropped his head,
lips pulling back in a snarl. Fehra's corvet hissed and
scratched needle claws in the air. The crowd, so hostile
to the *ahalad-kaaslane* moments before, hushed and
cowered away from the wizard, averting their eyes and
making signs to ward off evil.

Kvepi Mastone ignored them utterly and spoke to
Karalis Vasalis, taking little notice of Karaliene Pavadone.

"I am sure, Your Grace, that you cannot possibly believe this fantastic drivel. It's clearly a ploy to prevent
you from doing as you must righteously do. Kvepi Buris's absence is particularly worrisome to us. It is very
convenient that both he and the Dure Vadonis should
not be present. Neither man is here to refute these extravagant tales."

"Murdering maggot-eater! Do you call us liars?" Kebonsat leaped forward, grappling at the wizard's neck.

An inferno exploded between them, bright orange and
scarlet flames spinning outward like a whirlwind. Kebonsat flew into the air, arms flung wide. A whoosh of heat

and an echoing boom shuddered through the floor of the pavilion.

Kebonsat landed in the midst of the gathered nobles, knocking them about like ninepins. Kvepi Mastone sniffed and smoothed his robe, adjusting the twisted three-pointed pin on the folds of his collar.

"One should remember that using magic in Our Royal Presences is strictly forbidden." Karalis Vasalis spoke dispassionately still, but something in his voice struck Reisil like a wall collapsing. With chill certainty, she understood that he meant to challenge the Guild here and now, and there was no cost too high to curtailing the wizards' unchecked power. No cost too high.

Reisil's gaze swept the pavilion and beyond, to the close-gathered troops. It could be a bloodbath, a second Mysane Kosk. Should she stop it? Could she?

Reisil felt a trembling begin deep in her stomach. The scene unfolding was larger than she had expected, larger than she had dreamed. This was no simple matter of declaring a traitor—as if that would have been simple—but something much more cataclysmic. A crossroads of shadow and light, of disease and health, of futility and hope. What happened now would change everything that came after. Reisil felt the moment yawning before her like a stone teetering on the edge of a pit. A prickling began deep inside her healer's soul. Would the change be for the better? Or for much, much worse?

Chapter 18

Kvepi Mastone met Karalis Vasalis's condemnation with something akin to unconcern. Reisil could feel the wizard weighing his answer. She saw arrogance and irritation vie with discretion and expedience.

After several long, weighted moments, a basilisk smile curved his lips and Reisil's blood chilled. The Karalis had thrown the gauntlet, and Kvepi Mastone was picking it up. There was a delighted malignancy in the wizard's narrow, piggish eyes, a greedy anticipation, and she was reminded of a wolf licking its lips.

"Surely I must protect myself from outrageous attacks, Your Grace?" he asked, his nasal voice high with counterfeit astonishment.

"Surely you must do as required," came the implacable reply.

"Ah, yes, what is required," the wizard said, tapping his fingers against the pale, loose flesh of his cheek. And then he made the first feint, crossing the line beyond which there was no going back.

"And just what is required in a situation such as this? When to all appearances you consort—nay, shall I not say it—*conspire* with the Kodu Riikian vermin, our nation's greatest enemy? When so many loyal members of the Guild, loyal subjects of Patverseme, lie dead, burned to ashes, and the culprit stands unchained? When Kvepi Buris is missing, probably murdered? Your Grace, what would you have me do? I must serve, yes, that is true. But do I serve a tainted crown? Or do I serve the people?" He shook his head sagely.

"I believe, though I doubt many here would agree, that your own Dure Vadonis would never *willingly* treason his venerable house by allying secretly with our enemies. No more than you would *willingly* do so. But I say now that these Kodu Riikian charlatans have cast a spell over you! They have convinced this panting pup that they have saved him and his sister from death and torture. All to discredit the Guild, Patverseme's greatest defense. I ask you—what evidence do they offer of the Guild's guilt?"

He swung his arms wide and twisted so that he was talking more to the avid audience than Karalis Vasalis.

"None. They wish to make you doubt your right hand, blaming the Guild, which has always been loyal and steadfast. But I say that the fault lies with these Kodu Riikian charlatans! I say they have cast spells to confuse and deceive us all."

The watchers gasped and looked at one another with hard suspicion.

"I say that they use dark magic to hide their lies so they can lure us into a terrible trap! They want nothing more than to see Patverseme fall, to put their boot to our throat and crush us. Revenge, Your Grace, on the Guild for Mysane Kosk, for keeping the wolves at bay. Indeed, your own altered behavior, so mysterious and distrustful in these last months, offers greater proof that they have cast a spell over you than any tales of wizardry and kidnapping."

His voice rang out as he waved his arm dramatically at the royal pair, and Reisil saw sharp, angry looks darting from the crowd. Much as they feared the power of the Guild, when that weapon was turned on someone else, it gave them pride, gave them a sense of strength and fed their hatred for Kodu Riik.

Kvepi Mastone continued without a pause, his voice falling sorrowfully, manipulating the crowd's long-established resentment, fear and hatred of the *ahalad-kaaslane* and Kodu Riik.

"I beg your humblest of pardons, but I cannot but doubt that you are of sound mind. There are no trust-worthy witnesses to the so-called miracles these *ahalad-*

kaaslane supposedly wreaked, but everyone saw the destruction that whore of dogs visited on the brave, poor souls who were meant to guard *you* from harm."

He pointed an accusing finger at Reisil, his voice resonating with bitter condemnation. Behind him and all around, the already heated Patversemese people shouted encouragement. Suddenly a goblet crashed to the ground at Reisil's feet. Another struck her chest a glancing blow, the metal cup clattering to the wooden floor.

Saljane mantled and screamed. *Kek-kek-kek-kek!*

~*Easy,* ahalad-kaaslane.

Bethorn stepped closer and blocked her from further bombardment, his wolf snarling at the assembly. Edelsat flanked him and then the other four *ahalad-kaaslane* threaded a protective line in front of the Iisand and Mesilasema. Kebonsat, coughing, his clothes burned, ugly blisters rising on his blackened cheeks and chin, stumbled back out of the crowd. Chamberlain Dekot caught him around the waist and passed him into the supportive arms of a blocky guard. A rain of objects pelted him—a candle, a goblet, a boot, a rock.

"Kodu lover! Pox on your cods! Deserves to be hung. Hang him! Hang him!" More objects flew through the air as the stirred mob took up the refrain. Kvepi Mastone smiled, turning a triumphant look on Karalis Vasalis. That the nobility were so easily turned to rabble, turned so easily against one of their own. The wizard clearly anticipated success in trimming the royal wick once and for all.

The rock on the chasm of chaos teetered and Reisil felt the situation slipping beyond control, into the abyss of hatred and evil.

"There she is! Let us go!"

A scuffle began on the edge of the pavilion, breaking the tension as the *ahalad-kaaslane* faced off against the ugly Patversemese crowd. Kvepi Mastone frowned and turned to discover the unwelcome source of the disturbance. Reisil saw the Karalis flick his fingers to beckon forward the old, white-robed cleric who bent to hear whispered words and then slipped away into the crowd, leaning heavily on the shoulder of his sharp-featured young *chela*. Then she turned her attention to the knot of guards struggling with two intruders who shouted for the attention of the assembly.

"We must speak!" called a woman's strident voice. Reisil cocked her head, frowning. She sounded familiar. "Please! Let us through! We must speak!" The man echoed his companion's pleas in a rusty-sounding voice.

"Let them through," commanded Karaliene Pavadone in a quiet, carrying voice. The guards responded with alacrity even as Kvepi Mastone whirled around, his mouth working.

"This is no time for—"

Karaliene Pavadone leaned forward, skewering the wizard with her black gaze.

"For what? What *is* it time for, do you think?" she asked.

He snapped his mouth shut, his cheeks turning white. He'd lost the momentum of the mob's roiling resentment and would have to regroup. His eyes bulged with the force of his frustrated fury. Karaliene Pavadone sat back, smiling at his discomfort, arching her eyebrows as if daring him to act. His cheeks changed from white to red and he fingered the pin on his collar.

He hated her, Reisil realized suddenly. He resented the power of the Karalis, but he hated her with a perfect, relentless, ruthless loathing that made him lose all sense of himself. And so mistakes might be made, she thought, clutching at the hope of reprieve.

"That's her! She did it. Look at his arm! She—she grew it back!" Turbid silence fell as the woman pointed at Reisil and the man held up his arm, pulling it free from his shirt to expose the pale, new skin, unblemished by callus or scar. The arm protruded from a shoulder that had been wasted by illness. His face was thin and haggard, his eyes sunken in pits of bruised shadow. But he stood straight, eyes glowing as if lit from within. He came forward, kneeling before Reisil, who colored and shifted back and forth uneasily.

"Dear lady, how can I ever repay such a gift? All I

have is yours. You have only to ask." Tears slid down his cheeks and his wife sank to the floor beside him, her own thin, sallow face radiant, reminding Reisil of the early sweep of green on a winter-barren field—of life returning. She recognized them now.

The couple from the decrepit hut on the edge of the plains. She hadn't thought of it since—hadn't wanted to. Reisil remembered the unbearable call that drew her into their ramshackle grass dwelling. There she had given him what was demanded, too consumed by the magic to know what she'd done. She looked at his arm in awe.

"Give gratitude to the Blessed Amiya, for it is her gift and I am merely her messenger," Reisil said in a low voice, reaching down to urge the couple to their feet. "I deserve nothing."

The woman clutched Reisil in an awkward hug, sobbing her broken gratitude. With her husband whole, her family would not starve. In the dark she'd expected death and worse from the riders, and instead there had been light and joy and hope.

Her husband pulled her away, holding her tightly as she continued to cry. He ducked his head in an awkward bow.

"I will offer the Blessed Lady my gratitude, but my word still stands. Anything of mine, anything at all—you have only to ask. I am called Reimon and my wife is Clayrie. Anything—anything at all," he said again, nodding his head and gazing at Reisil until she nodded back reluctant acknowledgment, and then, with a self-conscious bob at the assembly, he retreated, drawing his wife with him.

"Very touching," Kvepi Mastone said, eyeing the assembled nobles to gauge their reaction to the scene. Brows were furrowed and there was a growing murmur—not angry this time, but wondering. More than one reached out a hand to touch the couple as they were led away, and then turned marveling eyes on Reisil.

"Indeed, very touching," said the Karalis. "And timely. There is now proof of the miracles these *ahaladkaaslane* can do for Patverseme. And proof of goodwill—that they seek to aid us, rather than kill, as you would have it, Kvepi Mastone. For she performed this miracle with no fee required."

"A ruse," Kvepi Mastone scoffed. "A child's trick to buy our trust. Smell the burned bodies of the Guild members who died protecting us all!" He pointed imperiously at the darkness. "Their scorched flesh is the real story, not this miraculous healing. She gifts one man an arm, and incinerates a hundred in a single moment. A poor exchange indeed. Do not be deceived. Only one in league with them could assert that such monstrous murder could ever be justified."

"Mysane Kosk," Bethorn muttered beside Reisil, and she started, glancing at Kvepi Mastone. But he had not heard.

"That is twice that you have suggested We have betrayed Patverseme and Our people," Karalis Vasalis observed. Still that frozen, uninflected tone and that dreadful formality. He had done nothing, made no moves. Still everything about him resonated with an unspoken, unnamed threat, a horror barely leashed.

"Once might be overlooked in Our generosity and goodwill—We are nothing if not forgiving, and We understand that emotions may on occasion overwhelm even the best of Our subjects. But Our patience is stretched thin. Unless you can produce the Dure Vadonis and Kvepi Buris, we suggest that you retire. Now."

Reisil held her breath again, seeing an angry flush sweep Kvepi Mastone's face, then leach away into icy whiteness. He opened his mouth, then closed it. The Karalis sat back, turning his attention to Iisand Samir. Having dismissed the wizard, he had no intention of acknowledging him further. Did he know how that would grate? How enraged the wizard would become?

Yes!

Kvepi Mastone clenched his fists and straightened, veins standing out on his forehead. He stepped forward. Then he let out a laugh—a hard, gloating, echoing laugh.

"It is time, Your Grace, that you learned your place."

Karalis Vasalis turned back to the wizards, one brow raised.

"I know *my* place, wizard. Do you know yours?" For

the first time Reisil heard a hint of emotion in his voice as he discontinued the royal plural pronoun. But rather than fear or concern, as might be expected in a show-down with such a powerful force as the Wizard Guild, it was something else. Something more akin to the gloating anticipation she heard in Kvepi Mastone's voice. Reisil glanced at the other *ahalad-kaaslane,* wondering what to do, but all were riveted on the unfolding scene.

~Be ready, she told Saljane and herself both.

"I will show you what I know," Kvepi Mastone replied.

His two black-robed companions stepped forward as if this moment had been rehearsed. One had pale, almost translucent skin, with threadings of blue veins tracing across his cheeks and forehead. The other was younger than Kvepi Mastone by a handful of years. He stood tall and stiff, more like a military man than a wizard. Together they formed a triangle, with Kvepi Mastone at its point.

Kvepi Mastone muttered a few words under his breath and gestured in a wide circle, smirking. The pavilion went eerily silent—no more rustling of rich fabrics, no more voices or the clank of guard armor. "That will leave us undisturbed by the rabble."

The crowd appeared frozen like sculptures in a tableau, but infinitely more horrible. Reisil's stomach curdled. It was like a wax display, funereal in its stillness. People were caught arguing, a man there lifting a cup to his mouth, another with his arm cocked back as if to scratch his head. One woman clutched the arm of another, her mouth open as she bent close to the older woman's ear. The swing and lift of the clothing remained caught in time, like paint on a canvas.

Reisil's eyes flicked back to the wizards and she found Kvepi Mastone staring at her, waiting to see what she would do. He smiled, his parchment-colored teeth glistening. The tip of his tongue emerged slowly to moisten his lips.

"Do not fear on their account, demon slut. You have yourself to worry about."

He glanced at the other *ahalad-kaaslane,* then at Ii-sand Samir and Mesilasema Tanis, who clung weakly to her husband's arm, her pale face drawn. None of them had been caught in his spell, though Reisil did not know if that had been his intent, or the hand of the Lady.

The wizard deliberately turned his back on Reisil, showing how little he feared her. Reisil's heart pounded. Should she do something? Now, while his back was turned and he was vulnerable? But her power did not spark to life, and the hand that had driven her to heal Reimon and to strike down the wizard circle did not materialize to give her guidance. She searched within herself, but could not find the key to turn the lock on her power.

"Let us obey your royal command," Kvepi Mastone said to the Karalis and Karaliene.

He snapped a quick order to his two companions. With practiced symmetry, they widened the triangle, each of the three stepping three paces outward. Kvepi Mastone held his hands out over the open space between them, muttering.

Suddenly, in the space between two heartbeats, a body appeared on the floor at the center of the triangle.

It was Kvepi Buris.

He still wore the bloodstained crimson robes he'd worn earlier in the day. The blood had dried on the fabric in black patches, and his face remained as it had after Saljane's attack. Skin curled in ragged, moist shreds at the edges of the terrible wound, and blood bubbled from the ragged hole where his nose had been. He was unconscious. Each breath rattled loudly in the silence of the pavilion.

No one spoke or moved as the Kvepi Mastone re-moved the twisted triangle-shaped pin on his collar. He reached out to take the pins of the other two wizards and fit them together like a pyramid. He bent down, dabbing the wires with blood from Kvepi Buris's wound. When he was satisfied that they were sufficiently coated, he jabbed the sharp prongs of the base into the flesh of the unconscious wizard's ruined forehead. As he did,

Reisil's stomach lurched and she swallowed hard against the nausea.

Then, with a nod to the other two, the three wizards began to chant, loudly this time, but in no language Reisil understood. The hair on her arms and scalp prickled and a wave of cold fear washed her skin. The air clogged in her throat as if it had grown too thick to breathe.

Still the chanting went on, growing louder, then fainter, higher pitched, then lower, faster, then slower—a discordant harmony of syncopation, music and noise.

Reisil struggled to fill her lungs as the air heated and filled with a gray haze of sulfur and smoke. Soon she could no longer see the injured wizard's body at the center of the triangle. The three conjuring wizards and the rest of her companions were no more than ghostly shapes in the smoke. She touched Saljane, clinging to the anchoring power of her *ahalad-kaaslane*'s clean, sharp mind. It touched her own like a north wind, sweeping it clean of the mesmerizing effects of the smoke, sulfur and hypnotic spell-casting. But it did nothing for her fear.

She felt power swirling, gathering tighter as if in the heart of a whirlpool. It felt as though it would split her skin with its force, but still the wizards chanted, faster and faster, louder now. Whatever they were doing, they demonstrated no fear of the two royal couples, no fear of the *ahalad-kaaslane*. *Why should they?* she asked herself. *After Mysane Kosk—who could stand in their way?*

~We can, ahalad-kaaslane.

And into Reisil's mind came the image of a red-eyed Saljane flying to her as she stepped into the wizards' barrier circle. The thundering eruption of power as Saljane clutched her fist and together they struck the wizards down.

She felt a sudden surge of heat in her feet; then power ignited inside her like a shaft of lightning, crackling and untamed, burning her up in its cleansing white brilliance. This time no thundering blast of sound accompanied the surge of volcanic energy—it had come before only when she stepped into the wizards' circle and struck her might against theirs. But the power of the lightning roared into Reisil and, fearing her ability to control it, she reached for Saljane.

Her *ahalad-kaaslane*'s strength flowed into her and they wrestled the sizzling energy to containment. Unlike her attack against the wizards of the circle, what came next could not be a swift, righteous strike. She must wait to find out what the wizards conjured. Only then would she know what must be done.

The thought made her heart flutter. Would she know? So many lives hung in the balance. She sent a prayer to the Lady for guidance, then focused on the wizards.

They were shouting the final words of the spell in hoarse voices, the thick, acrid air tearing at their lungs and throats as they reached their crescendo.

Silence, but for the rattling of Kvepi Buris's breath and the heavy panting of the three wizards. The smoky yellow haze swirled and then began to settle, like a heavy mist into the cupping hands of the swampy lowlands. The magic they had summoned screwed tighter, pressing inward like the coils of a strangling snake.

Reisil felt herself twitching as the power flowing inside her demanded release. But she held still, waiting. Saljane's eyes glowed red and her beak flashed gold. Reisil knew that her own eyes had also turned red and that the vining on her face and neck glowed gold to match her *ahalad-kaaslane*.

Tighter. Tighter. Tighter still.

"Can you do something?" Bethorn murmured, his voice sounding breathless.

Before she could respond, the tension broke.

A deep, guttural, stomach-twisting sound rose up as if from the bowels of the earth—a grating, churning sound like a dam breaking, like the wash of floodwaters spewing white waves through a boulder-toothed gorge. The pavilion trembled, and then shook in earnest. The floorboards convulsed, cracking apart until Reisil thought the entire structure would collapse.

Still no one moved. The wizards stood as still as the ensorcelled nobility, facing one another across the trian-

gular space, arms raised in supplication, heads thrown
back, eyes wide. Sweat rolled down their faces.

A blackness swirled between them, concealing Kvepi
Buris's prone body. It grew dense, then . . . solid. A
shape formed itself from the amorphous mass. Slowly
limbs elongated, a bulb on the top for a head, a trunk
for the body. It was out of proportion—the arms too
long, the legs uneven, the head long and twisted. It had
no ears, no clothing. Just an enormous wraith of solid
darkness. A creature from the Void.

It opened eyes—silver teardrops slashed by a knife
blade of ebony. Reisil's heart jumped and she gasped.

"Who calls me forth?" There was no mouth, only a
disturbance where the mouth should be, like black sands
drifting with the wind. The eyes lashed the room, ignoring the wizards and fixing themselves on the Karalis and
Karaliene. To Reisil's shock, the two monarchs had
dropped to the floor, bellies and foreheads touching
the floor.

"Praise the Lord of the Dark who births the light,
who dies each year and is born again new, waxing dark,
waning light until he burns up in the bright sun and the
dark sun rises again. Praise Pahe Kurjus, Lord of the
Dark, Lord of Demons, Lord of Death, Lord of Life."

The words shocked Reisil, rocked her to the soles of
her feet. That they worshiped the Dark Lord, that the
wizards had summoned him forth. Summoned him! The
Demonlord himself. Their master.

The unspeakable arrogance of such boldness stole her
breath. One prayed to gods. One did not demand their
service. What did they expect in return? To be served
by the Dark Lord? She shook her head, unaware of
the action.

"Pretty words," the shadowy giant jeered at the two
groveling monarchs. "Do I tear my name from your
faces? Do I rip it from your bones where I wrote
it in the ancient language, so that you could speak
it at great need? And yet you have not spoken it;
you have done this other thing. This *summoning*. You
sacrifice the blood of another, when I gave you my

name and set the price: your blood—only your blood. Only it may be spilled to balance the exchange. Tell me, what has made you do this thing? What do you call the need that calls me thus, but refuses to speak my own name?

The words burned like acid, softly spoken, flaying in intensity. The wizards said nothing and Reisil could feel their consternation. They had not known that the tattoos on their monarchs' faces were anything but ceremonial, affectation. They had not known that there was a bond to the Dark Lord. They had believed themselves to be favorites, alone blessed. They had set themselves above the Karalis and Karaliene.

"We obey Pahe Kurjus in all things," Karalis Vasalis said in a surprisingly strong voice. "He holds us in the warmth of his hands, gifts us blessed night and births the precious day, he who guards our souls from evil. We would not disobey his commands. We worship at his feet and we rejoice in his presence. But we did not draw him here."

The Dark Lord was silent, surveying again the group gathered before him. His gaze rested on Reisil and she shook with the pressure of it. Still she stood, feeling the lightning within her snapping back, refusing to be crushed. There was a gusty sound like a sigh. It whined through the pavilion with the strength of a winter wind off the high ice, bleak, desolate and bitter.

"Speak then. Whose insolence calls me thus? And why have you allowed it?" The condemnation in his voice was unmistakable. A rime of frost formed on the floor and turned the black thrones white. Reisil felt it coat her skin and hair. Moments later the lightning within her flared and the frost on her evaporated.

"Greatest Lord! It is we, your faithful servants, who have called you here in great need!" Kvepi Mastone croaked in his overtaxed voice. Claiming his prize, Reisil thought. Stupid. But perhaps the Guild was special to the Dark Lord, as the *ahalad-kaaslane* were to the Blessed Lady. Perhaps, like a child, he wanted a reward for performing a particularly tricky feat.

The massive shadow head of the Dark Lord whipped around like a snake and the silver eyes fixed Kvepi Mastone, a handbreadth away from his face. The wizard choked, turning green as he breathed the fumes.

"You? And *who* are *you*?" His next words shocked Reisil. For all she'd ever heard of the Demonlord, she did not think he valued life. "What soul did you send to me too soon? What right do you claim in stealing away what I have given?"

"Gr . . . Greatest of Lords! I beg humble forgiveness for offending. Kvepi Buris gave his blood willingly so that we might seek your aid."

Reisil snorted low. Willingly. The injured wizard had merely been unlucky enough to be unconscious and available.

"Speak then, wizard. What do you wish of me?"

Reisil didn't miss the threat in the unworldly voice. She clenched her fist tighter beneath Saljane's talons.

Kvepi Mastone bowed his head low, submissive. A ploy, Reisil thought. The wizard was trying to manipulate his own god. Did he think it possible?

She watched the silver eyes in the smoking blackness and was glad that they were not turned on her. She saw in them a mind that was so remote to all she knew that it made her stomach clench in fear. And a knowingness. A testing. A judging. He would let the wizard say and do all that he would, she realized. And then there would be judgment.

Bile rose in her throat as the fear clawed up from her stomach. Then she calmed herself. Whatever the judgment, she would do what the Blessed Lady had given her to do—protect and heal Kodu Riik and its people. Unthinkingly, she took a half step forward, putting herself in front of Bethorn and her companions, and a terrifying half step closer to the Dark Lord.

When Kvepi Mastone spoke again, she heard brittle triumph in his voice, as if he realized the danger, yet still felt himself in control and winning.

"Greatest, we had no alternative but to ask for your aid and guidance. Our enemies have come from Kodu

Riik with deceitful words of peace, ensorcelling many of our people, including Karalis Vasalis and Karaliene Pavadone. We of the Wizard Guild, your chosen children, stood against this vermin, but they destroyed fully a hundred of us in a monstrous, unprovoked attack. Alas, we cannot guard against such magic. And now the Karalis plans to sign a treaty, enslaving us to the Kodu Riikian creatures. It will tear the heart right out of us."

He pointed at the two monarchs, still in a position of abasement on the floor. They neither moved nor made a sound to deny his accusations.

Kvepi Mastone quickly began reciting the tale of Ceriba's kidnapping, this time laying the plot at the feet of the *ahalad-kaaslane* in collusion with Iisand Samir, aided by the ensorcelled Karalis Vasalis and Karaliene Pavadone. The wizards, he argued, had tried to first guard the ambassadorial party from assault, then to rescue Ceriba before lasting harm had been done. Two wizards had been thus foully murdered and the brave martyr Kvepi Buris dreadfully wounded. How far the corruption of this ensorcellment and treason had gone, he sadly could not tell. But clearly the very leaders of the land had been compromised, as well as many of the nobles.

He spoke confidently, rapping out each detail of his lie with the plausibility of practice, the practiced ease of truth.

Reisil clenched her teeth, feeling for Saljane.

~The Demonlord can't be so gullible as to believe that tripe!

~Patience, ahalad-kaaslane. *The reckoning is not yet made. Do not suppose the Dark Lord is easily fooled, any more so than the Lady.* There was a cool edge to Saljane's mindvoice that cut across Reisil's sudden panic, calming her with its patient strength.

Kvepi Mastone completed his oration. Smothering silence weighted the air as the Dark Lord considered this new information. His silver gaze raked the assembly. "Is this true?"

"No! No, it is not, on my honor, and the honor of House Vadonis."

Kebonsat struggled out of the supportive hands of the guard to fall to one knee, his raw, blistered forehead bent low. He spoke with a slurred voice, his lips swollen and bleeding.

"The wizard speaks lies. The Guild sought to prevent the treaty, and thus they worked with rebel *ahalad-kaaslane* to kidnap and torture my sister, hoping to provoke an attack. They would see the war continue, and with it, their growing domination of Patverseme." His voice broke off into a thick, rasping cough.

"Rebel *ahalad-kaaslane*?" The Dark Lord's voice was both dubious and menacing as he eyed the group of *ahalad-kaaslane*.

Sodur stepped forward, bowing low, though not with the deference he might give the Lady. Lume crouched at his side. The cat kept his shining green eyes fixed on the shadow figure, his lips curled in a snarl. "It is true, great Lord. At least one *ahalad-kaaslane* aided in this treachery. He was . . . mistaken . . . in his conclusions concerning the matter of this treaty. The Blessed Lady has punished him." The finality of his tone brooked no doubt of Upsakes's death. "We have come here by the Lady's wish, to seek peace between Kodu Riik and Patverseme, to heal the wounds of war. The wizard speaks lies."

The silver eyes contemplated Sodur for a long moment, then skipped to the two monarchs lying facedown, then to Kvepi Mastone. The air in the pavilion grew searingly cold. Reisil's lungs hurt with every shallow breath—all she could manage, as the cold cut like razors.

The Demonlord reared up and up, a massive black shape blotting out the sparkling stars. They stared up at him as he billowed and swelled, hovering above them like a malignant wraith, his insubstantial body churning like a sandstorm to sweep them all away. Kvepi Mastone spoke, arguing, pleading, but Reisil couldn't hear his words over the rush of her blood and the crackle of the lightning within. She tensed, feeling the hot, white power flickering in her hand.

"Someone speaks lies. To Me." The contempt in his

voice hummed through the pavilion like a deep-struck note, setting teeth on edge, making the cracked and buckled floorboards shudder. "The *ahalad-kaaslane* are not to be touched. . . ." The silver eyes darted to Reisil. "Foolish is the one who ignores the mark of Amiya."

A thick smoke hand like a horse-sized spider on a boneless, writhing arm stretched out and Reisil shrank from its touch. But it only skimmed the air above her.

"But I *shall* have the truth, and I shall have it *now*." For a moment, in the shifting maw of the Dark Lord's mouth, Reisil thought she saw the whiplike shape of a serpent's tongue rolling between great, curving tusks of teeth.

Then the Dark Lord stretched out two hands, now fingerless, like snakes. So quickly Reisil could hardly see them, they darted out to Kvepi Mastone and Kebonsat. The fingerless hands split their lips apart and drove down their throats. The two men rose up on tiptoe, arching over backward at impossible angles, blood trickling from the corners of their mouths as the Dark Lord wriggled deeper inside. Reisil's stomach turned and she turned aside, retching.

When she turned back, she cried out. Agony and terror masked Kebonsat's features, his eyes bugging from his burned face. The lightning danced eagerly in her hand.

The silver eyes flashed at her. "Do not think to interfere, *ahalad-kaaslane*. What is mine is *mine* and I will suffer no interference."

Reisil pulled the power back unwillingly. He was right. It was not her place, and the Blessed Lady would not protect her from him if she took it upon herself to challenge him. She'd thought Kvepi Mastone arrogant! What would she be if she interfered with the Demonlord's own justice?

She held herself rigid and unmoving. The two men hung from their mouths in painful, twisted gracelessness and unrelenting silence. Kebonsat's arms were flung wide, fingers spread and curled like talons as he clawed at the air. His throat was bloated and stretched, screams battling the thrust of the Dark Lord's probe. Reisil's heart ached for him and all he'd been through. He had been tortured by Ceriba's kidnapping, by both Kvepi Buris and Kvepi Mastone, and now again by the Dark Lord. She bit her lips to keep from crying out protest while tears coursed down her cheeks.

Then Kvepi Mastone convulsed, flailing his arms and feet in the air. He grabbed at the impaling arm of the Dark Lord, but his hands passed through the limb as if through smoke. He convulsed again and Reisil gasped as a finger of black smoke screwed its way out his chest. Another sprouted from his back.

Like roots from a tree, the tendrils twisted and curled through his skin as he bucked and jerked in silent agony. More tendrils thrust through, eating his flesh and drinking his blood. Soon there was nothing but a sliding, writhing knot of black snakes, coiling and weaving together in voracious hunger. When there was nothing left, they withdrew, retracting back into the shadowy shape of the Dark Lord.

The tattered rags of the wizard's silver and black robe dropped to the floor and Reisil found herself holding Saljane against her chest, a protective arm around her *ahalad-kaaslane*'s feathered body, panting as if she'd been running.

The Dark Lord set Kebonsat back down on his feet, retracting the probing tentacle of his hand. As he let go, Kebonsat collapsed to his hands and knees and retched over and over with a wrenching, raw sound.

Reisil twitched, wanting to go to him, heal him, but the Dark Lord stopped her with a searing silver glance.

"Mine, *ahalad-kaaslane*," he said softly, like a gust of hot, desert air, buzzing with the razor-edged teeth of driven sand. Reisil recoiled. "Mine."

He turned back to contemplate Kebonsat's battered form, coughing and retching with convulsive force, chest heaving as he sought for cleansing breath. The Demonlord stretched out his hand again.

Kebonsat saw it coming and clenched his fists, digging his nails into the splintered wood floor. He neither flinched from nor evaded the Dark Lord's touch, but gritted his teeth and held himself still, every muscle rigid with effort. Reisil felt a rush of fury for the Demonlord, and pride in Kebonsat's pride. The hand brushed across Kebonsat's tense face, and beneath his touch, the blistered, bruised and burned skin turned whole and unbroken, ruddy with health.

"Mine," the Dark Lord repeated. "Of this one I have great pride. A warrior true, brave, devoted and strong. In this one I have found the truth." He turned to Karalis Vasalis and Karaliene Pavadone.

"Rise and answer." The two monarchs stood with alacrity, facing the Dark Lord without reserve. "You are my hands in Patverseme. You have the power of my name, and it is no small matter. Yet you permitted these wizards to summon me when you could take my name from their lips, smooth it from their minds forever."

Karalis Vasalis answered with the same swiftness with which he had obeyed the Dark Lord's command to rise. "Yes, Greatest Lord. It is so. We allowed the wizards to make their summons and knew that our own lives would be forfeit—for *we* pay the blood price for calling your name and no other."

A knife was suddenly in the Karalis's hand. He set its point against the bare pulse at the base of his neck. A tendril of smoke reached out and leisurely coiled around his wrist, squeezing so that the blood drained from the Karalis's face. Reisil heard bones cracking. The knife clattered to the floor.

"There will be time enough for blood later. Explain. Did you not know I would be angered?"

"We did, Greatest Lord." The Karaliene's voice rang out, unsubdued. She took the Karalis's free hand in her own and held it, for his comfort, not hers, Reisil realized, admiring her strength and courage. "In the last century, the Guild has become evil, corrupted by its love of power alone, with no sense of its proper purpose— serving Patverseme. In recent years, they have excluded altogether the order of the Whieche, the bright sun of the waning year."

She paused, choosing her words. "For many years they have selected only those who would blindly follow, murdering those who would stand apart or follow the path of the Whieche. But long has the Guild claimed independence from us, following your secret teachings. We did not know what tasks you had set them and feared to meddle in your concerns."

She paused again, a crease between her black brows. She took a slow, careful breath and continued. "Still we worried they had managed to hide their corruption from you, for your trust is vast in those who have pledged themselves to you. So we chose to allow them to summon you, that you might say what must be done. We did so, knowing the price. For the safety of Patverseme, we will gladly pay it."

Her words revealed no fear, no reticence, no accusation or challenge. They rang with the serenity of truth. The Dark Lord did not respond for long moments and Reisil felt the hair on her arms rise. Karalis Vasalis's breath wheezed between his lips as his hand withered and curled into a shrunken, white claw.

"It is true that the Guild has stepped from the path. It may be that I have granted too much power to those chosen souls. Even Amiya has been betrayed by her own."

He glanced at the *ahalad-kaaslane,* still standing in a loose chain before Iisand Samir and a pale, shaking Mesilasema Tanis.

"Yet she still has faith, to bring forth one as powerful as you, to invest you with so much of her own essence. Such cannot be withdrawn again. The damage you could do . . ." he mused aloud, skewering Reisil on the blade of his silver gaze. Her mouth was dry, her tongue felt thick and unwieldy, but she felt compelled to answer, as indeed he seemed to be waiting for one, something to prove her worth.

Reisil reached up and set Saljane on her shoulder, dropping her hands to her side. Closing her eyes, she let the lightning go, pushing it down and away until it drained from her. When she opened her eyes again, she knew they were clear, jade green.

"If you are asking me why the Blessed Lady trusts me, I cannot answer. If you are asking whether I can be trusted, I can only say that the Lady gifted me with a friend I did not want, a power I did not seek, and a responsibility that weighs heavily. I have come to cherish Saljane, as I do the Lady's faith in me. I have always loved Kodu Riik, and I love life. But I am a healer, and I know that when disease takes a tree, it must be cut down, and when limbs become twisted and dangerous to the rest of the tree, those limbs must be pruned, if the tree is to live and thrive." She paused, thinking of Kaval's betrayal. "It is true that we sometimes trust those who are unworthy of it." Her eyes slipped to Kebonsat and her heart contracted. She swallowed the sadness that rose in her, remembering his chill withdrawal and his courage in withstanding the Demonlord's trial. "It is also true that sometimes we trust those who are worthy and deserving."

The Dark Lord continued to watch her as if expecting more, and Reisil suffered his scrutiny, her cheeks stained red, her eyes still and level. Then he turned away, heaving again that gusty sigh of chill, bleak nights on the high ice. Reisil shivered as the frost crystallized on her hands, cheeks and eyelashes.

"Greatest Lord," came a thin, ancient voice. The white-robed cleric had returned, leaning heavily on the shoulder of the boy, accompanied by a young wizard in black robes, marked at the wrists, collar and hem with patterns in white. The twisted wire triangle that Kvepi Mastone and Kvepi Buris had worn was not in evidence on his collar. The young wizard stood shoulder-to-shoulder with the white-robed cleric, his handsome young face pale, but resolute. "I greet you with gratitude and joy." The old man bowed, held steady by the wiry strength of his *chela*.

"Priest of Whieche, it pleases me to see you, though I wonder, what is your part in this?"

"Greatest Lord, it sorrows me to say that you look now upon almost the whole of the Order of Whieche. Myself, my *chela*, who is not yet pledged, and a handful of others who continue to follow the Bright Path in hiding, are all that remain. The rest have been drawn down the Dark Path or killed. Ah, it has been a wasting time for the order. But at last there will be a reckoning, a return to balance. We come before you: I, high priest of Whieche, and Kvepi Chollai, wizard of Nethieche, two halves of a whole, the Bright and Dark Paths circling endlessly in the sacred wheel of life and death, birth and withering. We stand before you at the will of Karalis Vasalis and Karaliene Pavadone, their marriage itself a pairing of the Bright and Dark Paths, as they each trained in one of our orders, so as better to serve you, Greatest One."

Reisil started, her eyes flickering back and forth between the two monarchs of Patverseme, her mind racing at this revelation. Wizards? The both of them?

"Greatest One," the young Kvepi Chollai said, kneeling to the floor. "I have come here not only at the behest of Karalis Vasalis and his Lady. I come here also for my brothers, who have long felt the taint of corruption within the Guild, but had no means to act, no means to know if doing so violated your trust. I come to you to beg guidance, to say that there are many of us yet who serve you faithfully and wish to see balance again between the Orders of Nethieche and Whieche."

The Dark Lord stared down at the two men, his thick form shifting and pulsing like billowing smoke from a funeral pyre. At last he spoke into the waiting silence.

"I am pleased by your words. For gifts given cannot be withdrawn, and I should not like to destroy the Guild. But be assured, a cleansing will be done." Reisil licked dry lips, remembering Kvepi Mastone's death. "In the future, the gift shall be sown with more care. I, unlike Amiya, neither care to involve myself in human cares, nor do I find it so easy to give trust where it has been broken. But I warn you now, and let there be no mistake. My eyes will travel unblinking along the path of the sun and I will destroy the weeds that grow in my garden."

His silver gaze flashed to Reisil and sharpened a moment, then passed to Karalis Vasalis and Karaliene Pavadone. "What you have done or not done has been answered, and the punishment stands as given. Let it serve as a reminder." He turned to the priest of Whieche and his companion wizard. "See that the Guild is cleansed, for I will not be patient if I find you unequal to your words. Do not take overlong."

With that, the shadow form lost cohesion, erupting upward like a gout of ash and smoke from a volcano. It rose higher and higher, then turned and plunged downward like a sea serpent diving into the ocean depths. Into the great hole in the center of the wizard's summoning triangle he dove, down into the earth until he disappeared, and with him, the bodies of the three wizards.

All that was left was Kvepi Mastone's shredded robe and a glowing hole that sank deep into the nether depths, and from which a glowing heat pulsed, parching skin and eyes, charring the edges of the wood around the hole until they burst into flame.

For a long moment no one spoke, staring into the distorting waves of heat rising from the hole. In the soles of her feet Reisil felt a vibration, and almost beyond the reach of her ears she heard a faint, faint grumble. Karalis Vasalis glanced about, seeing the frozen nobility beginning to move, faces tight with fright and confusion. He called guards and instructed them to escort the nobility safely away.

"We had best depart at once," he suggested to his companions as the boards around the whole began to burn in earnest. "This place is no longer safe."

He led them down from the pavilion, cradling his white, withered hand in the crook of his left arm. "Let us adjourn to camp farther up the river. We will speak and decide what must be done next. And sign that treaty." He gave a grim smile to the Iisand. "I will have men prepare tents and food for us. There is a carriage for your lady."

He turned away without waiting for an answer and snapped an order to Chamberlain Dekot, who had materialized beside him. The gaunt courtier nodded and then hurried away without a word.

Reisil took a breath, her gaze snagging on Karalis Vasalis's ruined hand. "I might be able to—"

"No." He gave a slight smile to soften his abrupt reply. "You are kind to offer, but it is a little enough price to pay. And one that I am meant to pay. Better to look to Mesilasema Tanis, who appears to have need of you."

But when Reisil stepped to her side, the Mesilasema shrank away, moaning inarticulately and clutching at her husband. Reisil bit her tongue and stayed behind when the carriage came and Iisand Samir lifted his lady inside. Fehra clambered up on the driver's seat, accompanied by Reikon. Juhrnus and Bethorn mounted horses and followed after the carriage.

"There will be peace." It was not quite a question, mumbled through stiff lips as Reisil watched the carriage disappear into the night.

"For now, for a while," Sodur answered, standing beside her and scratching Lume's ears. "No little thanks to you."

Reisil gave a sad smile. "Thanks to the Blessed Lady. Without her, I could do nothing."

"Perhaps. But you proved yourself worthy of Her trust, of Her gifts. You did not fail Her, or us. You were what Kodu Riik needed. So thanks go to you as well." The ice in Reisil's chest warmed with his words and impulsively she gripped his hand.

"Thank you for that."

"Anytime. You are leaving now?"

"No reason to stay. I fear for the Mesilasema, but she will not let me help her, and Edelsat's family is suffering greatly. If things are settled here—"

"They are, nor can you stay in the hopes of helping someone who won't be helped. I too fear for her." He shook his head. "But it is right that you should give aid to Edelsat's family, and right that you should go now." He looked around, seeing Edelsat standing a distance off, watching them uncertainly, his eyes like black wells in his pale, gaunt face. Sodur nodded at him and turned back to Reisil. "Come to us in Koduteel when you are

able. There is much yet for you to learn, and many
friends for you to meet."

"I'll do that. Give my farewells to . . . everybody."
Tears pricked Reisil's eyes, for Kebonsat and Ceriba had
gone away with the Karalis and Karaliene. She would
have liked to speak once again to Kebonsat, to say . . .
what? What could she say? She would see Ceriba again,
she knew, in two weeks' time. If Ceriba still wished to
go to Elutark.

"Bright journey," Sodur said as she gripped his hand
again, and then she crossed to Edelsat.

Saljane tipped her beak to caress her *ahalad-
kaaslane*'s cheek. Reisil wiped a trickle of tears away,
feeling the warmth in her chest expand. She had Saljane,
would always have Saljane.

Edelsat welcomed her with a tired, tight twist of his
lips and led her away to find the remnants of his men,
and to begin their journey back to Mekelsek Keep.

Chapter 19

Reisil finished rubbing down the dun gelding, smiling when he butted against her leg, demanding a scratch on his ears. She complied and he let out a groan of satisfaction. When her fingers were tired, she patted his forehead and went to build her fire.

It was early yet for her to stop, but the ride from Priede had been swift, and she wasn't due to meet with Ceriba until the following morning. She liked this spot. From her vantage point on the bluff, she could see across the river to the pink walls of Kallas. Below it her former cottage nestled amidst the fruit trees rustling in the light breeze.

"It is pretty, isn't it?" she said idly to Saljane, dangling her legs over the edge of the cliff. Green tangles of berry bushes and cottonwoods screened off the sides of their camp. Saljane sat on a limb, tearing hungrily at a silver grayling she'd pulled from the river. Reisil munched on a handful of squashed strawberries Odiltark had sent with her. In her bag she had rosemary-roasted chicken, a sharp lemon cheese, a loaf of nut bread baked just the evening before, and a sack of tart chokecherry wine from last year's pressing. Odiltark had pressed the foodstuffs into her hands, lamenting her scrawniness while still exclaiming over the seeds and sprouts she'd harvested on the leisurely ride from Mekelsek Keep.

"Funny, isn't it? Seems like a year since I left Kallas, instead of just weeks. I hope someone has remembered my garden. I'd hate to see it all go to waste," she said to Saljane, who did not answer, absorbed in gobbling her feast.

It did seem like a year to Reisil. She thought of how homesick she'd been, how much she had resisted walking the path the Lady had set for her. And now?

Now she eyed her former cottage with a tinge of regret, the kind of fond regard that is for bygone times, which are remembered better than they were, and which comfort in times of pain and fear. But the gnawing ache of it was gone, and in its place was a joy in being strong, in being the means of defeating evil and returning joy to those who had lost hope.

She did regret that she could no longer take the time to stay in one place and grow things. She took such satisfaction in watching the green curls unfurl from the earth, tending them as they spread leaves and opened delicate flowers. She thought of Kaj Mekelsek, crying heavy tears as she banished the plague from his home. Too late for his wife, but not so for his children and grandson. Not so for his servants, men-at-arms and retainers.

She smiled to herself, stretching and cracking her back. Things would always grow, wherever she was, and she would tend what green things she could when she could. But now her garden was all of Kodu Riik.

She thought again of Edelsat's father. Proud Kaj Mekelsek had wept unabashedly, offering gifts of gold, silver, horses and jewels. She refused all, accepting in the end only a saddlebag bulging with travel supplies, at the bottom of which she later discovered a fat pouch of gold and silver coins, and a necklace of heavy silver links, to which she attached the Lady's gryphon amulet. The last was a gift of Edelsat, she knew, feeling a pang of sorrow.

He had come to her in the velvet darkness as she walked beneath the stars, stretching tired muscles, gratified that Edelsat did not have to watch his family die a torturous death. He had taken her hand, touched her face with gentle fingers. And in the darkness she had wanted his touch, wanted to be held, to stroke his warm skin, feel his heart beating beneath her cheek.

But it could not be so. He continued to hold her hand when she'd spoken in pained fits and starts of her bruised heart, already given to another, sent to a cold shore where it found no welcome, no comfort, only rocky indifference.

"I wish it were me, but if it is not, then a better harbor your heart could not have found. Kebonsat is not thinking well—his sister stolen away and so abused, his father missing, perhaps dead. His own torture and near death. Ellini help us all. But his heart is large and I have seen his eyes on you. They are not the eyes of indifference."

"It doesn't matter," Reisil had replied hopelessly, grateful for the comfort. "For our lives must be separate, his to grow sons and take the title of his house, mine to serve Kodu Riik in the Lady's name."

Still, when she rode away, she had taken the knowledge of Edelsat's deep friendship with her, and the rebellious hope of something else.

She quickly sloughed her melancholy like an old skin, letting the sun warm her spirits. She stopped often to dig plants, to listen to the unfamiliar patter of the mountain birds, to sit by a still mountain pool and gaze at the reflection of the sky in its depths. She had nearly two weeks to make the journey and no sense of urgency.

It was a healing time, to reflect, to fly with Saljane— and no more fear of heights. She walked to the edges of precipices, gazing into deep-cleft forest valleys, across vistas of rock to faraway purple mountains she didn't know the names of. It was a time to feel herself, to know herself, to walk in silence in the green cathedrals of towering redwoods, sleep beneath the sweeping boughs of traveler pines, breathe the sharp, red cedar–scented air, drink of crystal mountain streams and watch the gamboling antics of growing fawns and playful river otters.

At the little village where Upsakes and Glevs had died, she traded the leggy, smooth-gaited sorrel mare for the rough-gaited dun gelding she'd ridden from Priede. It was a poor trade, with her coming out of it with the lesser bargain, but she had missed the dun, and remembered fondly his trust and loyalty during the wizard night. The farmer who made the trade protested, fearing a retaliation from Mekelsek Keep—for purchasing a stolen animal, or swindling for it. Reisil smiled gently and insisted, the gelding lipping at her hand as she fed him a handful of grain, touching velvet-black nose to beak with Saljane.

In the end, the farmer had acquiesced, letting her go only after refilling her slack packs so that she could hardly tie them shut, and offering to reverse the trade at any time if she desired. She agreed, and before she left she went among his herds, pleased at the care he took of them, touching a lamb here, a horse there, a cow—mending small hurts and larger, hidden ailments. Then she left in the dawn, avoiding the camp where Upsakes and Glevs had tried to kill them all.

In Priede, Odiltark had fussed over her, then sat clicking his tongue as she related her story. They'd talked well into the night, and then she'd accompanied him on his rounds the next day. She did little healing. Odiltark argued that he didn't need it, that the patients would mend well enough with his care.

"Have you thought what will happen when everyone knows what you can do? You'll have no rest. They'll use you up. Think about it. Have a care for yourself."

The next morning he'd given her messages for his sister, then closed her in a powerful hug before sending her on her way, admonishing her to look after herself.

Now Reisil watched the lowering sun flame on the Sadelema, feeling Saljane's constant presence in her mind like a sparking fire. Below on the river she heard the creaks of the boats, stevedores shouting, and the clop of hooves as teams of draft horses drew heavily loaded wagons up into Kallas. Behind her the dun cropped the lush meadow grass. She thought of Roheline and Raim, suddenly craving a meal from the kohv-house. She considered riding into Kallas and eating there, and returning for Ceriba the next day. But the memory of her last days in Kallas, the suspicion, the condemnation, stopped her.

No, she wasn't ready to confront that yet. She sighed.

They would already have the news of the treaty. They would know some, if not all, of her part in it. Still . . . Raim and Roheline had been friends and she had lied. Lied to them, lied to herself.

~*Fledglings fly not well, nor gracefully,* Saljane said in her mind, and Reisil smiled, feeling her companion's sated fullness as Saljane cleaned her talons and beak.

"I am not a fledgling," she replied aloud. Sometimes their conversations were silent, mind to mind. Other times Reisil spoke out loud, just to hear the sounds of the words.

~*No?*

Reisil laughed, tossing a pebble over the edge of the cliff.

"All right. I'd like to think I have enough experience and judgment to be called full-fledged, but I'm not sure that will ever happen. I *have* come a long way since we left Kallas. You know that as well as I. But how will I know when I get all the way there?"

There was a merriment in her mind, a steel-edged amusement. Reisil felt her stomach tumble and her heart swelled at the gift of Saljane.

~*Ahalad-kaaslane, it is a journey we shall ever make, and one that finds no end.*

"You sound like an oracle. Much wiser than I."

In the last weeks Saljane had spoken more often. Reisil remembered how she'd wondered if their communication would ever be more than a terse one or two words. She smiled now. Their slow journey from the keep had been one of mutual discovery, of many questions, of much sharing. Reisil wasn't even sure that Saljane used words, or merely thought her thoughts in Reisil's mind. Sometimes they seemed so intertwined that it was hard to know where she stopped and Saljane began.

~*In some things,* Saljane answered thoughtfully. ~*But different from you. We guide each other to better wisdom.*

Reisil sighed, feeling smugly contented, like a cat lolling in the sun. "Just so. May we make the fewer mistakes for it."

~*We will make many mistakes,* Saljane said. ~*It is vanity to think otherwise.*

"I was afraid you'd say that."

~*It is the truth.*

"Yes, it is, and it always finds us, no matter how much we might hide from it."

Reisil's thoughts slipped away to Kebonsat, and she touched the edges of the sadness she had not allowed herself to feel. Edelsat's confident words had buoyed her, but still she remembered Kebonsat's cold distance. Whatever friendship had rooted between them seemed to have evaporated in that last long day. A bitter irony that she should retrieve her heart from Kaval, only to give it to a man who feared and distrusted her.

She let the sadness take her, let herself cry, the dun wandering over to stand behind her and breathe warmly on her neck. Saljane embraced her mind, sharing the sadness.

After a while, Reisil wiped away the tears, feeling strangely better.

~*Saljane, we need a name for our friend.* She patted the gelding's forehead. ~*Do you have any ideas?*

The goshawk cocked her head at the horse, her white brow flashing.

~*I had not thought. Do you have a name for him?*

~*I thought perhaps . . . Indigo.* Reisil smiled as she sensed Saljane's doubt. "It doesn't seem to match, I know. He's not blue. But Indigo is a valuable dye, hard to come by: it doesn't fade, boiling won't hurt it, and you can't wash it away with any kind of soap. Steadfast, loyal, precious. Is that not a good name for our friend?

~*A good name. So he shall be called.*

Before rolling into her cloak, Reisil fished a rosemary candle from her pack and set it on a stone. She lit it, the flame standing still and tall. She'd burned it every night since leaving the Vorshtar plain. It never went out, never depleted.

She cupped her fingers around the warmth of the flame, then touched the silver tree-and-circle tark's brooch on her collar. In the heart of the tree burned a candle like this one. She smiled.

The next morning Reisil woke early before the first

gleams of dawn. She stirred up the fire, setting a pot of tea on a tripod to heat. When flames of gold and pink burned bright along the eastern edge of the world, Saljane flung herself into the sky, spiraling in great lazy circles. Reisil dined on the remnants of the nut bread and cheese, washing them down with three hot cups of sweet tea. Afterward, she saddled Indigo and rode down off the bluff.

She wondered, not for the first time, how Ceriba's family had responded to her decision to study with Elutark. She did not wonder whether Ceriba had been strong enough to hold to her choice. Given the alternative, she did not think that Ceriba would allow herself to be dissuaded.

Reisil cantered Indigo across a wide, fallow field to the road, Saljane's shadow skimming the ground beside her. A line of birch trees screened the road from view, and thus she was surprised to see a camp of six tents and two-score horses on the other side. A pennant flew above the central tent, the rich hues of indigo and gold in a diamond pattern, with red rampant lions and a crown of red.

House Vadonis.

Reisil slowed Indigo to an amble, eyeing the collection of men and tents askance. There was a shout as she came out of the trees onto the road and soon a horse galloped out to meet her.

Kebonsat.

She pulled Indigo to a halt. Kebonsat pulled up opposite and for a long moment neither spoke. She could not read his expression. His face was a mask of angles and reserve.

"Bright morning," she managed at last. "I had not expected to see you here."

"You thought I would send my sister alone?" *After what has already happened to her?* He didn't say the last, but Reisil heard it anyhow and colored.

"No, I suppose not," she said quietly. "May I inquire after your father?"

The reserve cracked a bit, and for a moment he smiled

with real warmth. "He is well. Kvepi Buris did not have
opportunity or strength to do more than hit him over
the head. Kvepi Chollai had him found and healed.
Thank Ellini, my father has a hard head, and the damage
was not too great."

"That is welcome news."

Silence descended between them again and Reisil
found herself squirming as he watched her with that un-
readable gaze. Finally she urged Indigo forward and
Kebonsat fell in beside her.

"Ceriba is also well?" she asked when he made no
effort to speak.

"She informed us of her decision several days after
the treaty signing, when my father had found his feet
again. It is a sign of her healing, perhaps, that she did
not bend to my mother's protestations, and that she
would have come here alone." Again, Reisil could read
nothing in his tone. She looked up as Saljane coasted
down to land on her fist. Reisil transferred her *ahalad-
kaaslane* to her shoulder, touching her mind affectionately,
glad of the mental support in the face of Kebonsat's
chill reception.

They arrived at the central tent without another word
spoken. Ceriba emerged as Reisil dismounted and the
two embraced, Reisil in her dusty travel leathers, Ceriba
in a tailored riding habit of pale blue with the Vadonis
crest embroidered along the cuffs and neckline. Ceriba
led her inside and offered her cool juice, a plate of mel-
low cheeses and an assortment of melon and berries.
Reisil ate little, unnerved by Kebonsat's hovering
silence.

"How far is it to Elutark's cottage?" Ceriba asked in
a low voice. Gone was the merriness that had illumi-
nated her features when Reisil first met her. There was
a furtive, diffident air to her now.

"Two days, if we ride hard, three if we take our time.
But I am not certain it is a good idea to go with such
a group."

"I alone will accompany you. The rest of our retinue
will wait here," Kebonsat stated shortly. Reisil nodded,

feeling the food in her stomach turning. That meant several days in Kebonsat's company by herself on their return journey. She did not know if she could stand his coldness.

They set off several hours later. Ceriba brooded, staring down at her saddle. Kebonsat rode ahead on the excuse of scouting the way, and Reisil tried to make herself relax and enjoy the beauty of the summer day. It grew warm, much warmer than it had been in the mountains, and soon she shed her cloak and vest and rolled up her sleeves.

They camped early, catching rainbow trout in a lazy stream. After supper Reisil dug soaproot and bathed in a quiet bend in the stream. The water was not warm, but neither was it as frigid as the mountain streams, and she felt some of her tension wash away with the dirt. She slept well that night, peaceful in the tall grass buzzing with insects and rustling with ground squirrels and grouse.

The next day went much the same way, but Reisil spent more time with Saljane, flying high and seeing Kodu Riik spreading out like a quilt in patterns of brilliant red and yellow, blue and green, gray and brown. That night they fished again, having come to the foot of Suur Hunnik. Elutark lived in a small cottage in the foothills above the town of Manniokas. The next day they skirted the quiet town and arrived in Elutark's yard just after noon.

Reisil took the horses into the barn, leaving her companions to get acquainted with Elutark. Reisil took her time, unsaddling and rubbing down the horses, checking feet for rocks. She turned them loose in a grassy paddock, leaning on the fence as Indigo galloped through the grass, then dropped to the ground to roll. She returned reluctantly to the cottage, but soon Elutark had peppered her with so many questions that time passed swiftly until supper.

Elutark gave Reisil and Ceriba Reisil's old room, and sent Kebonsat out to the barn to sleep. Reisil and she sat up for several hours after the other two had gone to bed.

"Ceriba's had a hard time of it. She's strong, though. Isn't going to break. She'll make a good tark in time, I should say," Elutark pronounced without looking up from her small handloom. "And you will on to Koduteel?"

Reisil nodded. "I'll return to Kallas with Kebonsat and see my friends there. Then I'll go."

Elutark said nothing of the tension between her former pupil and the handsome brother of her new charge, sending them away the next morning without ceremony. Ceriba hugged Reisil.

"I'll see you again?" She sounded fearful.

"Of course. As soon as I am able, I will visit."

Ceriba drew a deep breath and nodded, collecting herself.

"Thank you."

She hugged Kebonsat, sending messages of farewell to her parents. Then Reisil and Kebonsat mounted and retraced their path of the day before.

That night they sat in silence, much as before. Reisil blew on the hot fish, almost too hungry to wait for it to cool. Kebonsat sat on the other side of the fire, watching. Reisil had come to assume the silence, not bothering with any more attempts at conversation. It was as if she shared the fire with a speechless shadow. So when he spoke, she started, dropping her dinner.

"I haven't properly thanked you—for your aid with Ceriba, for healing me," he said in sharp, surly tones, sounding more accusing than grateful. Reisil pressed her lips together and picked up her fish, picking off the stray bits of grass that clung to it.

"No, you haven't. But there is no need." She recognized the steel in her tone, the sharp-edged asperity, and was pleased. It was a no-nonsense tone she'd acquired from Saljane.

Kebonsat didn't respond and Reisil finished her dinner, though she was no longer hungry. Afterward, she went down to the stream to wash her hands. She sat on the bank, watching the moon in the water, unwilling to go back to the fire. She flinched when Kebonsat joined her, close beside her so that his thigh touched hers.

"I remember how I was when I first met you. I was rude, to you, to *him*—Kaval."

Reisil stiffened as he spoke the name. She hadn't asked what had become of the traitors, hadn't wanted to know. Death at the least.

"I didn't like him at all. Didn't think about why. Then you served us at the kohv-house and I got my comeuppance." Reisil heard the smile in his voice and knew he remembered Ceriba as she was then, laughing and carefree. "Then there was that endless journey—hopeless, it seemed. You reminded me of Ceriba then. Determined, strong, unbreakable. That gave me hope when I thought there was none. Then all of a sudden you weren't the pretty girl in the Kallas square anymore. You turned into something more, something out of legend, out of the pages of books. You did such *things*. . . . Such things. Then . . . you disappeared in the night, and I hadn't said anything. Nothing."

He fell silent and Reisil sat unmoving. She felt cast afloat in the ocean, helpless for the wind to carry her one way or the other. The silence stretched on, thinning, fraying. Nearly unbearable. Then he spoke again.

"I was left to think. You know, I didn't suspect *him*— Kaval. Not until you told me that you'd seen him among Ceriba's captors. What I didn't like from the moment I laid eyes on him was the way he touched you, the way you looked at him. I didn't like the way you regretted him.

"I am not skilled at speaking my heart. When I saw the things you did . . . it was overwhelming and I— I didn't know how to think or feel. You had never been anything but caring, honest and loyal—you had nothing in common with Kvepi Buris and the others. Except your magic. I doubted you. But I learned well enough what my heart wanted when you disappeared with Edelsat. To return to Mekelsek Keep to aid his family—I knew that. But my heart spoke of Edelsat's feelings for you, told me that I had waited too long, that I had lost my chance to speak and Edelsat would not be so foolish as to waste his chance."

He paused, as if waiting for her to speak, to confirm his suspicion, but Reisil remained silent, her head ducked down, twisting a grass stem between her fingers, cheeks hot.

"I determined that when I saw you again, I would speak, tell you at least of my gratitude and my friendship. But still I had not learned my lesson, for when you arrived to guide Ceriba to Elutark, I faltered. You seemed so happy, so replete. I thought surely Edelsat must have spoken to you, surely this was a sign of an understanding. Such are the obstacles foolish men make. And mayhap I was not wrong. But I must speak, for my heart will have it so. So I tell you: Reisiltark, *ahalad-kaaslane,* friend of my sister, you are my heart's ease and I yearn for you." His voice deepened and he took her hand, pressing his lips against her cold fingers.

Then Reisil answered without words, meeting his lips with her own in a kiss of deepest longing.

They traveled together for the next two days, talking constantly, making love in the brilliant sunshine at the noon stop, again into the small hours of the night, the stars cartwheeling above. Reisil felt such a deep delight in the bottom of her soul, matched by the rich joy in Kebonsat's dark gaze.

"Tell me about your family."

"What would you know?"

They sat in the shade of a tree, Reisil between Kebonsat's legs, her back pressed to his chest, head resting on his shoulder, his arms wrapped warmly around her waist.

"I don't know. What about the man you fought with outside the wizards' circle? Edelsat said you both had blood ties to the throne."

Kebonsat growled and made a sucking sound with his teeth.

"Both our houses go back to the first Karalis Vasalis. He had two brothers. Both were ambitious, both hated each other. But they also loved Vasalis. He had charisma and power to unite the clans. His brothers became his henchmen. Vasalis made them his first Dures, ranked higher than any other lord. Covail and Vadonis weren't the brothers' original names. As a sign of loyalty and respect, each house adopted a name rooted in Vasalis. Covail, meaning 'dawn of victory,' and Vadonis, meaning 'service to glory.' But new names didn't change how we feel about each other. Our families have a long history of hating each other."

"How close are you to the throne?" Reisil asked in a diffident tone, tracing his laced fingers with a fingertip. Kebonsat's arms tightened, sensing her purpose in asking. His voice was tight as he answered.

"Close enough. Far enough that I don't worry overmuch about it."

"But you will be the next Dure Vadonis, right?"

He nodded. "But in between me and that chair are the Karalis's brother, his two sons, his daughter and Covail. I don't lose sleep over it." His tone was clipped and his fingers turned beneath hers and clutched them tightly.

Reisil nodded, feeling something inside curling up into brown dust. She had never expected their relationship to be permanent or even long-lasting. Hadn't she told Edelsat the same? But deep down, somewhere she hadn't even realized it existed, she had hoped against hope. But that was gone now.

She twisted in his arms, urgency pushing at her. Time was so precious! She pressed her lips to his and lost herself in the fire that swept them up.

There came a time, too soon, when they neared Kallas.

Reisil dismounted, her expression pained, her pace stumbling and slow. Kebonsat walked beside her. Saljane skimmed high on the summer breeze. Too soon they came within sight of the town and, on the other side of the river, the collection of tents. Kebonsat's retinue, waiting for him to return home. In the opposite direction, in Koduteel, Reisil's friends and teachers waited. Her duty waited.

They stopped, hearts twisting, fingers caught together. They watched the Vadonis pennant snapping in the breeze. A caravan trundled down across the bridge, wheels echoing hollowly as it headed into Patverseme. A kingfisher twittered and was answered. A cloud of chickadees swarmed into a cottonwood tree, chattering loudly.

Reisil turned to face Kebonsat, tears tracking down her face. He brushed at them with a finger, even as he caught his breath on heart-splitting pain.

"We'll see each other," he whispered. "I will come to Koduteel, and surely you will come to Patverseme."

Reisil nodded, though she thought again of the words she had said to Edelsat. *Our lives must be separate, his to grow sons and take the title of his house, mine to serve Kodu Riik in the Lady's name.*

"We will see each other again," she repeated back to him. Not as lovers, but as old, honored friends. For each had their duties, and neither would shirk them. For as much as she loved Kebonsat, she loved the Lady better, just as he loved his family.

She touched dry lips to his in farewell, then mounted, galloping toward Kallas, calling Saljane to follow. She didn't look back, but kept her back straight, rigid with misery.

She came to the road and turned Indigo up the hill, dust puffing in tiny clouds from his hooves. For a moment she reined him in, bowing her head. It wouldn't do to ride into Kallas tearstained and morose. She wrestled with her grief, balling it up and setting it far down inside herself to feel later, when she could do so in private. She clucked to Indigo to continue on.

~I will miss him too, Saljane said.

Already it was shared, and in the sharing, less difficult a burden. Reisil breathed deeply, feeling the caress of the sun on her head. Her heart lifted.

She rode through Kallas's open gate, waving a greeting at Leidiik, Saljane perched on her shoulder. He limped down to meet her.

"Bright day, Reisiltark. And welcome home."

It wasn't home anymore, but the words warmed her in a way she hadn't expected. She grinned at him.

"Thank you, Leidiik. It is nice to be back."

He eyed her face where the golden vining traced its way down to her collar.

"I heard things turned out all right. You found the Vadonis girl, got the treaty signed."

Reisil nodded. "We did. And now there will be peace. For a while, at least."

"Good news. Won't be sorry to see the fighting done with. Glad to see you're okay, too. Had some worries. But I guess you probably don't want to dawdle. Want some kohv, I expect. Hot meal. Won't be staying long."

Reisil shook her head. "Not long." She nudged Indigo forward and then paused. "Leidiik, if you should see Nurema, tell her I'll be back, would you? Tell her she was right, about everything."

He grinned. "I'll tell her, but likely she already knows. That woman has a sixth sense."

Reisil chuckled and nodded, and then rode on.

By the time she reached Raim's kohv-house, she was being trailed by more than two dozen people, all calling greetings, asking questions faster than she could answer. When she dismounted, Indigo's reins were whisked away along with her packs. Raim met her at the door.

"Bright day, *ahalad-kaaslane*. Be welcome here." He bowed, gesturing with a flourish. Reisil found herself smiling. She missed the familiarity of his old address, "tark of my heart," but change was to be expected. At least he wasn't still angry with her.

He sat her at the head of a great table, and a crowd collected around her, pressing in from beneath the arcades to hear the story she told. She related as much as she could, leaving out the horrors done to Ceriba and playing down her own role. But the winds had carried the stories far in advance and many came forward to beg healing aid. Well enough did Reisil know of the wounds, old and new, that plagued them all. But she quailed under the demand. She did not know if she could do so much and she remembered Odiltark's warning.

Suddenly Varitsema was there, smiling and bustling. He chased them off like a sheepdog harrying a pack of wolves and carried her off to sleep in his own house.

She came to the front stoop with trepidation, remembering the day she'd shoved her way in, the day she'd become *ahalad-kaaslane*. But Varitsema was most cordial and guided her to a bedroom, leaving her to bathe and sleep. Which she did.

The next day she rose before dawn and wandered through Kallas, Saljane on her shoulder. That day she performed many healings, miracles the town called them, and would continue to call them. She was fed, stuffed full, her pockets filled with trinkets and bits from grateful wives, fathers, daughters, brothers, sons and mothers.

The end of the day found her back in Raim's kohvhouse, eating a thick soup of beans and vegetables, smearing a thick layer of butter on the chewy flatbread fresh from the oven. Saljane ate strips of meat on a perch nearby. Otherwise, Reisil ate alone, watched on all sides by those who came to see her, to be near her. In her exhaustion, she hardly realized the attention.

"I have something for you." Roheline slid into the chair opposite Reisil. "Welcome back to Kallas. I hear you've been busy. Tark indeed, greater than we ever imagined. And *ahalad-kaaslane*." She spoke quickly, as if afraid of silence, as if the speech were planned.

Reisil nodded tiredly. "The Blessed Lady has been generous."

Roheline put her hand over Reisil's. "Since you left, I regretted my coldness. I didn't understand. I still don't—as children we all dream of becoming *ahalad-kaaslane*. But it would be hard to give up my home, give up Raim."

Reisil turned her hand to grip the other woman's, eager to confess her feelings. "I feared it so much. I didn't want to give up what I had here. All my life I had worked so hard to have a place of my own, somewhere that I belonged. I thought I couldn't have that as *ahalad-kaaslane*. But I've grown a bit since then. Now I wouldn't have it any other way."

Roheline squeezed her hand and pushed a paper-wrapped package across the table. "All the same, I want you to remember us. So I made this for you. You might want it in Koduteel."

Reisil unwrapped the package, gasping. It was a long wrap, to be worn as a skirt or shawl. It was the color of spring plums, dark and alluring. She turned it over in her hands, the soft, sturdy fabric sliding like silk. "It's beautiful!"

"You'll be seeing more of the purple coming out of here. We're going to have a dye cooperative. Everyone who wants work will have it, and no one will go hungry. Thanks to you. Already traders have begun pounding on the doors wanting the first shipments."

Though she wanted to hear more, Reisil's jaw cracked on a sudden yawn and Roheline stood. "I'd better go. Time you were asleep. Come here in the morning before you go and Raim will have food for your journey." She came around the table and hugged Reisil. "I'll miss you, my friend."

Reisil slept well that night and woke refreshed, well before dawn. She thought of Kebonsat, her dreams filled with him. Their parting still ached, but no longer with the rawness of a fresh wound.

She dressed in the new clothing that had been delivered the day before while she walked the streets. New soft boots, supple doeskin trousers and a vest of dark green, a buff-colored cotton shirt laced tightly down her arms and at the neck. She pulled on her gauntlet and lifted Saljane to her shoulder before retrieving the newly shod Indigo from the warm comfort of Varitsema's stable. She trotted him through the cool morning to the kohv-house, the clopping of his hooves echoing down the deserted streets. Raim fed her an enormous breakfast of sausages, eggs, berry tarts, seedcakes with honey, and hot kohv with cream and nussa spice.

"You have turned into a ghost of yourself. Eat it all or I shall be mortally offended," he pronounced dramatically, and then hovered as she ate.

When she was through, he handed over her packs, bulging once again with food to feed an army.

"Thank you, Raim."

"No thanks are necessary, tark of my heart. Come back soon, when you can. You are always welcome here." He hugged her. Reisil hugged him back, a silly grin splitting her lips.

Then she was back on Indigo, heading southeast toward Koduteel. She rode into the dawn that streaked the sky in a blaze of glorious purples, reds, oranges and yellows. Indigo pranced, the rest of the past days making him eager to run. Reisil smiled and tossed Saljane into the air.

Home was Kodu Riik. Home was Saljane and Indigo. Home was in the Blessed Lady's service, no matter where that might take her.

She urged Indigo into a gallop, feeling the wind tossing her long black braid. Above her Saljane skimmed like an arrow into the dawn, into tomorrow.

Behind her, a figure sunk down beside the wall unfurled itself, pushing to its feet with a groan. The tough old woman watched Reisil as she grew smaller and smaller and finally disappeared. She continued to stare at the empty horizon, still as a frozen lake. At last she pulled her shawl tight about her shoulders, though the sun bloomed warm in the dawn sky.

"That's the way of it then. Good girl. You've done well, as I told my Lady you would before you were ever born. But mind you keep a sharp eye out. You came into this world for more than to rescue that little girl. Mind my words. Keep to the path. But step lightly. The way rises steep, slick and treacherous. Watch your footing girl, and keep your wits about you. When the time comes, we'll meet again, you and I."

With that, Nurema retreated back inside Kallas, muttering to herself as she went.

About the Author

Diana Pharaoh Francis grew up on a cattle ranch in northern California. She has a Ph.D. in Victorian literature and currently teaches literature and writing at the University of Montana–Western. She lives in Montana with her husband, son and an oversized lapdog. For more information, see her official Web site at www.sff.net/people/di-francis. This is her first novel.

Roc Science Fiction & Fantasy
COMING IN MAY 2004

CHOICE OF THE CAT
by E. E. Knight
0-451-45973-3

In Book Two of *The Vampire Earth*, David
Valentine, a member of the human resistance, is
sent on his first mission—to investigate a new
force under the alien Reaper's control.

COVENANTS: *A Borderlands Novel*
by Lorna Freeman
0-451-45980-6

This exciting new series features Rabbit, a
trooper with the Border Guards. But this
trooper is different than the others—he is the
son of nobility and a mage who doesn't know
his own power.

NIGHTSEER
by Laurell K. Hamilton
0-451-45143-0

New York Times bestselling author
Laurell K. Hamilton's spellbinding debut
novel—a tale of a woman known as a
sorcerer, a prophet and an enchantress.

R642